"Val is definitely your type, Scott."

Jeff leaned over the pool table, trying to hide his grin. Poor old Scott looked shocked. "C'mon, Scott, you can't tell me you haven't noticed Val is one fine-looking woman."

Scott shook his head. "No. But romance is out of the question. She's my manager. And I have definite ideas about employer-employee relationships."

"Hell, man, I'd be thinking—come on to her, and if things worked out, you might have a mom-and-pop operation here . . . to say nothing of a handy squeeze nearby." Jeff chuckled.

Scott didn't smile. "And I'd be thinking, if things didn't work out, I'd probably lose a good manager."

Jeff chalked his cue deliberately, considering Scott's words. "Yeah," he said finally, "I guess you would. So, if you're not interested, I guess you wouldn't mind some other guy making a play for her?"

Scott's eyes narrowed. He wondered if Val would actually accept a date with Jeff. It shouldn't matter to him one way or another.

So why the hell did he suddenly feel like punching his brother?

Special thanks and acknowledgment to Barbara Kaye for her contribution to the Crystal Creek series.

Special thanks and acknowledgment to Sutton Press Inc. for its contribution to the concept for the Crystal Creek series.

Published August 1993

ISBN 0-373-82518-8

AFTER THE LIGHTS GO OUT

Printed in U.S.A.

After the Lights Go Out

Barbara Kaye

Harlequin Books

TORONTO • NEW YORK • LONDON
AMSTERDAM • PARIS • SYDNEY • HAMBURG
STOCKHOLM • ATHENS • TOKYO • MILAN
MADRID • WARSAW • BUDAPEST • AUCKLAND

Dear Reader,

Welcome back to Crystal Creek! In the heart of Texas Hill Country, the McKinneys have been ranching, living and loving for generations, but the future promises changes none of these good folks could ever imagine!

Crystal Creek itself is the product of many imaginations, but the stories began to take shape when some of your favorite authors— Barbara Kaye, Margot Dalton, Bethany Campbell, Cara West, Kathy Clark and Sharon Brondos—all got together with me just outside of Austin to explore the Hill Country, and to dream up the kinds of romances such a setting would provide. For several days, we roamed the countryside, where generous Texans opened their historic homes to us, and gave us insights into their lives. We ate barbecue, we visited an ostrich farm and we mapped out our plans to give you the linked stories you love, with a true Texas flavor and all the elements you've come to expect in your romance reading: compelling, contemporary characters caught in conflicts that reflect today's dilemmas.

The Hole in the Wall Dude Ranch, Scott Harris's dream-come-true, is finally open for business in Barbara Kaye's *After the Lights Go Out.* Scott has appeased his neighbor's concerns, hired a top-notch manager in the person of Valerie Drayton and is looking forward to a spectacular first season. But a couple of worms seem to have appeared in Scott's perfect apple. One is his always-difficult brother Jeff, and the other is a gentleman guest determined to pay an inordinate amount of attention to his very capable—and very attractive—ranch manager.

In September, we'll strike it rich with the story of the oilman and the beauty queen. Old Hank is making book on Jeff Harris. The boy has the right instincts. 'Course he has a hankerin' for the marriage-minded Miss Beverly, too, and that might just thoroughly mess up Hank's plans!

C'mon down to Crystal Creek—home of sultry Texas drawls, smooth Texas charm and tall, sexy Texans!

Marsha Zinberg
Coordinator
Crystal Creek

A Note from the Author

As the mother of five children, I am amazed by the dissimilarities in all of them. That children born of the same parents and raised in the same environment can grow to be such different adults has always intrigued me. So it is with this story. Scott and Jeff Harris are as different as day and night—one serious to a fault; the other seemingly without a serious thought in his head. Jeff considers Scott a stuffed shirt, and Scott thinks Jeff is too undisciplined to be trusted. To a certain extent, both are right. The only thing they have in common is a mutual attraction to Valerie Drayton. But Val is one woman who knows exactly what she wants.

I loved exploring these relationships and hope you will find them appealing, too.

Barbara Kaye

Cast of Characters

AT THE DOUBLE C RANCH

John Travis (J.T.) McKinney	Rancher, owner of the Double C, his family's ranch. A man who knows his own mind.
Cynthia Page McKinney	J.T.'s wife. An ex-Bostonian bank executive learning to do things the Texas way.
Tyler McKinney	J.T.'s eldest son, a graduate of Rice University. Now he wants to grow grapes in his daddy's pasture.
Cal McKinney	J.T.'s second son, an irresistible and irrepressible rodeo cowboy.
Serena Davis	The bootmaker who turned Cal's head.
Lynn McKinney	J.T.'s only daughter. She bucks the trend by raising Thoroughbreds in quarter horse country.
Hank Travis	J.T.'s ancient grandfather. Old Hank has seen and done it all.
Ruth Holden	Californian vintner, daughter of Dan Holden, J.T.'s old army buddy. Ruth is visiting the Double C to help Tyler plan his vineyard.

AT THE CIRCLE T RANCH

Carolyn Randolph Townsend	J.T.'s sister-in-law and neighbor.
Beverly Townsend	Carolyn's daughter and a former Miss Texas.
Vernon Trent	Real-estate agent, and childhood friend of Carolyn's.

AT THE LONGHORN

Dottie Jones	Owner of the Longhorn Motel and Coffee Shop.
Nora Jones	Dottie's son's ex-wife.

AT THE HOLE IN THE WALL

Scott Harris	He's exchanged his pinstripes for chaps and a Stetson, to create his dream, the Hole in the Wall Dude Ranch.
Valerie Drayton	Ranch manager extraordinaire and Scott's right hand.
Jeff Harris	Scott's brother. Once the Hole in the Wall puts a few bucks in his pocket, he's heading for his true love: the Texas oil fields.

CHAPTER ONE

SCOTT HARRIS STOOD in the center of the lodge's lobby and slowly pivoted, a satisfied smile on his face. After six months of the hardest physical work he had ever done in his life, he now had all this.

"All this" was the culmination of a dream. The Hole in the Wall Dude Ranch was going to knock everybody's socks off. The lodge, spanking new, had purposely been built to look rustic. The lobby was dominated by a massive native-stone fireplace. Two leather sofas faced each other on either side of it, and a Navaho rug lay on the floor between them. Groupings of leather chairs were scattered around the room, and game tables stood in front of the huge picture window. There was Western paraphernalia scattered about—a steer head stared down from the mantel, and Western art adorned the walls.

The rusticity was all for show. The lodge was chock-full of every modern convenience, and the dozen double and four single guest rooms upstairs were the latest word in comfort. At any given time, the Hole in the Wall could play host to twenty-eight people in the lodge, more in the family cottages out back, and Scott figured if he could keep paying guests booked at eighty-percent capacity during the spring, summer and fall, he might turn a tidy profit. Everything was working out better than he had dared hope. He'd finally appeased his neighbor, Carolyn Townsend, and convinced her that the exotic animals wouldn't be hunted nor would they threaten the health of her cattle, so as opening day loomed, he couldn't have been more pleased.

He crossed the foyer, went through the dining room, then through the gleaming, restaurant-size kitchen and out the back door. It was mid-May, and the weather had been cooperating beautifully. The extended forecast called for more of the same—fair and mild. Abundant spring rains—including a torrential storm several days ago—had turned the Hill Country of Central Texas into a verdant paradise. Perhaps Providence was smiling down on his dream.

The entire building was encircled by a covered veranda. Here on the rear portion a dozen cowhide chairs were propped against the wall. From this spot parents could watch their children in the pool, which was only a short distance away. Scott's boot heels tapped out a staccato rhythm as he crossed the porch and descended the steps.

The sound brought a grin to his ruggedly handsome face. Until six months ago he had never worn cowboy boots, jeans and a Stetson on a regular basis, but he'd surmised that guests at a dude ranch would expect the owner to be a cowboy. Scott wasn't, not by a long shot, but he could sit a horse well, and he had real cowboys to take care of the stock, the roping, the trail rides, the campfire cookouts and the like. And he was even beginning to be comfortable with the clothes.

He was by profession an attorney, but the lucrative Austin practice that had made him, if not wealthy then extremely well-off, was a thing of the past. During the past twelve years he had seen more meanness, avarice and heartbreak than most people would see in several lifetimes, and he had finally fled in horror, fearing he was becoming cynical and jaded. Here at the Hole in the Wall, families would come together for a good time, not shatter asunder.

Scott's eyes took in everything at once. It had been a very long time since he'd loved a *place*. In the distance, the ranch buildings seemed to be dozing in the late-afternoon sun. Guests would expect a ranch to have corrals, a barn and stable and a bunkhouse, and the Hole in the Wall had them all. It also had riding trails and hiking trails, picnic tables around a huge barbecue pit, six family-size guest cottages and another one for his manager. Another small building adjacent to the lodge housed the custom boot-making enterprise run by Serena Davis and Cal McKinney.

On beyond it all, far out of sight of the lodge, was the area reserved for the exotic game he had imported. Blackbuck antelope from India, wild Corsican rams, East African oryx and axis deer were some of the species that roamed the two-hundred-acre preserve. Guests would be invited to participate in photo safaris. Closer in, nestled in the trees that partially obscured them from the rest of the compound, were the four tennis courts, with their bright light. Scott had briefly considered doing away with the courts altogether, feeling they didn't really belong in the rustic surroundings, but then he'd decided that a guest ranch would have to have them. A young pro named Mark Whatley had been hired to give lessons four days a week. Val had assured him the courts weren't a jarring note, and Scott had learned to trust her judgment completely.

His gaze wandered toward his manager's cottage. He wondered where Val was. She had been all over the place all day, issuing orders in that sweet, soft drawl of hers, but he hadn't seen her in a couple of hours.

As if on cue, the door to the cottage opened, and Valerie Drayton stepped out. Seeing him, she waved and headed in his direction. She seemed to lope rather than walk, as though she was imbued with enormous unused energy, and she truly was the hardest-working person Scott had ever known. She had been with him a month now, and he had no idea how he'd managed without her.

Scott had interviewed half a dozen people for the job of general manager before he'd received her résumé. She had answered his ad in a farm-and-ranching publication. He had read all the dry statistics—thirty-two years old, five foot seven, auburn hair, green eyes, single. She had never done anything but ranch work, and for the past three years she had been assistant manager of a dude ranch near Bandera. She knew her way around livestock, had excellent organizational skills and was accustomed to handling a payroll. On paper, Valerie Drayton had sounded too good to be true.

In person, she was that and more. Scott smiled as he recalled their first interview. She had been enthusiastic about the concept of the ranch and had made several suggestions he had since put into practice. Perhaps it was that very enthusiasm that had prompted him to hire her on the spot, one of the wisest decisions he'd ever made.

Val had turned out to be something of a jack-of-all-trades. She worked well with people, knowing instinctively when to lavish praise and when to employ a little subtle arm-twisting. Qualities like that simply didn't show up on a résumé.

And nothing in her résumé had told him of her full-breasted, sleek-as-a-colt figure that filled out a pair of jeans about as well as any he'd ever seen. Her appearance alone was an asset because people were naturally attracted to her. Though Scott hadn't particularly thought about having a woman manager, he now thought of his hiring her as a stroke of genius.

"Good evening, boss," she called as she neared. "Doesn't everything look great?"

"That it does, with many thanks and a tip of the hat to you."

Her face flushed slightly. "I've loved every minute of it. Are you getting excited?"

"You bet."

"I thought I'd check on the upstairs guest rooms one last time, just to make sure I haven't forgotten anything. And there are a few things in my office that need attention."

Scott shook his head. "Val, you must be dead on your feet. I know how tired I am, and a slip of a thing like you . . ."

"Hey!"

Scott chuckled and drew himself up to his full six-foot height. "Sorry. To me, you're a slip of a thing. I know you can work circles around anyone on the place, me included, but enough's enough. I think we're both entitled to an evening off. I'll make a deal with you. I won't go into my office all evening, and you won't go into yours."

"Okay, it's a deal."

"How about coming inside and having a drink with me? Then Carla can fix us something to eat. Okay?"

Valerie hesitated, but only for a few seconds. "That sounds wonderful, Scott. Thanks."

He took her by the arm, and together they climbed the steps.

JEFF HARRIS TAPPED a toe on his pickup's brake as he approached the boundaries of Crystal Creek. Apprehension churned inside him. He'd never found asking for help easy, and asking for his brother's help promised to be excruciating. But he had no choice. He had exhausted all other re-sources.

As he drove into the small community he glanced around without much interest. He guessed he was about forty miles west of Austin, out in the boon-docks for sure. What had prompted Scott to pick this place? he wondered. He'd always pegged his brother for a city man.

Crystal Creek was a nice little town, he supposed, if one liked nice little towns. Jeff didn't particularly, nor did he particularly like big towns. He never allowed himself to get attached to places . . . or to much of anything, for that matter.

An intense growling in his stomach reminded him how long it had been since he last ate. Facing Scott on an empty stomach wasn't appealing, so he began looking for a place to get a meal. He finally saw something—the Longhorn Motel and Coffee Shop. It had been his experience that motel coffee shops were pretty good bets when one was in unfamiliar territory. He parked in front of the establishment, went inside and took a stool at the counter. Within a minute a pretty brown-haired waitress had placed a menu, silverware and a glass of water in front of him.

"Hello," she said. "Do you need a few minutes to decide what you want?"

"No, just bring me chicken fry with gravy on the side."

The waitress turned and called the order through the serving window, then again faced Scott. "Something to drink?"

"Ice tea, I guess."

While she filled a tall glass with ice, she said, "You're not from around here, are you?"

"No."

"Just passing through?"

"No, I have a brother living in the area. I came to see him. Can you tell me how to get to the Hole in the Wall Dude Ranch? He owns it."

"Scott's your brother?"

"Yeah. You know him?"

"Oh, almost everybody knows Scott. We're all excited about that place he's opening. It promises to be a real boon for this town." She set the glass of tea in front of him. "Funny. Scott was in here yesterday and didn't say a word about expecting a visit from his brother. By the way, my name's Nora Jones."

"Hi, Nora. Jeff Harris. And Scott's not expecting me."

"Ah," she said with a smile. "You're going to surprise him."

Jeff chuckled quietly and stared at the wall over Nora's shoulder. "Yeah, I guess I am. I figure it's going to be quite a surprise, all right."

TWO VODKA AND TONICS had left Valerie feeling more relaxed than she liked to be around Scott. It was too easy to dwell on her boss in anything but an employer-employee manner. Try as she might, she simply couldn't be indifferent to Scott Harris. When she had arrived at the Hole in the Wall for her interview with him, he had almost taken her breath away. Tall, ruggedly handsome and impeccably mannered, he was unlike any rancher she had ever known. In fact, he wasn't like any man she had ever known.

Of course she had later learned that he was about as much a rancher as she was a Rhodes scholar. But then, the Hole in the Wall wasn't a working ranch. It was a place for city dudes to come and play at ranching, a far cry from what she was used to. Even though the place near Bandera had taken in guests, cattle had been the serious business there. Here it was a sideline, just part of the big show.

"Another drink?" Scott asked.

"No, thanks. I'm not used to much alcohol."

They were seated in the lobby, Val on one sofa and Scott across from her on the other. He looked completely relaxed and happy, unusually so, for he was by nature a serious, rather reserved man. Val was accustomed to the casual untidiness of working cowboys, so Scott's suave sophistication was new to her. Sometimes when she looked at him if she was sure he didn't know he was being watched, she would somewhat wistfully wish she had the luxury of regarding him as simply an interesting man who had entered her life, someone she wanted to know better.

But that was impossible because he was her employer and she wanted to keep this job. He had made it very clear from the beginning that he expected them to maintain a strictly professional posture with the hired help and with each other. But that wasn't the sole reason Val kept her distance from the most attractive man she had ever met. Scott was dating Beverly Townsend, Crystal Creek's reigning goddess, and Val harbored no illusions about her ability to compete. Beverly had everything she herself lacked—stunning beauty, money, a solid family and a college education.

"Did you hire that man who applied for a job this morning?" she asked. "What was his name... Harte?"

Scott nodded. "Luke Harte, and, no, I didn't hire him."

"We really need another hand. Why not?"

"I thought he'd worked for J. T. McKinney for a while, but J.T. wasn't on the list of Harte's references. I wondered why, so I called J.T."

"And?"

"He says he never hired Luke. The man has a reputation for being lazy and more interested in women and hell-raising than in getting a day's work done."

"Well, we certainly don't need someone like that around here."

"My thought exactly."

"Mr. McKinney's the man who had the heart attack about the time I got here, right?"

"Right."

"How's he doing?"

"He says he's doing great, and Carolyn says the same thing."

Scott looked up to see Fiona Daly, one of the housemaids, standing timidly in the foyer. "Yes, Fee."

"Carla says you can have dinner whenever you like."

"Thanks." He quizzed Val with a raised eyebrow. When she nodded, he turned back to the maid. "Tell her we'll have it now," he said, and Fee left.

The big dining room could seat forty people at two enormous tables. Another half-dozen tables for four stood in front of the big windows. The room was the size of a small restaurant, and its walls were papered with photographs and newspaper clippings about the citizens of Crystal Creek, another of Val's ideas.

In spite of its size, the dining room had a homey feeling to it, as did most of the rooms in the lodge. One of the tables in front of the windows had been set for two. Scott and Val had no sooner sat down than the kitchen door flew open, and Carla Moreno came out of her bailiwick, carrying two plates laden with food. While they ate, Scott and Val discussed every aspect of the Hole in the Wall operation, trying to decide if there was something they'd overlooked.

There wasn't, Val was sure of it, but they went over everything again. Guests would check in by noon Monday and out by noon Saturday. Stays of one or two nights were not encouraged; this wasn't a hotel. Then the staff, both household and the cowhands, could have Saturday afternoon till Sunday night free. So could Val and Scott.

Huge ranch-style breakfasts would be served; there would be box lunches for those who wanted them, and at night family-style meals would be served in this cavernous dining room. On Friday nights, weather permitting, an outdoor barbecue would be held; if rain threatened, a lavish buffet would be served in the lodge instead. Scott and Val had gone over the arrangements again and again, with each other and with the staff, and yet Val was certain there would be glitches that neither of them had foreseen.

They talked through the meal and were still talking when Carla served dessert and coffee. They didn't often dine together, but when they did, they discussed business and only business, so Val knew very little about Scott. He was as handsome as Adonis and drove a sleek black Lincoln that fit his newly acquired cattleman persona like a glove. He was in his mid-thirties and had never been married. He had given up an Austin law practice to build the Hole in the Wall. His father had died some years ago, and his mother lived in a town house in Austin. He had a brother whom he seldom spoke of, but from a word dropped here and there, Val assumed the brother was something of a black sheep, in Scott's estimation, at least.

Those little tidbits of information were the sum total of her knowledge about the man. And she guessed he knew even less about her—just the dry, pertinent facts on her résumé. He'd never asked her many questions, so she supposed he simply wasn't the curious type. Or maybe he wasn't interested in her personal life. He was very business-oriented.

"Now think, Val...have we covered everything?"

"I've been racking my brain trying to think of something we've missed, but I haven't found anything. But things can look perfect on paper and still fall apart when you start applying them to people."

Scott nodded thoughtfully. "Yeah. Well, as long as nothing major goes awry, I guess we're okay. We'll learn."

At that moment the doorbell rang. Scott frowned and waited for someone to answer it. A second or two passed, then he stood up. "I guess Carla and Fee can't hear the bell. I'll get it." He strode out of the dining room, across the foyer and threw open the door.

The sight that greeted him nearly floored him. He blinked once to make sure his eyes weren't deceiving him. The last person on earth he expected to see stood before him. "Jeff?" he said, disbelieving.

"Hello, Scott."

"Good Lord, I . . . This is . . . quite a surprise."

"I figured it would be."

Scott struggled to regain his composure. He stood back, holding the door wider. "Come in."

The two men shook hands. "How've you been?" Scott asked.

Jeff shrugged. "I've been better."

"It's been a while, hasn't it?"

"Try two years," Jeff said.

"Had dinner?"

"Yeah, I stopped in town for a bite."

"How about some coffee?"

"Thanks, that'd taste good."

"Come on. We're just finishing up."

Scott led the way to the dining room where Val waited. "Jeff, this is Val Drayton, my manager. Val, this is my brother, Jeff."

Val glanced at the newcomer in surprise, and she could tell from the expression on Scott's face that he was still stunned. The brothers didn't resemble each other. Scott had ash blond hair and gray eyes. Jeff's coloring was darker, and he was taller than Scott by about an inch. He was more athletically built, too. Scott's physique was lean and trim. And Val definitely thought Scott the handsomer of the two. "It's nice to meet you, Jeff."

"Thank you, ma'am. My pleasure."

"How'd you know where to find me?" Scott asked.

"Mama told me."

"Where are you headed?"

"Here, I hope."

Scott pursed his lips and made some kind of unintelligible sound in his throat. Val looked from one man to the other, puzzled. They were staring at each other, seeming to have forgotten she was in the room. This, she knew instinctively, was anything but a warm family reunion. In fact, Scott and his brother reminded her of two fighters sizing each other up before the big contest, eyeing each other warily, trying to anticipate the other's next move.

The tension in the air could have been cut with a knife.

Baffling, to say the least, but none of her business. Placing her napkin beside her plate, she stood up. "Well, I think I'll be going. Thanks for asking me to dinner, Scott. See you in the morning."

"What? Oh . . . sure, Val. In the morning."

"I'll go through the kitchen. I want to thank Carla for that delicious dinner."

"Ask her to bring us more coffee, okay?"

"Sure. Good night, Jeff."

"Good night, Val. Nice meeting you."

When Val had left, Scott gestured toward one of the dining chairs. "Have a seat."

Jeff sat down. The look on his brother's face, Scott noticed as he took a seat, was one of a man walking the last mile. The devil-may-care aura that was Jeff's hallmark was absent tonight. If it was possible for Jeff Harris to look contrite, he did at that minute. Scott could tell he was uncomfortable, and in his discomfort he made a show of looking the place over. "Nice," he finally said.

"Thanks. It's been a lot of work," Scott said.

"What in hell made you leave Austin? Man, you had it made."

Scott smiled. "Let's just say I got tired of helping wives milk their soon-to-be exes for all they were worth...or of helping husbands keep as much of their loot as they could."

Jeff shrugged as if he had run into a concept he couldn't understand. Carla entered the room just then, carrying a carafe of coffee and another cup. The men remained silent while she was in the room, but the minute she was gone, Scott fastened his gaze on Jeff.

"What brings you here?"

There was a pause, then Jeff said, "I won't mince words. I'm broke, and I need a job. Mama told me to try you." He met Scott's gaze. "You gotta know this isn't easy for me."

"I know."

Scott knew Jeff had to be down on his luck to come here, of all places. He sighed wearily. Their relationship over the years had been so difficult and complicated that he wouldn't have dared try to explain it to anyone. He had been very protective of Jeff when they were kids, and maybe that was part of his brother's problem. To his knowledge, Jeff had never had a serious thought in his life, and there always seemed to have been someone to get him out of the many scrapes he'd gotten himself into. Sometimes it had been Scott, sometimes one or both parents; often it had just been someone Jeff had conned into helping him. The younger of the Harris brothers had always been able to get people to do what he wanted them to do. There had been a time when Scott had admired that trait and been a little envious.

But as years passed, the admiration and envy had gradually given way to exasperation and resentment. The brothers had worked in their father's grocery stores when they were in school. Scott figured he'd saved ninety cents out of every dollar he'd made in those days. Jeff's Friday-night paycheck had rarely lasted until Monday morning, so he'd usually found it necessary to borrow a little from Scott. That had gone on until Scott had realized that to Jeff the words "lend me" meant "give me." He'd begun refusing the requests, and that had brought on more difficulties between them.

And while Scott was struggling through undergraduate work, then law school, Jeff was out in the West Texas oilfields, stringing pipe, chasing women, boozing it up and spending his money as fast as he made it. Life had always been a lark for him, an endless round of fun, and Scott knew that was part of the problem, too. It was all but impossible to accept responsibility when you'd never been given any.

But at some point in time, a man had to grow up. His brother, it had always seemed to Scott, had his priorities all wrong. "Work, huh? Well, Jeff, I'm not sure what you have in mind. This place may look like fun and games, and I hope it will be for our guests, but those of us who run the joint are going to have to work our butts off.''

''You ever work a rig, bro? Now *there's* some hard work.''

''Maybe. But you could always walk away from it and have plenty of times. I can't afford to hire someone who might not be here in two weeks. Everyone I've hired has signed a contract stating that, except for an act of God, they'll stay through the season, and that's from now till Christmas. I can't see you staying put in one place that long.''

Jeff passed a hand over his eyes, a weary gesture. ''I'll sign a contract. I'll stay. I've turned over a new leaf.''

''I've heard *that* before.''

Scott watched his brother's hands flex, saw the working of the jaw. He fully expected an outburst and was surprised when Jeff, with some effort, relaxed and said, ''This time you can count on it. I'll stay. I have to.''

''Just how broke are you, anyway?''

''Broke enough. I've got my truck, my clothes and maybe two hundred dollars in cash. Period.''

''Jesus!'' Scott exploded. ''What in hell did you do with the money you've already gotten from Dad's estate?''

Jeff's eyes dipped for a second, then came up. "I . . . er, made some bad investments."

And Scott would bet at least half the "investments" wore skirts. Jeff had always been a sap when it came to women, absolutely foolish. Scott remembered one of them, a flashy young blonde named Sally or Sissy or something. By the time she and Jeff had finally decided they weren't meant to walk hand and hand through life together, she'd had her teeth fixed and owned a new mobile home and Jeff's old pickup. And that was just one incident. There had been too many to count.

So two-thirds of Jeff's inheritance was down the drain, and when he received the final third, that doubtless would soon be gone, too. Scott was striving for patience, but he couldn't help what next popped out of his mouth. "Don't you see the difference, Jeff? My share of Dad's estate is now *this!*" And he swept his arm around to indicate the Hole in the Wall in its entirety.

Jeff seemed to be having some difficulty with his own patience, but he swallowed his pride. "I know. I know I've never had any sense when it came to money...or maybe anything else. But I'm going to change. I've got to. I need a job."

For what seemed an eternity but could only have been a few seconds, Scott said nothing, just stared into space across the vast room. Then he pushed himself to his feet. "Okay. Get your stuff and take one of the guest rooms upstairs. Tomorrow you can move into the bunkhouse, and I'll turn you over to Earl."

Relief was written all over Jeff's face. He, too, stood. "Who's Earl?"

"Earl Waddell. He's an old-timer I hired to sort of oversee the ranching part of this operation."

Jeff grinned. "I thought that's what the good-looking chick . . . er, Val, was for."

Scott stared at him icily. "That 'good-looking chick,' as you so charmingly described her, is my general manager. And a damned good one. But I can't very well expect her to rope calves and cuss out the cowhands, can I?"

"Sorry. I forgot how good you are at separating business from pleasure."

Scott ignored that. "You get three meals a day except for Saturday night and Sunday. Pay's four hundred dollars a week and you draw it on Friday night. You're off from noon Saturday until six a.m Monday. In return, I'll expect unreserved loyalty and plenty of work. You'll sign a contract. I, on the other hand, can fire at will."

"Sounds like it'll be a blast."

"No, it won't be, and if you try to turn it into one, you're history."

Jeff's grin broadened, which only served to irritate Scott. He'd often suspected his brother of getting a huge kick out of infuriating him.

Jeff turned to go back to his truck and get his gear, but at the threshold he paused and looked over his shoulder. "Man, do you ever loosen up? Ever?" Then he was gone.

Scott braced his arms on the table, dipped his head and took a deep breath. The simplest confrontation with Jeff always left him exhausted. Then he straightened and walked to the kitchen door. Peering inside, he looked first at Carla, then at the maid. "Fee, my brother's going to sleep in one of the rooms upstairs tonight. Sorry for the extra work. He'll move into the bunkhouse tomorrow."

"It's no trouble, I promise."

"Thanks. Have a good evening, ladies. Good night."

"Good night," they chorused.

As Scott crossed the foyer, the front door opened and Jeff came in, carrying a suitcase. "Is that all you have?" he asked.

"No, there's more. I'll get it tomorrow."

Scott nodded. "Good night, then."

"Good night." Jeff walked to the stairs, stopping when he reached them. "Scott?"

"Yes?"

"Thanks."

"You're welcome."

Then Jeff climbed the stairs. Scott checked the front door, then went through the lobby, turning off lights as he did. That done, he went down a short flight of stairs that led to a hall. His office was on one side, Val's on the other. At the end of the hall were his private quarters—living room, bedroom and bath. In his office, he turned on a desk lamp and settled into his comfortable swivel chair, where he sat brooding in silence for a minute or two, his mind a jumbled hodgepodge. It seemed whenever Jeff showed up, something major happened, and it was seldom anything Scott welcomed.

Lord, he hoped he wouldn't regret this. He had burned a lot of bridges when he'd left Austin, selling his law practice, leaving friends he had known his entire life. Just about everyone he knew had predicted either the ranch would fail miserably or he would get bored and return to law. Scott had vowed neither would happen. He had almost everything he owned tied up in the Hole in the Wall. It *had* to be a success, and to ensure that it would be, he had vowed to surround himself only with the most competent people he could find.

So what had he done just before the opening? Hired a man who he personally knew to be too undisciplined to ever settle down and do something useful. He must have mush for brains.

His morose thoughts overtook him, making him feel even wearier than he had half an hour ago. He reached for the telephone and punched a button.

VALERIE WAS already in bed, propped against the headboard, reading a paperback novel. Thoroughly engrossed in the story, she gave a little start when the phone on the bedside table rang. Noticing which of the buttons was flashing, she knew Scott was calling from his office. She reached for the receiver.

"Hello."

"Val? Scott."

"Yes, Scott."

"I just hired my brother."

"Good. We need someone else. That's nice."

"No, it isn't nice," the masculine voice on the other end of the line growled. "I think I've lost my friggin' mind."

Valerie frowned. "Well, I . . ."

"Remember everything J.T. said about Luke Harte? That goes for Jeff, too, in spades. But what could I do? He's my brother, and our mother sent him here."

"I understand."

"So I want you to turn him over to Earl in the morning with these instructions."

"All right."

"Jeff's not to be granted any special concessions because he's my kid brother, okay?"

"Of course."

"Give him a chance...maybe two. He's no cowhand, so he'll have to be led around for a while. But if he can't cut the mustard, don't hesitate to can his ass. Got that?"

"Ah...yes, Scott, sure."

"Fine. See you in the morning."

"Yes. Goodnight, Scott."

Val hung up the phone. Whew! she thought. *Whew!*

CHAPTER TWO

THE FOLLOWING MORNING, at Scott's request, Val had breakfast in the lodge with him and his brother. Jeff Harris was the biggest flirt she'd run across in some time. He flirted with her, with shy Fiona, with plump Carla and with one of the upstairs maids who happened to wander through. They all blushed and giggled furiously, but Val herself hoped she fielded his blatant flirtations with a little more decorum. She hoped so because the look on Scott's face told her exactly what he thought of his brother's flirting.

After breakfast, Scott immediately secluded himself in his office, and Val led Jeff across the grounds to the bunkhouse behind the stable. There she introduced him to a character named Earl Waddell. Earl was fifty-eight, had a weather-worn face, salt-and-pepper hair and a faint stubble on his chin. He'd worked ranches for forty years, and there was little about the occupation he didn't know. He was especially adept at turning greenhorns into good hands in record time.

"'Mornin', Val," he said in a raspy voice. "Don't you look like spring sunshine today."

"You're a sweetheart, Earl. I want you to meet someone." She touched Jeff's arm. "This is Jeff Harris. He's Scott's brother, and he's going to be working for us."

"Do tell." He stuck out his hand. "Pleased t'meetcha, son."

Jeff shook Earl's hand, noticing that its texture was like old leather. "Hello, Earl. It's nice to meet you, too."

"Scott never told me he had a brother in the ranchin' business. Where'd you last work?"

"I've never worked on a ranch before," Jeff said.

Earl blanched, but quickly recovered. "Well, you look like a strong'un. We'll see what we can do with you."

Val stepped back and smiled. She'd pass on Scott's special instructions to Earl later. Maybe Jeff would surprise all of them. "I'll leave the two of you to get acquainted, and I'll be talking to you later."

Turning, she strode across the grounds in the direction of the lodge. Jeff stared after her admiringly, watching the movement of her derriere under her jeans. She had the kind of body any man would love to get his hands on. He let out a soft whistle.

"That is one fine piece of equipment," he muttered.

Earl's eyes narrowed. "That there is Val, my boss and your boss and ever'body else's boss . . .'ceptin' Scott, of course. Don't be gettin' no notions, hear?"

"Hey, it doesn't hurt to look."

"Jus' make sure that's all you do. Got a vehicle, son?"

"Yeah, a truck. It's out in front of the lodge."

"Reckon we can always use another truck. What kinda shape's it in?"

"Well, it's seen some rough duty in the oil patch, but I figure it's got some years left in it."

"You're an oiler, huh?" Earl considered this for a minute. "Filthy work, the oil business. Wouldn't be caught dead in it, m'self." He glanced down at Jeff's athletic shoes. "Got any boots?"

"Yeah. Not the pointed-toe kind, but they're good, sturdy boots."

"Put 'em on. Go get your truck and park it over there where you see them others. Then come on inside and I'll introduce you to the rest of the men. After that I'll see what I can find for you to do to earn your pay. Personally, I ain't never yet seen an oiler who made a decent ranch hand, but you never know. Surely don't."

IT WAS LATE AFTERNOON. Val sat in her office, checking the RSVPs against her master list. The replies to the invitations had been pouring in all week, most of them acceptances. When the last names had been checked off, she sat back in her comfortable chair and smiled with satisfaction. The lodge was as quiet as it would ever get. Muted sounds came from the kitchen in the distance, where Carla, Fee and their helpers were no doubt taking a much needed break. Tomorrow promised to test everyone's mettle to the limit. Scott had told the women to take this evening off; he would bring something from town for Val and himself to eat for dinner. The ranch hands, of course, would eat in the bunkhouse dining room where the ranch's ersatz "chuck boss" would fix them the evening meal.

Val stared across the hall through the open door of her employer's office, focusing on Scott's empty chair. Then her eyes all but caressed her own office. Not much bigger than a large walk-in closet, it nevertheless had quickly become her quiet little corner of the world. Scott had given her carte blanche in decorating it, and she'd had a ball buying its furnishings in Austin. Her desk was whitewashed oak, as were the long table behind her and the bookcases flanking it. On the table sat a lone framed photograph, an enlarged snapshot actually. It was of her father and herself, taken when she was thirteen. It was the only family photograph she owned.

Val would have been hard-pressed to explain what this office meant to her. It was light, airy, feminine and a far cry from what she'd worked out of on the ranch in Bandera. That had been little more than an unadorned box of a room situated at one end of the bunkhouse. This room gave her spirits an immediate lift every time she walked into it. The cottage out back was nice, of course, and she had worked hard to add finishing touches that would make it "hers." But it had already been furnished when she arrived. But this room was different. For the first time in her life she was surrounded by items she herself had chosen.

And that was what made it so special. Except for clothes and her blue Ford, she'd never owned anything. And she didn't actually own the things in this room. When and if she ever left the Hole in the Wall, they would stay. But she had picked them out. For someone who had never owned much more than she could carry, that was something.

Besides, she couldn't bear thinking about ever leaving this place. She'd never lived anywhere half so nice or been given so many varied duties. She'd never made so much money. And she'd certainly never worked with anyone she liked as much as she liked Scott.

Perhaps *like* wasn't the word. When she was alone she could get downright dreamy-eyed just thinking about him. But there was more. She was learning a lot from him, from his manners and educated speech, watching the way he handled important people. She tried to emulate him, and in so doing she felt a little more self-confident, a little more poised than before.

Just then she heard the front door open and close, then footsteps across the lobby, heading, it seemed, in her direction. At first she thought Scott might be returning, but then she realized the footsteps were too light to be his. Within seconds she saw Beverly Townsend stop in front of Scott's office, peer inside, then look around. Val smiled in self-derision. Every time she started thinking about Scott as anything but her boss, Beverly showed up to bring her down to earth.

"Hello," Val said.

Beverly's head came around. "Oh, hi, Val. I'm looking for Scott."

"He had errands to run in town. I really don't know when he'll be back."

Val studied the woman. Beverly was drop-dead gorgeous in the way of a former beauty queen, but being arguably the prettiest woman for miles around didn't seem to be enough for her. She had to be noticed big time, so she dressed in a manner that Val could only call startling.

Today's outfit was pure Beverly—striped knit top that showed an inch of midriff, plaid belt and print pants. It was outrageous, the kind of garb Val wouldn't have dreamed of even trying on, but on Beverly the clothes somehow looked perfect.

Besides being beautiful, she was undoubtedly vivacious and fun. Those were the adjectives that usually came to Val's mind when she spotted the woman. But there were others, too. Air-headed and self-centered. But what surprised her more than anything about Beverly was that she had attracted a man like Scott. To Val's notion, it simply didn't fit. That only served to remind her how little she really knew about the man she often fantasized about.

"Oh, shoot!" Beverly said, with a little pout and a toss of her fantastic blond hair. "I'm so bored and restless I could jump out of my skin. I was hoping I could count on him for a little diversion."

Val forced a smile. "He's awfully busy. The grand opening's tomorrow night, you know, and the first paying guests arrive Monday."

Beverly rolled her eyes. "He's *always* busy."

"Well, he might show up any minute. I'm ready for a break. Why don't I fix us some ice tea, and we'll drink it out on the back veranda. It's a beautiful day."

Beverly's expression clearly said that while it wasn't what she had in mind, it beat doing nothing. "Sure, why not."

It *was* a beautiful day, fresh and clear with the temperature in the high seventies, the kind of day they needed to enjoy before the heat of summer settled in. The two women sat in the cowhide rockers and stared out over the grounds of the Hole in the Wall. Val thought the pastoral loveliness was magnificent, but Beverly didn't seem impressed. She was in fact wrinkling her nose as she looked around.

"What are people going to *do* here?" she asked.

"As much as they want. They can go horseback riding, hiking, swimming, have picnics, play tennis. There's a game room in the lodge, an exercise room, a media room. They can watch the cowboys work the livestock. Or they can do nothing but commune with nature. And every Friday night there'll be a big barbecue with songs around the campfire afterward."

"Sounds like fun," Beverly said, her tone implying that it sounded like anything but fun. "I do so wish Scott would show up."

Val didn't know how old Beverly was—mid-twenties was her guess—but she was certainly too young to be bored so much of the time. Val knew the woman did volunteer work at the hospital, but that wouldn't satisfy Beverly's penchant for fun, shine and glitter. She wondered why Beverly stayed in Crystal Creek, for she seemed far more suited to Austin or San Antonio, even Dallas or Houston.

But those big cities were full of gorgeous women. Maybe that was the answer. A Beverly Townsend would be one of many in those places. In Crystal Creek, she stood out, was a celebrity.

And why do I spend fifteen seconds wondering about her one way or another? But Val knew the answer to that one. Because Beverly was involved with Scott, that was why.

At that moment, two men came into view—Earl Waddell, with Jeff hard on his heels. They were striding purposefully in a northeasterly direction, headed it seemed toward the east-gate area where the feeding pens were located. Earl spotted the two women and waved. Jeff turned, then did a double take when he saw Beverly. A rakish grin spread across his face and, ignoring Val altogether, he touched the brim of his hat with a forefinger in a salute aimed squarely at Beverly. Earl tugged at his sleeve, and they continued on, but Jeff cast one last glance over his shoulder before they moved out of view.

"Wow!" Beverly exclaimed. "Who was that?"

"Don't you know Earl Waddell?" Val asked with a wry smile.

"Oh, of course I know Earl. Who was that man with him?"

"He's Jeff Harris, Scott's younger brother."

Beverly's head snapped toward Valerie. "No kidding?"

"No kidding."

"When did he get here?"

"Last night."

"Well, I'll be," Beverly said, a bemused expression on her face. "Scott didn't say anything about his brother coming."

"I don't think Jeff was expected."

"He's good-looking . . . but not as good-looking as Scott." Beverly shifted to look at Val. "I think Scott must be the most ideal man in the world, don't you?"

"He's an excellent employer, and that's all I know him as."

"Oh, come on. No woman's that indifferent to a man like Scott. Admit it—he's one handsome devil."

"All right, he's very good-looking." Which was the understatement of the century to Val's notion.

"He has only one fault that I can see."

"And that is?"

"He's too serious. I just wish I could get him to unbend and have a little fun."

"Well, Beverly...I guess it depends on your definition of fun. It seems to me Scott really enjoys this ranch and what he's done with it. Certainly he's enthusiastic about it. Maybe that's his idea of fun." Val felt very uncomfortable talking to Beverly about Scott.

"Oh, I'm talking *fun*," Beverly said. "Parties, fancy restaurants, night spots, things like that. Places where you really have to dress up. I adore gorgeous clothes, and I like being around people, lots of people."

Val could understand that. Beverly was the center of attention wherever she went. It probably would be fun to be around a lot of people under those circumstances. And no one wore clothes better than she did. "Then you should love tomorrow night's opening."

"Yeah...but that's *tomorrow* night. What about tonight?" Beverly shoved herself out of the chair. "Well, I'm probably keeping you from something. I think I'll drive into town and see what I can scare up. Thanks for the tea. Be talking to you."

"Bye." Val watched her leave the porch and round the house, and she shook her head in wonder. She found it so hard to believe there were people who couldn't stand having one idle evening on their hands. Hadn't the woman ever heard of curling up with a good book? *Maybe she can't read,* Val thought, then immediately scolded herself for her cattiness.

"Now, SON," Earl said, "this here's a calf."

Jeff shot the older man a look of disgust. "Hell, Earl, even *I* know that. And there's another one . . . and another one."

"They's jus' as curious as puppies and frisky as colts. Can't leave 'em alone a minute 'cause they don't know nothin' yet about barbed wire and such. Looks like they's wandered away from their mamas." Earl reached out and rubbed one of the calves, then straightened and pointed toward a gate. On the other side of the fence, backed up to the gate, was a red pickup, its bed loaded to capacity with bales of hay that Scott had purchased from the Circle T Ranch next door. Earl walked to the gate and swung it wide. "I gotta go check on a couple'a other things, so what I want you to do while I'm gone is back that truck through this gate and start unloading that hay. Jus' pitch it down on the ground there. I'll be back 'fore long. Got that?"

"Sure. No problem."

"Watch them calves," Earl said over his shoulder as he ambled off.

Jeff opened the door to the truck and climbed in, then backed through the gate. Getting out, he swung open the tailgate, hopped up on it and started picking up and tossing. The truck bed was about empty when Earl returned.

"You work pretty fast, son," Earl said with a hint of admiration.

"In spite of what my big brother thinks, I'm not afraid of work."

"Well, now that's done, we'll..." He stopped and took a look around. "Where're them calves?"

"Huh?" Jeff's eyes scanned the area. "Hell, I don't know. They were around here a minute ago." He tried to remember when last he'd actually seen them. The truth was, he'd forgotten all about the damned calves.

"Shee-ut!" Earl suddenly exclaimed. "Them little dogies have done wandered over onto Miz Townsend's place. Should'a closed the goldanged gate, son."

"Well, *you* should'a told me," Jeff said, jumping down and spying the little animals in the distance. "Won't whoever finds them bring them home?"

"How're they gonna know where they belong?"

"Don't they have brands?"

"Nope. We're savin' the brandin' till there's some city dudes around to watch it. That's part of the show."

"Then . . . how're we going to catch them?"

"Good question. Gotta get me a rope. You get over there and herd 'em together," Earl said, walking hurriedly away.

"How?" Jeff cried.

"Figure it out."

Feeling hopelessly inept, Jeff set off across the field in the direction of the straying calves. They looked pretty harmless with their blocky bodies, childlike faces and limpid eyes, but he knew zero about livestock. For all he knew, those little fellows might charge him any minute. He had no way of knowing that they were more afraid of him than he was of them, or that his biggest concern should have been that their mamas would come looking for them. Clustered together, perhaps no more than a few feet from one another, they stared at him suspiciously as he approached.

Jeff's heart beat frantically. "Hi there, boys and girls, as the case may be. Now, I'm not going to hurt you, but y'all need to stay right here until Earl comes, so we can take you back to your mamas."

He began circling them, holding out his arms and talking gibberish. For a minute the three little animals stood as docilely as lambs, watching him.

Suddenly one dashed away from the others, and like birds on a wire, when one flew they all did.

"Come back here, dammit!" Jeff yelled in hot pursuit. The calves ran a few yards, then stopped and again clustered together. "Now I'm telling you guys, you have to stay put!"

The little animals let him get within a few feet of them, then playfully dashed away again. "Goddammit!" Jeff sputtered and took off after them.

"Having some trouble, young man?"

A feminine voice behind him startled Jeff, who turned to see a handsome blond woman of about forty sitting astride a horse and watching him with some amusement.

"Yes, ma'am. These calves got out of that gate over there, and I'm supposed to try to keep them together until Earl gets here with a rope."

A broad smile spread across the woman's face. Even in his present unnerved state, Jeff recognized her as an extremely attractive woman. "Let me see if I can't give you a hand," she said.

A rope—lasso, he guessed it was called—was looped around her saddle horn. Unrolling it, she fashioned a noose, then twirled the rope in the air a couple of times and settled the loop over a calf's neck as smoothly and easily as slipping a coin in a slot. Then she tied the other end of the lasso to the saddle horn. Jeff was absolutely fascinated.

"One down, two to go," the woman said. "Now, I want you to bend down and grab that calf's fore-legs with one arm, its hind legs with the other, and carry it over here to me."

Jeff wasn't at all sure about this, but he did as the woman told him and discovered it wasn't difficult at all. He was somewhat clumsy, and the poor an-imal let out a little bleat, but he didn't have any real trouble picking it up. He carried it to the horse and rider.

"Just lift it up here," the woman said, and she positioned the animal across her saddle in front of her. "There. Now if you'll just pick up the other one..."

But just then Earl came hurrying toward them, carrying a rope. "Howdy, Miz Townsend," he said. "Sorry for the trouble."

"No trouble, Earl."

Earl walked up to the third calf and it let him loop the rope around its neck without protest. The woman nudged her horse's flank, and the trio moved toward the gate, Jeff and Earl falling into step beside her.

Once the calves were safely behind fence again, the woman smiled down at Jeff. "My name's Car-olyn Townsend," she said. "This is my property."

"How do you do, ma'am. I'm Jeff Harris, and I'm sorry about this."

"Don't be. Had I found the calves, I'd have figured they belong to Scott since they're unbranded." She cocked her head and studied him a second. "Harris? Are you related to Scott?"

"I'm his brother...and this kind of work is sorta new to me."

"Well, I'm happy to meet you, Jeff, and I'm sure I'll be seeing you again soon. Goodbye. Goodbye, Earl."

"Bye, Miz Townsend, and thanks."

Carolyn reversed direction, and with another nudge to her horse's flanks, trotted off. Jeff looked at Earl rather sheepishly. "Sorry."

"No harm done, but remember this, son. The A-number-one rule on a ranch is never, ever leave a gate open, not for a second. You drive up to one, you get out and open it. You drive through and get out and close it. I don't care if you drive through twenty gates a day, that's what you gotta do. Got it?"

"Got it."

"Good. Now, can you ride a horse?"

"Oh, I have a time or two."

Earl simply stared at him for a second, then raised his eyes and arms skyward. "Lord, I sure wanna thankee for sendin' this here greenhorn to me." Then his eyes settled on Jeff, and he heaved a sigh. "Well, you gotta ride. Folks'll expect it. So, I guess you and me are gonna spend the rest of the afternoon on ridin' lessons. Come on." He slapped Jeff on the back. "Ever'thing's, fine. You gonna do all right, son. It may take a spell, but you gonna do all right, 'cause I'm gonna see to it."

Somehow Jeff had his own doubts about that.

IN HIS OFFICE, Scott sat behind his desk, phone in hand. "Thanks for calling, Carolyn. I'm looking forward to seeing you tomorrow night.... Yes, me, too. Goodbye." He hung up, giving a growl of disgust as he stood. Clomping out of his office, he glanced in Val's, saw she wasn't there, so he went outside, scanning the property in all directions.

He found what he was looking for—Earl and Jeff. To his surprise, his brother was on horseback. He hailed them, and they reined in their mounts, then trotted over to him.

"I didn't know you could ride," he said to Jeff.

Jeff grinned. "I didn't, either. Earl here is a master teacher."

Scott shifted his attention to Earl. "What's this I hear about a gate being left open and some calves getting out?"

Jeff opened his mouth, an apology ready, but Earl preempted him. "Sorry as I can be about that, boss. I sure didn't have my head on straight. Won't happen again, promise you that, and we got them calves back all right. No harm done.''

"Mmm." Scott looked from one man to the other. He didn't for a second believe the open gate was Earl's doing, but it wasn't important enough to raise a stink over. "How're you coming along?''

"Oh, we're doin' jus' dandy, boss," Earl assured him. "Jeff and me, we're getting along great."

Scott was skeptical, but he only said, "Well, be careful. We can't afford to lose any livestock."

"Right, boss." Earl gave him the finger-to-hat salute. "C'mon, son. It's about time for chuck, and you and me could stand a shower."

Scott watched them ride off and slowly shook his head. Then he chuckled as he recalled his conversation with Carolyn. "I wish you could have seen it, Scott," she'd said. "Your brother was out in the pasture, on foot, no rope or anything, trying to get those little critters to stay in one spot. It was the funniest thing I've ever seen. But when I learned that Jeff hadn't done any ranching, I really felt for him."

Yet, apparently Earl thought enough of Jeff to cover for him, so maybe this wouldn't turn out to be the total disaster Scott had expected. He continued around the house and strode toward Val's cottage.

He had to knock twice before she came to the door. She looked sleepy-eyed, rumpled...and a little embarrassed. "Oh, Scott...I'm sorry. I...just lay down for a minute, and I'm afraid I dozed off."

"I shouldn't wonder," he said.

"Have you been back long?"

"Half hour or so. I brought us something to eat." Scott was slightly shaken by the sight of her. Of course he knew she was an unusually attractive woman, but it had never been difficult to think of her as only his manager, because she was so businesslike. She'd also never given him any reason to think she regarded him as anything but her employer.

Now, however, seeing her as she'd just tumbled out of bed... She looked so appealing. He gave himself a shake. "It's barbecue, and I'll heat it up whenever you're ready to eat."

"Thanks. I'll be along in just a minute. Let me...comb my hair or something."

"Fine. There's really no hurry." Backing off, he headed for the lodge.

SCOTT AND VAL ATE their meal at a round oak table in the kitchen where Carla, Fee and the rest of the household staff ate. They were the only two people in the lodge. That being the case, supper shared between two attractive single people might reasonably have been cozy and intimate. Instead, it was all business.

"All the RSVPs have been returned," Val said, "and there have been very few regrets. We are going to have quite a crowd."

"Isn't that what we hoped for?" Scott asked. "These people all have friends who have other friends. If tomorrow night is a success, word will get around."

"But tomorrow night won't tell us a thing about how paying guests are going to react. Tomorrow night, everyone is just going to be enjoying your generosity. Like two people living together before getting married—that might teach you a lot about each other, but it won't teach you what being married is like."

"No, I guess not." He looked at her with an odd little smile. "Have you ever lived with anyone, Val?"

"My dad."

"That's it?"

"That's it."

"What was he like?" It occurred to Scott that this was the first really personal question he had ever asked her. It also occurred to him that he was studying her with an unusual amount of interest. She had a little indentation in her bottom lip that he found intriguing. Why hadn't he ever noticed that before? When she smiled, she showed teeth so white and even she could have posed for toothpaste ads. And her hands were slender and graceful, not at all the hands of a woman who had never done anything but ranch work. He wondered if she had to spend a great deal of time taking care of them.

"Daddy was...oh...something like Earl, I think. Yes, sometimes Earl reminds me of Daddy. He worked ranches and dragged me along."

"Where was your mother?"

"Gone." Val smiled sadly. "I don't really remember all that much about her—I was only seven when she left—but Daddy carried a picture of her for a few years, and she was very pretty. Her name was Vivian. She loved people and parties and doing things." She caught herself just before saying, "like Beverly." That would have been a gauche mistake. "I guess Daddy bored her after so many years. I hate saying that because he was the dearest person in the world to me, but he . . . well, he didn't have a lot of ambition, and he found it very easy to pick up and move whenever the mood struck."

Like Jeff, Scott thought. Maybe there just were people like that in the world, those born with itchy feet and the urge to roam. Maybe some never got over it. At least, no one else had to suffer because of Jeff's roving instincts. Jeff had only himself to take care of.

"I guess that kind of life is hard on a woman. Was it hard on you?"

"In some ways."

Scott watched Val as she talked. She seemed to be pouring out her soul . . . but behind a veil. As much as she was saying, he had the feeling she was keeping even more to herself. "Where is your dad now?" he asked quietly.

"He died three years ago. A fall from a horse. It's so odd that he should have died that way. He was the best horseman I ever saw, but he got hold of a mean one. Right after that I got a chance at the job in Bandera."

Scott didn't know what made him continue asking questions, but there was one more that wouldn't remain unasked. "And your mother?"

"I have no idea where she is. She stayed in touch for a while, even sent money, but we moved around so much, and Daddy never would tell anyone where we were headed. He used to say that when he was through with a place, he was *through*. Maybe she just lost track of us. Last I heard she was working as a cocktail waitress in Fort Worth, but that was a long, long time ago."

"No brothers or sisters?"

"No, whatever ranch hands were around acted as my brothers. I used to regret being an only. I think I would have loved having a sister. You're so fortunate to have your brother."

Scott pursed his lips, and a distant look came to his eyes. "Well, brothers don't always act brotherly. I have to think it's the same with sisters."

"Perhaps. I used to just long for female friends of any kind. I had one once. Her name was Dixie June, and her dad owned the ranch we were working on at the time. Of course there was a world of difference between our stations in life, but that doesn't matter so much when you're a kid. I sure hated to leave that place." She sighed. "But Dixie June and I would have gone our separate ways eventually. I heard her dad sent her to some fancy school in the East. I was lucky to get out of high school, considering all the ones I went to. Five, if you can believe it."

Abruptly Val stood and carried her plate to the sink. Scraping the scraps into the disposer, she rinsed her dish and put it in the dishwasher. "Thanks for the barbecue. It was delicious."

"Don't mention it."

She indicated his plate. "Finished?"

"I'll rinse it."

Wiping her hands down the length of her jeans, she said, "Then I guess I'll be going. There are some things I want to do before bedtime."

"Sure, Val. Get a good night's sleep."

"You, too. We're going to need it."

Scott sat in the kitchen for five minutes or so after she had gone out the back door, wondering what had prompted him to question her. Now the things he knew about her—the itinerant life with her father, the mother who had left, only one girlfriend in her whole life—touched him in a way he didn't like. He felt sorry for her, and until tonight she had been a woman who'd inspired anything but pity.

Many years ago, in the early days of his law practice, he had learned the hard way that business and pleasure didn't mix. Since then he had always chosen to keep his distance and not learn too many personal facts about the people he worked with. Getting too close inspired confidences, like tonight. And confidences, in turn, inspired making allowances, overlooking inefficiencies, forgiving trespasses, so to speak.

Now Valerie Drayton was more than just an employee; she was a real person with a real past. He felt somehow closer to her now than he had before.

And that wouldn't do at all.

CHAPTER THREE

IN SPITE OF all the weeks of intense preparation and planning, Friday morning was full of frantic activity. Val's first order of business was making out the payroll checks. She paid each of the household staff herself, and took the rest of the checks to Earl for disbursement among the hands. Then she consulted her checklist, which was several pages long, and only when every last item had been dealt with, did she go to her cottage to get ready for the festivities.

Though some activities had been going on since midday, the main event was a barbecue that called for casual dress. Val knew the jeans and cotton shirts that served as her working attire wouldn't do. She had never owned a lot of clothes and no really expensive ones, but she did have a pair of black designer jeans and a bright black-red-gold-and-white print shirt. She also owned black designer boots. The outfit, she decided after studying herself in the mirror, was appropriate—not flashy but not dull, either. As an afterthought, she exchanged the gold studs she usually wore in her earlobes for a pair of dangling silver earrings.

As she crossed the grounds between the cottage and the lodge, she was unaware of two men who had just stepped out of the bunkhouse, whose eyes followed her every step. "Oooh, mercy, that's some fine-looking woman," Jeff said.

Earl glowered at him. "Son, I told you—"

"I know what you told me. I can't do anything but look. Well, hell, that's all I'm doing."

Oblivious to the masculine attention, Val stopped at the barbecue area where dozens of long picnic tables covered with oilcloth were ready for hungry guests. The barbecue pit, a steel structure the size of a pickup bed, was giving off some irresistible aromas. A team of "cowboys," all with red kerchiefs tied around their necks, were tending the proceedings. Actually, the men were professional caterers from a company called the Chuck Wagon Gang. The Gang worked events like Cheyenne's Frontier Days and the Calgary Stampede. Scott was lucky to have been able to book them. Satisfied that the barbecue process was in capable hands, Val climbed the steps to the veranda and entered the kitchen.

Six women were hard at work under Carla's watchful eye. The caterers handled the meat, beans and bread. It was left to Carla and her crew to turn out gallons of potato salad, coleslaw and other side dishes. "How're things going, Carla?" Val asked.

"Muy bien, señorita," the woman assured her. "This is a good group. You and *el señor* don't have a thing to worry about."

"Gracias. You let me know if you hit a snag, okay?"

"Okay."

"Where is *el señor,* by the way?"

"In his office, I think."

He was—sitting behind his desk, a forefinger curved over his mouth, so deep in thought he didn't hear her enter. She cleared her throat. "Scott?"

He gave a start, then seeing her, he stood. "Oh, Val..." His eyes roamed her in unabashed scrutiny. "Good Lord, you look wonderful!"

"Thanks."

She could have said the same for him. He wore Western-cut gabardine slacks and a silk shirt with a string tie at the neck—Sunday best, Western-style, the basic young cattleman look. Of course the garb was affected, as was most everything at the Hole in the Wall, but he managed to look as though he'd worn such attire all his life. Val pictured him in a business suit and came to the conclusion that he must have cut quite a figure in courtrooms. She wished she could have seen him in action. Crossing the room, she took a seat facing his desk. "Well, the big day is upon us."

Scott sat down and clasped his hands in front of him. "So it is."

For the first time, Val realized fully what a momentous evening this was for him. All the work he had done. She had come on late in the game, after he had done months of groundwork. A great surge of emotion for him swept through her. "Everything's going to go great. You've done a good job."

"*We've* done a good job."

Val loved that "we," and she hated herself for loving it. "But you did so much before I got here."

Scott glanced at his watch and again got to his feet. "Well, it's here, the trial by fire. The first guests should be arriving any minute. Ready?"

"Yes, as ready as I'll ever be."

FOR THE NEXT HOUR or so, a steady stream of vehicles drove through the gate and up the road to the lodge. Soon the parking area was full, and a horde of people milled about the grounds. Apparently almost everyone in Crystal Creek and its environs were curious about the posh new dude ranch that had sprung up in their midst. Scott threaded his way through the crowd, stopping for a word with everyone. Val had positioned herself unobtrusively in one corner of the veranda, her watchful eyes taking in everything at once, ready to intercede if anything seemed to go awry.

But a party like this almost took care of itself. There were plenty of snacks to keep everyone satisfied until the feast. A well-stocked bar had been set up, tended by a hired barkeeper, and the guests entertained one another. From the looks of things, everyone knew everyone else.

Val spotted Carolyn Townsend and Carolyn's cousin, Lori Porter. She knew the man with them was Vernon Trent, a local realtor and the special man in Carolyn's life. Cynthia McKinney had put in an appearance, but she hadn't stayed long. Her husband's recent heart attack kept the McKinneys close to home these days. Of course, Beverly made a late grand entrance, roaring up in her Cadillac, honking and waving gaily to the throng. She was wearing a tomato red jumpsuit with plenty of gold jewelry, and was impossible to miss. When she got out of her car, it seemed every head turned in her direction. All that was missing, Val thought, was a trumpet fanfare. The woman truly was sensational.

Val realized that with the exception of Jeff, whom she had yet to see, she was probably the only outsider. She knew very few of the townspeople, since she rarely left the Hole in the Wall except to go to Bandera on the weekends, and that was about to stop. It was a chapter in her life that needed to be closed.

Val shook her head. She had to concentrate on the present.

It looked as though Scott was organizing a grand tour for those who wanted it, so she went inside the lodge to give it one last going-over, trying to view it as someone seeing it for the first time might. As she wandered through the rooms, she thought everything was just about as perfect as human hands could make it. It was the kind of place she would have enjoyed spending a week in as a guest...if she could have afforded it. A week at the Hole in the Wall didn't come cheap, but she couldn't in her wildest dreams envision its being anything but a resounding success.

PROMPTLY AT SIX-THIRTY, the Austin band Scott had hired arrived in a chartered bus and began setting up their instruments near the front veranda. At the side of the lodge, guests started drifting toward the picnic tables in anticipation of being fed. Shortly afterward, one of the caterers rang a brass dinner bell, and the feast began.

The amount of food served was staggering, but it didn't seem to Val that much of it would go to waste. She mingled with people who, unless they asked, didn't have the slightest idea who she was.

Finally, when it looked as though everyone had been served, she got a plate for herself. Suddenly a voice beside her said, "I don't believe we've met."

She turned to see a tall, attractive man dressed in uniform. A glance at the emblem on his shirtsleeve told her he was the sheriff of Claro County. "I don't believe we have, either. I'm Valerie Drayton."

"And I'm Wayne Jackson. How do you do, Valerie. I've noticed you watching over these proceedings like a mother hen."

She smiled. "I'm the general manager here. It's my job." Looking again at the uniform, she asked, "Are you on duty?"

"I'm afraid so. But I couldn't pass up the opportunity to let Scott feed me. Do you have a dinner partner?"

"No, I hadn't planned to sit down. I thought I'd keep an eye on things."

"That's no way to enjoy food like this," Wayne said. "Let's fill our plates, find a seat and get acquainted."

"I'll take you up on that, Sheriff."

Val decided she couldn't have found a more pleasant dinner companion. Wayne Jackson apparently knew everybody. One woman had piqued Val's curiosity simply because she kept to herself and wore a rather sad expression. Val had noticed that many of the women present made a point of going over to speak to her, but the woman herself had positioned herself on one of the benches and hadn't moved from that spot all evening.

"The woman over there, Wayne...the one in blue. Who is she?"

Wayne looked in the direction Val had indicated. "That's Mary Gibson. Why?"

"She doesn't appear to be having a very good time, and my job is to see that everyone does. I'd best have a word with her after the eating's over."

"Have a word with her, by all means, but if you want to know why she's keeping to herself, you have only to look as far as the fellow who's talking to Scott and Beverly right now."

Val scanned the sea of faces, then spotted the man. "Oh, yes...his name is Bubba, right?"

"His name's Al, but everyone calls him Bubba."

Val had been introduced to him earlier and had been a little put off by him. Bubba seemed to consider himself the epitome of charm, but it certainly wasn't apparent to the naked eye. He'd done nothing to indicate he had a wife with him tonight. In fact, he had flirted with most of the women present, young and old. She glanced again toward Mary Gibson and felt surprisingly sorry for her.

Wayne turned to speak to the man on his right, and Val continued studying Bubba, Scott and Beverly. The beauty had stuck so close to Scott's side all evening one might have thought them joined at the hip. Val's eyes moved on and focused on a group of six people who had chosen to sit on the veranda steps to enjoy their food. She recognized Lynn McKinney, and she knew the man sitting beside Lynn was Dr. Sam Russell. She had also met Cal McKinney and Serena Davis because of the boot shop they had opened at the Hole in the Wall. But she had never seen the other two people before, so when Wayne returned his attention to her, she asked about them.

"The dark-haired man is Lynn and Cal's brother, Tyler, and the woman next to him is his fianceé, Ruth."

"Ah, the vintners."

Wayne smiled. "The McKinneys are sort of Crystal Creek's first family. I've often wondered what it must be like to grow up in a clan like that . . . or any kind of clan, for that matter."

Val, who had been studying the McKinneys, turned to him. "Sounds like you might be like me— an only child."

"I didn't have a family of any kind. I grew up in foster homes."

How awful, Val thought. She might not have had a conventional childhood, but she'd at least had a father who had doted on her. But she hadn't detected any wistfulness in Wayne's voice. His statement had been very matter-of-fact. The minute the words were out of his mouth, he spotted an acquaintance, smiled and waved and called out, "How're you doing, Charlie?"

Val and Wayne spent another twenty minutes or so eating and talking. He was a fountain of information about Claro County and its citizens. Val hated to see the pleasant interlude end, but Wayne soon declared he had to get back to work. "Thanks for having dinner with me, Val. I enjoyed it."

"So did I, Wayne. It's been very nice meeting you."

"We'll be seeing each other again."

"Sure. Good night."

The band struck up its first number, and diners began rising from tables and moving to the front veranda where the dancing would take place. Val thanked the members of the Chuck Wagon Gang for the fantastic job they'd done, then went into the lodge to heap praise on Carla, Fee and their helpers. When she came back outside, she felt a hand at her elbow. Turning, she looked into the grinning face of Jeff Harris.

"Well, good evening, Jeff. Where've you been?"

"Earl's been riding herd on me like a Spanish governess. I don't know what in hell he thinks I'm gonna do—abduct some local princess and hold her ransom? But he finally got tired and went to the bunkhouse. Now I'm gonna have me some fun. Want to dance?''

"Well . . . yes, thanks. I'd love to."

Jeff was a smooth, self-confident dancer. Val was a little embarrassed by her lack of skill. "I'm a bit rusty," she confessed.

"Hey, you're doing great! Tell me something— what's it like working for ol' Scott?"

Val suppressed a smile. "Ol' Scott" was hardly the way she regarded her employer. "He's a marvelous boss. Very competent and very serious about what he's doing."

"Yeah, that's Scott, all right. Competent and serious. And something of a stuffed shirt, if you ask me. I wonder if he ever relaxes and has fun . . . whatever fun is to him."

Over Jeff's shoulder, Val watched Scott and Beverly dancing. Beverly didn't just dance like everyone else. Her body slithered and slid, and her hair swung around her head like waves of wheat in a field. Scott didn't even try to match her movement for movement. Although he held on to her, he seemed to be watching rather than participating in her performance. Several couples stopped dancing to watch them.

Val turned her head away. "He seems to be having fun now," she commented.

Jeff's head swung around. "Yeah, who is that gal anyway? Every time I've seen Scott tonight, she's been right there."

"Her name is Beverly Townsend. Check out the dining room walls sometime. You'll find out all about her."

"Are she and my brother . . . you know, close?"

"I have no idea what their relationship is, Jeff. None whatsoever. Scott never talks about his private life, and I wouldn't dream of asking."

"She sure likes to be noticed." Jeff made a scoffing sound. "There's one like her in every crowd."

That remark surprised Val. Most men, it seemed to her, were struck dumb by Beverly's incredible beauty and became instant admirers. Jeff seemed to be an exception.

The music stopped, and Val stepped back. "Thanks, Jeff. Now I really must tend to duty."

Jeff didn't release her. Instead, he gave her an odd look, half amused, half questioning. "You know something—you remind me of Scott in a way."

"Oh?"

"Yeah. All business."

Val took another step back, and this time Jeff's hand dropped to his side. "That's what I'm paid to be—all business. Thanks again for the dance. Now, if you'll excuse me..." She strode off and disappeared into the crowd, searching for Mary Gibson and trying to think of a way to get the poor woman into the party mainstream.

How odd, Val thought. *I don't even know the woman, and I'm already thinking of her as poor Mary.*

Mary was still sitting in the spot she had occupied all evening. She appeared to be in her late forties or early fifties, Val thought as she approached the woman, and was...well, *plain* was the kindest adjective Val could think of. Her graying auburn hair was carelessly styled to cover her rather sallow complexion. Though Val was certainly no clotheshorse, even she knew that Mary's blue dress had not been fashionable for years. The overall picture she presented was one of absolute colorlessness.

"Hello," Val said gently. "I don't believe we've met. I'm Val Drayton, Scott's general manager."

Mary looked up and smiled. The smile transformed her face to an astonishing degree, making her look sweet and almost pretty. "How do you do, Val. I'm Mary Gibson."

Val took a seat across from her, noticing that Mary had the saddest eyes she had ever seen. "Nice party, isn't it?"

"Very nice. This is such a lovely place. So unusual for Crystal Creek."

"Have you lived here long?"

"All my life," Mary said.

"Crystal Creek is a great little town."

"I suppose it is. But I have nothing to compare it with."

"Do you have children?"

"Yes, I...we have a daughter, but she's married and lives away."

Mary's eyes darted over the crowd, then settled again on Val. To Val it seemed the woman's manner toward her was unusually cautious. Perhaps she was one of those people who found making conversation with strangers almost painful. "Tell me, Mary, what do you do?"

"Do?"

"Do you have a job or a special interest, hobby, something like that?"

"No, I...I'm a housewife."

Once again Mary's eyes wandered over the crowd. This time, Val noticed, they settled briefly on her husband, Bubba. The look on Mary's face was one of defeat. Val made a mental note to find out more about Bubba Gibson. Though she talked to Mary for another ten minutes or so, she couldn't say it was a very satisfactory conversation. Certainly she didn't feel as though she'd made much progress toward getting to know the sad-eyed woman. When they parted, in fact, Val realized that even more than before, she thought of her as "poor Mary"... but she didn't know why.

THE HOUR WAS LATE. Most of the guests had gone, leaving only about two dozen hard-core party types. The Chuck Wagon Gang had loaded up and driven away hours ago, but the bar was still open, and the band was booked to play until midnight. From her vantage point on the veranda, Val spotted Jeff and a couple of the ranch hands, but they were keeping to themselves, drinking beer and avoiding the rest of the guests. In fact, Jeff had stayed away from his brother all evening.

She then looked toward the picnic tables where Scott was entertaining Beverly, the McKinney clan and the Gibsons, plus a few others she hadn't met. She was glad to see Mary had joined them. Everyone seemed to be having a good time. They were hanging on Scott's every word. He didn't look much like a "stuffed shirt" right now. Val didn't think she had ever seen him so animated.

She envied him in a way because she was absolutely dead on her feet. There were still final details to be taken care of. She told Carla and her crew to close up the kitchen and get to bed. She paid the band and the bartender, thanking them all profusely. She checked on her office and locked it for the night. Then she slipped away from the lodge and went to her cottage. Once the door was closed, she all but collapsed.

But as tired as she was, she was elated, too. The opening had been a huge success. Val had heard nothing but raves all evening, so word of mouth should get the ranch off to a grand start. She had done a good job, and that always gave her a sense of satisfaction. It might even help get her through tomorrow.

Undressing, she put on her favorite robe—a ratty old faded blue terry-cloth thing she'd had forever. She often thought the robe was like a child's security blanket for her. When she curled up in it, she just seemed to think better.

And she had plenty to think about. She wouldn't allow herself the luxury of sleep until she had decided exactly how to handle tomorrow. Tomorrow was Saturday and she would drive to Bandera, as usual. Only this time she wouldn't stay the weekend. She was going to tell Bruce it was over.

Val and Bruce Flannery had been lovers for almost a year. Bruce, a good-looking, fun-loving cowboy, had once seemed the answer to her dreams. He was thoughtful, kind, a lot of fun to be with and a marvelous lover. They'd had some wonderful times together.

But then, about three months ago, things had begun going flat. Outwardly, nothing appeared to have changed, but inside Val knew better. She had begun to suspect Bruce would never settle down and commit to anyone or anything for a lifetime. In many ways he reminded her of her father. Perhaps that had been the attraction in the first place, but that wasn't what she wanted for the long haul. It was one of the reasons she had so eagerly applied for the position of general manager here at the ranch. A separation, she'd felt, would force her to take a good hard look at her relationship with Bruce and decide if she wanted to pursue it.

Now she knew she didn't. Her attraction to Scott had shown her that. Oh, she knew that was pure fantasy, that nothing would ever come of it. But Scott had introduced her to a kind of man she hadn't known existed—industrious, focused, principled. There *were* men like that in the world, and with luck, she'd find one of her own someday.

She didn't expect Bruce to be heartbroken, but tomorrow was going to be difficult anyway, another ending. Whenever Val looked back on her life, she envisioned it as chapters in a book—her mother's departure, the ranches she had been forced to leave just about the time she'd begun making friends, the schools where she had always been the new kid, her father's death. Now Bruce.

The knock at the door startled her. *Lord, no problems,* she hoped. Scrambling to her feet, she hurried to the door. "Yes?" she called.

"Val, it's Scott. Open up."

"But, Scott, I...I'm not dressed. I have on this old bathrobe...."

"I've seen old bathrobes before. Open up!"

She turned the knob and opened the door. He stood in the soft glow of the porch light, hands on hips and a puzzled expression on his face. "Well, are you going to ask me in?"

Val cinched the robe tighter around her waist. "Yes, of course. Please come in."

He brushed past her, then turned to her. "What *is* this?" he asked with a frown.

"I...what's what?"

"Why are you in here? Why aren't you outside? The band's still playing, and there are still guests here."

Oh, Lord, he was angry. Had he expected her to stay until the last guest left? That hadn't crossed her mind. "Scott, I'm sorry if you expected me to stay. I just thought...well, it seemed the crowd had boiled down to a few of your friends, and I was tired.... I took care of everything. I paid the band and the bartender and—"

He made an impatient sound. "That's not what I mean. Why aren't you out there celebrating with me? You're more responsible for tonight's success than anyone.''

"It *was* a success, wasn't it?" she said, relaxing. He wasn't mad, after all.

His expression softened, and he smiled. "A roaring one." Stepping toward her, he put his hands on her shoulders. "I couldn't have done it without you. That's why I wanted you to share the glory."

Val felt her face flush, a maddening trait of hers that she hated. "No, tonight's *your* party and your glory. I'm just hired help."

He stared down at her a second before saying, "I never want to hear you say that or think it. You're much more than hired help, Val. You're my right hand."

And then he kissed her.

It wasn't all that much of a kiss. He simply pulled her to him, bent his head and dropped the kiss on her very startled mouth, then straightened and smiled at her. But for a fleeting second she had felt his lips, warm and hard, on hers, and she had felt the contours of his body. And she knew that kissing Scott felt better than anything had in recent memory. Val was completely unnerved.

"Please get dressed and join us," Scott implored.

Right now, Val thought, the last thing she needed was a heavy dose of Beverly Townsend. "Scott, let me beg off. I'm leaving in the morning, and I'd like to get an early start,'' she fibbed.

He backed away. "Oh, that's right. I forgot you always go somewhere over the weekend."

"I'll be back early, but I really do have to go."

"You're not staying away until Sunday night?"

"No, I'll be back tomorrow afternoon. I have to get ready for Monday, you know. Tonight was fun. Monday the serious business begins."

"Hmm." Scott reached and put his finger on the indentation in her bottom lip, tapping gently. "You know, Val... it wouldn't hurt you to forget work for... oh, twenty minutes every month or so."

"Well, I do. I..."

"All right. I won't pressure you. Get a good night's sleep, and I'll see you when you get back. Again, thanks for everything."

"You're welcome."

A second later he was gone. Val dazedly walked into her bedroom and sank to the edge of the bed. *This won't do, my girl, not at all. Get these thoughts out of your head. They'll only lead to disappointment and the possibility of losing the job of your dreams. Even if it's one-sided, romance and business don't mix.*

Yes, the thoughts were dangerous. And they certainly underscored the necessity for breaking off with Bruce. Never had one of his kisses made her heart pound this way. So Scott had unwittingly taught her something else. Somewhere there was a man whose kisses would make her feel like this—and she wasn't going to stop looking until she'd found him.

CHAPTER FOUR

THE DRIVE from the Hole in the Wall to the Trail's End Dude Ranch outside Bandera took well over an hour, though the distance was only fifty miles. But they were very crooked miles of two-lane highways traversing the kind of scenery that brought out weekend gawkers. Val had driven the route so many times she felt she knew every bend in the road like the back of her hand, and this morning she was too preoccupied to notice the scenic splendor around her.

As she drove through the ranch's main gate, Val honked and waved at some of her former co-workers. Braking, she rolled down the window and stuck her head out. "Anybody seen Bruce?"

"He was down by the branding chute a while ago," someone called out.

"Thanks." Val parked her car, got out and strode over familiar territory to the branding area, behind one of the barns. Bruce, she saw, wasn't doing the actual branding, but merely standing by, watching. She walked up behind him and put a hand on his shoulder.

He turned and gave a start. "Well, hello, darlin'. You're kinda early today, aren't you? I don't get off work for a couple'a more hours."

"I ... I'm going to have to get back, Bruce. There's an awful lot that needs doing."

"You're not staying tonight?" he asked with a frown.

Val shook her head. "But I do want to talk to you."

"So...talk away."

The lowing of the cows and bleating of the calves set up a frightful din. "Could we go someplace else?"

"I suppose so," he said, searching her face, as if he had heard something unusual in her voice. "This way."

A peeling wooden bench encircled the thick trunk of an ancient tree. Bruce gestured toward it, and they sat down. "So...what's up?" he asked bluntly.

"Something is."

Val took a deep breath. "The truth is, I won't be coming back at all, Bruce."

A ponderous minute of silence followed. Then he sighed. "So that's it. Another guy?"

"No, nothing like that."

"What then?"

Lord, how could she explain it? Bruce deserved an honest answer.

"It's not just one thing, Bruce. It…it hasn't felt right for some time."

Bruce rubbed his chin and smiled ruefully. "Well, babe, maybe it's best. I've been having an awful itch lately, like it's time to move on."

Val didn't know if that was the truth or if he was engaging in some male face-saving, but it didn't matter. She chose to believe him. "I've been moving on all my life," she said quietly. "I'd like to get set in concrete somewhere."

They sat under the tree and talked for perhaps twenty minutes, then parted with a light embrace. As she walked back to her car, Val felt as though some tremendous weight had been lifted from her.

Her hand was on the car's door handle when she heard her name being called. Turning, she saw Jerry Cooper, the foreman of Trail's End, advancing on her. "Wait up, gal. I got somethin' to tell you."

"Hello, Jerry. How're things going?"

"Not too bad. Glad I caught you. There was a lady here this past week askin' for you."

Val frowned. "Who was she?"

"Got no idea. Judgin' from that fancy foreign car and her clothes, I don't 'magine she lives from payday to payday. Wouldn't give me a name or telephone number or nothin'. And you know what, I flat couldn't remember the name of the place you're workin' now. I told her it was a new place northeast of here, but 'course that didn't help much. And Bruce was off that day, so I couldn't ask him.''

"Mmm. Can't begin to imagine who it could have been.''

"She sure was actin' peculiar, seemed to me. Nervous, you know. Ain't got somebody you owe money to, do you?''

Val smiled. "Not that I'm aware of.''

"She asked me all kinds of questions about you.''

"What kind of questions?''

"Oh...how well did I know you, for one. I told her I guess I know you pretty good since you worked here so long. Then she started askin' me what kind of person you were and a bunch of things like that. I figured I didn't have any business answerin' that kind of stuff. I finally told her you're usually around on the weekends, and she said she might be back.''

"Really puzzling,'' Val said with a little frown. "And I'm not going to be here this weekend, Jerry. Tell you what, though...'' Opening the car door, she got her handbag and rifled through it until she found a notepad. "I'll write down my address and phone number. If she happens to come back, you'll have it.''

"Thanks. Sorry about it. My memory ain't what it used to be.''

"It doesn't matter. Here you go. I can't believe it was very important anyway.''

"I'll put this someplace where I won't forget it,'' Jerry promised. "You take care, hear?''

"Sure, Jerry. You, too.''

Val naturally was mildly curious about the woman, but, since she couldn't imagine why anyone could be looking for her, she decided it was probably a case of mistaken identity and she put the entire incident out of her mind.

Feeling as free and light as air after her session with Bruce, she decided to indulge herself. She'd stop at a sinfully wonderful German smokehouse in Fredericksburg for lunch. Wurst, sauerkraut, potato pancakes and something chocolate for dessert. Then when she got back to Crystal Creek, she might not go straight to the Hole in the Wall. Maybe she'd do some shopping. She really felt as though this was the first day of the rest of her life.

SCOTT SAT BROODING in his office. Beverly had left about fifteen minutes ago—stormed out was more accurate—and he had been doing some heavy thinking about their relationship. It wasn't going anywhere and never would, he now admitted. They had basically different outlooks on life, and though opposites might attract, it had been Scott's observation that they didn't wear well together.

In many ways Beverly reminded him of Jeff—forever wanting to do something fun, always accusing him of being too uptight. She was breathtakingly lovely and exhaustingly vivacious. It was impossible not to be taken with her, but Scott often wondered if she had ever entertained a serious thought for more than five minutes...the very same thing he'd so often wondered about Jeff.

So he knew the relationship was about to wither on the vine. He suspected he was beginning to bore Beverly. She had dashed in, wanting him to take her to Zack's or to Austin or *somewhere, for heaven's sake,* and all he'd wanted was a pleasant evening at home. Pleasant evenings at home were hardly her style, so he was sure she'd end up at Zack's tonight with a gaggle of her cronies. And the thought didn't bother him at all. That ought to tell him something.

Swiveling in his chair, Scott stared out the window at the quiet grounds of Hole in the Wall. Hardly anything stirred. Earl was probably around somewhere; he usually was, having no family that Scott knew anything about. Just then two men came into view. Both were dressed in white shorts and carried tennis rackets. Jeff and the pro, Mark Whatley. Scott hadn't known his brother played tennis, but he figured Jeff was probably good at it. Jeff had always been good at games, sports, dancing ... or anything that didn't involve serious commitment.

But he had to give his brother credit for one thing. Jeff's ability to ingratiate himself with total strangers had to be second to none. Scott had noticed that, in the space of only a few days, Jeff had established a hail-fellow sort of camaraderie with the other men. It was amazing. Jeff couldn't rope a steer, brand a calf or do anything that was of much use on a ranch, but men who could do all of it had apparently accepted him as one of them. That was a real talent, and Scott had often thought if Jeff would only channel it in some worthwhile direction, there was no limit to what he could accomplish.

Just then a streak of blue flashed by the window. It was Val's Ford. Scott smiled, quite surprised at how pleased he felt about having Val back. He had often wondered where Val went every weekend, and now he wondered why she was back on Saturday afternoon instead of Sunday evening.

Maybe he'd take advantage of her early return, he thought. After giving her plenty of time to get to her cottage, he reached for the phone and punched a button.

She answered after one ring. "Yes?"

"I saw your car, so I knew you were home. Any plans for tonight?"

"No, not a thing. Do you need me to do something?"

"Yes, have dinner with me. This place is as quiet as a tomb."

There was a pause before she said, "Well . . . all right, Scott. Maybe we can go over—"

"Go over nothing. Not tonight. Come prepared to tell me about a book you've just read or how you feel about the Mideast situation or the fall of communism or anything but work."

He heard a chuckle on the other end of the line. "Okay. I'll be thinking about thoughtful and provocative subjects."

"Come on over at six-thirty and we'll have a drink."

"Fine. See you then."

After hanging up, Scott sat with his hand resting on the phone for several minutes. Damned if he knew why he was doing this. It went against all his concepts of the way to conduct business, especially when one's business associate was a beautiful woman.

But he'd led an awfully solitary life during the months he'd worked on the ranch. The dates with Beverly had begun fairly recently and showed signs of terminating soon. Maybe he just wanted someone to talk to. One never simply sat down and held a meaningful conversation with Beverly. Beverly's conversations leaned heavily toward who was doing what, where and with whom.

It occurred to Scott with something of a start that he might possibly just need a friend. He guessed he had to go all the way back to law school to recall chums, buddies, pals. And Valerie Drayton seemed to be the sort of woman who knew how to be a friend.

But friends and only friends, he cautioned himself.

AFTER TALKING TO SCOTT, Val spent the next hour or so on household chores that she usually saved for Sunday nights. Those done, she changed into starched jeans and a fresh shirt. Leaving the cottage, she had intended taking a walk around the grounds—she never seemed to tire of that—but hearing some activity on the tennis courts, she strolled in that direction.

Jeff and Mark were finishing up a match. Val didn't get to watch them play long, but it seemed to her that Jeff was holding his own with the pro. After shaking hands over the net, they strode past her, faces flushed with exertion. Mark greeted her warmly and headed for his car, but Jeff lingered.

"How're you doing, boss lady?"

"I'm fine, thanks. I don't know much about tennis, but you looked like you're pretty good at it."

"Oh, I am," he said with his charming grin. "At that and a lot of things. Now it's Saturday night, my night to howl. Wanna come along?"

Val smiled. "No, thanks. I have plans."

"Too bad. Your loss, sorry to say. Come what may, I always manage to have fun on Saturday night. So long." He walked away, grinning at her over his shoulder.

Val watched him until he disappeared into the bunkhouse. Brash and cocky as the devil, Jeff was. It wasn't difficult for her to see why he and Scott had a strained relationship. But Jeff was also good-natured and likable. Earl liked him and so did the other hands. Scott, she thought, ought to loosen up a little. It seemed to her that no differences should be so great that they couldn't be resolved. The two men didn't even have to like each other a whole lot, but they were *brothers*, for heaven's sake.

Val turned and looked in the direction of the lodge. Scott's call had surprised her. Where was Beverly? But there could be any number of answers to that. She could be filming a commercial in Austin, modeling in a fashion show, anything. Scott probably was at loose ends and needed some company. With that in mind, she crossed the grounds to the lodge, entered the back door, walked through the deserted rooms and found her employer in his office.

He looked up when he heard her. "Is it six-thirty already?"

"On the dot."

"Now why did I ask that? You're always very punctual. Have a seat and I'll fix us a drink." Uncurling from his chair, Scott stretched his arms and flexed his shoulders, causing a rippling of muscles beneath his shirt. "You had vodka and tonic the other night. Is that what you want?"

"Yes, thanks."

There was a wet bar behind louvred doors. As Scott mixed their drinks he said, "I'll be spending tomorrow in Austin with my mother."

Val wondered why he was telling her that. "Oh? Is there something you want me to do for you while you're away?"

"No. I just thought if you came looking for me, you ought to know where I was."

"Well...have a nice visit."

"How was your day?"

"Oh...so, so."

He carried her drink to her. "I wondered if there was a problem since you always stay away all weekend. I'm not prying, just wondering."

Val took her drink and sipped it while Scott sank down in his chair again. "I don't mind questions, Scott. There's little about my life that isn't an open book. As a matter of fact, I spent this morning breaking up with a boyfriend."

He looked over the rim of his glass. "Your idea or his?"

"Mine. It wasn't very dramatic."

A second of silence passed. Val was itching to ask how come it was Saturday night and he was reduced to asking his manager to have dinner with him. But she wouldn't. She searched her mind for a safe subject. "That picture over there, Scott... I've always meant to ask about that."

He smiled. "That was my dad's first grocery store. He went on to build two more. Those stores were what put me through law school."

"Then they were successful."

"They were, but that's not what I meant. Dad let me work in those stores, and I saved my money. And since he wanted me to go to law school in the worst way, he was very flexible about my hours. I worked a lot."

"Did Jeff also?"

Scott's expression altered in a subtle way. "Sort of."

"What happened to the stores?"

"Dad sold out to a big chain. He sure didn't want to, but there was no way a family enterprise could compete. I'm convinced that watching what the chain did to his beloved stores is what killed him. That or boredom."

"Did you enjoy law school?" Val asked idly.

"I hated it!" Scott blurted out, surprising her. "Every law student with half a brain hates law school. The professors are arrogant despots, and the course loads are impossible. But if you love the idea of the law, you have to go through it."

"If you loved the idea of the law so much, why did you quit?"

The question caused Scott to lapse into deep thought. He sipped his drink and furrowed his brow. "A lot of reasons," he finally said, telling her nothing.

"Were you good at what you did?"

He snorted. "Oh, yes. At the risk of sounding immodest, I was the best. When I finished in a courtroom, my client got the kids, the house, the car, the boat, the VCR, the whole enchilada. That kind of stuff gets around. I couldn't handle all the cases that came my way."

He sounded bitter, but Val couldn't tell if he was bitter toward the system ... or himself for using it so successfully. "Well, Scott, people are going to get divorces, and they need representation," she offered weakly. "I'm sure the other side was always trying to do the same thing."

"True, but you can only spend so many years doing that kind of thing before it gets hard to look in the mirror. That is, if you've got a shred of fair play left in you. There's going to be a moment of truth."

"What was yours?"

Scott stood up and drained his glass. "Want another drink?" he asked.

"No, this is fine, thanks."

He walked to the bar and mixed a drink. "It was a routine divorce, or as routine as the breakup of a thirty-year marriage can be. At least I thought it was going to be routine. The family was rich as Midas—oil, gas, real estate, cattle, insurance, you name it—and the divorce so alarmed the old grandmother that she made out a new will."

Scott returned to his seat with a fresh drink. "Then she died not long after that. The new will left five million a year to her daughter, bought off her soon-to-be-ex-son-in-law with a lump sum of five million, and gave each of her grandkids four hundred thousand dollars a year for life. The rest went to three hospitals, a couple of museums and a ballet company. That's the kind of money that was involved.''

Scott took a deep breath. ''The daughter and grandkids wanted to sue the estate. They said it wasn't enough money to get by on. That's when I completely lost it and told them what a bunch of money-hungry bloodsuckers I thought they were. A week after that I went looking for something, and I found this.''

Val had to admit it was quite a story. It was hard for an ordinary working person to imagine how five million a year wouldn't be enough to get by on. ''Did they sue?'' she asked.

''Yeah.''

''Did they get more money?''

''Yeah.'' He took a hefty swallow of his drink, then slapped the desk with his palm. ''Enough of this. I have an idea. Forget rummaging around in the kitchen to see what Carla left. Let's go somewhere for dinner.''

''All right, thanks.''

''Got a favorite spot?''

''Well…there's not a lot to choose from, but I'm sort of partial to that steak house out on the highway.''

''You're on.''

"But I want to change first. That's a pretty nice place."

"You look fine to me, but whatever makes you feel better. Just don't get too gussied up. I'm going to wear what I have on. Sure you don't want another drink?"

"I'm sure," Val said. "It won't take me long to change. I'll be back in twenty minutes or so." She turned to leave, then paused at the threshold. "By the way, did you know your brother's a better than average tennis player?"

"Figures," Scott said.

IT WAS SATURDAY NIGHT, Zack's was packed, and Jeff had three days' pay burning a hole in his pocket. Earl had told him Zack's was the place to be on Saturday night, "if that's the kinda thing you find interestin'," and had given him directions. So here he was.

At the entrance he gave the joint a good going over with a practiced eye. The music was country and loud; customers were standing three-deep at the bar; and there seemed to be enough unattached women to keep things lively. Jeff threaded his way into the crowd. This was definitely his kind of place.

After a few minutes' wait, he managed to elbow his way up to the bar and order a beer on tap. While waiting for it, he reflected on the past three days. Scott had stayed completely out of his way, so that was all to the good. He didn't see much of the boss, Val, either, but he had a feeling if he screwed up big time, she'd be on his case in an instant. Earl rode him like a drill sergeant, but he was mostly bark and no bite. Actually, the old-timer and the green-horn got along pretty good, all things considered.

And the guys in the bunkhouse were his kind of people—devil-may-care types who didn't take themselves or life very seriously. Plus, the work wasn't very demanding. It was more like playact-ing than anything. This interlude in life was going to be a piece of cake.

And it *was* going to be an interlude. There was no way on earth he was going to work for Scott one minute longer than necessary. The one driving force in Jeff Harris's life was the sure knowledge that there was a big oil well out there just waiting for him to find it. And when the sweet SOB came along, that contract he'd signed with Scott would be just a piece of paper.

His beer delivered and paid for, he turned, propped his elbows on the bar and surveyed the passing scene. He didn't know a soul in the place, but that didn't faze him. He'd walked into count-less honky-tonks where he hadn't known anyone, and left in the wee hours with a sweet thing on his arm. It was part of the game.

The band had been playing "Waltz across Texas." When that ended, they lit into some good ol' Bob Wills Western swing. That emptied the floor of the less adventuresome dancers. Jeff's eyes moved over the tables and stopped at one. He recognized Beverly Townsend; who could forget her? He looked around for Scott, but his brother was nowhere to be seen. Beverly was seated at a table with three other women. Jeff thought he recognized one of them from last night's party. The other women he'd never seen before; he was sure of it. Taking a long drink of beer, he worked his way across the room and stopped at their table.

"Hello," he said.

All four women raised their eyes to him. He was met by blank stares from three of them, but Beverly smiled. "Hello. You're Jeff, aren't you? Scott's brother?"

"Ah, yes, the story of my life. Scott's brother."

"I'm Beverly Townsend."

"I know." Jeff could tell that his knowing who she was pleased her.

Beverly then introduced him to the other women. The one he'd thought he recognized was Beverly's cousin, Lynn McKinney. After only three days in the area, Jeff had heard plenty about the Mc-

Kinneys. He acknowledged the introductions and wondered if he should ask one of the women to dance or if he should just move on.

But Beverly was adept at the social graces. "You probably don't know anyone here, right?"

"Right."

"Why don't you join us?"

"Thanks, ladies. I'd like that." He found an empty chair and pulled it up to the table. "Where's Scott?" he asked Beverly.

"I'm sure I don't have the slightest idea," she said testily. "Apparently he prefers a quiet evening at home to Zack's."

"Figures," Jeff said.

Beverly then proceeded to bombard him with information about the other women at the table. Lynn, he learned, was engaged to someone named Sam Russell, and had Sam not been out of town, Lynn would not have been at Zack's. In fact, she looked a little bored, and shortly after Jeff sat down, Lynn excused herself and left.

The other two women's names were Shirley and Abby, and they had known Beverly "forever." They were both pretty in a way that screamed of sunshine and fresh air. Neither of them said much, only followed Beverly's lead. She, of course, sparkled like a diamond.

Jeff had taken the time to scan the clippings on the walls of the lodge's dining room. At least half of them seemed to have concerned one Beverly Townsend, starting back when she looked about fourteen, a beauty even then. While looking at those clippings, he had formed some preconceived notions about her, and she wasn't doing a thing to change any of them.

First, he'd bet she always surrounded herself with friends like Shirley and Abby, women she could outshine. Secondly, she was pulling out all the stops in an attempt to captivate him, something she doubtless did with every man she met. Forget that most of her captives would be dismissed without a second glance once they were under her spell. It was the captivation that counted.

It surprised him that Scott had taken a liking to her. Sure she was beautiful, unusually so, and Scott wouldn't be any more immune to that than other men. But when he thought back over the women his brother had been interested in, Beverly didn't fit. Scott had always gone for the ones who liked deep discussions about issues and ideas. But maybe there was some substance under Beverly's gorgeous, flirtatious exterior.

Jeff turned to Shirley. "So, Shirley, what do you do?"

"I'm a paralegal," came the soft reply.

"And you, Abby?"

"I'm a secretary at Southwest Bank."

"And you, Beverly?" He suspected the answer was nothing, but it would have been rude not to ask.

Beverly looked surprised for a second, then said, "I do volunteer work at the hospital... with children."

"That's all? You aren't employed somewhere?"

"I don't need to be," she said coolly. "I do occasional modeling and television commercials. I daresay I make more doing those than I ever could in a stuffy old office."

Jeff suppressed a smile. And, of course, not being tied down to an office meant she was free to pursue fun whenever it presented itself. He was on familiar terms with that line of reasoning.

He sensed he was rubbing Beverly the wrong way, probably because he was giving her no more attention than he was Shirley and Abby. After a decent interval had passed, after he'd bought them a round of beer, he stood. "Since I can't dance with all three of you lovely ladies at once... Shirley, would you like to dance?"

She gave him a timid smile and held out her hand, allowing him to lead her out on the dance floor. Beverly glared after them, then leaned toward Abby. "What in the devil makes him think any of us want to dance with him?"

"I thought that was nice of him," Abby said sincerely. "Not a lot of guys ask Shirley to dance. And he's cute."

Next Jeff asked Abby to dance, saving Beverly for last. But when he finally held out his hand to her, she ignored it. "Thanks, Jeff, but I just spotted some old friends I haven't seen in ages. I simply must speak to them. Will all of you excuse me?" She stood and was swallowed up in the crowd within seconds.

Grinning, Jeff sat down and focused his attention on Shirley and Abby. Once out from under Beverly's overwhelming presence, they turned out to be interesting company. He gave momentary thought to making an evening of it with one of them, but then he thought better of it. Shirley and Abby didn't seem the type who allowed themselves to be picked up in honky-tonks, and he was a newcomer still looking to ingratiate himself with the locals. So he contented himself with making pleasant conversation with two extremely nice women.

If Beverly felt snubbed, that was more her problem than his. The snub had not been intentional and wouldn't have been considered such by anyone else. But Jeff knew people like her, the compulsive flirts who enjoyed hogging the limelight and couldn't stand not to be noticed above others. He was one of them.

Beverly did not yet know it, but she had met her match.

CHAPTER FIVE

IT WAS only a quarter past nine when Scott's Lincoln drove through the ranch's main gate toward the lodge. But instead of parking it in its usual spot, he drove on toward the cottages in the back.

"You don't have to do this," Val protested from the passenger seat. "I certainly don't mind walking to my place. In fact, it's early enough that I might take a walk. I often do late at night."

"Really?" Scott pulled up in front of her cottage and parked.

"It's one of the things I love about living here at the ranch. I'd hate to live in a city where walking at night was dangerous." Val opened her door just as Scott opened his. "Thanks so much for dinner. It was delicious."

"You're welcome. I enjoyed it." They met in front of the car. "A walk sounds great. Mind if I join you?"

"Love to have you."

They walked aimlessly for a time, talking about nothing in particular. Mostly Scott told her anecdotes of his law school days. It was so difficult for Val to picture him in the middle of a group of law students, hanging out at the lake on the weekends and, in his words, "making asses of ourselves in front of the sorority girls, who were hugely successful at ignoring us." She wondered what an even younger Scott Harris had been like.

He shoved his hands into his pockets. "God, I used to love Saturday afternoons and Sundays when classes could be forgotten. We all thought we were so stressed out. Years later when I was paying for an apartment, a car and a law practice, I wondered what in hell I had found so stressful about school."

They had strolled in a circular path and now were headed back toward Val's cottage. Suddenly she stopped, frowning. "Scott, look over there at cottage four. Is that window cracked? It's hard to see in this dim light."

Scott crossed in front of her and went to inspect the window. "Sure is," he said over his shoulder. "Great!" He touched the window, and a jagged triangle of glass fell out, nicking him on the back of the hand. "We'll never get anyone out on Sunday to fix it."

Val came up behind him. "Maybe we can. I can fix the window if I can get the glass cut. And the lumberyard's open tomorrow afternoon. They darned well ought to cut it for us, considering the money you've spent with them. I'll see what I can do."

"You can fix a broken window?"

"Oh, I'm the handiest little thing you ever saw. I can rope a steer, brand a calf, mend a fence and . . . Scott, you're bleeding."

He glanced down at his hand. "Just a little nick."

"You're getting it on your shirt. Come on inside and let me put something on the cut."

"I'll do it when I get back to the lodge."

"Come on in and let me do it. You're dripping all over the place. I've got peroxide and bandages inside." Val pushed open the cottage door, leaving Scott little choice but to follow her.

Her cottage was furnished much the same as the others, like a nice motel suite. But Val had filled her living room with plants, pillows and books—small things that made the room warmer than the others.

"In here, Scott," she said, beckoning him into the bedroom.

It was that room that personified Val, Scott thought as he followed her through it and into the bathroom—quiet, neat, feminine. Although the furniture was the same as in the bedrooms in the other cottages, Val had introduced her own color scheme. She had complemented the basic white with bold accents of peach, green and blue, the same colors she had used in her office. And she had carried the colors into the white-tiled bathroom. Both rooms smelled so fresh and clean—a mixture of soap and floral fragrance.

As Val took peroxide, a cotton ball and a metal box of bandages out of the medicine cabinet, he noticed certain things—a lipstick and a cosmetic brush lying on the vanity; a pair of panty hose over the shower curtain rod, to dry, he supposed. He couldn't understand why the sight of that intimate garment unnerved him so. It wasn't as though he'd never seen such things before.

Val took his hand and dabbed the cut with a cotton ball soaked in peroxide. Then she lifted his hand to her lips and blew on the cut. Feeling her warm breath on his skin had the most unsettling effect on Scott.

Twisting to her right, she reached for a bandage. As she did, her blouse opened slightly, giving him a glimpse of a gentle mound of flesh. With great effort, he forced himself to look over the top of her head.

Using her teeth, Val ripped open the wrapper and peeled away the protective strips. Then she smiled as she gently pressed the bandage over the cut.

"There you go."

"Thanks. You're a wonderful nurse."

"You'd better soak that shirt in cold water tonight."

"Right."

"You have a good visit with your mother tomorrow and don't worry about that window. I'll take care of it."

And she would, too, he knew. "Thanks. Well, good night. I'll let myself out."

"Good night, Scott. Thanks again for dinner. I really enjoyed it."

He nodded distractedly, turned and left the bathroom, crossed through the cottage and let himself out the front door, feeling curiously as if he were escaping from something. He was halfway to the lodge before he remembered his car. Sheepishly, he reversed direction and went back to it.

This is nuts, he thought as he turned the key in the ignition. He had the feeling something profound had just happened to him, and all she'd done was put a damned adhesive strip on the back of his hand. What in hell was the matter with him?

Thank God, he had something to do tomorrow that would take him away from the ranch. He was on the verge of screwing up big-time. He knew. He'd done it before.

LILLIAN HARRIS lived in a two-bedroom town house in Shady Oaks, an Austin adult community of some eighty such dwellings. There were precious few shady oaks on the premises, but the complex came complete with a clubhouse, a swimming pool and a nine-hole pitch-and-putt golf course, all beautifully landscaped and immaculately kept. For the first six months after moving in, she had hated living there, had longed for the house she and her husband had shared for twenty-nine years.

Now she loved it. There were other widows living there, women who had become her friends. They got together for coffee, lunch, bridge and dinner. She and some of "the girls" were even planning a Caribbean cruise during the fall. She was secretary of the Shady Oaks Homeowners' Association and served on its architectural committee, a grand name for four people who okayed residents' personal projects, like privacy fences, patios and flower gardens. Like many women her age, Lillian's life had been centered around her husband and children. She'd never earned a paycheck, chaired a committee, joined a club or had a social life separate from her family. Now she had an active one, and she was having a wonderful time.

But a visit from one of her sons still made for a red-letter day. She had spent Sunday morning cleaning house and preparing far more food than two people could consume. "I really wish you hadn't gone to all this trouble," Scott said when he saw all the elaborate preparations. "I would have taken you out to eat."

"Nonsense. I love to cook when there's someone to cook for. I eat out so much nowadays. Not many of the girls like to cook, but I have them over about twice a month, and then I really pull out all the stops." Lillian paused and smiled. "You know, I used to complain that I never got to go out to dinner. Your father was always too busy. Now I look for excuses to stay home and cook."

"I guess that's normal. How're you doing, Mama? You look great."

"Thanks, hon. I feel pretty good."

While Lillian put the finishing touches on their Sunday dinner, she quizzed Scott about the Hole in the Wall. He told her about the grand opening, how well his general manager had turned out, everything but the one thing she was most curious about. It was during the meal that she brought it up. "You hired Jeff."

"Yes."

"Good. How's he doing?"

Scott shrugged, digging into roast beef and mashed potatoes. "I guess he's doing fine. I haven't heard any complaints."

"You don't see him?" Lillian sounded dismayed.

"Of course I see him . . . off in the distance."

Lillian put down her fork. "That distresses me, really it does, Scott. The two of you are *brothers*. It seems to me you should get together over coffee or drinks or something."

"Mama," Scott said patiently, "that would look bad. Others would resent what would seem like preferential treatment. He's a hired hand." He didn't bother to add that whenever he and Jeff had "got together" in the past, they'd usually wound up pissed off at each other for days.

"I had hoped you might find some sort of . . . well, *position* for him."

"Like what? There aren't any 'positions' at the ranch. I own it, Val manages it, and everyone else is a hired hand."

Lillian sighed and returned to her food. "It would have been wonderful if Jeff could have been your general manager."

Scott blanched at the thought. "Sorry, Mama. The position is filled, and I wouldn't dream of letting Val go. She's quickly becoming invaluable to me." He wanted to change the subject. "I'd like to tell you this is one of the finest meals I've ever had."

Lillian smiled, pleased. Although she had never favored one son over the other, she admitted to having a particularly soft spot for Scott. Perhaps that was because he'd given her so little trouble. He had been a placid baby who'd wake and play in his crib until she came for him. As a youngster, his toys had to go back exactly where they'd come from the minute he was finished with them. She couldn't remember all the teachers who had told her, "If I had a class full of Scotts, I'd have the easiest job in the world." He was just such a serious, responsible person and had been from day one.

Too much so, she sometimes thought. Lillian would have been the last to wish any of Jeff's mischievousness and lack of restraint on her older son. Her younger son's antics and his restlessness had almost driven her crazy. A squeaky wheel, he had demanded—and received—a lot of attention from his parents. For every teacher who'd praised Scott, there had been at least two who'd complained that Jeff "is a disruptive influence in class, Mrs. Harris."

But she did wish something or someone would come along and loosen Scott up a bit, teach him how to have fun.

Then if something or someone would come along to settle Jeff down and teach him there was more to life than fun, maybe her sons would get along a little better. That Scott and Jeff found it impossible to relate to each other was the most distressing part of Lillian's life.

"I hope you'll be patient with Jeff and give him the benefit of the doubt sometimes."

"I'm going to try, but part of his problem is that people have always been willing to give him the benefit of the doubt. He's come to expect it."

"Oh, I don't know. It seems to me he's changed a lot. He's more... humble."

"He's broke. That'll humble anyone."

Lillian sighed. "Scott," she said, reaching out and covering his hand with hers, "I want to tell you something. I don't know if you'll listen to me or not."

"I always listen to you, Mama."

"Friends come and go, but family is forever. I'm not going to live forever, and then the only blood kin you'll have, besides hopefully your own children, will be Jeff. I just want you to think about that."

Then she moved on to local gossip that meant absolutely nothing to Scott, but he listened and made appropriate comments. And Lillian didn't mention Jeff again.

VAL WAS CERTAIN that Sunday was the longest day of her life. Part of that could be attributable to her apprehension over tomorrow's arrival of the first paying guests. Mostly, however, it was because the ranch was almost deserted, and though she'd never minded being alone, she didn't think she'd ever been *this* alone. She made up her mind right then to find some activity to fill up subsequent Sundays.

But then she reminded herself that once the ranch was open for business, she might very well welcome a quiet Sunday.

She knew the lodge and cabins were in as perfect condition as human hands could make them, but she decided to check them again anyway. As she went from cottage to cottage, then room to room in the lodge, she experienced a feeling of proprietary pride. The place was the last word in inviting comfort, and she knew all the guests would be impressed down to their toes.

She went into her office, sat behind her desk and pulled her inventory out of the middle drawer. Then she gave a growl of disgust. The thing had been checked and rechecked so many times she had committed it to memory. She slipped the sheets back into the drawer and closed it. Just then the telephone rang. She glanced at it to see which light was flashing. It was the number of the lodge, not Scott's private line. Val sent up a silent prayer that it wasn't a last-minute cancellation, then picked up the phone.

"Hole in the Wall Ranch," she said crisply. "This is Valerie Drayton. May I help you?"

A few seconds of silence ensued, but she definitely could hear someone breathing. "Hello," she said.

Another second of silence, then a click and the dial tone. Val frowned her irritation, wondering why the caller hadn't had the good manners to say, "Sorry, wrong number."

Satisfied that everything was in order, she left the lodge and was crossing the grounds when she spied Earl. She was so glad to see a real-live human that she quickened her step to catch up with him.

"Good afternoon, Earl," she said brightly.

His index finger touched the brim of his well-worn Stetson. "'Afternoon, Val. Nice one, ain't it?"

"Beautiful. Pray the weather holds. I don't suppose it's reasonable to hope it only rains on the weekends from now until Christmas."

"'Fraid that'd be askin' a bit much."

"Do you have the bunkhouse all to yourself today?"

"Oh, Jeff's in there nursin' a granddaddy of a hangover, so he's about as much fun as a case of strep throat." Earl chuckled. "'Course I gotta give him credit for bein' smart enough to sleep it off to-day."

"How's he doing in general?"

"Aw, he'll be okay. Don't know beans from wild honey about bein' a cowpoke, but he'll do all right. I'll keep him on the straight and narrow. 'Least I will here at the ranch. 'Fraid I can't do nothin' about them weekends, though."

Val smiled. "Thanks, Earl. I'd sure hate to have to fire the boss's kid brother. What have you told the men about tomorrow?"

"I told 'em that ever'time they see some dude walkin' by, they's supposed to start doin' some cowboyin'. Don't worry. We'll put on a show for you."

"Great. See you tomorrow."

Earl headed for the bunkhouse, and Val turned to go to her cottage. She was crossing the grounds when she heard a horn toot. Stopping, she saw Beverly and her Cadillac heading toward her. Val waved and waited for the car to pull up beside her.

"I don't see Scott's car," Beverly said. "Does this mean he isn't here?"

"No, he isn't. He went to visit his mother."

"Oh, shoot!" Beverly slammed her palm against the steering wheel. "Wonderful! Another night with nothing to do. When's he due back?"

Val shrugged. "I don't know, Beverly. Sorry."

Beverly rolled her eyes. "Splendid!" she exclaimed irritably.

"You know...he might come along any minute. Would you like to wait? I was just on my way back to my cottage. You're more than welcome to wait there."

Beverly considered this a second, then shook her head. "No, thanks. Maybe Lynn will want to do something."

At that moment, the bunkhouse door opened, and a very bedraggled Jeff stumbled out, squinting in the bright sunshine. Beverly snorted disdainfully. "I met that one last night. He was at Zack's. He's a real ass."

"Jeff?" Val asked in surprise.

"Yeah. He's a God's-gift-to-women type, more in love with himself than with anyone."

Takes one to know one, I guess, Val thought. It would be amusing to get Beverly and Jeff together and watch them try to establish territories and jockey for position.

Beverly shifted the car into reverse. "Well, if Scott comes back, you might tell him I was looking for him. Maybe he'll call...and maybe I won't be there." With a toss of her head, she backed up and drove off.

Yes, Val decided, there had to be a frivolous side to Scott Harris that she'd never seen, because there was no way the serious, thoughtful workaholic she knew would have been attracted to Beverly beyond one evening.

WHEN SCOTT RETURNED to the ranch late that afternoon, he deliberately went in search of Jeff. He found him in the bunkhouse playing cards with Earl. None of the other hands had yet returned from their free weekend. The two men were just finishing a hand of gin rummy. They both looked up when the door opened and did double takes when they saw who their visitor was.

"'Afternoon, boss," Earl said, as he gathered up the cards. "Somethin' wrong?"

"Not a thing." Scott looked at his brother. "How about a game of pool?"

Jeff could hardly have been more surprised if Scott had come at him with his fists. He looked at Earl, then back at Scott. "Man, I'm just now beginning to feel human again. I don't know what the crack of the cue against the ball would do to my head."

"Hangover?"

"How'd you guess?"

"Last night was Saturday," Scott said. "Come on. It'll be good for you. Care to join us, Earl?"

"Nope, thanks jus' the same. Never got any good at the game. My daddy used to say bein' a good pool player was the sign of a misspent youth." He cackled.

"Sure you don't mind, Earl?" Jeff asked.

"Nope. I'll switch to solitaire."

"What are you gonna do about eating?"

"Never in my life have I had trouble rustlin' up some grub. I'll manage."

Jeff stood. "See you later, then." And he followed Scott out of the bunkhouse, curious as hell about what had prompted Scott's invitation.

In long strides, the two men walked to the back of the lodge. "Where'd you go last night?" Scott asked.

"Zack's. It's pretty nice for a honky-tonk. It's the goddamn Ritz Carlton compared to some of the watering holes I used to frequent out in West Texas. Zack's even has pretty good food. I ran into your girlfriend there."

"Beverly?"

"How many girlfriends you got? Sure Beverly."

Scott only grunted.

"I gotta tell you something, bro. Now don't take offense. This is just an offhand observation, but she sure doesn't seem like your type. "

Scott opened the back door and stood aside to let Jeff precede him into the kitchen. "We've done some dating, that's all."

Scott led the way to the game room. It was spacious and held many tables where the guests could play checkers, dominoes, cards and the like. But the room's focal points were the two regulation pool tables that occupied the center. Balls lay neatly racked on both. Scott took two cues off the wall and handed one to Jeff. "Rotation okay with you?"

"Sure."

"You break 'em."

Jeff leaned into the breaking shot and with a crack sent the balls scattering over the green felt surface. He considered the position of the one ball and gauged his shot. Having spent a goodly amount of his life hunkered over a pool table, he was roughly as good at this game as he was at tennis. He easily pocketed the one.

"I spent the day with Mama," Scott said, circling the table, eyeing the position of the two balls.

"She's fine, right?"

"Looks good to me," he said, bending over the table and tapping the two into the corner pocket. "She asked how things were going with you here."

"What did you tell her?"

"That you were doing okay."

The game continued mostly in silence, the two players circling the table like predators stalking prey. Scott scratched his six ball and cursed when

Jeff easily pocketed it. Jeff had always been the better pool player, just as he'd been better at baseball and basketball than Scott had. And with his gift of gab, he'd been better at getting the girls. Only when it came to schoolwork had Scott come out way on top. And Scott had always had to work hard for his success. Jeff, on the other hand, had scored his victories effortlessly.

But that afternoon, Scott had promised his mother that he would work hard at establishing some kind of communication with his brother, and this was the first step. Jeff would doubtless win the game, but that sort of thing no longer bothered Scott. He circled the table, noticing he was in good position to nail the ten ball. Just as he cocked his cue, however, a door somewhere in the lodge opened and closed. The tip of his cue glanced off the side of the ball. He cursed again, and Jeff laughed.

Light footsteps sounded down the hall, and Val appeared in the doorway. "Oh, I'm sorry," she said. "I'm interrupting."

"Not at all," Scott assured her. "Come in."

"No, I won't bother you. I heard voices and was curious. I didn't think anyone was here." She looked at Scott. "Did you have a nice visit with your mother?"

"Yes, thanks. Very nice."

"That's good. I took care of the broken window."

"Somehow I was sure you would."

She favored them both with a smile. "Well, I'm just going to get some things out of my office and go back to my place. Both of you have a nice evening."

"You, too," they chorused.

Footsteps again sounded down the hall. "You know something," Jeff said after a minute, *"that's* your type."

"Val? Impossible."

"Why? She got a boyfriend?"

Scott shook his head and studied the table. "As a matter of fact, she just broke up with one. But that doesn't have a thing to do with it. She's my manager."

"So?" Jeff wanted to know.

"So I have definite ideas about employer-employee relationships."

"Such as?"

"Such as distance. I don't mean you have to be cool and aloof. But if you get too close, then it's hard to criticize, hard to fire. And romance is out of the question."

"Hell, man, I'd be thinking—come on to her, and if things worked out, you might have a mom-

and-pop operation here...to say nothing of a handy squeeze nearby.'' Jeff chuckled.

Scott didn't crack a smile. "And I'd be thinking—if I came on to her and things didn't work out, I'd probably lose a good manager."

Jeff digested that, chalking his cue. "Yeah," he finally said, "I guess you would. But you can't tell me you haven't noticed that she's one fine-looking woman."

"No, I won't tell you that. Val is extremely attractive."

"And you can work with her all the time and never think about sneaking a feel or grabbing a kiss?"

Scott thought about the night of the opening when he'd grabbed a kiss. But that didn't count. It had been an impulsive thing, a by-product of his exuberant spirits. He was certain Val had taken it as such. "I work hard at keeping my more earthy instincts on hold when it comes to business."

"Then if you're not interested, I guess you wouldn't mind some other guy making a play for her."

Scott's eyes narrowed slightly. "Are you talking about yourself?"

"Why not? Earl told me I couldn't do anything but look at her, but what I do off duty should be my own business. Val's, too."

For some reason, the thought of Val and Jeff together absolutely appalled Scott. Of course he had no right to tell his employees what they could and couldn't do off the job, but Val was Jeff's boss. "That's not a good idea."

Jeff grinned. "Sounds like a hell of a one to me."

"Val's not the kind of woman a man toys with."

Jeff pretended to be offended. "Who said I'm going to toy with her?"

"Remember, I've watched you with women all my life. It's the chase and capture that counts. Once caught, the woman becomes dispensable. That's not good enough for Val."

Jeff's grin only intensified. "Seems to me you've taken a sort of proprietary interest in her."

Scott grunted and pretended to study his next shot. Perhaps he *had* come to care about Val's welfare to an unusual degree, the result, no doubt, of those shared confidences. But she was so different from the kind of woman Jeff normally sought out, and the thought that Jeff might possibly hurt her emotionally alarmed him. "I've learned a lot about Val during these past few weeks, not from asking questions but from a word dropped here and there. She's got a thing about family, probably because she never had much of one. Some widower with five kids to raise might seem like the catch of the century to her."

"And you say you're not interested in her?"

"I didn't say I wasn't interested in her as a person, but I do have definite ideas about—"

"About employer-employee relationships, I know. Maybe Val doesn't harbor those feelings."

Scott considered that a minute. He wondered if Val actually would accept a date with Jeff. It shouldn't matter to him one way or another... but it did. However, even if Val went out with Jeff, Scott personally doubted she would be interested in him long. Jeff was frivolous, and Scott didn't think Val had a frivolous bone in her body.

But what did he really know about Val off duty? He shrugged. "As long as it doesn't interfere with the ranch's operation, I suppose you can ask out anyone you like. Your shot."

They finished the game. Jeff won, naturally, having made all his shots, plus Scott's six and ten. They replaced their cues and left the room. "Enjoyed it," Scott said, "but I'm rusty. Let's go into the kitchen and see what we can find for dinner."

"One more question," Jeff said.

Scott halted. "Yes?"

"Do you ever take a chance on anything?"

"Chance? Well, I suppose there are those who would list the Hole in the Wall under the heading of taking a chance."

"Yeah, but you thought about this, planned it for months. I'm talking about doing something a little rash on the spur of the moment. You know—seize the moment and tomorrow be damned."

Scott recalled the one time he had and the regrets that had prompted. "No, not any longer."

"Somehow I didn't think so." Jeff followed his brother through the lodge. He still didn't have the first clue what all this was about. Their mother probably was behind it in some form or fashion. But he *was* aware of one thing: he and Scott had occupied roughly the same territory for five entire days without so much as a snarl or harsh word passing between them. That had to set some kind of record.

CHAPTER SIX

THE FOLLOWING MORNING, Val woke before dawn and was unable to go back to sleep. Getting out of bed, she slipped on a pair of jeans and a T-shirt, then made a cup of instant coffee and carried it outside to sit on the stoop and watch the sunrise.

This was her favorite time of day, when all was hushed and still. She and her father had often shared a cup of coffee in the predawn hours while she listened to his cowboy yarns. And when he tired of them, she would tell him about whatever book she was reading. He was one of the few people who seemed to understand what books meant to her. They were her window on the world. When she'd read *Anne of Green Gables,* she'd rushed to an atlas to find out where Prince Edward Island was. The same with *Heidi.* She'd *had* to find those Swiss mountains on a map. She still did that today. She was a great reader of maps, but even as a child she'd known that was all the world travel she and her father would ever experience.

Harry Drayton had been the son of a cowboy who had been the son of a cowboy. Neither of them had ever owned a piece of land, although Harry had once made a down payment on a town lot in Abilene, promising to build his young wife a real house "someday." But when she left, he'd sold it, never dreaming, Val guessed, that his daughter might enjoy living in a real house that belonged to them and not to the owner of some ranch.

Val's eyes made a sweep of her surroundings. Everything was so quiet. The scene looked like a painting. Scott had a treasure in the Hole in the Wall, an absolute treasure. Val couldn't imagine actually owning something so wonderful, so *permanent*. How different might her life have been if Harry had ever actually built that house? Would her mother have stayed?

Val couldn't understand why she'd been thinking of her mother lately, not with any great longing or resentment, just thinking. Mostly she wondered if Vivian Drayton had ever found what she was looking for. It was so odd to think about a person she could barely conjure up a picture of.

Val had been doing an unusual amount of soul-searching lately, and that wasn't like her. Maybe it was because she was in a new place and didn't know many people. Or maybe it had to do with her age. At thirty-two she was searching for something she couldn't give a name to, just something to call her own. She, the daughter of two nomads, longed for roots above all.

The first rays of dawn peeped through tree branches, and somewhere in the far distance a rooster crowed. A light came on in the bunkhouse, then another. Val glanced toward the lodge in time to see a light come on in the kitchen. The day had begun. She drained her coffee and went inside.

A wellspring of excitement rose inside her. The first guests would begin arriving in about four hours, and then all her and Scott's plans would be put into practice. Everything had to go perfectly for Scott. He deserved that much.

After having breakfast, then showering and dressing for the day, she left the cottage in time to hear Earl giving the men a pep talk. She stood some distance away and listened.

"Okay, fellers, we're through dress-rehearsin'. Now it's show time, and I want all'a you lookin' sharp. Ever' one of you men, 'ceptin' this one here—" he pointed to Jeff "—been around cows and horses all your lives, and you know what to do with 'em. There's gonna be lots'a little kids around the place, and they's gonna be curious as the devil. You can't go losin' your patience with 'em or nuthin' like that. So get to work, and I'll see you at lunch." The men scattered, and Earl again looked at Jeff. "You stick to my heels, hear?"

"Right," Jeff said, and he walked off, one pace behind the old-timer.

Val smiled as she headed for the lodge. The guests were absolutely going to love Earl. He really belonged in one of those old Westerns on late-night TV, as the hero's sidekick. Earl was another treasure.

THE FIRST WEEK the Hole in the Wall was in business was a study in perfection. The guests were a convivial bunch who threw themselves into the spirit of the place and seemed to be having a wonderful time. Val saw to it that those who wanted to participate in organized activities were kept busy from waking to sleeping. And the guests who had come for fresh air and quiet R and R got plenty of that, too. She put in fifteen-hour days and loved every second of them.

Scott unobtrusively watched her, marveling at her stamina and vitality. She seemed to have an inner sense that told her what to do and what to say at any given moment. She was as good with little children and teenagers as she was with their parents. Nothing escaped her watchful eye. She lavished praise on the household staff; with the zeal of a hyped-up cheerleader, she inspired them to do their best. Once he'd overheard a brief exchange between Val and Carla.

"Oh, *señorita*, I've been so nervous. All these people! What if something is overdone or underdone?"

"Relax, Carla," Val had said. "I've heard nothing but raves about the food. I'm convinced that once word gets around, *Bon Appétit* will be knocking at the door, wanting to do a feature on Hole in the Wall's kitchen."

"Oh, *gracias, gracias*. Now I must go make sure there's enough cumin in the rice." And the cook had scurried away, elated.

What had instilled in Val that way with people? Scott wondered. She was the daughter of an itinerant ranch hand. Her mother had deserted her when she was seven. She had only a high school education. She'd had minimal feminine influence in her life, had never even had a home in the accepted sense of the word. Yet she had more poise, more polish, more grace under pressure than anyone he had ever known. She amazed him.

Unbidden, Jeff's words came back to him. *That's your type*. Was she? Sadly, he'd never find out. He would never take the chance of losing Val as manager of the Hole in the Wall.

By the time the last guest checked out Saturday morning, Scott, Val, Earl, everybody couldn't stop congratulating themselves and one another. It wasn't until Tuesday of the second week that Val regretfully had to report major glitch number one to Scott.

"Mark's going to have to quit, at least temporarily," she announced as she walked into his office.

Scott scowled. "He can't quit. Dammit, he has a contract!"

"An act of God, remember? His mother in Houston is sick, and he's the only one available to take care of her. He says he might be able to get back in three or four weeks. Depends on how she does. It can't be helped."

Scott slammed his fist down on the desk. "Damn! How many people have signed up for lessons this week?"

"Ten."

"What are we going to do, Val? I hate to disappoint guests."

Val sat down and crossed her legs. Scott watched the movement. Now that the ranch was open for guests, she had taken to wearing dresses or skirts and blouses instead of jeans. She always looked bandbox fresh and professional from head to toe. She also had just about the shapeliest pair of legs he'd ever seen. He'd noticed she couldn't walk across the grounds without many pairs of masculine eyes, young and old, following her.

"I have an idea," she said quietly, "but I don't know if you'll like it."

"Try me. Right now I'm pretty desperate."

"Jeff."

"Jeff?"

She nodded. "I asked Mark about him, and he says Jeff's good, certainly good enough to give beginner lessons."

Scott lapsed into thought, then said, "Well, I don't know what else we can do. Would you mind running Jeff down and sending him in here?"

"Not a bit." She stood up. "One more thing. You know the Beasleys in room ten?"

He nodded. "Middle-aged couple. He's a... dentist?"

"Optometrist. Her birthday's tomorrow. I know that because her husband asked me to order flowers for her as a surprise. I'd like to call that little German bakery across from the courthouse and order a cake, too. One big enough for all the guests. Present it to her at dinner tomorrow night."

"That sounds great, Val. I'm glad you thought of it. It'll be a nice touch."

"That's what I thought, too. I'll find Jeff and send him in right away." Pivoting, she left the office.

Scott stared after her and wondered if Jeff had asked her out yet. Or if she had accepted. Or if they'd actually gone out together. He didn't have any idea what she'd done Saturday night, and dammit, why did he even care?

He knew what he'd done Saturday night—escorted Beverly to a party at the Crystal Creek Country Club. It had been a benefit for...he'd forgotten...but the tickets had commanded an exorbitant price. All for a good cause, Beverly reminded him, and he had agreed. They'd made the date weeks before, when they'd just begun dating and anything had seemed possible between them.

Now he knew better, and if he'd needed solid proof, Saturday night had been it. The party had been top-drawer, very posh for Crystal Creek, and Beverly had been radiant. God, she loved that kind of thing, but he had very quickly tired of the festivities. Was he getting old? Forty wasn't all that far away.

But Scott knew he couldn't attribute his dislike of constant socializing to age. He'd never liked it, not even back in the Austin days when it had been a necessary part of building a society law practice. And Beverly doubtless never would never tire of it. So he didn't see much hope that their relationship would progress beyond casual dating.

"You wanted to see me, Scott?"

Scott looked up to see Jeff framed in the doorway, looking as if he'd worn cowboy garb all his life. "Yes, I do. Come in and have a seat."

Jeff sauntered into the room and looked around, letting out a little whistle. "This is a pretty elegant office."

"Thanks. I spend a lot of time in it."

Jeff didn't sit down; instead he stood in front of the desk, a curious expression on his face. "What's up? Have I committed a serious goof?"

"Not that I know of. I need your help."

"That's a switch," Jeff said with a grin.

"I hear you're a pretty fair tennis player."

"You didn't hear that from me."

"As a matter of fact, Mark told Val and she told me. Just how good are you?"

Jeff shrugged. "Well, no one's ever mistaken me for Jimmy Connors, but...I guess I'm pretty good."

"Good enough to give beginner lessons?"

"Oh, sure. Good enough for that."

Scott sat back in his chair and regarded his brother. "Mark's having to leave us for a few weeks...I hope it'll only be a few weeks...and we have a lot of people signed up for lessons. Want the job? It pays better."

Jeff's face broke into a delighted grin. "Hell, yes! I've had about all this get-along-little-doggie crap I can stand."

Scott chuckled. "You realize it's only temporary, just until Mark gets back."

"Suits me."

"And you won't want to continue staying in the bunkhouse, I'm sure. You can take one of the singles upstairs . . . temporarily."

"Man, this is great—in more ways than one."

"What do you mean?"

"It might improve my social life. I asked Val out last Saturday, but she said it wouldn't look right to the other guys. So she isn't interested in dating a cowpoke. But a tennis pro might be more up her alley. Thanks, bro. I'll go get my stuff and move upstairs."

With a thumbs-up gesture, he turned and left the office, leaving Scott to wonder if perhaps Val had suggested Jeff for the job for the precise reason his brother had just mentioned.

"Now, EARL," Jeff said, advancing on the old-timer, "I don't want to upset you, but you're about to lose your best hand."

"Huh?"

"You're looking at the new tennis pro."

"You?"

"Yep, me. You're just going to have to muddle through without me as best you can."

"Well, that sure as hell ain't gonna be hard to do." Earl began to cackle. "So you gonna dress up in them little white shorts and teach little kids how to hit a tennis ball."

"You bet."

"That there's somethin' you might be good at. You sure ain't worth the powder it'd take to blow you to hell as a cowpoke."

"Earl, I think that's the nicest thing anybody ever told me. Be talking to you, podnuh."

Jeff crossed the grounds to the bunkhouse where he packed in record time, then stowed most of his things in his truck. Carrying a large suitcase and a hang-up bag, he hurried toward the lodge. As he approached the swimming pool, he saw Val talking to a group of guests who seemed to be on a morning hike. Jeff stopped and waited until they'd left.

"Good morning," he said, walking up to her.

"Good morning." She eyed his luggage. "Are you our new pro?"

"Yeah, and I want to thank you for suggesting me to Scott."

"Don't mention it. We were in a bind, and Mark said you could handle it."

Jeff flashed her his most charming smile. "So, now that I'm no longer a lowly cowhand but am employed in a loftier position, how about Zack's Saturday night?''

"Zack's? What's that?''

"A honky-tonk.''

Val wrinkled her nose. "I'm not much for honky-tonks.''

"In Crystal Creek, Zack's is socially acceptable. Or I guess it is. Beverly Townsend goes. So does Lynn McKinney and that crowd. Now that I've moved up in the world, the least you can do is accept a date with me.''

She smiled. His being employed as a cowboy hadn't had a thing to do with her declining to go out with him. She had dated cowboys all her life. But he was a Hole in the Wall cowboy, and that made a difference. He was also Scott's brother, and why that made a difference she didn't have a clue. It just did.

But why shouldn't she go out with Jeff Saturday night? As tennis pro, he answered only to Scott, so she no longer was Jeff's boss. She didn't have a thing to do this weekend, and Jeff probably knew how to show a date a good time. "All right, Jeff. Thanks. I accept with pleasure.''

"Hot damn! See you at dinner tonight. Guess I'll be eating in the dining room from now on." He strode off in the direction of the lodge, his face alive with triumph.

SCOTT WAS a huge hit with all the Hole in the Wall guests, not only because of natural politeness and his willingness to talk and listen to everyone, but because in his big white Stetson, starched jeans and crisp white shirts, he fit everyone's idea of what a cattleman should look like. Many of the middle-aged ladies all but simpered when he stopped to have a word with them. And their husbands warmed to him because he seemed every inch a man's man.

He was in his element. He loved being in charge, and here he was in charge of something that was wholly *his*. And he kept his finger on the pulse of every facet of the ranch's operation, ready to pounce before tiny problems became big ones. That was why the episode with the Price girl did not escalate into a major to-do.

The Prices were a wealthy Austin family in cottage three. The husband was a builder and the wife a socialite, and they had brought along their two cute teenage girls. Ben Price introduced them to Scott during Monday's registration.

"Mr. Harris, I'd like to introduce my daughters. This is Molly. She's fourteen. And this is Dusty, who's sixteen."

"Almost seventeen," Dusty quickly said, glaring at her father.

Scott was surprised. Dusty could easily have passed for early twenties. Her jeans clung to her figure so tightly he wondered how she had managed to get into them, and her brilliant green T-shirt stretched tightly across ample breasts. She had enough reddish blond hair for three girls, pouty red lips and predatory eyes under heavily mascaraed lashes. Scott wondered why her parents let her wear so much makeup and dress that way.

Then he met her mother. Sandra Price was an older version of Dusty. She worked as hard at looking young as her daughter did at looking older. Her eyes were just as predatory as Dusty's and much more frank. They roamed Scott in blatant admiration, leaving him feeling rather sorry for Ben Price, who seemed like such a nice guy.

That night at dinner, Dusty flirted with Scott so openly that he was embarrassed. The way she leaned toward him, making certain her breast crushed against his arm, telegraphed an unmistakable message. She had to be discouraged quickly. When the meal was over, Scott approached the Prices. "Mr. and Mrs. Price," he said smoothly, "your daughters are lovely young girls. I'm sure they'll be beautiful women when they grow up. They remind me of my nieces. Kids that age are so cute."

The look Dusty gave him was murderous, but his remark was effective. Scott was given a thorough leave-alone for the remainder of the evening, prompting him to breathe a sigh of relief and bless his nonexistent nieces.

Then Dusty saw Jeff and immediately signed up for tennis lessons, even though she had been playing since she was eight. Now she had a far more receptive audience. Jeff could no more not flirt back with her than he could not take his next breath. Seeing the two of them together alarmed Scott more than he could say, and at the first opportunity he called Jeff into his office.

"Stay away from the Price girl," he commanded tersely.

"Aw, hell, Scott. We're not doing anything, just flirting."

"Do you have any idea how old she is?"

Jeff shrugged. "Dusty said she's almost eighteen. I was surprised. She looks older."

"She's sixteen. That's what her father told me when I was introduced to the family."

"Well, gosh...how was I to know? Somebody tells you how old they are, you believe them."

Scott, having made promises to their mother, did not want to be guilty of lecturing his brother, but dammit, he didn't trust Jeff when it came to the opposite sex. "Jeff, you're going to have to be careful with our female guests. I know how you are with women. Not one from puberty to senility is safe with you. All it would take is one irate father or one incensed husband, and this operation would be deep in more crap than we could handle. I know Dusty's a flirt just asking for trouble, but she's not going to get any here. Understand?"

"Sure, Scott. I understand," Jeff said, a bit irritably. "What do you think I am, some kind of pervert who chases after teenage girls? Val's much more to my liking."

Scott stiffened. "Val?"

"Sure. I told you she wouldn't go out with a cowboy. But she'll go out with a tennis pro. I'm taking her to Zack's Saturday night." Jeff grinned effusively. "Don't worry about Dusty Price. I'll be nothing but professional from now on."

"And with all the women guests from now on?"

"Sure. Like I said, Val's a real foxy lady... and she's here all the time. Plus, she isn't sixteen." Jeff shot his brother a little salute and left the office.

Scott stared morosely after him. It had been on the tip of his tongue to order Jeff to stay away from Val, too, but he couldn't do that.

Funny. He would have bet anything that if Jeff asked her out again, she'd still have said no. But she had accepted, and now that he thought about it, he wasn't really surprised. Jeff had such a way with women. And Val was a woman, after all. Increasingly, he was all too aware of that.

THE SECOND WEEK ended on as much of an upbeat note as had the first, with many satisfied guests promising to return. Once the last of them had departed and the staff had fanned out through the lodge and the cottages to ready them for next week, Scott went into his office for a much needed rest.

He loved what he was doing, but it was exhausting staying forever on the alert. He was beginning to get jealous of his weekends. Removing his big hat, he sat down in his comfortable chair, propped his feet on the desk, leaned back and closed his eyes. He supposed he should go to Austin tomorrow to see his mother, but he just might commandeer Jeff into doing that. As long as one of her sons visited, Lillian was happy, and God knows, Jeff had visited her far less than Scott had over the years.

Ah, hell, Scott thought. Tomorrow was Sunday. Jeff would have a crushing hangover.

Or would he? He was going out with Val tonight, and she just might be a sobering influence on him. Scott couldn't imagine her putting up with the kind of Saturday night hell-raising Jeff had always been so fond of. It was possible his brother might be reasonably clearheaded tomorrow.

Scott closed his eyes and dwelt on the delight of doing absolutely nothing tomorrow. Then there was a tap on the door. Swinging his feet off the desk and straightening, he called, "Come in."

Beverly swished into the room, eyes afire. "Are you avoiding me?" she demanded.

Scott got to his feet. "Avoiding you? No, Beverly, not at all."

"Do you have any idea how long it's been since you've asked me to do so much as have a Coke with you?"

"Want a Coke?" he asked with a grin. "I'll be glad to get one for you."

"Don't be cute." She plopped in a chair facing his desk. "You know what I mean."

Scott sat down. "Yes, I know what you mean. I'm sorry, but I've been very, very busy. There's simply no chance to get away from here during the week."

"And I suppose it's going to be that way from now on," she said icily.

"I'd like to think the day's going to come when the ranch will almost run itself, but we've only been open two weeks."

Beverly fumed a minute, then said, "I don't often find myself in the position of having to ask men for dates, but do you suppose we might *possibly* go somewhere tonight?"

Scott actually didn't want to. It had been a long, long time since Saturday nights were anything special to him, and he liked it that way. But he *had* been unfair to Beverly, he supposed. After many weeks of fairly steady dating, he'd suddenly just wrapped himself up in the ranch and all but ignored her. He was normally kinder than that.

"All right," he said smoothly. "Tonight I'll take you to Zack's. How's that?"

Her eyes brightened. "Wonderful!"

Scott honestly hadn't known he was going to suggest that until the words were out of his mouth.

THERE WAS SOMETHING about honky-tonks, mused Jeff as he escorted Val through the entrance to Zack's. He had been in hundreds of them, and even the seediest ones were magically transformed when the sun went down and the lights came on. And Zack's was so respectable people stopped there for lunch. It was at night, though, that the joint started jumping. This was the third Saturday night running he had spent here, and being the glad-hander he was, he was beginning to be known. Several people at the bar waved to him as he and Val made their way to a table.

Val was less enthusiastic about such places. Even though her dad had liked them, Bruce had liked them and virtually every man she'd known gravitated toward them like moths to flames, they'd never been her favorite form of entertainment. To her they seemed like dens of forced hilarity. She liked going to the movies, liked some television, and she loved to read. But if one wanted to socialize in Crystal Creek and wasn't a member of the country club set, Zack's was about it.

"Where do you want to sit?" Jeff asked.

"Not too close to the band, okay?"

"Sure, fine." He found a table far enough away from the stage to guarantee at least a little conversation. Holding her chair for her, he asked, "Want a beer?"

"I'd prefer vodka and tonic, please."

Jeff grinned. "You really aren't much of a honky-tonker, are you?" He glanced around the crowded club. "Looks like it'll take a waitress some time to get around to us. I'll go order at the bar."

While he was gone, Val studied the gathering throng. She saw a few familiar faces, not many, but she was used to that. It was a youngish crowd, few over-forties, she guessed. Suddenly one couple came through the entrance, and Val felt a momentary pang in the region of her heart. Was it always going to be this way? Lord, she hoped not. Surely the day would come when she could look at Scott without a twinge of longing.

He and Beverly made the most beautiful couple imaginable. And they seemed to know everyone—at least Beverly did. They could scarcely move a foot without being stopped by someone who wanted a word. At this rate it would take them an age to maneuver through the crowd and reach a table.

Not that there were many tables available. Val realized that since she and Jeff had a table for four, the logical thing to do would be to ask Scott and Beverly to join them. She wasn't sure she wanted that, but perhaps if she actually listened to the give-and-take between them, she might better understand why they were together. She didn't have to wonder what Beverly saw in Scott, but the other remained a mystery to her.

Val was spared having to decide whether or not to call them over, for the minute Beverly spied her, she pounced. "Well, hi, Val. You're not here alone, are you?"

"Of course not," Val said quickly, then wanted to bite her tongue. She sounded priggish. "Jeff's gone to get our drinks. Hello, boss."

One corner of Scott's mouth twitched. "Hello, Val."

"Jeff?" Beverly asked. "Are you talking about Scott's brother?"

"Yes."

"Hmm," Beverly said.

Now what was that supposed to mean? "Won't the two of you join us?" Val invited.

Scott frowned, but Beverly immediately accepted. "Thanks. I was wondering if we were going to be able to find a table."

Scott pulled out the chair across from Val. Beverly sat down and he sat between the two women. Just then Jeff returned with his beer and Val's cocktail; he did a double take when he saw Scott and Beverly.

"Ah, we have company."

"Do you mind?" Beverly asked, an edge to her voice.

"Shoot, no," Jeff said affably. "The more the merrier, right, Val?"

"Of course."

He looked from Scott to Beverly. "Want me to go get you something at the bar?"

"We can wait for the waitress," Scott said.

"Might take a while. I know what Scott drinks. What'll you have, Beverly?"

"Oh, a beer, I guess. I like beer about as well as anything."

The four of them eventually settled down to sipping their drinks and surveying the local scene. Beverly did most of the talking, and her conversation was heavily laced with gossipy tidbits about people who meant nothing to Val, Scott and Jeff. That didn't seem to trouble her. "Oh, look, there's Lacey Cullen. I haven't seen her in ages. She and her husband live in that big stone house on Robert Road, and I guess you know Robert Road is *the* residential street in Crystal Creek. Lacey's mother was once married to a Greek industrialist...or maybe he was Italian. Anyway, the Cullen money actually came from the mother's divorce settlement, although from the way they all act you'd think the whole clan had been born to the purple. Hi, Lacey!" Beverly waved gaily, then turned to Scott. "Would you like to meet her?"

"Why on earth would I want to meet her?" he asked.

"The Cullens are very important people."

"To whom?"

Val struggled to hide a smile, and Beverly made a sound of impatience. "Honestly, Scott..." Pushing back her chair, she stood. "Well, *I* must go say hello. All of you please excuse me for a minute." She turned and threaded her way through the crowd.

Jeff's eyes followed her. He chuckled, shook his head in amusement and raised his glass to his lips. Scott resumed a serious contemplation of his Scotch, and Val watched him discreetly. He looked as though he would prefer being anywhere but

Zack's on a Saturday night. If that was the case, why *was* he here?

Scott was wondering the same thing himself. Inviting Beverly to Zack's had been an impulsive gesture, and now he couldn't imagine what had prompted it. He refused to believe it had anything to do with knowing Val would be here with Jeff.

He thought longingly of the comforts of the lodge. He could fix himself a drink—a good one, not this watered-down bar stuff—and heat up whatever Carla had left for him. He could even have cooked himself a steak on the grill; he wasn't helpless when it came to putting a meal together. Then he could have watched a movie. The lodge's media room had an extensive video library.

He looked at Val, who quickly looked away. Had she not had a date tonight, he might have asked her to join him in his restful evening.

Suddenly Jeff gave a start. "Holy cow!" he exclaimed. "I think I just saw Buck Dalton."

"Who's Buck Dalton?" Scott asked.

"An old buddy from the oil patch. Yeah, I'm sure that's Buck. What in hell could he be doing here?" Jeff jumped to his feet. "Y'all excuse me a second, okay? I've gotta go talk to him." Picking up his beer, he scurried off.

Scott knew his brother would be gone far longer than a second, just as he knew Beverly would not be back in a minute. The two of them were party animals, at their best when surrounded by people. He cast a sideways look at Val. She was such a serene person, relaxing to be with, and she looked especially fetching tonight. Her auburn hair was a shining maze around her winsome face. A stranger might look at her for the first time and think her delicate, but Scott knew she was anything but that.

She turned, and their eyes locked briefly before she looked away. "Having a good time?" he asked quietly.

"I just got here," she said. "I'm not having a *bad* time."

"I was surprised when I heard you and Jeff were coming here... together."

Again she turned to look at him. "Do you disapprove?"

"It's hardly my place to approve or disapprove."

"Of course it is. You're the boss. If you have rules about employees dating, I'll certainly abide by them."

Scott hesitated a second, then said, "I have no such rules. I imagine they would be completely unenforceable, anyway."

"You're right. One owner of a ranch Daddy and I worked had a rule like that. He employed a lot of single cowboys, and there were quite a few single

women on his household staff. The party line was—
no fraternization. But once everyone went into
town on Saturday night, you'd be surprised how
many of them 'accidentally' ran into each other.''

Beverly and Jeff were still table-hopping, and Val
was fighting a major case of ennui. Suddenly the
thought of her ratty old bathrobe and a good book
held tremendous appeal. The only thing she could
think of that would be more appealing was having
Scott all to herself this evening, and that was the
most ridiculous thought that had crossed her mind
in some time. She recalled the evening they'd had
dinner at the restaurant out on the highway. They'd
been alone for hours, and what had they talked
about? The Hole in the Wall, what else?

Suddenly she felt the pressure of his hand on
hers. ''Our dates seem to have deserted us. Dance
with me, Val?''

''Yes, boss,'' she said a little breathlessly.

''Stop calling me that.''

He stood and gently pulled her to her feet. Out
on the dance floor, he opened his arms, and she
walked into them, loving the feel of them as they
slid around her. As she moved with him in time to
the music, she was acutely aware of his strong legs
brushing against hers. Like his brother, Scott was
a smooth, accomplished dancer, but there was a
difference. Jeff, she imagined, had learned to dance

in places like this, while Scott doubtless had learned at senior proms, frat parties and sophisticated dinner dances. There was just something about the way he moved. Why, she'd bet he could even waltz...and in a tuxedo at that. She guessed he was the only man she'd ever known who probably had actually worn a tux. For a moment she allowed herself a flight of fancy. As in an old movie, one day Scott Harris would look at her across the expanse of his mahogany desk and suddenly see the woman of his dreams.

A shriek of feminine laughter brought Val down to earth. Over Scott's shoulder she saw Beverly holding court in a circle of admirers, most of them men. *That,* Val reminded herself, or someone very like her, was the woman of Scott's dreams.

BEVERLY REALIZED it was time to get back to the table and try to breathe some life into Scott. What was wrong with him, anyway? He sometimes exasperated her. He was handsome, sexy and successful, just what she'd always wanted in a man, and when he was in the right mood, he could be a lot of fun. Tonight he was about as much fun as an itching rash.

When she returned to the table, neither Val nor Scott was there. Jeff was, along with a couple Beverly did not know. Two more chairs had been pulled up to the table, and the three were in deep conversation. Jeff spotted her. "Oh, hi, Beverly. I want you to meet some old friends of mine. This is Buck Dalton and this is Bettina."

"Just call me Bebe," the pretty brunette said. "Everybody does."

Beverly acknowledged the introductions with her famous smile, then spoke to Jeff. "Where's Scott?"

He jerked his head toward the dance floor. "Out there."

Beverly craned her neck, then saw Scott's head. *Who in the devil is he dancing with?* she wondered irritably, her view obscured by the other dancers. Then a couple glided away, and she saw that the woman in his arms was Val. Well, Beverly supposed it was only polite of Scott to ask Val to dance since she and Jeff had left them alone. She watched them a second, then tensed.

It wasn't so much Scott's dancing with Val that bothered her; it was the way he was looking at her. Warmly, confidentially, privately, as if the two of them were in on things that no one else knew anything about. Beverly felt her face grow warm. She didn't remember his ever looking at *her* that way.

Jeff, too, was watching the two dancers. There was something about the look on Scott's face that arrested his attention. Val tilted her chin up, and Scott smiled down at her. It was no ordinary smile, either. Jeff knew his brother's way with women; they had competed for a few over the years. Scott could turn on the charm when he wanted to, and it looked as though he wanted to tonight. He claimed to have no romantic interest in Val, so why that look?

If there was one thing Jeff was as expert at as getting petroleum out of the ground, it was the man-woman thing. There was more between Scott and Val than they let on. Hell, they might not even know it yet. They both were pretty starched.

Jeff's mouth set in a tight line. *Employer-employee relationship, my ass,* he thought sagely.

CHAPTER SEVEN

ACCEPTING A DATE with Jeff probably hadn't been the smartest thing she'd ever done, Val decided the following morning, and it wouldn't happen again. She'd been uncomfortable the entire night, and she couldn't put her finger on the reason.

It definitely had been a strange evening. The most memorable moments of it were the brief ones she had spent in Scott's arms while they were dancing. She had wished the music would never stop. But when they had returned to the table from dancing, the atmosphere had changed in some imperceptible way. Jeff had acted rather peculiar, for Jeff. He'd kept looking at Scott, then at her, and smiling a rather secretive smile. And Beverly had slipped into something of a blue funk. Maybe on her table-hopping rounds someone had said something to get her in a snit. Or maybe it was the third woman at the table.

The woman named Bebe had chattered incessantly about the most insignificant things, hogging the spotlight that normally was reserved for Beverly. And Jeff and Buck had swapped enough oil-patch yarns to fill a short book, leaving Val, Scott and Beverly to make conversation as best they could. Finally, Beverly had stood and demanded that Scott take her home because she had a crushing headache. Beverly the first to leave any gathering? Yes, it had been a strange evening indeed.

So Val determined there would be no others like it. She wouldn't accept another date with Jeff. Of course, she thought with a wry smile, he'd given her no reason to think he'd ask her out again. He'd simply deposited her at the door to the cottage, dropped a light kiss on her cheek and sped off, presumably to return to Zack's and find more spirited company. The evening had probably seemed as strange to him as it had to her.

Now it was Sunday, and Val was restless. The ranch, as usual on Sundays, was as quiet as a cemetery. She supposed Scott was in the lodge, but she hadn't seen him. Earlier she had found herself fabricating half a dozen excuses to go search him out, but none was plausible. It bothered her that she allowed such thoughts to cross her mind. It also bothered her that she attached such importance to one dance with one man.

She decided to go into town. Crystal Creek wasn't much livelier on Sunday than the ranch, but the Longhorn Coffee Shop would be open. She

could have lunch there, and afterward she would go
to the discount store out on the highway and buy
some books. She realized that with a little effort she
could probably find something more productive to
do, but where was it written she had to be productive all the time?

Down deep in her heart she knew what she actually was doing was putting some distance between herself and the disturbing man in the lodge.

VAL ARRIVED at the Longhorn ahead of the after-
church crowd. She took a table for two by the window and scanned the daily specials scrawled on a
blackboard behind the long lunch counter. A young
waitress brought water and silverware and took her
order. While she waited for her food, Val viewed
the empty streets of Crystal Creek through the
window. Then the First Baptist Church's bell
started pealing, and in a very short time, the streets
were no longer empty. Cars streamed past the window as churchgoers drove home to Sunday dinner... or stopped at the Longhorn.

Val was familiar with small-town life, never having lived in a big city. The largest town she'd ever
lived close to was Abilene. In those days, a trip to
Fort Worth had been to her what a trip to New
York or San Francisco would have been to someone else, but she'd never once thought she'd want

to live there. What she wanted to do more than anything was to sink down roots in a small, friendly town where she eventually would know everyone. And Crystal Creek filled the bill perfectly. World travel would be glorious, of course, but only if she had a home to come back to.

"Well, hello, Val," a voice said. "How are you this morning?"

Val turned and looked into the sweet, smiling face of Dottie Jones, the owner of the Longhorn. "Good morning, Dottie. I'm fine, thanks."

"Seeing you is such a coincidence. There was a fella having breakfast in here who asked about you."

"Asked about *me?*"

"Yeah. Asked me if I knew you."

"Who was he?"

"Don't have the slightest idea. Just asked me if I knew you. I said I did, but you'd only been here since April, so I didn't know you well like some of the characters who've been coming in here for twenty years. Then he paid his check and left. Looked pretty prosperous to me. The place was packed at the time, so I didn't have a chance to quiz him. Anyway, just thought I'd tell you."

The café was filling up fast, so Dottie moved away just as the waitress brought the food. Val ate in thoughtful silence. How strange! First a woman had been asking about her at Trail's End; now a man was asking about her in Crystal Creek. She couldn't think of one soul on earth who would be looking for her, much less two.

Well, if it was a mystery, she had to assume it would resolve itself one of these days. She finished the meal, which was delicious, paid the check and left the café. Once back in her car, she momentarily considered just driving on back to the Hole in the Wall. But there was a long afternoon ahead with little to do. She headed for the bookstore.

THAT AFTERNOON while Val was browsing the bookshelves in the discount store, Scott was in the lodge's exercise room, riding a stationary bicycle with the air of a man doing penance. For the first time since he'd bought the Hole in the Wall, he'd had a day all to himself...and he'd been bored silly. Since he'd never gotten around to asking Jeff to go see their mother, he'd briefly considered making the drive to Austin, but let a phone call suffice instead. Some time before noon he'd rung Val's cottage, thinking they might have lunch together, only to get no answer. He wondered if she was spending the day with Jeff. The mere thought had a dispiriting effect on him.

Glancing at the bicycle's gauge, Scott satisfied himself that he had pumped the obligatory number of miles. Crawling off the machine, he threw a towel over his bare shoulders and strode through the lodge to his private quarters. He showered quickly, changed into fresh clothes and went into his office. There were a dozen things he could be doing, but nothing held much appeal. Instead, he sat behind his desk and thought about last night.

Memories of the way Val had felt in his arms flooded him. His physical reaction to her had been immediate, uncomfortable and startling. All evening, while that blasted Bebe woman had prattled, he had wanted to ask Val to dance again, just to feel the warmth of her close to him. He hadn't, of course. He'd forced himself to dance only with Beverly and had endured the sight of Val in Jeff's arms.

Back at the table he'd had ample opportunity to compare Val and Beverly. Of course Beverly was beautiful; there wasn't a man alive who wouldn't think so. But next to Val she seemed rather insubstantial, the difference between jug wine and a vintage Burgundy. Once during the evening, when Bebe had launched into another of her inane stories, Scott had caught Val's eye, and they had shared a secretive smile. As insignificant as that was, at the time it had seemed a very special, private moment. He'd wished he could take her by the hand, lead her out of the nightclub and take her back to the ranch where they could just talk.

To make matters worse, after he had deposited a somewhat ticked-off Beverly on her doorstep and returned home, he hadn't been able to sleep. He had no idea what had happened to peeve Beverly, nor did he much care. He had wanted to rest, but his thoughts wouldn't let him. He'd felt discontent and had instinctively known that the reason for his discontent was not something he wanted to acknowledge. Normally he was a sound sleeper, but last night his restlessness had kept him awake; long enough to hear Jeff's truck drive by his window and drive past it again in only a few minutes. Well, he'd thought, at least Jeff and Val weren't spending the night together.

It had been early for a Saturday night. As soon as he'd known she was home, he'd given some thought to ringing her cottage and asking her to have a nightcap with him. But better sense had prevailed.

I'M GOING TO GET this under control, Scott vowed as he stared at the papers on his desk. He and Val had a beautiful working relationship, and he wasn't going to spoil it.

At that moment the front doorbell rang. Scott's initial impulse was to ignore it, but when it rang a second time, he stood up. It might be Cal McKinney. Though Cal and Serena spent most of their time in their boot shop in Wolverton, leaving the ranch's shop in the hands of an employee, one or the other often came out on Sunday afternoon to make sure everything was going smoothly. Scott found himself hoping it was Cal. The ex-rodeo superstar was good company, and Scott thought good company was exactly what he needed.

But when he opened the door, he found a stranger standing on the porch, a dapper-looking gentleman in possibly his fifties, nattily attired in tailored slacks and sport coat. Tall and handsome, very distinguished looking. His thick mop of dark hair was graying, which only enhanced his good looks.

"May I help you?" Scott inquired, thinking the man probably needed the use of a phone.

"J. Martin Dodson, at your service, sir. Are you the owner of this establishment?"

"Yes, I am."

"I've come to inquire about accommodations."

"We don't open until tomorrow morning," Scott explained.

"I'm quite aware of that. I've read your brochure."

"I see." Scott stepped back, holding the door wider. "Please come in."

J. Martin Dodson stepped into the foyer and looked around. "Splendid. Absolutely splendid."

"Thank you. By the way, I'm Scott Harris, Mr. Dodson."

"How do you do." The two men shook hands. "As I told you, I wrote for your brochure. I've been in the area a few days and now find myself with some free time. I wondered if you might possibly have a vacancy for the coming week."

"I'm not sure. Miss Drayton, my manager, handles the reservations. Come with me, and I'll check."

Dodson followed Scott into the lobby. The lodge had no registration desk as such. There was a big oak desk where Val sat every Monday morning and registered arriving guests. Scott opened her registry, scanned it quickly and turned to Dodson. "It seems we do have a single that hasn't been booked, but nothing else. If your family is with you . . ."

"No, no. I'm alone, so the single will be fine. I consider myself fortunate to get it."

Scott opened drawers until he found the registration cards. "If you'll just fill this out, please."

Dodson took a seat and bent over the desk to write. "I believe the brochure mentioned payment in advance."

"Yes, but if something comes along that prevents your staying the entire five days, a refund will be worked out."

"Splendid. There you are, young man. I suppose you take credit cards."

"Yes, we do. I'm not sure where the gizmo is. Val takes care of all this stuff." Again Scott opened and closed drawers.

A feminine voice sounded behind them. "Just what is it that Val does?"

Scott looked up. "Oh, Val. I didn't hear you come in. I'm looking for the credit card thing. This is Mr. Dodson. He'll be in eleven this week. Mr. Dodson, my manager, Valerie Drayton."

Val stepped toward Dodson, her hand outstretched, her welcoming smile on her face. "How nice, Mr. Dodson. We'll enjoy having you."

Dodson took her hand, and then the most peculiar thing happened. Instead of shaking it, he merely held it, and the look he gave her so surprised and stunned her she was speechless. She felt as though she had been placed under a high-powered microscope. He studied her face so intently he might have been counting her eyelashes. It was the strangest thing that had ever happened to her.

Scott noticed it, too, and was completely taken aback by the way the man looked at Val—like a thirsty man who had just stumbled upon a water fountain. He was smiling at her in an awestruck sort of way. For some reason, it irritated the devil out of Scott. Dodson was at least twenty years older than Val, old enough to have better manners. Val could have been forgiven if she'd slapped the old boy's face.

"Miss Drayton," Dodson finally said. "What a distinct pleasure."

She withdrew her hand and mumbled, "Thank you."

"Val, where in hell is that credit card gizmo?" Scott asked sharply.

She turned with a start. "I'll get it."

Scott made way for her from behind the desk, and she completed the transaction and handed Dodson his card. "Check-in begins any time after ten," she told him, still unnerved and unable to look him in the eye. "That's when you sign up for any of the organized activities you wish to participate in."

"I don't anticipate taking part in any activities. This will be a week of rest for me." Dodson executed a little half bow. "It's been a pleasure meeting both of you, and I am looking forward to my stay."

He left then, but not before casting one last unabashedly admiring glance in Val's direction. For on't nor-

from men.

nd with nar-

haps that was

"Why, thank you,

nice thing to say."

." Scott cleared his throat. It was

his tongue to ask her to have dinner

but the alarm in his head said no. The less

he spent alone with her, the better. The un-

bidden, unwanted feelings she elicited made him—

how he hated the word—vulnerable. "Did you have

something you wanted to talk to me about, Val?"

he asked in his crisp businesslike voice.

"No. I just came in to look around, check the

rooms, that sort of thing. I don't seem to be able to

stay away long."

"Well, when Dodson showed up, I was working

on some personal accounts," Scott fibbed. "Guess

I'll get back to them."

"Of course."

"I'll see you in the morning."

"Yes."

"Scott?"

"Yes?"

at him.

"Do you k

"A first?"

"Yes. Now th

have a full house for the

very pleased."

"We will, won't we? A full h

pleased."

Scott continued on to his office. He

pleased as he should have been. As far as h

concerned, eleven could have stayed empty. There

was something about J. Martin Dodson that both-

ered him, which was pretty ridiculous when he

thought about it.

J. MARTIN DODSON DROVE away from the Hole in
the Wall and into Crystal Creek, where he got a
room for the night at the Longhorn Motel. He did
not unpack his car but merely carried in an overnight bag that contained toilet articles, pajamas, a
change of underwear and a bottle of Scotch. He
took off his sport coat, mixed a drink and settled
down to read the Sunday edition of *San Angelo
Standard-Times* he had grabbed before leaving

The last guest to register that morning was J. Martin Dodson of San Angelo. "Good morning, Miss Drayton. It's nice to see you again."

"Good morning, Mr. Dodson. Please sign our register, and I'll have someone take your things to your room. And on that table over there you can sign up for special activities. We offer trail rides, hikes..."

Dodson shook his head. "No, thanks. This is strictly for rest, relaxation and research. I might give the sauna a try. Tell me, Miss Drayton, what do *you* do with your time?"

"Me? Well, I keep an eye on things."

"Now that sounds interesting. Would you object to my joining you on your rounds sometime? I've often wondered how an operation like this works."

Val chuckled. "Mr. Dodson, I'm afraid you would find what I do terribly boring."

"I assure you, Miss Drayton, I would not. I dabble in writing, you see. And a dude ranch would make the perfect setting for a story I'm currently working on. But I don't know a thing about how one runs. Precisely why I wanted a stay at this delightful place, to get a feel for it. If you wouldn't mind my accompanying you as you go about your business, I promise to make myself unobtrusive."

"In that case, Mr. Dodson, feel free to dog my footsteps anytime you please. I rather like the idea of the Hole in the Wall being used as the background of a story."

"Thank you, Miss Drayton. And I feel I owe you an apology."

"An apology, Mr. Dodson?"

"Yes. Yesterday when I first saw you, I'm afraid my reaction to you was a bit...excessive. But the moment I laid eyes on you, I knew I'd found Sylvia."

Val blinked. "Sylvia?"

"My heroine. I haven't really been able to get a handle on Sylvia, really a delightful girl, but the minute I saw you, I knew I'd found her."

Val's face flushed. "I'm...flattered."

Dodson stepped back and executed another of those courtly half bows. "Then please don't be startled if you see me at every turn. I'll probably annoy you with hundreds of questions."

Val stood and extended her hand. This time he shook it and released it quickly. "I'll be glad to have you along, Mr. Dodson. Welcome to the Hole in the Wall. I hope your stay will be a pleasant one. Shall I have someone show you to your room?"

"Oh, my dear, I think I can find number eleven on my own. See you later." And he strode off, an air of importance about him.

Val giggled. She could hardly wait to tell Scott. As soon as Dodson had gone upstairs, she closed the registry and hurried to Scott's office. "Guess what!" she blurted out as she entered the room.

He looked up. "What?"

"Our mysterious Mr. Dodson turns out not to be so mysterious after all. He's a writer. He wants to use a dude ranch as the background for one of his stories, and he thought this would be the perfect place. He's here doing research. Lots of good publicity, Scott."

"Well, I'll be."

"And he apologized for his rather inappropriate reaction to me yesterday. Seems he took one look at me and knew he'd found Sylvia."

"Huh?"

"His heroine. I'm a dead ringer for her. He wants to follow me around this week."

A suggestion of a frown furrowed Scott's brow. He recalled the way Dodson had looked at Val yesterday and wondered if research was all the man had in mind. "Well, don't let him get in your way. He seems the pushy sort to me. We have a lot of other guests, you know."

Stung by his words, Val bristled. "I know how to do my job, Scott."

"Yes, I know. Sorry. What I meant to say was don't let him monopolize your time and make a nuisance of himself."

"Count on it," she said, turned and left the office.

UPSTAIRS in room eleven, J. Martin Dodson inspected the comfortably furnished small room and its equally small but adequate bathroom. Then he unpacked. That done, he checked to make sure he had enough loose change, and hurried downstairs. The room had no phone, but he'd noticed a bank of phone booths in the hall outside the game room. He slipped inside one, closed the door and placed his call.

When it was answered, he said, "I'm here at the ranch. You have the phone number, but please don't call unless it is absolutely necessary." He listened for a minute, then said, "It won't be a problem, I assure you. I gave her a cock-and-bull story about being a writer, wanting to do research on the operation of a dude ranch—a stroke of genius, don't you think?...yes, she bought it. She'll be very cooperative and won't think a thing about all the questions I'm going to ask." There was a pause while he listened. "I'm going to do my best, and I can be very persuasive when I want to, as you well know. Just go on about your business, try not to think about it, and I'll see you Saturday...yes, me, too. Take care."

Dodson hung up, then went into the lobby to wait for lunch.

THAT WEEK Val had an almost constant companion in J. Martin Dodson, but true to his word, he never intruded. In fact, she began to welcome his presence. He was handsome and witty, an intelligent man who asked thoughtful questions. True, he seemed far more interested in her than in the Hole in the Wall's operation, but she attributed that to his wanting to "get a handle" on Sylvia.

"Shouldn't you be taking notes or something?" she once asked.

But he only smiled and said, "I find that if I take voluminous notes, I try to work every single fact into my story, which bores readers. I have a good memory. I assure you, my dear, I will forget nothing about this week."

"You didn't list writing as your occupation on your registration card."

"That's because writing is a hobby with me. I've made very little money from it. It's simply fun."

"You said you're retired. Retired from what?"

"The United States Navy."

"A Navy man? You must have seen a lot of the world."

"Quite a bit, yes. And much more water than I ever want to see again."

"How exciting! I think if I were to suddenly come into a lot of money, I'd spend some of it seeing the world."

"And what would you do with the rest of it?"

She smiled. "Buy a house. I've never owned one. Tell me, if writing is only a hobby with you, what do you do with your time?"

"For the past five years I've been restoring a fine old stone house near San Angelo. That's where I live and raise Angora goats."

"Do you have children?"

"A son. He's a doctor in Connecticut. I'm afraid I don't see him very often."

"And his mother?"

"She died many years ago."

At his request, Val now called him Martin, but when she asked him to call her Val, he insisted on Valerie. "It's such a lovely name. Why shorten it?"

Martin made a point of sitting with her every night at dinner, and the first thing he did every morning after breakfast was seek her out. He didn't participate in any of the ranch's activities, and he had pumped her for so many details of her personal life that Val was certain he now knew more about her than any other soul on earth.

"When your mother left, Valerie, how did you feel?" he asked her at one point.

"I really don't remember, Martin. I was only seven."

"And over the years have you harbored resentment?"

"I don't think so. Certainly I don't feel any now."

"Do you know where she is?"

"No, I have no idea. Why?"

"Sylvia needs a past. I might give her yours."

Val laughed. "I've always wanted to be someone's heroine."

"Do you believe in knights in shining armor?" Martin asked teasingly.

"Oh, indeed!" she teased back. "I'm a realist about most things, but I firmly believe that someday my prince will come."

Martin was endlessly fascinating to her, so she naturally was curious about the kind of background that had formed such a personality.

"Oh, my childhood was quite ordinary," he told her when she inquired. "I was born in San Angelo, just as my father and grandfather were. They were pharmacists. Dodson's Pharmacy was a local institution. It was naturally assumed that I would follow in their footsteps, but as young boys are wont to do, I had other dreams. Above all I wanted to see the world. The United States Navy provided me with that opportunity. Yes, I had a very ordinary childhood.''

To Val, of course, it sounded anything but ordinary. People were strange creatures. Martin had dreamed of leaving the kind of world she had always dreamed of entering.

At one point it vaguely crossed Val's mind that Martin might be wooing her a little, because she'd never been on the receiving end of such constant male attention. Of course there was a great deal of difference in their ages, but no more than there was between, say, J.T. and Cynthia McKinney, and from what Val had heard, they were the happiest couple on earth. May-September relationships often worked out beautifully.

After mulling over this possibility, however, Val dismissed it. Martin's manner toward her was courtly and gallant, more paternal than romantic. It was a rare woman who didn't know when she was being courted, and she knew with certainty she wasn't. She was just enjoying an unexpected friendship. And she feared she was going to miss the gentleman when he was gone.

SCOTT HAD WATCHED Dodson with Val all week, and *he* hadn't dismissed the possibility that the man was wooing her, not by a long shot. In fact, he was sure that was exactly what was going on, and he didn't like it worth a damn. He shouldn't have cared. There was no good reason for him to care. But he did.

Unfortunately, he mused, Dodson would probably appeal to Val—an intelligent, distinguished older man, someone who would represent security and stability to a woman who'd had precious little of either in her life.

And the fact he was a writer probably impressed her. Scott had been around her long enough to know she stood a little in awe of anyone with an education, and she was totally in love with books. Yeah, she'd probably think the guy was hot stuff. Scott wondered what in hell Dodson wrote.

He also wondered *when* he wrote. The day before, one of the housekeepers had summoned him to room eleven to check a leaking bathroom faucet. He'd noticed there were no signs of the tools of a writer's trade. If Dodson really was doing research, wouldn't he have to write it down somewhere, on something? A laptop computer, a notebook, something? Nothing of the sort was in evidence in his room. Scott had never even seen the man take down notes. He'd once had a client who was a writer, and the guy had never been without a notebook.

But, he conceded, there was always the possibility that Dodson simply had an outstanding memory.

He swiveled his chair and glared out the window. There they were, Val and Dodson, walking toward the corral where a dozen or so guests were lining up for a trail ride. If Val ever stopped suddenly, Dodson's chin would crack on the top of her head.

Scott had tried to think of a plausible reason to tell her to ask the guy to back off, but what? Dodson didn't interfere with her work; she was as efficient as ever. She didn't neglect the other guests. She knew everybody's name, where they were from and what they did for a living. Her patience seemed limitless. She was the first one up every morning and the last to go to bed at night, and during the day she appeared to be everywhere at once. He knew she had to have a dozen things on her mind at any given minute, but they all seemed to be neatly organized in the cubbyholes in her head.

He had considered telling her there had been complaints about the special attention she was giving Dodson, but it would have been a lie, and she probably would have known it. So to complain about Dodson's attention would be petty... and would tell Val how much he, Scott, had been watching her.

Scott passed a weary hand over his eyes. He'd had a terrible week, feeling cross and out of sorts most of the time, and that wasn't like him. He'd snapped at a couple of people he'd later had to apologize to. The apologies had been graciously accepted, so no harm done, but it served to make him aware that something was troubling him. He was accustomed to being at peace with friends, co-workers, his life and himself. He wondered if he was coming down with something. He didn't much like himself this way.

FRIDAY NIGHT'S farewell barbecue and sing-along around the campfire were enormous hits with the guests. Val enjoyed watching everyone enter into the spirit of the occasion. Many friendships had been formed during the week, and she had heard some couples make plans to stay in touch and meet again at the Hole in the Wall the same time next year.

She herself seemed to have made a wonderful friend, one who was full of adventurous tales of his Navy days. He had opened up a broad new world to a woman who'd never been farther from Texas than a ranch in eastern New Mexico. He had spent a lot of time in the Orient and in Mediterranean countries. His favorite cities, she had learned, were San Francisco, Hong Kong and Seville. She couldn't even imagine actually visiting places like that. It had been great fun hearing them described by someone who'd been there. Next week it would seem strange not to have Martin dogging her footsteps, and she wondered if it would be appropriate to ask him to write to her occasionally...or at least to send her postcards from his travels.

Tonight, even as she kept a watchful eye on the festivities, Val found herself searching for Scott. She'd scarcely exchanged a dozen words with him all week. She had the oddest feeling that he'd been avoiding her, which probably was a figment of her imagination. Why would he deliberately avoid her? It must simply have been that he'd been busy, and she'd been busy, and now that the ranch's operation was settling into a groove, there was less need for them to consult.

Now, scanning the crowd, she spotted him. He was pretty hard to miss in that spanking-white cowboy hat that had become his trademark. He was so handsome he made her heart ache, and *that* really was ridiculous. This unwanted attraction to him was the only discordant note in a life that was humming along nicely right now.

"A penny for your thoughts, my dear," a familiar voice said from behind her.

Val turned and smiled at Martin. "Oh, I was just thinking how nice this week has been. You've been very entertaining. Will you be glad to get home?"

"It's always good to get home. And since I will be leaving in the morning, there is something very important I must tell you."

"What is it?"

"Can we go somewhere and talk? Somewhere private? It's personal."

Val looked at him. He sounded so serious. Important, private and personal? Lord, had she been wrong? Was he going to make some sort of romantic move, after all? What would she say? As much as she liked Martin, she knew she would never feel romantically inclined toward him.

She glanced around. The chairs on the porch were occupied, as were most of the picnic benches. The outdoor festivities were winding to a close, and some of the guests had gone back into the lodge to watch television or play games. She couldn't think of any place really private except for perhaps her office... or her cottage, which was closer. "My place," she said. "We can talk there without being disturbed. Come on."

"Excellent, Valerie. Excellent."

She led the way across the grounds to her cottage. She pushed open the door and invited Martin inside. "This is very nice, Valerie," he said, looking around. "You have wonderful taste."

"Very little of what you see is actually mine. The cottage came furnished. I've only added a few personal touches. Sit down, Martin. I'm anxious to hear this important thing you have to tell me."

He sat on the sofa, and she took a chair next to it. "In the first place, I must confess to having lied to you about a number of things."

Val's eyes widened. "Lied to me, Martin? Whatever about?"

"I'm not a writer. I can't even compose a very memorable letter, much less write a book."

"But...why on earth did you tell me you were?"

"I needed an excuse."

"For what?" Val didn't think she'd ever been so bewildered.

"To get close to you, to get to know you, to become your friend, to get you to trust me. You'd have thought it suspicious as the devil if I'd followed you around like a cocker spaniel without a good excuse, something you'd believe."

"This isn't making much sense, Martin."

"I knew who you were and where you were long before we met last Sunday, just as I knew tonight I was going to ask something of you that would be impossible if we weren't friends."

Val was puzzled, but she was beginning to wonder if she should also be worried. This sounded very mysterious. "What is it?" she asked warily.

"Tomorrow I want you to come home with me."

So that *was* it! Val couldn't have been more dismayed, and she quickly decided to handle the situation lightly, not to make a big deal out of it. She simply stared at him a minute, then uttered a little laugh. "Oh, Martin, I couldn't! We hardly know each other. Goodness, what did I do to make you think I would consider such a thing?"

He smiled. "You misunderstand, my dear. Even though you are a very lovely young woman, you *are* young. Much too young for me, I'm afraid. No, I have no romantic intentions toward you. I want you to come home with me so you can meet my wife."

"Your wife? I thought you said you were a widower," Val said testily, beginning to wonder what kind of scoundrel her new friend actually was.

"I said my son's mother died many years ago, and she did. But six months ago I remarried. That's the woman I want you to meet."

"Why on earth would you think your wife and I would want to know each other?"

He paused, smiled again, then leaned forward. "I know she wants to meet you. I'm *hoping* you'll want to meet her. When I first met her she introduced herself as Vivian Drayton. You see, Valerie, I married your mother."

CHAPTER NINE

VAL GASPED. For a minute she thought her chest would explode from pressure. "My *mother?*" she cried.

"Yes, I married Vivian Drayton six months ago. I fell in love with her the moment I laid eyes on her. She was tending bar in a swanky little watering hole I frequent. Actually I later discovered she owned a piece of the place. It was a quiet evening, not many customers, and we fell into conversation. I returned the next night, and the next. The courtship lasted several months before I proposed. Our marriage has been a six-month fairy tale... with the exception of one ogre. You."

Val put a hand to her chest but said nothing.

"Viv told me about you shortly before we were married," Martin went on. "She had stayed in touch with you for a number of years, but then she lost track of you. Apparently your father was a bit of a roamer. Viv accepted the estrangement for a time because she had nothing to offer you. She hasn't had an easy life, and now I'm trying to make up for that.''

"She hasn't seen me in twenty-five years!" Val exclaimed. "Why now?"

"Why not now? You're her daughter. And now she has plenty to offer you. Right after we were married, she began searching for you in earnest, beginning with a ranch near Abilene. It was during our search that Viv found out about your father's death. We ran up against many stone walls and dead ends, I'll tell you, but we finally thought we had you cornered at a place near Bandera. Viv and I went there one day, a Wednesday, I believe it was. The foreman said you'd quit to work somewhere else, but he couldn't remember where. However, he said you were most always around on the weekend, to come back then. We did, but you weren't there.''

Val closed her eyes, and her heart began to pound. The woman who had been looking for her at Trail's End was her mother! It was too incredible.

"This time, though," Martin went on, "the foreman had your address and phone number. When we returned home Sunday, Viv called you. But when she actually heard your voice, she lost her nerve and hung up.''

"If…if she wanted to see me, why didn't she just come here? Why did she send you? I assume that's what happened."

Martin shook his head and sighed. "Fear of rejection, I suppose. Fear that you might harbor some resentment toward her and not want to have anything to do with her."

He paused and looked at her. "Now I'm convinced you don't."

"No, I don't. Maybe I did early on, I don't remember, but Daddy never did, so how could I? Daddy always said she just did what she had to do."

"Thank heavens for that! I couldn't bear watching Viv fight resentment. Anyway, she asked me to come and meet you, to try to judge for myself what your reaction to seeing her after all these years would be. It was my idea to sign up for a week here. I reasoned it would give me a chance to really get to know you. And I'm afraid my very inappropriate reaction to the sight of you last Sunday was prompted by your startling resemblance to her. I turned and found myself staring at Viv some eighteen years ago."

"Sylvia, indeed! All those questions." Something occurred to her just then. "Were you the man who asked about me at the Longhorn Coffee Shop?"

"Yes. You've told me a great deal about yourself this week, Valerie, enough for me to know what a fine young woman you are, enough for me to know that you and Viv would like each other a lot. As I said, you favor her a great deal . . . same hair and eyes, same mouth. She's a beautiful woman at fifty, and I adore her. I would do anything for her."

Val looked at him suspiciously. "What other lies did you tell me? The son who's a doctor?"

"A neurosurgeon."

"The Navy?"

"No, I was in the Navy for twenty-five years."

"The Angora goats?"

"Some of the finest."

"The big stone house near San Angelo?"

"It's there. A wonderful house that was built in 1900 by one of the area's more successful sheep ranchers. I spent five years on its restoration, and it's a showplace. People driving by slow down to look at it." Martin leaned forward and gently touched her hand. "Valerie, I am not a wealthy man, but I *am* well off. I have my retirement pay. The goat raising is profitable, and over the years I've made some very good investments. For the first time in her life, Viv does not have to worry about money, and I think she'd like to share some of that with you. Please come home with me tomorrow.

Just let her see you. Is that too much to ask? We've gone to a lot of trouble to find you."

Valerie didn't know what to say. It was such a stunning surprise. Her mother! Suddenly she recalled how much she had been thinking about her mother lately. She wasn't much of a believer in fate or Kismet or whatever it was called; she was much too much the realist for that. But for her mother to find her just now, when she'd been longing for something that was hers ... Well, the coincidence was overwhelming.

Still, she had reservations. "Oh, I don't know, Martin. It's all very dramatic, but...what...what if we don't hit it off, don't mesh?" Val asked. "Wouldn't that be worse for us than not knowing each other at all?"

"My mission, if you'll recall, was to find out if I thought that a possibility. It isn't. Personally I think the two of you are going to adore each other."

Val hesitated, chewing her bottom lip. It was all overwhelming, but she knew she'd never be able to live with herself if she didn't go. Wouldn't she always wonder? She took a deep breath. "All right, Martin. I'm ... I'm very nervous and unsure about this, but since you think it will be all right, and since I trust you ... I'll be happy to go home with you."

Relief engulfed him, and a warm smile wreathed his face. "Oh, Valerie . . . you can't begin to imagine how happy that makes me."

Val thought what a truly handsome man her stepfather was. Her stepfather! She almost laughed out loud. She did have family after all! "I'll follow you in my own car. I have to be back Sunday night, and there's no sense in your having to make the trip again. How long a drive is it?"

"A little more than two hours." Martin clapped his hands together, then stood up. "If we leave by ten we'll get there in time for lunch."

"That might be a problem. Normally I'm on duty until the last guest departs."

"Surely Mr. Harris, who seems to be a nice man, would understand the enormity of the occasion."

"Martin, I . . . I don't think I want to tell anyone about this just yet. It's very private, and I . . . I don't want anyone to know about it until my mother and I have actually seen each other." Despite what he said, Val thought it entirely possible that all this might not work out exactly as Martin hoped. Besides, who else would be interested in knowing she'd found her long-lost mother?

"As you wish, Valerie. But it would be nice if we could leave by ten. Ask. Asking can't hurt anything."

"All right. I'll see if I can leave at ten."

"Now I must go to the room and call Viv. Poor dear has been a bundle of nerves all week. She'll be so pleased."

Val, too, stood. "And I need to get back to the guests."

Smiling fondly at each other, they left the cottage.

SCOTT HAD SEEN Val lead Dodson to her place, and he'd been aghast. How could she? She must be out of her mind. He was oblivious to the conversation swirling around him as he kept his eyes riveted on the cottage door. If it didn't open pretty damn quick, he...

What would he do? Kick down the door? Make an ass of himself? They were two adults, for Pete's sake. Miserably, he kept watching the door. When it opened and they stepped out, he expelled his breath. He hadn't even realized he'd been holding it. They hadn't been in there very long, not long enough for... for anything major to have transpired.

Scott continued watching them, the way they were smiling at each other. They strolled toward the picnic tables, then stopped. Dodson took Val's hand and lifted it to his lips. Scott had never seen anyone actually do that except in movies. Then Dodson walked on in the direction of the lodge, and

Val headed for the tables. Scott realized she was looking for him, so he stood up, and she hurried toward him.

"Boss, I'm going to ask a big favor of you."

"Ask away."

"May I leave at ten in the morning? I'm going out of town for the weekend."

Scott tensed. "Where are you going?" he asked, though he was terribly afraid he knew. And if he'd thought a second before asking the question, he would have realized it was none of his damned business.

"To San Angelo. I'll be back Sunday night, but I've been invited to lunch tomorrow. It would be so nice if I could leave at ten, but if you would prefer I didn't, of course I'll..."

So Dodson had done it, wormed his way into her heart to the point she was going to spend the weekend with him. Why didn't the guy pick on someone his own age? At that moment, Scott would have given anything if he could have thought of something to keep Val at the ranch over the weekend. But there was, of course, nothing, and her weekends were hers.

He lifted his hand and touched the side of her head. "Val... I..."

His touch was electrifying, and the look on his face was...almost pleading. Her eyes widened. "Yes, Scott?"

He checked himself. What in the devil was he going to say? He was getting ready to make a complete fool of himself. "Nothing. Leave at ten, by all means," he said brusquely. "Take the whole morning off. I'll say goodbye to the guests." Then he sat down and resumed talking to the group at the table, giving her the back of his head.

Val's mouth dropped. She stood rooted in place for a few seconds, unable to believe his sharp manner. Did he perceive the request as shirking her duties? She worked harder than anyone on the ranch. Fighting back tears, she forced herself to join the group and make a stab at conversation.

But later, as the guests began to disperse, she caught up with Scott, forcing him to turn and look at her. "If you're angry about the two hours, I naturally won't take them."

"I'm not angry."

"You're giving a good imitation of it. How can we possibly work together if you aren't honest with me? Those two hours aren't that important to me."

"You mean, if I asked you to wait until noon, you would?"

"Of course. How can you think otherwise?"

He stared at her a minute, his face a mask, his eyes like iron. Finally he said, "Take the two hours, Val. Good night. I'll see you Sunday."

And he strode off, leaving her even more bewildered than before, even more certain she had done something to displease him. If not the two hours, what? Dejectedly, she turned and crossed the grounds, heading for her cottage.

Nearby, with his rump propped against a tree trunk, Jeff had heard the exchange between Scott and Val. Now she passed within only a few yards of him, head down. "Problems?" he asked.

Val turned with a start, her face a dark cloud. "Oh, Jeff. To tell you the truth, I don't know if I have problems or not. Scott is...well, he's just not acting like himself, hasn't all week. I've never seen him like this."

"I have, a bunch of times. Do yourself a big favor. Don't let ol' Scott's moods get to you. If you do, and you keep working for him very long, you'll be upset a lot of the time."

Val miserably digested that. "Yeah, thanks, Jeff. I'll try to remember that. Good night."

"Good night."

Val thrust her hands in her jeans pockets and continued on to her cottage. Several times during the past month, she'd deluded herself into thinking she and Scott were growing closer, but she really didn't know him at all. Maybe she never would. Maybe she wasn't supposed to.

SATURDAY MORNING dawned clear and unseasonably warm. Val rose before the sun and carried her coffee out onto the stoop. Tucking the terry-cloth robe snugly around her, she held the cup in both hands and sipped slowly. Her insides bubbled with excitement and anticipation, but there was some apprehension in there, too.

Vivian Drayton Dodson. The name rolled around in her head. Val knew she had read a lot of stories about a parent and a child being reunited after many years, but she couldn't remember how any of them had turned out. Martin was so sure it was going to be a joyous occasion, but it was bound to be awkward at first.

Whatever else it was, though, it surely would be memorable, something to tell her kids and grandkids someday.

Her thoughts moved on to Scott and the hurtful way he had treated her last night. It didn't make much sense. For more than seven weeks they had shared a wonderful working relationship, a meeting of the minds, almost perfect. Now she couldn't shake the feeling that things might never be the same between them again, and that disturbed her more than she could say.

But then, Scott hadn't been himself the entire past week. Maybe he had problems she knew nothing about. Maybe he'd had a fight with Beverly. Val knew her own request had not been out of line. Maybe tomorrow night he would be his old self again. For sure she wouldn't allow this to spoil her reunion with her mother.

Tossing the contents of her cup on the ground, she stood and went back inside the cottage to shower, dress and pack an overnight bag. She passed up breakfast in the dining room and made do with coffee and doughnuts in her own kitchenette. Shortly before ten, she tossed the bag on the back seat of her car, wheeled the car around and drove to the side of the lodge to meet Martin.

"All ready?" he greeted, leaning through the window and giving her a peck on the cheek.

"All ready."

"Excited?"

Val beamed at him. "Very."

"And Viv, bless her, is about to pop. Let's not make her wait any longer than necessary." Martin got into his own car, and they drove off, unaware of Scott glaring at them from the window of his office.

THEY HEADED WEST, leaving cattle country behind and driving into an area known for its fine sheep and goats. Just before noon they entered San Angelo, a handsome city that was greened by the Concho River and crisscrossed by broad boulevards. Some five miles west of the city stood Martin's gray stone house.

The sight of it took Val's breath away. It was magnificent, standing far back from the road, looming tall and proud over the surrounding terrain. A sweeping curved drive led to it. Val followed Martin, who parked at the foot of the steps leading to the porch. She parked behind him and looked up at the house. Behind those massive double doors with their stained-glass panels her mother waited!

Throughout the two-hour drive, she had rehearsed what she would say when she caught her first glimpse of Vivian Drayton Dodson. She knew her mother had to be on pins and needles, and she wanted to put her—them all—at ease as quickly as possible.

Martin came up to her car and opened the door. "Be it ever so humble, there's no place like home," he said with a smile.

"Martin, it's magnificent."

"Let me get your bag and we'll go in."

Val slid out from behind the wheel, and Martin reached inside for her bag. Then, cupping a hand under her elbow, he led her up the steps, across the porch and into the house.

They stepped into a gleaming tiled foyer. In the center of it stood a round polished oak table, and on that was the most enormous vase of flowers Val had ever seen. Ahead of them rose a curved stairway. "Grand" was the only adjective she could think of.

"This way, Valerie," Martin said. "I'm sure Viv will be waiting for us in the conservatory."

Conservatory? Val had read of houses that had a conservatory, but she'd never expected to be in one. In fact, she wasn't at all sure what a conservatory *was*. At the threshold, she balked momentarily, but after receiving an encouraging nod from Martin, she squared her shoulders and stepped forward.

The room she entered was something like a greenhouse—windowed on three sides and full of tropical plants. One majestic ficus almost reached the ceiling. Out of the corner of her eye, she saw some sort of movement. She turned in the direction of it.

A woman of her own height and coloring rose from a chintz-covered chaise. Martin had been right about her mother. Vivian was an extremely attractive fifty-year-old woman—slender, with delicate features. Right now she looked awestruck, her lips slightly parted, her eyes wide. A dainty manicured hand was placed against her chest.

"Viv, darling," Martin said, "this is Valerie."

The woman took a step forward. "Oh, I... Oh, Valerie, I...don't know what to say. You've grown into such a beautiful woman."

Whatever Val had expected her immediate reaction would be, it wasn't the sudden misting over of her eyes. Her chest rose and fell, then she smiled. "Hello, Mother."

IT HAD BEEN as simple as that. After an awkward embrace and a few nervous giggles, with Martin standing by grinning like a Cheshire cat, Vivian had taken her daughter by the arm, and the three of them had gone into the dining room for lunch, which was served by a diminutive woman in a white uniform.

Now, after a wonderful meal of Spanish omelet, sautéed potatoes and salad, they lingered over coffee and conversation. "Viv, you must see that place where Valerie works," Martin enthused. "It has everything. I didn't get to really take advantage of it this trip. I want to go back and take you with me."

"Then you really enjoy your work, Valerie?" Vivian asked.

"Oh, it's a wonderful job, the best I've ever had. I'd like to think I'll be working at the Hole in the Wall for years to come."

Vivian and Martin exchanged a glance that Val didn't see. "You don't think about marriage?" Vivian asked.

Val smiled. "I don't guess there's a woman alive who doesn't *think* about it."

"So you aren't seriously involved with anyone now?"

"No," Val said and was surprised by the look of relief she saw cross her mother's face.

"More coffee, Valerie?" Martin asked.

"No, thank you. That was a delicious meal." Her eyes swept the beautifully appointed dining room. "I must confess to wanting to explore every nook and cranny of this house. You're right, Martin. It is a showplace."

"I'm going to leave you two alone this afternoon," he said. "I've been gone a long time and am sure there are things requiring my attention. Feel free to explore all you like, my dear. Make yourself at home."

"Yes," Vivian agreed. "Nothing would please Marty and myself more than to have you begin to think of this as home, a place to come to whenever you want, a place where you'll always feel welcome."

A strong surge of emotion swept through Val at that moment. Home. Such a simple word, she thought. No one could possibly know how good it sounded to her...or how long she had waited to be able to say it.

CHAPTER TEN

ALL OF HIS adult life Jeff had dreamed of having a lot of money. But the stuff had a way of slipping through his fingers. In order to make more than even he could spend, he would have to make a bundle. That was why he had gravitated to oil prospecting. It was the only way he knew of that a guy with nothing but a high school education, looks, charm and luck could get to be a millionaire.

And he *was* lucky. Always had been—in cards, with women, in sports, name it. And everyone knew that those who were successful in the oil patch were not the smartest nor the hardest-working, but the luckiest. It was almost as though he had a sixth sense about where oil was, but he'd also picked up some solid knowledge of geology through the years. Of course, he'd had some failures, too, but his overall record was good, and his name was well-known in the industry.

And somewhere along the way he had discovered it wasn't only the prospect of money that motivated him. He loved the business, everything about it—the excitement, the uncertainty, even the rootlessness. And after talking to Buck Dalton that night at Zack's, he'd felt the itch again. It was almost like a chronic disease. This time it wouldn't let go.

He had been one hundred percent sincere when he'd told Scott he would settle down and work till Christmas. At the time it had been what he wanted to do because he hadn't been able to foresee another opportunity presenting itself. But he hadn't counted on the itch. Could he dare hope Scott would understand? Maybe not, but nothing ventured nothing gained.

Leaving his room, Jeff bounded down the stairs, crossed the deserted lobby and went into Scott's office. His brother looked up from his desk when he entered.

"Seen Val?" Jeff asked.

"Not since early this morning," Scott said, scowling.

"I wonder where she is. Thought I'd see if she'd like to go somewhere tonight."

"She wouldn't. She's in San Angelo." The bite in Scott's voice was unmistakable.

"San Angelo. Wonder what she's doing there."

"I'm sure I have no idea."

Jeff snapped his fingers. "Say, isn't that where that old boy who took such a shine to her lives?"

"Yes."

Jeff whistled and sank into a chair facing the desk. "Man, he came and saw and conquered in record time, didn't he?"

"Apparently."

Jeff eyed his brother speculatively for a minute. He was finely attuned to Scott's darker moods, having been on the receiving end of them countless times. He didn't know what was stuck in his brother's craw, but something sure was. Could it possibly be Val and that guy Dodson? In spite of what Scott said, Jeff couldn't shake the notion that his brother had the hots for ol' Val. He might never act on them, but the feelings were there, Jeff would have bet on it.

He hesitated. This probably wasn't the best time to ask anything of Scott, but when was? Scott was never the jolliest person alive, and this past week he'd been a bear. But what the hell? Jeff had never walked on eggshells around his brother, and he didn't intend to start doing so now. "I want to ask you a question," he said.

"Okay. What is it?"

"You know, when ol' Mark comes back, I'm going to find it hard as hell to go back to playing cowpoke."

Scott glared at him. "So?"

"Remember Buck Dalton, the guy who sat with us at Zack's the other night?"

"I remember."

"He told me there were a few deals in the oil patch that are opening to individual bids. So I was wondering—since everything seems to be chugging right along without me, would you entertain the notion of letting me out of my contract...when Mark comes back, that is?"

Scott's scowl intensified. "I thought you needed a job."

"Well, I've put a little aside since I got here, some of my salary and some poker winnings. Not a lot but enough to keep me going a couple of months while I hunt up some action."

"Goddammit, Jeff!" Scott barked. "You've been here what? Four weeks? And already you're slipping back into your old ways. You came looking for me, remember? I told you at the outset what I expected of you."

"Hey, I was just asking. Does that hurt? I'm not any good at ranching, so I figured I wouldn't be missed."

"Jeff, I knew you wouldn't be worth screw-all when I hired you. Your worth to the operation never entered the equation. I gave you a job in order to help *you,* not the Hole in the Wall."

"Okay, okay. If the answer's no, it's no. Just say so."

"No!"

"Splendid." Jeff got to his feet. "See you around the campus."

He left the office. Out in the hall, he made a fist and slammed it into the palm of his other hand, cursing under his breath. Then he crossed through the lobby, the dining room and kitchen and out the back door. He met Earl coming up the steps. "Boss in?" Earl asked.

"Yeah, but I wouldn't go in there wanting any favors or handing out problems."

"Why not?"

"He's about as friendly as a grizzly this afternoon."

Earl considered that a second. "Jump all over you 'bout somethin'?"

"You could say that, yes."

"What'd you do... if it's any of my business."

"I didn't *do* anything. I wanted out of my contract when Mark gets back. I don't want to go back to the bunkhouse and try to pretend I know what I'm doing. Earl, you know what kind of cowhand I am."

Earl nodded solemnly. "'Bout as pitiful a one as I ever seen."

"So why won't he let me out of my contract?"

"The boss said no?"

"In spades. Man, I've got to get busy and do something. I've got to make some real money, and I heard of a deal that might make me some."

"What kinda money you talking about?" Earl asked.

"A cool million would do."

Earl cackled. "You sure ain't gonna make that kind of money playin' at cowboyin'."

Jeff glared at him. "I know that! That's why I want out of my contract."

"Son, come over here and sit down. Let ol' Earl tell you a few things about money." The two men sat down on the top step, and Earl put a companionable hand on Jeff's shoulder. "I've been around a spell, and I've known lots'a guys who professed to wantin' great wealth. Most never got close. Most never even tried. But lemme tell you somethin' else about money. Guys I've known who had it spent all their time worryin' 'bout someone takin' it away from 'em. And a million won't do 'cause there'll always be someone with two. And two won't do 'cause then there'll be someone with three."

"I wouldn't know," Jeff said glumly, "never having come close to a million."

"But let's say you do get all that money." Earl was warming to his role of folksy philosopher. "What're you gonna do with it? Most ol' boys I know either spend it and then ain't got it no more...or they let it make 'em heaps more to leave to their kids. And the kids think, lookee here at all the money Daddy left me. Now I don't have to work no more. So they turn out to be lazy, ungrateful bums. But leavin' it to their kids is the next best thing to takin' it with 'em, which is what they'd all like to do in the first place."

Earl sat back and let that sink in. Then he leaned forward and spoke like a Dutch uncle. "Do yourself a favor, son. Forget makin' all that money. Find yourself some sweet little gal, marry her and start makin' babies."

Jeff fumed for a second or two, then shook his head. "I've never been able to take good advice, Earl," he said. "I've got to do something. The restless itch is back. I'm going stir-crazy. Want to come into town and have a beer with me?"

"Naw, I don't drink much. Had a real problem with the stuff some years back, so I pretty much stay away from it now."

Jeff fumed some more. "It just doesn't make sense for Scott to hold me to a contract when he doesn't need me. He's doing it out of meanness, orneriness, to teach me a lesson, something."

"Well, mebbe you ought'a wait and talk to him again some other time."

"I don't know...when he gets in one of these moods..."

"Bad 'un, huh?"

"Dark and sinister."

"Hmm. It's been my experience that only two things in this whole world can put a man in a mood like that. One's money problems, which I don't figure Scott has. And the other's a woman. Yep, I betcha next week's pay that the burr under ol' Scott's saddle was put there by a woman."

"Yeah, I think you might be right."

"That purty Beverly, Miz Townsend's kid?"

Jeff slowly shook his head. "Nope. I think Scott's problem is Val."

Earl's eyes widened. "Val?"

"Val."

Earl scratched the stubble on his chin. "Naw...I don't think so. I've been around the boss and Val a bunch in the last couple'a months. I ain't never seen nothin' like that between 'em. Seems to me they treat each other kinda, well, respectful, you know."

"Yeah, but let me tell you something, Earl. I know a little bit about boys and girls, if you get my drift. Do you remember the guy who followed Val around all week?"

"Older feller, right? Yeah, I remember him."

"Val went home with him."

Earl looked completely taken aback. "Val? Hell, the guy's old enough to be her daddy."

Jeff shrugged. "Some women like older men. Anyway, she's gone off with him, and suddenly Scott's meaner'n a snake for no reason I can think of. Figure it out for yourself."

Earl pondered this. "Well, if that don't beat all."

The two men lapsed into silence for a minute. Then Jeff stood up and stretched. "Yeah, I think my brother's problem is his manager...only he doesn't know it yet." He gave an unmirthful little laugh. "Only Scott would fall for a gorgeous gal and not know what was happening to him." Bending, he slapped Earl's back. "See you later, podnuh. I'm going to go see what kind of trouble I can get into." And he strolled off in the direction of his truck.

THE BIG STONE HOUSE was a treasure chest of delights, Val decided. Every room seemed grander than the last. During all those years in the navy, Martin had acquired so many splendid possessions it would have taken her weeks to study them all. Objects of art abounded. There was even a room designated the library, with floor-to-ceiling shelves crammed full of books. Val could have spent all day in that room alone.

Yet for all the house's luxury, there was no feeling of ostentation, no touch-me-not elegance. Martin and Vivian lived, really lived in the place, so there was a surprising coziness to it. The bedroom that had been given to Val contained a beautiful antique armoire, an easy chair upholstered in a bright print and a four-poster bed made up with ivory, lace-trimmed linens. She had not been able to resist touching them, and never had she felt anything so soft.

She couldn't even imagine living in such a house. "It's so... beautiful," she told her mother as they toured the rooms. "And that's a very inadequate description."

"Isn't it, though?" Vivian said. "When Martin brought me here, I was dumbfounded. This house looked like something that had been constructed on a back lot in Hollywood. Can you imagine? Six months ago I was tending bar. It was a very swanky one, but a bar nevertheless. And now here I am."

"That's quite a story," Val said. They had entered a small sitting room whose walls were covered with what she guessed to be expensive artworks. The paintings certainly *looked* expensive.

"Yes, it is," Vivian said. "I remember so well the first time I saw Marty. It was a very quiet Monday night. We'd only had a few customers, and I had been giving serious consideration to turning the bar over to the new kid I'd hired and just going home."

"And if you had..."

"Possibly I wouldn't have met Marty. I'm living proof that fairy tales come true. Shall we sit down for a minute? Would you like tea? That's a nice custom Marty has introduced me to."

"That sounds wonderful."

Vivian walked to an intercom and placed the order. Then she sat on the sofa and faced Val. "At the risk of repeating myself, I can't tell you how happy you've made me. I don't know what I would have done had you refused to come."

"Well, think about it, Mother." It was amazing how easily that word tripped off her lips. "A person would have to be very coldhearted and totally lacking in curiosity to have refused." Val glanced down at her hands, then back up. "But... why now?"

"Now?" Vivian asked, puzzled.

"Why not a year ago, two years ago?"

Vivian lapsed into silence for a minute, then folded her hands in her lap and sighed. "Actually I did start looking for you about eighteen months ago, long before I met Marty. I was making some real money for the first time in my life, and I wanted to share it with you."

"What happened?"

"I ran into a dead end in Abilene and quickly got discouraged. And, too, I went through a period of wondering if perhaps I shouldn't let sleeping dogs lie. Then grim determination would take over, and off I'd go again. But it wasn't until Marty came along that I began to let myself believe I might really find you. My husband is very resourceful, and Marty doesn't know the meaning of the word *no*."

"Those years when you were alone...what were they like?" Val asked.

This time Vivian's silence lasted longer. Finally her gaze wandered to a point somewhere over Val's shoulder, and her eyes became distant. "Hard," she said tersely. "There were many times when it was difficult just to feed myself. I was terribly naive and trusted many people I shouldn't have, but I wised up in a hurry. I grew up, it now seems, overnight, and I'm afraid some of my experiences left me damned cautious about people and their motives."

Val shook her head in wonder. "How on earth did you manage?"

"I managed because I had no choice. And luckily, I'm a lot smarter than a lot of people gave me credit for. But I had to claw for every inch of ground I took." Vivian's gaze then met Val's squarely. "Whenever I thought of you—and I did a lot, Valerie—it was with a mixture of pain and the sure knowledge I had done the right thing. At least I knew you had your father and would always have a roof over your head. By the way, I was very sorry to hear about Harry."

"Yes, it was a sad time for me. When did you hear about his accident?"

"Not until we'd tracked you down in Bandera. That's when I renewed my determination to find you. Frankly, Marty was beginning to have doubts, but I wasn't about to be swayed. I told him if he wouldn't help me, I'd just have to do it myself. I'm afraid my husband doesn't know quite what to make of me half the time. He says I'm impulsive and stubborn, a dangerous combination, and he's right."

"He adores you," Val said.

"I know. I caution myself constantly against taking advantage of that." Vivian paused and gave Val an enigmatic smile. "I'm only successful part of the time. Adoration from another human being is almost impossible to resist."

Val could imagine that was so. She recalled the expression on Martin's face whenever he looked at Vivian, and she wondered how it must feel to be on the receiving end of such a look.

"Tell me about your life now, Valerie," Vivian said. "Oh, Marty called me every night he was at the ranch and reported everything he had learned about you, but I want to hear it from you."

As succinctly as possible, Val told her mother about the requirements of her job and about Scott.

"You like working for him," Vivian said. It wasn't a question.

"Yes, I like working for him." Which was true. Even though he disturbed her. Even though she didn't understand what made him tick. Even though he sometimes made her long for something that could never be, she always enjoyed working for him.

"And you like *him,* right?"

Val smiled a little sheepishly. "You're very perceptive."

Vivian smiled knowingly. "There was something in the tone of your voice when you were talking about him. We never can hide it completely."

"Lord, I hope you're wrong, Mother. I'd die of mortification if Scott suspected I ever thought about him as anything but the man I work for. You see, he has a girlfriend . . . a gorgeous one, I might add."

"I sure wouldn't let that stand in my way."

Wanting to change the subject, Val then told Vivian about her office and the little cottage she lived in. "The place came furnished, which was a blessing. Daddy and I never owned much. He thought belongings were too cumbersome." Once again her eyes swept the room. "You have to be settled to own lovely things, and I never have been."

"You're right. Possessions can come to represent security. When I first met Marty, I thought his feelings about the lovely things he owns were rather silly, but I'm beginning to understand." Vivian reached out and covered Val's hand with her own. "Valerie, the things you see represent a way of life that's very seductive. Marty and I meant it when we said we want you to think of this as home, a place where you're always welcome to come and stay as long as you like. Every weekend. All the time, if that suits you. You see how much room we have. You would not be in our way, and we would not be in yours."

The servant who had served lunch—Val seemed to recall hearing her called Sara—appeared in the doorway carrying a tray, which she placed on the coffee table. She stood aside, waiting for the mistress of the manor to inspect its contents. Vivian studied the assortment of sweets and savories, then smiled and nodded her approval. Sara silently left the room.

"Lemon or cream?" Vivian asked.

"I…ah, I'm not sure," Val admitted. "Lemon, I guess. This is a bit new to me."

"Sugar?"

"A little."

"Six months ago I didn't have the foggiest notion of what afternoon tea was. The first time Sara asked me if I wanted tea, I thought she meant a glass of iced tea. When she rolled a little cart in front of me loaded with goodies and a pot of tea, I felt a trifle silly." Vivian smiled at the recollection. "I'm sure there were many giggles and much shaking of heads out in the kitchen, not that I really cared. Marty loves the gracious life, but I only go along with it to a point. I've discovered there's a fine line between graciousness and stuffiness."

Vivian handed Val a cup and saucer, then picked up her own and settled back. "Whereas once I could offer you nothing, now I can offer you almost anything. Fine clothes, elegant surroundings, travel. Would you like to go back to school, perhaps get a degree? That can be arranged."

"Good heavens!" Val exclaimed with a little laugh. "My head is spinning."

"Think about it. Think about it *seriously*."

Val sobered. "I really don't want you to think . . . you owe me anything . . . or have to make something up to me."

"I don't," Vivian said firmly. "I don't spend a minute's time in the past. What's done is done. But this is something I want to do. In fact, both Marty and I want you to have whatever your heart desires. Marty is a very generous man, and from our phone conversations this past week, I know he's quite taken with you. He spoils me horribly... and it's fun."

"I like him," Val said. She also liked her mother. Meeting Vivian was the nicest thing that had happened to her in... she couldn't remember when.

"You'll like him even better the more you get to know him."

Val sipped her tea thoughtfully. A seductive way of life. Yes, she could certainly believe that. It was probably very easy to get used to and almost impossible to give up. She, who had never had much of anything, was being offered the moon.

It certainly gave her something to think about.

SCOTT STEPPED OUT of the shower, briskly toweled, then slipped on a robe and went into his bedroom where he lay on the bed with his arms behind his head. He had to snap out of this bitch of a mood. What did he have to be cross about? Things couldn't have been going better. He had everything he'd hoped for. Reservations were coming in at a steady pace. The lodge was booked solid through mid-August, as were several of the cottages. The family trade would slacken once school started in September, but then hunting season would be just around the corner. Unless something major happened, the ranch would show a profit after its first year of operation, and how often did something like that happen?

And why had he snapped at Jeff this afternoon? It had been totally uncalled for. His brother's request had been a reasonable one, probably even a desirable one. Hell, except as a tennis pro, Jeff was of absolutely no use to the Hole in the Wall, so why not let him out of his contract? Scott was a little disappointed that Jeff didn't want to honor a commitment, but even that was an improvement. In the past he'd often been *acutely* disappointed in Jeff.

And, in retrospect, whose fault was that? Jeff was Jeff—irrepressible, irresponsible—but people warmed to him. *Cut him some slack.* All things considered, Jeff had been remarkably well behaved during his stay at the Hole in the Wall—no fistfights or incidents involving women. No staying out all night or guzzling beer on the job.

So tomorrow Scott would tell his brother he would let him out of his contract when Mark came back. Another apology. He seemed to be doing an awful lot of that lately.

Then, inevitably, he wondered what Val was doing, and hated himself for wondering. He thought of Dodson. To Val the old boy probably represented the last word in polish and worldly sophistication. Judging from his clothes, his manners, his car, Scott had to believe Dodson was affluent. He doubtless could have Val's head filled with sugar-coated dreams in no time.

What if she fell for him, really fell? What if he asked her to marry him? Scott's gut clenched. None of his envisioned scenarios of the Hole in the Wall's future had ever included Val's marrying and leaving. Which was shortsighted of him, to say the least. She was young and pretty, sweet-tempered and efficient. She'd make somebody a hell of a wife. That thought settled suddenly on his mind and deepened his already black mood.

Today was the first Saturday in quite a while that Beverly hadn't been by. He guessed he'd thoroughly discouraged her by his preoccupation with the ranch, and that was just as well. Beverly shouldn't waste her time on him. And it was probably better to let their relationship wither, rather than make a big deal of splitting up. Maybe then they could remain friends.

He looked at the bedside clock. Six-thirty. There was a long evening ahead. He thought of possible ways of filling it.

There was the Longhorn Coffee Shop, where he was guaranteed to fall into lengthy conversation with someone. But no liquor was served at the Longhorn, and he felt unusually in need of a drink.

He thought of the bachelors he knew, the ones who weren't currently tied up with some woman. There weren't many of them. Only three came quickly to mind. Sheriff Wayne Jackson. Mayor Martin Avery. And Manny Hernandez, the veterinarian. Maybe he could call them and invite them out to play pool or poker. Open the bar. Then he'd rustle up something to eat. The ranch's kitchen was amply stocked at all times. Macho stuff. Have a stag party, albeit a subdued one.

But Scott felt restless and mean, like a coiled snake. Maybe it wasn't such a good idea to be around people tonight. Best he do something solitary, like have a few drinks and dinner at that steak house he and Val had...

Growling, Scott swung his legs off the bed and stood up. Hell, he'd just stay here. Get semismashed, eat a steak, then watch a movie and go to bed. Anything to keep from wondering what the devil was going on in San Angelo.

CHAPTER ELEVEN

IF VIVIAN and Martin had set out to seduce Val to their way of life, they were doing a masterful job of it. After spending most of the afternoon exploring their wonderful house, she accompanied Martin as he inspected his property in a Jeep Cherokee. He called it his farm, but it was the most beautifully kept farm she had ever seen. And his healthy herd of Angoras was a sight to see. Martin was justifiably proud of what he owned.

Her stepfather was every inch the country squire, Val had noticed. He carried himself with authority, and the people who worked for him treated him with the utmost respect. Her mother had to be one of the most fortunate women on earth.

At one point during the inspection, Martin suddenly halted the Cherokee, turned off the engine and twisted in his seat to face Val. "So, tell me about you and your mother. How are the two of you hitting it off?"

"I like her, Martin. Very much. I can't thank you enough for giving me the opportunity to know her."

He beamed. "It's more that I should thank you for giving *her* the opportunity to know *you*." Then he sobered, frowning slightly. "Poor dear hasn't had a life anyone would especially envy. I know there are those who would say she was more responsible for that than anyone, and to some extent perhaps they'd be right. But she has the kindest heart of anyone I've ever known."

"I wanted to ask her more about herself and her life after she and Daddy split up," Val said, "but I wasn't sure I should. I have no idea how she feels about talking about it."

Martin pursed his lips. "It's not something she often brings up, but I don't think she really minds talking about it. You see, after she left your father, she went back to her parents. Those were terrible days for her. They had never approved of her marrying so young, and there was a great deal of 'I told you so' and chastisement. Viv had never meant to stay, but she *had* hoped they might give her some moral support and time to decide what her next move should be. They only made her feel unwelcome, however, so she struck out on her own much sooner than she should have."

Val shuddered at the callousness of the grand-parents she barely remembered. "Where did she go, what did she do?"

"She went to Fort Worth first, because she imagined there would be more opportunities in a city. But, of course, with little formal education or training, she was able to secure only the most menial employment. She sent you money occasionally, but often there was none to send."

"To look at her now, you would think she was to the manner born. It's so amazing."

"Viv's smart and resourceful. Survivors always are, and your mother, Valerie, is above all a survivor."

The sun was lowering in the sky. Martin shifted in his seat and turned on the engine. "I do believe the cocktail hour approaches. Viv has planned a feast for dinner tonight. And afterward...well, afterward we have a little surprise for you."

Val glanced at him sideways as the Cherokee inched forward. "Martin, one more surprise might be more than my poor mind can absorb."

I GUESS I don't have to have a brick house fall on me to get the picture, Beverly thought morosely, staring at her image in her dressing table mirror. It was late Saturday, and she hadn't heard from Scott. Worse, something told her she wasn't going to, not tonight, maybe not ever again. It was a humbling thought for a woman whose man troubles had always involved having too many of them falling all over her at once.

Heaving a sigh, she sat and listened to the sounds an empty house makes. Her mother was out with Vernon. Sam was in town, so Lynn was with him. Beverly vowed she positively, absolutely wouldn't call Shirley or Abby or any of her other girl-friends. No way would she let anyone know she was probably the only woman in Claro County who had nothing to do on Saturday night, but God, she wished something would happen or someone would call. Even that conceited ass Jeff Harris would be a welcome diversion tonight.

She glanced around her bedroom. It had been her private corner of the world for twenty-five years. There had been a college dorm, of course. And, more recently there had been times when she'd thought about getting an apartment of her own; she certainly could afford it. But she'd never do it. The Circle T represented security, the one thing she cherished above all. Here she would stay until she found Mr. Right.

An involuntary sigh escaped her lips. Scott epitomized her ideal man, and she wasn't going to get him. Beverly wasn't sure how she knew that for certain, but she did. She would get over him, but she wished she didn't have to.

She also wished she knew what had happened. In April she would have sworn everything was perfect between them. Then he got so tied up in that ranch he just didn't have time for fun any longer.

At least that was what she wanted to blame it on. She refused to think he might have found someone else. Who? He hardly ever left the Hole in the Wall. He saw almost no one but the cowboys, the household staff and the ranch's guests.

The guests! Could he possibly have fallen for someone who had stayed at the ranch? But they were mostly families, weren't they? At least that was what Scott had told her. Mothers and fathers and their children. The lodge only had four single rooms.

Well, how many did it take? One lonely or stressed-out career woman who wanted a week of peace and could afford the Hole in the Wall. Scott would go for an upwardly mobile career woman who was as serious and successful as he was.

Your survival instincts failed you this time, girl, she thought. She should have hung around the ranch more and checked out all the check-ins. Beverly had no doubts about her ability to nip a budding romance before it flowered. Possibly she should have made a confidante out of Val and gotten Scott's manager to do a little snooping for her.

All of a sudden a light bulb went off in her head. Val! She and Scott were together all the time, day in and day out. She was probably the first person he saw in the morning and the last at night. And they were cut of the same cloth. Any woman who got Scott got that ranch on a twenty-four-hour basis, like it or not, and Val treated the place as if she'd personally driven every nail that held it together. She was also pretty in a homespun way that might appeal to a man like Scott.

Beverly's mind raced off on an uncharted course. Val? It couldn't be... could it? Suddenly she recalled the way Scott had looked at Val when they danced together that night at Zack's. Val! The possibility absolutely stunned her.

THE CHEROKEE PULLED to a stop in front of the stone house's front steps, and Val hopped out. "I want to go spend some time with my head stockman, but I'll see you at dinner. I'm sure by now your mother is completely jealous of the time I've had with you."

"See you later, and thanks for the tour," Val called as she bounded up the steps. She paused momentarily at the front door, wondering if she should just barge in. But of course, she decided.

Martin and Vivian had told her over and over that this was her home, and one didn't ring one's own doorbell.

Pushing open the door, she stepped into the foyer and looked around, seeing the house with newly opened eyes. *Her* home! It wasn't real to her yet. In the past, whenever she had thought of having a home to go to, she'd envisioned a bungalow, something with two or three bedrooms, perhaps a second bath. Never in her wildest flights of imagination could she have conjured up this house.

She wondered where Vivian was. The thought had no sooner formed than her mother appeared at the top of the stairs. "So Martin finally decided to bring you home, did he?" Vivian said with a smile. "Could you come up here a minute, Valerie? I have something to show you."

"Of course."

"Up here" was the master bedroom . . . or suite, Val supposed it should have been called. The room was enormous. Besides the king-size bed, there was a fireplace with two easy chairs flanking it. Separate baths and dressing areas were on either side of the room. Vivian motioned her to a door and opened it. Inside was a closet much larger than Val's office, and it held more garments and shoes than Pamela's Boutique in Crystal Creek. Val couldn't stifle a gasp.

"What size do you wear, Valerie?" Vivian asked.

"Eight."

"I thought so. It appeared to me we're the same size." She took down a garment and offered it for Val's inspection. "I wondered if you might like to wear this to dinner tonight. I've never even worn it except to try it on in the store. I'm afraid clothes are my main extravagance."

The garment was lounging pajamas in a silky sapphire blue, so exquisite Val couldn't resist touching it. The top was a kimono style, held closed by a sash. The pants were step-ins. "Do you mean you and Martin dress like this for dinner at home?"

"There's a certain formality to Martin's way of life. I can't imagine the man coming in from the fields and putting his feet under the table. He likes to dress, then have cocktails, then a proper dinner in the dining room. I've followed his lead and found that it's a wonderful way to live. Do you like this?" Vivian asked, indicating the pajamas.

"It's beautiful! I'd love to wear it if you're sure you want me to."

"I'm sure. If you like it, it's yours. I have too many clothes as it is, and I can't resist buying more. I suppose I'm like a child being turned loose in a candy store for the first time. Here, let me show you something else."

From a jewelry case, Vivian withdrew a pair of dangling gold earrings in which were set stones the same color as the pajamas. "I bought these to go with the outfit... and have never worn them, either."

Val's eyes shone. "Thank you so much, Mother."

"Don't mention it, dear. Now, I'm going to take my bath and get dressed. Martin and I usually meet in the conservatory at six-thirty for cocktails. Dinner is served at seven-thirty."

"I wouldn't miss it for the world," Val said, hugging the sapphire silk to her. She turned to leave, then had an afterthought. Turning back to Vivian, she gave her a quick hug. Her mother's face flushed with pleasure.

Down the hall in her own room, Val carefully hung up the garment, placed the earrings on the table beside her bed, then did a dance in the center of the room. Everything that was happening to her combined to create a feast for the senses. Sights, sounds, aromas, tastes that were foreign and heady.

Hurrying into her private bath, she drew water in the tub and sprinkled bath bubbles under the faucet's spray. Though the rest of the house was furnished traditionally, the bathroom was luxurious and modern...all tile and marble and mirrors. For the next forty-five minutes or so, Val indulged in a full-scale beauty treatment. She soaked in the fragrant water until it cooled, then got out, toweled and dusted herself with bath powder. Afterward she sat in front of a vanity and primped and preened as she'd never done in her life. The final fillip was stepping into the pajamas and feeling real silk against her skin for the first time. Once the earrings were in place, she stood in front of a full-length mirror and took a good look at herself.

That can't be Valerie Drayton, was her first thought. She looked beautiful. She sat on the edge of the bed and kept a watchful eye on the bedside clock, waiting until exactly six-thirty. When both hands reached six, she went to the door, giving in to a delighted giggle. Normally she simply left a room. This time she swept out grandly.

SCOTT WAS WELL THROUGH his fourth Scotch on the rocks when Jeff put in an appearance. The younger brother had seen the light and had come to see what was going on. He stood in the doorway of Scott's sitting room, taking in the scene. Scotch bottle on the end table next to the sofa. Scott on the sofa, empty glass in hand, a darkly brooding expression on his face. Only one small lamp was on. Interesting, Jeff thought... and obvious.

His brother hadn't yet seen him, so Jeff gave some thought to leaving before he did. Instead he took a few steps inside the room.

"Mind some company?"

Scott looked up and scowled. Jeff knew that look, and he fully expected to be told to get lost. Then Scott shrugged. "Suit yourself."

Jeff strolled into the room, took a seat facing the sofa and sized up his brother. He himself tended to be a happy drunk; three beers and he loved everyone in the world. But alcohol in anything but moderate quantities had always had the opposite effect on Scott. He didn't get mean, but he turned even more inward, became reflective and somber.

But Scott didn't often have more than a couple of drinks. Jeff glanced again at the bottle and wondered how much it had held before this drinking bout started. "Something wrong?" he asked.

"Yeah. The goddamn Astros blew it in the ninth. I lost twenty bucks to Wayne Jackson."

"B.S.," Jeff said, grinning.

Scott looked at him, as if suddenly remembering something. "What in hell are you doing *here* on Saturday night?"

"Everybody's got to be somewhere. I couldn't stir up anything in town, so I came back, figuring I might con Earl into a game of gin. I saw your light and came in. Got any beer?"

"I think there's some in the bar in my office. Help yourself. And while you're at it, get me some more ice." Scott stuck out his glass.

Jeff was gone a few minutes, then returned carrying a can of beer and Scott's glass. Handing it to his brother, he resumed his seat and watched as Scott poured a splash of liquor over the fresh rocks. "Wanna talk about it?"

"About what?"

"About whatever's eating you."

"Nothing's eating me."

"More B.S." Jeff took a hefty swallow of the beer. "Talking helps. That comes straight from the horse's mouth, believe me."

"Helps what?"

"Troubles. Especially women troubles."

Scott frowned at him. "Since when have you ever had women problems? And I don't have the slightest idea what the hell you're talking about."

"Yeah, you do. Maybe you won't admit it yet, but you definitely know what the hell I'm talking about. The symptoms are all here. Solitary drinking, for one. That snarl for another. Sitting here in semidarkness. So, I ask myself what could be wrong. What happened today that's unusual? And then it comes to me. Val sailed off to San Angelo with that old boy."

Scott's face looked like a summer thunderstorm about to break. "Now, just a goddamn minute..."

"Hey, it's nothing to be ashamed of. Admitting it, bringing it out into the open is the first step in dealing with it." Jeff was relishing being in the position of giving advice instead of getting a load of it. "I've suspected for some time you've thought about Val in ways that don't really jibe with that employer-employee crap you're always dishing out."

Scott's defenses were down, Jeff could see. Instead of lashing out at him or telling him to get out, his brother took a long swig of his drink, then said, "I've never touched Val...or almost never."

"Maybe that's the problem."

"I'm not following you."

"You've never given her any reason to think you think of her as a woman. So she finds someone who does."

"I'd like to remind you that Val's never given me any reason to think she would welcome my advances."

"Your fault, of course. I saw the way she was looking at you at Zack's that night. I've seen her look at you when you didn't know it lots of times. Longing, you know."

"I thought *you* had the hots for her," Scott growled.

"Well, I'll admit to hoping, but the lady's not interested, thanks. Believe me, I can pick up on that quick. That's another thing—that lecture you gave me about Val's not being the type a man toys with. When a guy starts having noble thoughts about a woman, he's a goner."

Jeff tilted his head and took a hefty swallow of beer. Then he settled back, fingering the rim of the can. "Tell me something, bro—this thing you have about business relationships—what got it started? What was her name?"

Scott looked startled. "What makes you think a woman had anything to do with it?"

"Don't give me the village idiot treatment. What was her name?"

"Linda." For a long wordless minute Scott stared moodily into his glass. Then he began to talk. "It was back in the early days of my practice, back before I became the one the rich and famous came to when they wanted divorces. Linda was fresh out of law school, smart, sharp and pretty. Idealistic, too... like I was in those days. We made a great team, in courtrooms and out, and we were making more money than two people in their late twenties had any right to. Then I made the mistake of falling for her."

For the first time in a long time, Jeff was seeing his brother as an ordinary mortal who had ordinary problems. "What happened?"

"Suddenly she became jealous of every female client I had reason to spend time with. Suddenly she was far more interested in what I was doing when she wasn't around than she was in working on our cases. The relationship soured immediately and so did the partnership. When she left she took some of my best clients with her. It taught me a lesson."

Jeff shrugged nonchalantly. "So Linda loused it up. Not all women would. I think you should give in to the inevitable."

"And I think you should mind your own business," Scott said rather wearily.

Silence fell over the room like a shroud. Jeff didn't know why he didn't just leave. Scott had never been his idea of the greatest company in the world, and when his brother was like this, he was unbearable.

But Jeff stayed. Then abruptly Scott drained his glass and stood, a trifle unsteadily. "Hell, enough of this. Let's cook some steaks and watch a movie. Go see if Earl wants to join us. Let's do something, for God's sake!" And he strode out of the room, leaving Jeff smiling knowingly in his wake.

THE MEAL that had been set before Val that night was the most elegant she could imagine. It began with corn velvet soup, followed by grilled salmon, then by a raspberry sorbet. Val naturally had thought the sorbet was dessert. She later discovered the sorbet was to cleanse the palate before the main course of a veal chop, tiny potatoes and peas from the garden on the premises. Then had come salad and dessert. That she could actually do justice to that much food amazed her, but the servings were small and artfully arranged on delicate china in the kitchen. There was much changing of plates and wines, and all was served on crisp white linen—a visual treat as well as a tasty one. She thought of the countless tin plates piled high with food she had consumed in her life. Compared to this, that seemed barbaric.

And before dinner she had sat in the conservatory sipping sherry. Val had never had sherry before, and she couldn't say she'd liked it much, but that was what Martin suggested, and it sounded so genteel. Her mother, she noticed, drank Scotch on the rocks, Scott's drink.

Throughout the meal she discreetly studied Vivian and Martin. Theirs was an unusual relationship. There was an abundance of love on both sides; that much was evident. After that, matters grew more complex. Martin apparently had set himself up as the designated care giver, the one who would lead his lovely, once deprived wife through a life without hills and valleys. Vivian, who probably had known more valleys than Val could imagine, humored him. But everything about Vivian Drayton Dodson pointed to a woman who didn't need anyone to take care of her.

When the meal ended, Vivian instructed Sara to serve coffee in the conservatory, and the three of them trooped out of the dining room. Conversation throughout the meal had been mostly limited to Val's answering more questions about her past, so she wondered what the surprise Martin had mentioned was. Maybe it was the meal. If so, it had been a delightful surprise.

Once coffee was served and the atmosphere relaxed, Martin looked at Val, beaming. "Remember I told you that your mother and I have a surprise for you, my dear?"

"And I think I told you I wasn't sure I could take another surprise. This is the most beautiful house. These are the most beautiful clothes, and that was the grandest meal I have ever, ever... Words fail me."

"Then hang on to your hat," Martin said, casting a fond glance at Vivian. "First of all, we meant it when we said we want you to live here with us, if that's what you want. But even if you don't choose to live here on a full-time basis, it will always be your home. In fact, Viv and I were discussing this while we were dressing tonight. This grand house that I love so much will someday have to belong to someone else. To Viv, of course, should I predecease her. But one day we'll both be gone. I can't leave it to my son. He would only sell it to the highest bidder. His roots are deep in New England, and he has a rather grand old house himself. Oh, there might be a few odds and ends here that he would enjoy, but the house itself would be nothing but a bother to him. So the logical heir is you, Valerie."

Val was stunned. What was being offered to her didn't even register for a minute. It was like a dream, not rooted in reality. Or maybe she'd had too much wine at dinner. "M-me?" she finally stammered.

"Of course," Martin said. "Monday I'll consult with my attorney about having my will changed. It rather pleases me to think of you in this house, then one of your children, a grandchild, and on and on."

Val was so overcome with emotion that tears welled, then spilled and ran down her cheeks. That she, Valerie Drayton from nowhere in particular, would someday own this house was...unbelievable. Something to call her own. Something permanent.

A three-room condo would have sufficed. This was too much.

Unable to speak, she stood and crossed the room to hug, first Martin, then her mother. When she returned to her seat, she composed herself with some difficulty. "I don't know how to thank you. I pray my ownership will be many, many years away, but be assured, when it *is* mine, it will be given the same care you've given it. Whew! You said you had a surprise for me, but this is a whopper."

Again Martin and Vivian exchanged glances. Then Vivian turned to Val. "But that's not all, Valerie." •

"H-how could there be more?"

Martin shifted in his chair, a cat-got-the-canary look on his face. He lifted the pot from the tray Sara had left. "More coffee, Valerie?"

"No, no, thanks."

Slowly, Martin refilled his cup, then sat back and sipped. "Several months ago, Viv and I began planning a trip. You see, like you, Viv's never been anywhere, whereas it sometimes seems I've been everywhere. I began waxing nostalgic about New England in the fall, and Viv said she would love to see it. But I'm afraid our plans have grown rather ambitious. They now include returning to New York and flying first to London, then to Paris,

Madrid, Seville—oh, most definitely Seville—then on to Rome. We plan to leave immediately after the fall shearing, and I rather imagine we'll be gadding around the globe throughout the remainder of the year. Possibly we'll spend Christmas in Rome."

Val heaved an exaggerated sigh. "That sounds fabulous. Mother, you're a very fortunate woman."

"I know," Vivian said, "but there's more. Marty and I want you to come with us."

"Oh, good grief!" Val let out a little shriek and a laugh. But then reality set in. "That's so sweet of you both, but I can't. I have a contract that calls for me to work until Christmas."

Vivian's face fell. "Oh, Valerie, surely the contract isn't ironclad."

"I certainly thought it was when I signed it."

"I've seen few of those things that couldn't be broken," Martin said. "I have an excellent attorney."

"Well . . . you see, it's not only that. If I left, I would be leaving Scott in the lurch. I . . . I just don't think I can do that."

"There's bound to be something we can do, Marty." Vivian cast a pleading glance at her husband, then back to Val. "We do so want you to come with us, Valerie. It's really the trip of a lifetime."

Yes, Val knew it was. London, Paris, Madrid, Christmas in Rome. Those were places she had visited vicariously through books, never dreaming she would ever actually see them. Now they were being handed to her on a silver platter. She'd be a fool not to grab this chance.

But obligations were obligations, and she had never been one to turn her back on them. "I can't jeopardize my job," she said with a sad shake of her head. "It's the best one I've ever had."

Martin smiled fondly. "Valerie, you might want to give some thought to your job's importance to you now. I don't believe you fully realize what's being offered you—not just a trip, not just an inheritance someday, but a brand-new way of life."

Val chewed her bottom lip. Normally a decisive person, she now was more confused than she'd ever been. They were asking her to give up life as she knew it, and while there were times when it hadn't been all that great, it was familiar and comfortable. "I...I'd like to ask you to let me think about it," she said weakly.

Martin reached over and patted his wife's hand. "Of course. Viv, dear, I'm afraid we've absolutely bombarded the girl today. Yes, I think she should sleep on it. I quite imagine by morning she'll have this all in clearer perspective. So enough for now. I think I'll have a brandy. Would either of you like one?''

Val accepted his offer and leaned back in her chair. For the next hour or so, she dreamily listened to Martin's reminiscences of other European jaunts, deliberately whetting her appetite, she knew. By the time they all went upstairs to retire for the night, she felt light-headed, almost giddy. That could be attributable to sherry, wine and brandy, but she didn't think so.

Someone had turned down her bed and left a small lamp burning. Sara, she supposed. Val hated to take off the luxurious pajamas, so she didn't immediately. She turned off the lamp and went to sit in a chair by the window. The grounds were bathed in moonlight that spilled through giant oaks, creating lacy patterns on the grass. The grounds of Martin's home stretched out in all directions. He referred to it as his farm, but to her it was an estate, a manor, as grand as Tara itself. That all this would be hers someday was incredible.

A brand-new way of life. Hers for the taking. Why was there any question in her mind? By October the Hole in the Wall would practically be running itself. She wouldn't be as indispensable as she was now. Scott wouldn't need her.

Scott. She vaguely wondered if he was still miffed over the two hours off. She hoped not. But if he was, she would just work twice as diligently in the days ahead and perhaps he would soon get over it.

Being honest with herself, Val knew it was Scott more than her job that caused her hesitation. She didn't want to leave him, and that was pure stupidity. If she stayed at the ranch "forever," as she'd once said she would, she'd only be forced to someday stand by and watch him marry Beverly...or someone very like her. How would she like working in the lodge under the watchful eye of Scott's wife? Val knew the answer to that one; she'd hate it. Truthfully, she knew she probably would leave the Hole in the Wall if Scott married. In the meantime, she would have turned her back on a dream any woman would kill for. Stupid.

Giving herself a shake, she stood and took off the pajamas and earrings, then put on her plain cotton nightie. They seemed to symbolize the decision she had to make. She could wear silk the rest of her life or plain white cotton. That there was any decision to be made stunned her.

She went into the luxurious bathroom, brushed her teeth then crawled into bed. Martin was right. Things probably would look clearer in the morning. Like Scarlett, she would think about it tomorrow.

CHAPTER TWELVE

SCOTT WOKE at seven o'clock the next morning and couldn't go back to sleep. Now he remembered why he didn't allow himself to get drunk as a rule. He couldn't sleep with a hangover. In college he'd had buddies who could sleep all day after a binge, but he'd never been able to. He'd just have to suffer the dull headache until noon or so, when he would renew his vow never to do it again.

Scowling at his ravaged countenance in the bathroom mirror, he switched on his electric razor. Its hum made his temples throb. As he went through the routine chore, his mind wandered back over the previous evening. It had been an interesting, if boozy one. Jeff had surprised him. He wasn't all superficiality and shallowness, after all. There *were* some ideas spinning around in that brain. Of course he was still something of a rogue and probably always would be. And he had the soul of a wildcatter, so he'd probably never be entirely settled—at least not to the extent Scott considered settled. But he *did* occasionally think and talk about something besides women and good times.

And Jeff had been absolutely right about one thing—Scott had fallen for Val, completely, madly, head over heels. He must have. What else would account for his mood, the stark terror when he thought of not having her around? And if he'd admitted it and acted upon it weeks ago, she wouldn't be off with Dodson this weekend...maybe.

On the other hand, if Dodson hadn't shown up, Scott wondered how long it would have taken him to forget the fiasco with Linda and own up to the way he really felt about Val.

So at last he acknowledged the source of his recent discontent. Dodson! Merely thinking about Val with that middle-aged dandy just flat killed him. Scott wondered if too much damage had already been done. Hopefully not. He was counting on her sensible nature. She never did anything impulsively. He simply couldn't believe that she would fall into bed with a man she'd only known six days. Maybe it wasn't too late. After all, he, Scott, was with her all week.

Scott now intended to woo Val with the same single-minded purposefulness that he had once employed in keeping his distance from her. He wasn't a ladies' man, not in the sense that Jeff was, but he'd always been pretty successful in getting the ones who interested him interested in him. Deep beneath that serious, somewhat starched exterior of his beat the heart of a natural romantic.

Once he'd had lunch, he felt almost human again. Val would be back by late afternoon, so he planned his next move. He'd ask her to have dinner with him, of course . . . not in the dining room or kitchen, but here in his own rooms. Scott eyed his quarters critically. A decorator from town had done the rooms for him, and they were comfortable, tasteful, masculine without being cold. He had not expected to do any entertaining here, but the decorator had insisted on putting a small round table and two chairs in one corner of the living room. "You never know when you might want to have a quiet dinner alone. Every place, no matter how small, should have somewhere to sit down and eat properly," she'd said.

Bless her. Scott cleared the table and covered it with the tablecloth she had also insisted he have. That done, he walked through the lodge and into the kitchen's supply room to get dishes, silverware and glasses. Then he decided what he would have to eat.

VAL FOUND IT difficult to say goodbye to Vivian and Martin, and she especially hated that she was leaving without committing herself to that "brand-new way of life." But she would be back next weekend, she promised, and surely by then she would have an answer for them.

Just before she left, her mother had taken her off to one side. "Valerie, if it's the man you work for who's causing your hesitation, I can certainly understand that. I strongly believe in following your heart. But if it's some misguided sense of loyalty or duty that's prompting you, forget it."

Once Val was back on the road to Crystal Creek and the Hole in the Wall, she relaxed. After two days of surprise heaped upon surprise, she was looking forward to getting back to the familiar, the routine. A mind could only be assaulted so long before it wanted to simply think about nothing.

It was just past five when she drove through the ranch's gate, past the lodge, and parked beside her cottage. She had returned with far more than she'd left with. Her mother had insisted on giving her a dozen or more garments, insisting that she never wore them. Val didn't know if that was true or not, but she'd sensed Vivian would have been disappointed if she had refused them.

Such clothes! She had no idea where she'd wear them. Certainly not here on the ranch or in Crystal Creek, but simply owning them was fun. She carefully unpacked, hung up everything, then set about deciding what she would fix for supper in the cottage's tiny kitchenette. She was in the midst of that when her phone rang. Checking the flashing light, she saw the call was coming from Scott.

"Yes?"

"Val, Scott."

"Yes, Scott."

"I'd like you to have dinner with me, if you can."

"How nice. I'd love to."

"We'll have it here, if that's all right."

"It's fine."

"Say, in an hour?"

"Thanks. I'll be there."

Hanging up, Val tapped her lips with a fingernail. He didn't *sound* miffed, just cordial and businesslike, as usual. She might be forced to endure a mild scolding, but she'd live through it. Now she didn't have to worry about supper. Now all she had to do was freshen up and change.

On her way to the bathroom, she threw open her closet and studied its contents. The sapphire pajamas fairly screamed at her, and an impish smile crossed her face. Did she dare? After a moment's consideration, she thought—why not? She ought to seize every opportunity to wear her lovely new clothes; there would be precious few of them. With a nod of satisfaction, she closed the door and went into the bathroom.

SOME FIFTY MINUTES LATER Val left her cottage and started across the grounds. The air was still and muggy, and she smelled rain. Looking skyward, she noticed dark clouds moving in from the north. Lord, she hoped it was just a late-afternoon thunderstorm and not one of those protracted spates of rain they'd had in April. Of course she and Scott had devised contingency plans for inclement weather, but making plans and putting them into practice were two different things. And guests at a dude ranch naturally expected to spend most of their time outdoors. Continuing on, she opened the back door and crossed through the lodge.

The door to Scott's private rooms was open, but Val hesitated at the threshold. This was as far as she'd ever ventured into his retreat. "Scott?" she called.

Getting no reply, she stepped hesitantly into the room and glanced around. A table in one corner had been set for two, with a tablecloth, china, silverware, and water and wine goblets. A bottle of wine was chilling in a silver bucket. Soft music came from somewhere, and the lighting was low. The atmosphere felt downright . . . intimate. What in the world was going on? "Scott?" she called again.

A rumble of distant thunder sounded as he emerged from the bedroom, wiping his hands with a towel. Accompanying him were the distinct aromas of soap and after-shave. "I'm running a little late. I..." He stopped dead in his tracks and stared at her, his mouth slightly open. "Lord, you look wonderful!"

"Thanks."

"I've... never seen you wear that."

"It's new. A present."

"A present?"

"Yes." She executed a little pirouette. "Like it?"

"It's... beautiful."

Sensuously, she ran a hand down the garment. "I've never owned anything so nice. And there are more clothes, a lot of them."

He had the most peculiar look on his face. Did clothes really make that much difference? He stared at her a second or two, then seemed to have some difficulty collecting himself. "I'll be right back. Have a seat." Then he turned and went back into the bedroom.

Instead of sitting, she walked around, studying the room. She and Scott had spent hours together, but she knew little about the private Scott, the man who lived in this room. He obviously enjoyed Western art and the colors of the Southwest. His book collection was eclectic, with spy thrillers and mysteries much in evidence.

Hearing him clear his throat, she turned and smiled. "This is a nice place, Scott. Funny I've never been in here before."

"Yes, it is, isn't it?" He gave her a small, lazy smile. "I'll go in my office and fix us drinks and be right back."

Val stared after him. There was something different about him tonight. He was back in a minute, carrying their drinks, which he placed side by side on the coffee table. He waited for Val to sit down and sat beside her.

His hair was slightly damp and curled around his ears. He wore dark trousers and a crisp white shirt that was open at the neck, showing tanned skin and a tuft of ash blond hair. Val would have given anything to touch it, to feel if it was as coarse as it looked. "Looks like we're in for some rain," she commented inanely.

"I hope it's only a little. So far we've not had to cope with a lodge full of guests on a rainy day."

"Bunch of teenagers coming this week. I imagine they can always find ways of amusing themselves. Besides, this time of year it'll probably be only a thunderstorm that'll blow itself out in an hour or so." Val took a sip of her drink. "How was your weekend?" she asked.

"Last night Jeff and I got gloriously smashed, so I spent this morning nursing a hangover."

She wondered what had prompted the toot. Jeff, she imagined, didn't need a reason, but Scott? Maybe whatever had been bothering him all week had finally gotten the best of him. "Well...at least the two of you got together socially."

Scott made some kind of sound deep in his throat. "I don't know. There's this gap that just can't be bridged. Sometimes we get close, but... Never mind. I don't want to talk about Jeff." He took a sip of his drink, then one arm casually snaked along the back of the sofa; his fingertips touched her shoulder as lightly as the brush of a butterfly's wings. A tiny shiver raced along Val's spine. "And this afternoon I slaved over a hot stove," he added.

Val's eyes widened. "You can cook?"

"I have a repertoire of about eight things I do well. Tonight you're getting one of them—veal piccata."

"I'm impressed."

"It was a case of necessity being the mother of invention. I've lived alone for a long time. Here at the ranch I feel like the member of a large family, but for years it was just me in a bachelor apartment. You can only eat out so much. Even really great restaurants begin to pall after a while."

Val smiled. "I'm not much of a cook. I've eaten bunkhouse chow most of my life. But last night... oh, Scott, last night I had the most memorable meal!'' She went on to describe the food down to the last exquisite detail. When she finished, she set her drink on the table and turned to him with shining eyes. "Scott, I simply must tell you about yesterday. It was the most incredible day of my life! But first—"

"I don't want to hear it, Val!" he said, more harshly than he intended.

She sat back, as stunned as if he had hit her. "Why not? It was—"

"I really don't care what it was. I don't want to hear about it. I didn't ask you here to hear about your weekend."

Val clenched her teeth together. "You don't want to talk about Jeff," she said quietly, "and you don't want to hear about my weekend. What would you like to talk about, Scott?"

"Anything but what you did yesterday."

Val's face had grown very warm. So there still was something bothering him. She couldn't imagine what it was, but at the moment she no longer cared. She sat in silence a minute before getting to her feet and facing him with puzzled eyes. "I don't understand what's going on here. There's been something all week, so there's no way it can simply be my asking for two hours off. If you're ticked off at me about something, I do wish you'd tell me

what it is. Why did you ask me to dinner tonight?
To snarl at me? For the first time since I met you I
don't know how to talk to you. How can we work
together with this...whatever it is between us? I'm
beginning to empathize with Jeff. Scott, you're...
unknowable!'' Skirting the coffee table, she
swished out of the room.

Had it been physically possible, Scott would have
kicked his own butt. In an unthinking instant he
had spoiled everything. Getting to his feet, he went
after her.

She'd barely gotten as far as the door to her office before he caught up with her. Taking her by the
arm, he swung her around with such force she fell
hard against his chest. Her eyes came up to his in
puzzled appeal.

"What *is* it? What's wrong?"

"I'm sorry, Val. I really am. And I'm not ticked
off at you. Please don't go."

She looked at him uncertainly. "Something's
wrong, I know there is."

He brushed a strand of her hair and tried to smile
reassuringly. "No, no...please believe me. I *have*
been in a mood this week, and I'm sorry. Seems like
I've had to apologize to half the people I know. But
I don't want you to leave, Val. Please stay. I really
want you to have dinner with me. I really want you
to spend the evening with me."

He was lying, of course, and she knew it. Something was bugging him, but his voice was gentle. She sensed he really did want her to stay, so perhaps whatever was troubling him had nothing to do with her. "Well . . . all right."

Another rumble of thunder sounded, this one much closer. Knowing Hill Country thunderstorms, Val realized it might be some time before she could leave the lodge without getting soaked.

"I really would like to tell you about yesterday, Scott. It was so fabulous, and it meant so much to me," she said as Scott took her hand and led her back to his room.

He sighed. "All right," he said in a resigned voice.

"But first, I want your advice about something."

A somewhat pained expression crossed his face. "Yes?"

"Let's say you were completely satisfied with your life. You liked your job, liked the people you worked with, were better off financially than you'd ever been. Then suppose someone came along and offered you something so incredibly wonderful that it would change your life completely. You would have things you had only dreamed about, but it would mean giving up the known for the unknown. Would you risk it?"

Scott tensed, afraid to ask the next question but knowing it must be asked. "What...what were you offered?"

Val laughed. "The world! Or at least a good part of it. London, Paris, Madrid, Rome. And the grandest house I've ever—"

Alarm raced through Scott like a forest fire. Damn Dodson for dangling those enticing carrots in front of a woman who'd had so little luxury in her life! The old boy knew exactly how to touch her most vulnerable area. Scott would have liked to strangle the man.

To hell with patience, mood and everything else. In a lightning-quick motion, he placed his drink beside hers and took both of her hands in his, squeezing them hard. "Don't, Val!"

The reaction was so extreme that Val's mouth dropped and her brow knitted. "Don't? Just like that? You don't know every—"

He released her hands and cupped her face, bringing his very close to it. "Please, don't. Look, I know how things like that must sound to you, how wonderful they must seem. But think of next year, the one after that, all the ones left to you. Think of what you'd be tying yourself to. You're young, you're beautiful, and you have all the time in the world to acquire things like that."

"But, I don't... You haven't heard—"

"I don't want to hear. I have things to tell you, too, Val. A confession of sorts. You're right. I *was* different all week. Something was eating at me, only it took my kid brother to make me own up to what it was. You."

"M-me?"

"I've fallen in love with you."

It was the last thing in the world Val had expected to hear. The confession knocked the breath out of her. "Oh, Scott...I don't know what to say. Wh-when did you discover this?"

"A long time ago, I think. I only admitted it yesterday."

His head came closer, then his mouth covered hers. It was nothing like the only other kiss they had shared. This was deep, prolonged, druggingly sweet. Val leaned into it, and they wound themselves around each other, kissing until they were breathless. Everything else evaporated from Val's mind. Vivian and Martin were forgotten. The trip, the house were forgotten. How often had she dreamed of kissing Scott this way.... The rest of the world melted away.

When he finally broke the kiss, he moved a hand to her nape, tucked her head into the curve of his shoulder. "I think..." she began when she at last could find her voice, "I think that's the nicest kiss I've ever had."

"That's why you can't give those other things another thought."

"Scott, I haven't told you everything. I—"

"Hush. I don't want to hear them. Not now." Then he kissed her again with unhurried thoroughness. When his lips left her mouth, he kissed the tip of her nose and her closed eyelids. "Val, I've fought this so long. It's a hell of a relief to get it off my chest."

Knowing he had harbored secret longings for her just as she had for him sent ripples of pleasure through her. Still, there were questions, doubts. "But what about Beverly?"

"What about her?"

"The two of you. I thought... you and she were..."

"It was never that way between the two of us, Val. We only dated casually. I think I've had you on my mind since... hell, I don't know. Maybe since the first day you showed up here."

Val could barely comprehend it. "You never gave any indication...showed any sign.... I was just an employee...."

"You were always more than that, but I wouldn't admit it." His hands stroked her arms and the side of her face. He looked at her as though seeing her for the first time.

"Oh, Scott... I'm so confused."

"I know."

"And . . . delighted."

"Are you, Val? Honestly?"

"I'm afraid I've been guilty of dreaming about you, boss."

"You're a very good actress."

Her eyes closed, and she took a deep breath. Maybe she was hallucinating. Maybe yesterday, which had seemed like a dream, was reality and this was the dream. It didn't seem possible that so much could happen so fast. "I've been in love with you since day one."

"You don't have to say that, you know. You don't have to make an honest man out of me. I'll give you time to learn to love me."

"I don't need any time."

"Val, look at me."

Her head came up. His eyes were like granite as they seemed to bore right through her.

"I really do love you," he said. "You've come to mean the world to me. I want you . . . and I don't mean just tonight."

Val's breath came out in labored puffs. Oh, Lord, she knew she should back off and take a good look at this, but if she did, she might find it slipping away. Her hands crawled up his chest and locked behind his neck. This time she instigated the kiss, parting her lips and inviting his tongue to invade her mouth. His arms went around her and crushed her to him. She heard a strange guttural sound deep in his throat. Heat radiated from his body. In a fluid motion, he stood, bringing her with him without breaking the kiss. On their feet, their bodies molded together, fitting like two pieces of a puzzle. His hardness pressed against her belly. Her body swayed involuntarily, seeming to have become disconnected from her brain. Val wasn't sure how much longer she was going to be able to remain on her feet.

Their mouths parted. "Come with me," Scott said hoarsely, taking her by the hand. The thunder grew louder, and a crack of lightning split open the sky...or perhaps, Val thought, what she heard was only the tumult in her own head. He led her into his bedroom and closed the door. It was then that Val at last let herself believe it was really going to happen, that he really was going to make love to her. She felt uncertain and sure, timid and bold all at the same time.

Scott led her to the bed. He jerked back the spread, then turned to her. Their eyes locked. Slowly, with great deliberation, she reached up and removed her earrings. He smiled and reached for the sapphire silk sash, untying it. The top of her outfit fell open, revealing a lacy wisp of a bra. His hands pushed the top off her shoulders; it fell to the floor in a heap. Scott stared at her in awe. "Val, you're beautiful."

She swallowed hard. "Th-thank you. Please do something with these." She dropped the earrings in his hand.

He reached behind him and let them fall on the bedside table. Val closed the space between them and reached for his shirt buttons. Flicking them out of their holes, she tugged the shirt free of his waistband and pushed it down his arms. Then her hands wandered luxuriously over his chest. It was warm, hard and smooth, with only the faintest sprinkling of hair. His flat brown nipples hardened when she touched them. He allowed her to caress him for a minute before reaching behind her and unclasping the bra. When that was dispensed with, he pulled her to him, crushing her breasts against his chest.

"We're a good team, you and I, Valerie Drayton," Scott said solemnly. "We have been from the first. This is another step in the collaboration."

Val watched in fascination as Scott finished undressing. In all of her dreams of him, she had never allowed herself to imagine him naked, but her imagination never would have done him justice. He had the physique of a much younger man, trim and solid. Not athletic in the usual sense of the word, but more graceful, like a dancer.

He joined her between the sheets and gathered her close to him. A bolt of lightning lit up the room, and a crash of thunder rent the sky above. Wind howled, and rain fell in hard drops, battering the windows.

To Val it was the most perfect union that had ever been made, a beautiful thing that she wished would go on forever. Scott was such a powerful yet sensitive lover, seemingly attuned to her every need. He brought her to the brink time and time again, only to withdraw, then plunge again. When she couldn't stand it a second longer, she held him with her legs, binding him to her. Arching off the mattress, she felt the first shower of sparks begin. "Scott!" she cried. The sound of his name triggered his own release. He thrust, lunged and, shuddering violently, collapsed on top of her. Golden fire bathed Val's limbs. The ecstasy was indescribable.

VAL WAS THE FIRST to wake. Outside, the storm was unleashing its full fury, but her insides had grown still. She sat up in bed, pulled her knees up under the sheet and laid her cheek on them, turning in Scott's direction. His eyes were closed. In repose his face took on a boyish cast. The mouth that had brought her such exquisite pleasure was slack. She allowed herself the luxury of studying him unguardedly. He was the handsomest man alive.

If this wasn't something! Valerie Drayton, who'd never had very much special happen to her in thirty-two years, had in the space of two days found her mother, become an heiress and made love with the man of her dreams. It was almost more than her mind could absorb.

It was ironic really. After so many empty years she now had been offered more than she would be able to accept. Of course Vivian and Martin would have to do Europe without her. She could never be away from Scott so long. It was then that she realized she'd never told him about her mother. Small wonder. Looking back, it seemed she had merely stepped into the living room and the next minute they were in bed.

Suddenly one of his hands moved, and he placed a warm palm on her bare back. She smiled down at him.

"You are wonderful." His hand stroked her cheek and he gave her a look of a satisfied man. "That was a beautiful collaboration."

"Scott, have we just bought ourselves a heap of problems?"

"Problems?"

"I've always sensed that you wanted to keep our relationship strictly business."

"Maybe that's what I thought I wanted, but...I could no more have stopped this than I could have stopped the earth from turning."

"So what now?" Val asked.

"I believe I told you I didn't want you just for tonight. For the time being, I guess discretion will have to be the watchword, but not for long. Val, I want you to marry me."

Val's eyes widened, then closed as her breath escaped in a sigh of wonder. "Oh, Scott, are you absolutely sure that's what you want?"

"In my entire life I've never been more sure of anything. The thought of your ever leaving scares the hell out of me. The thought of your ever marrying someone else makes me sick. Yesterday was the most miserable day of my life. When I saw you sail off with Dodson, I wanted to hit something or somebody."

She cocked her head and looked at him quizzically. "Why?"

"Why? How can you ask that? And then you come back and tell me he's offered you the world. You were wearing a garment he obviously gave you. And the look on your face... as though you'd just found Prince Charming."

Val placed her hand over his mouth and began to laugh. "Oh, my God! *That's* what you thought?"

Her shoulders shook, and her laughter bubbled up like a gurgling brook.

"I fail to see what's so funny about giving me the worst day of my life."

"You thought that Martin and I... And you were jealous?"

"Jealous as hell, but now I guess nothing must have happened or you wouldn't have made love with me."

Val threw herself down on him, crushing her breasts against his chest, and kissed him soundly. "Oh, plenty happened, Scott. So much that it boggles my mind. You see, Martin is married to my mother!"

He stared at her a minute. "Your mother?"

"I spent the weekend with my mother, isn't that something? After twenty-five years! It was the most glorious experience of my life . . . well, with the exception of tonight."

"Val, I... Your *mother?*" he asked incredulously.

"She and Martin were married six months ago, and they started trying to find me. But when they finally tracked me down, she got cold feet. So she sent Martin to look me over, get to know me, try to decide how wise it would be for us to meet again." She kissed him again. "I have so much to tell you."

"Apparently so." Scott's arms went around her, and he held her close. "Dodson is . . . your stepfather?"

"Yes. They're taking a trip this fall and want me to go with them."

"London, Paris, et al.?"

"Exactly. I told them about my contract, but they suggested I try to get out of it. I . . . I guess I gave it some thought, but . . . of course, it's out of the question now."

"You're damned right it is!" Scott pursed his lips and thought a minute. "But you'd like to go, wouldn't you?"

"No," Val said firmly. "Of course I'd like to see those places someday. But I wouldn't want to be gone from you so long. I might have considered a week maybe. But Mother and Martin are planning on spending Christmas in Rome, and they're leaving right after the fall shearing, whenever that is. October, I guess."

"The fall what?"

"Shearing. Oh, that's something else I want to tell you. Martin raises champion Angora goats. And the house . . . you have to know about the house. I'm an heiress, Scott. Or I will be someday. Me! Valerie Drayton! The mistress of the most exquisite manor you have ever seen . . . a very long time from now, of course. Still..." And she described the house in a rush.

Scott smiled and shook his head. "It's really been an exciting time for you, hasn't it?"

"It really has." She traced the outline of his mouth with a fingertip. "But this, us, is the most exciting of all. I used to wonder if it would ever happen to me...if I would marry someone I truly loved or would have to settle for someone solid and dependable and...dull."

Scott chuckled. "I'm afraid there are those who might describe me that way."

"Oh, no, Scott. You're the most exciting man I've ever known," she said seriously. "You're handsome, successful, focused, principled. You don't just sit around dreaming. You make your dreams come true."

"My, God, you make me sound like a paragon."

"And you can cook! Which reminds me...I believe you promised me dinner."

"So I did." He pulled her closer and kissed her hotly, wetly. A knee wedged her thighs apart. "Is that what you want to do now?"

Sighing, she melted against him. "No, not now. Dinner can wait."

CHAPTER THIRTEEN

VAL SOPPED the last of the veal's lemony sauce with a piece of crusty bread, popped it into her mouth and pushed her plate away. "Inelegant," she said, "but delicious."

Two hours had passed since she had stepped into the lodge, two of the most wonderful hours of her life. The storm had spent itself now, and only light rain fell. Across from her, Scott sipped his wine and stared at her over the rim of his glass, the corners of his mouth lifting in a small smile.

She had been talking almost nonstop throughout the meal, her eyes bright and alive with excitement. She had described Dodson's house down to the tiniest detail. Scott thought how wonderful it was for someone who'd had so little in life to suddenly find herself with so much.

"Tell me how you felt when you saw your mother for the first time," he urged.

Val gave it some thought as she pensively ran a fingertip around the rim of her wineglass. "It was so odd. I expected it to be awkward. All during the drive to San Angelo, I went over and over a dozen things I planned to say. Somehow 'How do you do, it's so nice to see you' didn't sound quite right. Then Martin showed me into the conservatory and introduced us. Do you know what I said?''

''What?''

'' 'Hello, Mother.' '' She smiled at the recollection.

''Just like that?''

''Just like that.''

''You didn't once think—hey, you walked off and left me twenty-five years ago?''

Val shook her head. ''Not once. Perhaps that seems odd, but... She's my mother... and I guess family means a lot more to me than it does to some. I want you to meet her, Scott. I want *her* to meet *you.*''

''I want that, too.''

''I promised I would come back next weekend. Will you go with me?''

''Of course.''

Impulsively, Val jumped to her feet, rounded the little table and plopped into Scott's lap, putting her arms around his neck. He gently rubbed her thigh. ''A family weekend,'' she said. ''I've never had one in my entire life that I remember.''

"From what you've told me about them, I guess your mother and Dodson will want to throw you a big wedding to-do, the works."

Val pulled a face. "Oh, I hope not. If they do, I'll just have to disappoint them again. It only seems right that you and I be married here at the lodge, where we met. Don't you think so?"

"I couldn't agree more."

"Mother and Martin will just have to come here. Your mother will, too, won't she?"

"Are you kidding? She wouldn't miss it. Mama'll be so glad one of her kids is getting married she'll walk here if she has to."

"Scott, are you absolutely *sure* this is what you want?"

He grinned. "You've asked me that four times in the past hour. Do I look like the kind of guy who lets himself be coerced into something he doesn't want to do, especially something as serious as getting married? As I recall, I'm the one who brought up marriage in the first place."

"There's just so much we don't know about each other's pasts."

"Good. Maybe we won't run out of something to talk about anytime soon. And it's not your past I'm interested in, Val. By the way, I don't see any point in dragging out an engagement for months, do you? I'd like to do it in a couple of weeks or so."

She sighed happily and laid her cheek on the top of his head. "This is going to be a very difficult week."

"How's that?"

"You know what this place is like during the week. It teems with people from early in the morning till late at night. It's going to be hard to find time to be alone."

He turned his head and kissed the underside of her chin. "I'm a very resourceful fellow when I want to be. I'll bet we find time . . . plenty of it."

THEY DID . . . once behind the locked doors of Scott's office while one of the maids vacuumed the hall outside. Several times late at night in Val's cottage. They had one thing going for them. It was customary to see one or both of them all over the place at all hours of the day and night, so no one noticed where they went or for how long, just as no one noticed the spring in their steps, the light in their eyes.

No one but Jeff. Toward the middle of the week, he cornered Val near the corral and favored her with his inimitable grin. "You know, ol' Scott's had a smile plastered on his face all week. I can't remember if that ever happened before. Why do I feel as though something momentous is taking place right under my nose?"

"Hasn't Scott talked to you?"

"I don't think we've said three words to each other since last weekend."

Val frowned. "Funny. I thought the two of you were becoming closer. I mean, Scott told me you spent last Saturday night together."

Jeff propped a foot on the first rung of the corral fence. "A couple of guys getting fried together is not the last word in camaraderie." Then he turned serious... or what passed for serious with Jeff. "It's been that way all our lives, Val. We'll spend a few pretty good days together and then something happens. Usually I do something that thoroughly chaps Scott's butt. I've learned to live with it, and I guess ol' Scott has, too. Well, seeing as you don't seem willing to answer my question, I'll have to speak to my big brother." With a wink he turned and was gone.

BY NOON SATURDAY the last of the guests had departed, and the lodge was back in the hands of the staff. Val bubbled with excitement. Earlier in the week she had phoned her mother to ask if she could bring a guest. Vivian had assured her she would love to meet Scott because Martin had already told her what a nice man he seemed to be. Val had to smile at that one. During the week Martin was at the Hole in the Wall, Scott had probably been at his absolute worst.

"Once Martin gets to know him, he'll like Scott even better, I'm sure," she told her mother.

"Is there . . . ah, any special reason for this, Valerie?" Vivian had asked.

"I'll talk to you when we get there. Don't go to a lot of trouble for us, okay?" she said, knowing perfectly well the household would pull out all the stops.

"All right. We'll make it very casual. See you Saturday afternoon, dear."

Now Saturday had arrived, and Val and Scott were on their way to San Angelo. Though she had described the stone house many times, words could never do it justice. When they pulled up in front of it, Scott stared at it a minute, then let out a low whistle. *This* was what Val would own someday? He was impressed . . . and very thrilled for her.

Scott was giving his hand to Val as she got out of the car when the front door opened and Martin burst out onto the porch. "Ah, there you are! Now maybe Viv will quit pacing." He clambered down the steps, embraced Val, then offered his hand to Scott.

"Martin, you remember Scott."

"Of course, of course. Nice to see you again."

"Thank you, sir. Nice to see you, too."

"Oh, come, come. None of that 'sir' nonsense. I'm Martin...or Marty, if you prefer." Martin placed a hand on each of their shoulders and ushered them up the steps. "I'll have someone see to your things. Let's go inside. Viv has refreshments waiting. Dreadfully warm day, isn't it? I'm afraid we're in for a scorcher of a summer."

Scott's reaction to the interior of the house was much the same as Val's had been the previous weekend. As Martin led the way down the hall to the conservatory, he tried to take in everything at once. Val had not exaggerated in her description of the place. It was magnificent.

And nothing had quite prepared him for Vivian Dodson. On being introduced to her, Scott knew he was looking at Val twenty-odd years down the road. He had to stifle the urge to embrace the woman.

After the usual pleasantries were exchanged, the four of them sat, sipping ice tea and making small talk until Martin asked Scott if he would like a tour of the place. Once the men had gone, Vivian crossed the room to sit beside her daughter and smile conspiratorially.

"Am I to assume you won't be going to Europe with us, Valerie?"

"I'm afraid not. Scott and I are getting married." Saying it, Val felt, made it seem more real to her, though she still woke up in the morning and pinched herself.

"Wasn't this sudden? Only last weekend you said you weren't seriously involved."

"It's very sudden, and I have Martin to thank for it all."

"Martin?"

Val chuckled. "It seems his hovering attentions to me alarmed Scott and prompted a proposal. I must remember to thank him."

"When is all this going to take place?"

"Very soon, according to Scott, within a few weeks."

"Martin and I would love to host a really nice affair for you, Valerie."

"I'm sure you would, and that's very sweet, but Scott and I want to get married at the lodge. You and Martin will have to be there, of course. And I'll meet his mother." Val's eyes shone. "Two weeks ago I had no one. Now I have a mother and step-father... and very soon I'll have a mother-in-law and a brother-in-law. I can't tell you what that means to me."

Vivian sat back and sighed. "I won't tell you that I'm not disappointed about Europe, but there will be other trips. Perhaps next year, or the year after that."

Val smiled secretively. She fondly hoped that for the next eighteen years or so she would be so busy raising a family she wouldn't have time to think about Europe or anywhere else. Wouldn't it be wonderful if the woman who'd had no one turned out to be the matriarch of a very large clan?

"WHAT WAS I to think?" Scott said at the dinner table that night. "I mean, here was this debonair gentleman lavishing all this attention on Val, and as far as I could tell, she was totally receptive. Then she tells me she's going home with him for the weekend. I ask you—what was I to think?"

Martin was chuckling so hard his shoulders shook. "I must say I'm flattered that anyone would think a pretty young thing like Valerie would seriously entertain romantic advances from an old codger like me."

"You're not an old codger," Vivian admonished.

"I imagine you would turn the head of any number of young women if you set your mind to it, Martin," Valerie said with a fond smile.

The four of them lingered over crème brûlée and coffee, enjoying the finish to another wonderful meal. "It has occurred to me," Martin said at one point, "that perhaps Viv and I should cut short our European jaunt in order to be home for

Christmas. This house is absolutely splendid when decked out in its holiday finery, and I usually host an open house the week before the big day. Now that Valerie and Scott are in our lives..."

"Oh, let's, Marty!" Vivian exclaimed. And to Val and Scott she said, "The first time I saw this house was last Christmas. It was so lovely. Marty works hard to maintain some of his own family's traditions. I was absolutely enchanted, and you will be, too, Valerie."

Christmas was half a year away, and already Val could feel excitement building inside her. A real Christmas with a tree, mistletoe, holly and all the trimmings was virtually unknown to her.

"What about your family, Scott?" Martin asked. "We have to take them into consideration."

"Well, Martin, there's only my mother and brother. Since Jeff and I grew up and Dad died, our Christmases have been rather quiet. I usually take my mother out to dinner, but that's about it."

"And your brother?"

Val quickly glanced at Scott, noting the rather pained expression that crossed his face. That so often happened when his brother was mentioned. It took him a few seconds to reply to Martin's question.

"My brother and I haven't spent the holidays together in a number of years. Jeff's usually... been away."

"A pity. I'm thinking how wonderful it's going to be for Viv and myself to have you and Valerie with us this year. It would be even grander if your mother and brother could join us. And if I could get my son and his wife down here... well, we'd have quite a gathering."

They talked for hours, and by the time everyone retired upstairs for the night, they had planned a Christmas holiday fit for a czar. Val couldn't help but wonder how many of those plans would really come to pass, and how many were pie-in-the-sky dreaming. She thought back to all the Christmases she and her father had spent with a handful of rootless cowboys in a bunkhouse dining room. Almost always there had been a small artificial tree on top of a television set, and everyone had exchanged gag gifts. She couldn't remember even one ranch owner who hadn't make an effort to give his workers a special meal on that special day—meaning turkey or ham instead of the beef they had eaten every day.

But the kind of Christmas her mother and Martin had described, the kind she'd seen in magazines—full of family, lavish decorations, festive food—was unknown to her. This year would be different.

Standing at the window in her darkened room, staring out over the sweeping grounds, Val smiled as she thought of what was in store. Behind her, she heard the door open. She turned and saw Scott step into the room and close the door behind him. He hadn't undressed, either, but his shirt was unbuttoned and pulled free of his waistband.

"Do you suppose Martin and Vivian expect me to sleep in that room across the hall?" he whispered.

Val held out an arm to him. "I doubt it, but Martin is very, very proper. Did you enjoy today?"

Scott crossed the room in easy strides and took her in his arms. "I loved it because it made you so happy. They are very nice people, and I know how much they must mean to you."

"Didn't Christmas sound wonderful?"

"That it did."

"Look, Scott." She gestured toward the window. "Isn't it something?"

"It," of course, was Martin's estate, and it really was something, even to Scott, who had known a certain amount of luxury in his life.

"Yes, it's really something."

"Do you suppose we'll ever actually live here, the two of us?"

"I can well imagine we will someday, when we're ready to retire and leave the Hole in the Wall to the kids."

They chuckled simultaneously, thinking about children as yet unborn. Then Val slipped both arms around his waist and grew serious. "Scott, there's something I want you to do for me."

He looked down at her, frowning slightly at the gravity he heard in her voice. An inner sense warned him that what she was going to ask of him was no little thing. "I'll do it if I can, sweetheart."

"I want you to make peace with Jeff."

Val felt him tense. She waited a second, but when he said nothing she plunged ahead. "I don't mean an uneasy truce. I don't mean détente. I mean real peace."

"Val, what you're asking might be impossible."

"It shouldn't be."

"Sometimes...sometimes it seems as though Jeff and I were raised on different planets."

"Oh, Scott, do you realize what's happening to me? I'm acquiring a family. It's only beginning to sink in. I have a mother, a stepfather, a step-brother. I'll soon have a husband, a mother-in-law and a brother-in-law. Someday Jeff will marry. There'll be a brood of us, and I want it to be a congenial one. I know I can't expect you to fully appreciate what that means to me, but..." She faltered, regretting her inability to adequately give voice to her feelings.

Scott sighed and drew her close, stroking her hair. "Val, you have some romantic storybook notion of what a family is. You're a victim of the Brady Bunch syndrome. I suppose that's understandable, given your past, but families are not always harmonious units."

Pulling away slightly, she looked up at him, her face a portrait of earnestness. "I want mine to be."

He stared down at her upturned face. The intriguing indentation in her bottom lip beckoned to him. He touched it with the tip of his tongue, then kissed her deeply. He wished he could promise her that he and Jeff would become close, but their differences were of long standing. Frankly, Scott had been pleased with their recent fragile truce, but Val wanted more. And he just wasn't sure it was possible.

Lifting his head, he smiled down at her. "I promise I'll do my best... but that's the best I can do."

"Fair enough." Val's gaze went again to the window. "Do you know what I'd like to do right now?"

"Well, I had my hopes."

"Before that, I mean. I'd like to take a midnight stroll. Just look out there. It's so beautiful."

"It's not midnight."

"An eleven o'clock stroll then?"

She was as enthusiastic as a young girl. Scott released her, buttoned his shirt and took her by the hand. "One eleven o'clock stroll coming up."

Quietly they left the room, went downstairs and found a rear entrance. The night air was soft and cool and permeated with unidentifiable smells of growing things. Arm in arm, Val and Scott strolled across the grounds, past a rose garden that was in full June bloom. Beyond that was an open meadow flanked by a stand of ancient trees. All was still and peaceful. Turning, they saw the majestic house silhouetted against the moonlit sky. They might have been the only two people on earth.

They halted, and Scott drew her into his arms. "Have you ever made love on the ground?" he whispered.

"Never."

"Have you ever wondered what it would be like?"

Val giggled and pressed her face against his shirtfront. "Not until this minute."

"Then let's not wonder any longer." Gently he laid her on a carpet of cool, sweet-smelling grass.

THE HOUR WAS LATE. Returning from his usual Saturday night on the town, Jeff halted his truck in front of the lodge and looked up at the big empty structure. Somehow the thought of spending the night alone in it turned him off. Glancing toward the bunkhouse, he saw a light in the window. To his knowledge, Earl was the only hand who ever spent Saturday night there. Pressing down on the accelerator, he drove past the lodge and parked in front of the bunkhouse.

Earl had a private room at one end of the building. The door to it was open, a light was on, and Jeff could hear the television set. Crossing through the deserted bunk room, he headed for it.

Earl was propped up in bed, watching TV. The remains of his dinner rested on a plate at his elbow. When he saw Jeff, he pushed the button on the remote, and the set went silent.

"Don't let me interrupt your program," Jeff said.

"Aw, weren't nothin' but a bunch of silliness, jus' people movin' around and makin' noise." Squinting at the clock on the wall, Earl said, "Kinda early for you, ain't it, son?"

Jeff shrugged. "There wasn't much going on. Or maybe there's just as much going on as there ever was, but tonight it was kinda boring."

"That kinda life gets that way after a while," Earl said. "I ought'a know. I sure lived it m'self a long time."

Sitting down in the room's lone chair, Jeff took a look around. Earl's quarters consisted of a box of a room and a private john with a shower. The furnishings were a bed, a chair, a dresser and a television set on a roll-around cart. There were no curtains at the window, no rug on the floor, no adornments on the wall. To Jeff's mind, it was, in a word, depressing. Yet Earl seemed like a very contented fellow.

"Podnuh, did you ever think about doing something besides cowboying?"

Earl scratched the stubble on his chin. "Don't think so. Least not very often and not for very long."

"You never thought about working the rigs or going into town and getting a regular job?"

Earl shook his head. "No, and that ain't the end of the song. I'll take a paralyzed oath that I never do. I ain't cut out for that sorta thing. Don't like too many folks around tellin' me what I ought'a be doin'."

Jeff hesitated before asking the next question, chiefly because bunkhouse conversation leaned heavily toward macho sexism and rarely included personal confidences. But he thought he and Earl had gotten pretty tight as the weeks had passed. If Earl didn't want to answer the question, he'd say so. "Did you ever think about getting married?"

"Yep, once, a long time ago." The old-timer squinted at Jeff, a funny sort of grin on his face. "Reckon now you're gonna want to know what happened."

"Well, I..."

"I got cold feet. I was about...oh, thirty, and she was a pretty little thing. But I got to thinkin' how marriage meant a mortgage and babies. Never yet saw a woman who didn't want a house and young'uns. Scared hell out of me. Then as years passed, I got even more set in my ways. If'n I was gonna do it, I should'a done it then. Remember that, son...you better settle down while you're young or chances are good you ain't never gonna."

Jeff pondered that a minute; a cold feeling raced up his spine. "Yeah, I'll remember. You got any beer in this joint?"

"Reckon there's some in the icebox since none of the hands can live without it. Go get you one. How about some cards?"

"You're on." Jeff went out into the main part of the bunkhouse, to the end of the building where a small refrigerator stood next to the door of the communal john. And he reflected on how easy it would be to end up like Earl. Only in his case he wouldn't be in a bunkhouse. He'd be just another monkey who worked the rigs until he was too old or too stove-in to keep doing it. And then what? He was almost thirty, and he owned nothing but his truck, his clothes and a small bank account. Moreover, he only had one more chance. Earl didn't know what scared was.

SCOTT HAD NEVER SEEN anyone transformed to such a startling degree as Val had been. She was as sweet and pretty as ever, but now she was radiant. During the drive back to the Hole in the Wall Sunday afternoon, she fairly bubbled over with plans. By the time they drove through the ranch's gate, Scott had made up his mind to try one more time with Jeff. It was the least he could do for Val.

While she unpacked in her cottage, he went in search of his brother. Surprisingly, Jeff wasn't hard to find. He was in his room upstairs in the lodge, stretched out on the bed, listening to a ball game on the radio.

"Got a minute?" Scott asked.

"I've got more than one. Come in." Jeff reached over and switched off the radio.

Scott walked in, closed the door and sat in an easy chair by the window. "Val and I are getting married," he said.

Jeff pursed his lips and nodded. "Can't say this is the most startling news bulletin I've ever heard. Congratulations."

"Thanks. It's going to be a small wedding here at the lodge. I'd like for you to be my best man."

"All right. I'm ... honored."

Scott clasped his hands in front of him and looked at his brother directly. "Look, Jeff, I know we've had our differences in the past, just as I know that's an understatement, but the point is ... Val's really excited about having a family now." He gave Jeff a capsulized account of Val's reunion with her mother, along with something about her past. "So you see, all this has more meaning for her than it might for some. She wants you to feel welcome to stay with us whenever you want, for as long as you want."

"And you?" Jeff asked guardedly.

"Yes. I want that, too.

"Not just because of Val?"

"No. My house is your house until you have one of your own. Look, I admit there were plenty of times when I could have ... given a little, not been so rigid. I apologize for them. How you chose to live your life was none of my business."

Jeff pursed his lips, saying nothing for several seconds. Then, "Well, I probably was a little hard to take at times."

It was an emotional moment, held in check in the time-honored masculine way, but each brother felt it. Scott actually had a lump in his throat, and he couldn't remember if Jeff had ever elicited such a thing before. He looked at his brother, really looked at him, and saw a good-looking, rakish devil who was beginning to mellow with age.

"Val would also like you to spend some time with us at Christmas," Scott said. "In fact, she wants you and Mama to spend the holiday with us at her stepfather's place."

Jeff looked surprised . . . and pleased. "Tell Val I said thanks. She's a classy lady."

"Yes, she is."

A slow grin spread across Jeff's face. "You're sure you're ready for all this?"

"All what?"

"A house and babies. A wise man once told me that's what every woman wants."

Scott, too, grinned. "Yes, I'm ready. Past ready."

"Funny," Jeff mused. "I bet you'll make a hell of a daddy. Like our old man."

Scott didn't know when a compliment had pleased him so much. He got to his feet, and Jeff uncurled from the bed. They stood facing each other uncertainly for a second, then Scott stuck out his hand. Jeff took it, and they shook heartily.

Suddenly Scott gave his brother's arm a jerk, enveloping him in a purely masculine embrace, complete with much back-slapping. Breaking the embrace, they simply stood and stared at each other a minute. Scott felt his eyes grow very warm, and he could have sworn Jeff's had misted over.

"Val and I are going to rustle up something in the kitchen for supper tonight. Why don't you join us?"

"I will. Thanks."

Completely shaken, Scott nodded and backed out of the room. When he went downstairs he felt ten pounds lighter. The old petty differences, so burdensome at times, had been put aside forever. Somehow he just knew it, felt it. It had been such a simple confrontation. Why hadn't they done it years ago? Why had it taken a woman with a deep sense of family to do it?

And that reminded him of something. Going outside, he walked to Val's cottage and knocked on the door. "Val, it's me," he called.

"Come in, Scott."

She had changed into jeans and a T-shirt, and had tied her hair at the nape with a print scarf. "Did you talk to Jeff?" she asked.

He nodded.

"Well . . . how did it go?"

Scott made a circle with his thumb and index finger. "He's having supper with us tonight."

"Oh, good!" She crossed the room and hugged him enthusiastically.

"But before we get around to supper, there's something I want to show you. Come on outside."

Val couldn't imagine there was anything on the ranch that she hadn't seen a hundred times, but she followed him. Scott led her to a pickup that had the ranch's logo painted on the cab doors. "Hop in."

"Where are we going?"

"You'll see."

He drove past the cabins and the tennis courts and headed toward the northeast quadrant of the ranch, following trails much better suited for horses and hikers than for a vehicle. At one point he drove across a narrow bridge that spanned the Claro River and continued on until they reached a small rise that led to a clearing surrounded by cedars and oaks. There he stopped the truck and turned off the engine. "Here we are," he said, opening the driver's door.

Val frowned in puzzlement. They were in the most remote part of the ranch now. Not even livestock ventured this far out too often. She recalled that in April the clearing had been a blanket of bluebonnets and Indian paintbrush, absolutely breathtaking in its beauty.

Scott stood with his arms crossed over his chest, gazing out over the clearing as though he'd just stumbled upon El Dorado. Val got out of the truck and went to stand beside him.

"It's pretty, isn't it?" he said.

"Yes, it is."

"The perfect place to build a house."

Val's eyes widened, and her pulse quickened. "A house?"

"Yes. Nothing particularly big or fancy. Three bedrooms and two baths, something big enough for a family. Rustic on the outside, cozy on the inside. Vernon Trent knows every builder for miles around. Sometime next week I'll get him to recommend one, and we'll get started on it right away."

"Oh, Scott!" Right before her eyes, Val saw the house begin to take shape. "The kitchen will have to go over there, to take advantage of the morning sun. And the master bedroom will go in back...."

"Guest room up front and a nursery between them."

"It'll have to have a fireplace."

Scott nodded. "And a front porch and a fence."

"And flower beds."

Val slipped her arms around his waist and hugged and hugged and hugged. Only a few weeks ago she had longed for something, *anything* to call her own. Now she had everything. "Thank you," she whispered.

If you enjoyed
AFTER THE LIGHTS GO OUT

don't miss
HEARTS AGAINST THE WIND
by Kathy Clark
the next installment of the
CRYSTAL CREEK series
coming to you in September

Hank Travis could see a lot of himself in young Jeff Harris. The boy had oil in his blood and lived only for the next big strike. There was nothing to keep him in Crystal Creek—except a certain marriage-minded Miss Beverly Townsend. Although Jeff seemed to have taken a shine to the former beauty queen, Hank wouldn't lay odds on Jeff sticking around much longer.

Watch for it next month wherever Harlequin books are sold.

Relive the romance...
Harlequin and Silhouette
are proud to present

by Request™

A program of collections of three complete novels by the most
requested authors with the most requested themes. Be sure to
look for one volume each month with three complete novels by
top name authors.

In June: **NINE MONTHS** Penny Jordan
                             Stella Cameron
                             Janice Kaiser

**Three women pregnant and alone. But a lot can
happen in nine months!**

In July: **DADDY'S**   Kristin James
           HOME   Naomi Horton
                         Mary Lynn Baxter

**Daddy's Home... and his presence is long
overdue!**

In August: **FORGOTTEN** Barbara Kaye
           PAST   Pamela Browning
                          Nancy Martin

**Do you dare to create a future if you've forgotten
the past?**

Available at your favorite retail outlet.

HARLEQUIN   Silhouette

Calloway Corners

In September, Harlequin is proud to bring readers four
involving, romantic stories about the Calloway sisters,
set in Calloway Corners, Louisiana. Written by four of
Harlequin's most popular and award-winning authors,
you'll be enchanted by these sisters and the men
they love!

MARIAH by Sandra Canfield
JO by Tracy Hughes
TESS by Katherine Burton
EDEN by Penny Richards

As an added bonus, you can enter a sweepstakes contest
to win a trip to Calloway Corners, and meet all four
authors. Watch for details in all Calloway Corners books
in September.

CA

HARLEQUIN SUPERROMANCE®

HARLEQUIN SUPERROMANCE WANTS TO INTRODUCE YOU TO A DARING NEW CONCEPT IN ROMANCE...

WOMEN WHO DARE!
Bright, bold, beautiful ...
Brave and caring, strong and passionate ...
They're women who know their own minds
and will dare anything ... for love!

e title per month in 1993, written by popular Superromance
thors, will highlight our special heroines as they face unusual,
allenging and sometimes dangerous situations.

ve into a whirlwind of passion and excitement next month with:
62 WINDSTORM by Connie Bennett
ailable in September wherever Harlequin Superromance novels are
d.

BE PART OF CRYSTAL CREEK
WITH THIS FABULOUS FREE GIFT!

The attractive Crystal Creek cowboy boot brooch—beautifully crafted and finished in a lovely silver tone—is the perfect accessory to any outfit!

As you share the passions and influence of the people of Crystal Creek ... and experience the excitement of hot Texas nights, smooth Texas charm and dangerously sexy cowboys—you need to collect only three proofs-of-purchase for the Crystal Creek cowboy boot brooch to become YOURS ... *ABSOLUTELY FREE!*

HOW TO CLAIM YOUR ATTRACTIVE CRYSTAL CREEK COWBOY BOOT BROOCH ... To receive your free gift, complete the Collector Card—located in the insert in this book—according to the directions on it. If you prefer not to use the Collector Card, or if it is missing, when you've collected three Proofs from three books, write your name and address on a blank piece of paper, place in an envelope with $1.95 (Postage and Handling) and mail to:

IN THE U.S.A.:
HARLEQUIN CRYSTAL CREEK PROMOTION
P.O. BOX 9071
BUFFALO, NY 14269-9071

IN CANADA:
HARLEQUIN CRYSTAL CREEK PROMOTION
P.O. BOX 604
FORT ERIE, ONTARIO L2A 5X3

Below you'll find a proof-of-purchase. You'll find one in the back pages of every Crystal Creek novel ... every month!

PREMIUM OFFER TERMS

Requests must be received no later than March 31, 1994. Only original proofs of purchase accepted. Limit: (1) one gift per name, family, group, organization. Cowboy boot brooch may differ slightly from photo. Please allow 6 to 8 weeks for receipt of gift. Offer good while quantities of gifts last. In the event an ordered gift is no longer available, you will receive a free, previously unpublished Harlequin book for every proof-of-purchase you have submitted with your request plus a refund of the postage and handling charge you have included. Offer good in the U.S.A. and Canada only.

Here's a proof of purchase— start collecting Today!

ONE
PROOF-OF-PURCHASE

088-KAW

Crystal Creek

CCPOP

"ENGAGING."
—*The New York Times*

"SUSPENSEFUL."
—*Chicago Tribune*

"EXTRAORDINARY."
—*Publishers Weekly*
(starred review)

"SUPERB."
—*Newsday*

Extraordinary praise for
CHAOS THEORY

"*Chaos Theory* combines corruption and kids dodging killers in a Grisham-like thriller that shares elements with *The Client* and *The Street Lawyer* but outshines both. Author Gary Krist takes things a step beyond those bestsellers, with an engaging ensemble of more complex characters. . . . *Chaos Theory*'s appeal lies largely in these characters, as well as Krist's agility with points of view. The coming-of-age aspects add humanity and humor."   —*USA Today*

"Accessible and engaging . . . Krist has considerable writing skills."   —*The New York Times Book Review*

"The traditional Washington novel is yielding to a different and far more interesting depiction of life in this part of the world. . . . [*Chaos Theory*] can be read as a thriller, and as such it reads quite well, but it is also about larger subjects."   —*The Washington Post Book World*

"Spinning a plausible situation into an extraordinary story while training a marksman's eye on character, Krist has conceived a sleek and thoughtful thriller. . . . Along the way, Krist . . . shows his flair for portraying characters under extreme emotional pressure."

—*Publishers Weekly* (starred review)

"Stunning . . . Krist has expertly envisioned and plotted the riveting tale of a sickly city brought to its knees by self-serving immoral politicians."   —*Chicago Tribune*

continued . . .

"Doubling the stakes of John Grisham's *The Client*, Krist plunges a pair of young heroes into peril that starts with a bang and ends with a bang-bang-bang. . . . A page-turner with new dangers and set-pieces every two minutes."

—*Kirkus Reviews*

"Action aplenty . . . thrills." —*Booklist*

"[A] deftly written thriller." —*Library Journal*

"Appealing . . . Mr. Krist . . . does several things well while untangling this mystery. He gives us striking snapshots of Washington scenery." —*The New York Times*

"A winner . . . *Chaos Theory* stirs up real terror. . . . Characters as well as locales in and around D.C. are vividly drawn . . . Superb." —*Newsday*

"A clever yarn . . . An exciting plot . . . All handled with aplomb . . . In the end, the superiority of Krist comes down to good writing." —*The Newark Star-Ledger*

Also by Gary Krist

THE GARDEN STATE
BONE BY BONE
BAD CHEMISTRY

CHAOS THEORY

GARY KRIST

JOVE BOOKS, NEW YORK

CHAOS THEORY

A Jove Book / published by arrangement with
Random House Trade Publishing, a division of Random House, Inc.

PRINTING HISTORY
Random House, Inc. hardcover edition / January 2000
Jove edition / March 2001

All rights reserved.
Copyright © 2000 by Gary Krist.
This book, or parts thereof, may not be reproduced in any form
without permission.
For information address: Random House, Inc., 201 E. 50th Street,
New York, New York 10022.

The Penguin Putnam Inc. World Wide Web site address is
http://www.penguinputnam.com

ISBN: 0-515-13085-0

A JOVE BOOK®
Jove Books are published by The Berkley Publishing Group,
a division of Penguin Putnam Inc.,
375 Hudson Street, New York, New York 10014.
JOVE and the "J" design
are trademarks belonging to Penguin Putnam Inc.

PRINTED IN THE UNITED STATES OF AMERICA

10 9 8 7 6 5 4 3 2 1

AUTHOR'S NOTE

The Washington, D.C., depicted in this book is fictional. Though it bears certain geographical, administrative, and atmospheric resemblances to the real capital city of the mid-1990s, it is a creation of the author's imagination. In no way are the individuals, offices, or governmental entities depicted in this novel to be identified with actual individuals, offices, or governmental entities. The truths of fiction and those of journalism may overlap, but they are not identical.

When you don't have controls, you have
an opportunity for severe mischief.

   —Stephen D. Harlan,
      vice chairman, D.C. Financial Control Board,
      October 7, 1997

The media likes to say it's sheer incompetence
and mismanagement. No, no, no. Someone thought
this through very clearly and made the decision
that good management wasn't in their interests.

   —Dwight Cropp,
      former adviser to Mayor Marion Barry,
      as quoted in *The Washington Post*, July 20, 1997

This is a vast wasteland out there.

   —Mayor Marion Barry,
      July 1997

ACKNOWLEDGMENTS

For various technical help and advice, I'd like to thank Detective Meredith Dominick of the Montgomery County Police Department; Loretta Berger; Susan Lloyd and Lisa Martin of the FBI; and Maria Foscarinis and the staff of the National Law Center on Homelessness and Poverty.

PROLOGUE

IT WAS A city of eyes. There were thousands of them—
the eyes of security guards, video cameras mounted on
the walls of government buildings, closed-circuit surveillance systems. HoJo, the eight-fingered Dominican
from the soup kitchen, claimed that every statue in Washington, D.C.—if you looked closely enough—had pin-
hole cameras for pupils, each one wired direct to the
office of the Mayor over in the New District Building.
On quiet nights the Mayor would sit in front of a wall
of video screens, drinking a vodka tonic and just watching. Of course, this was HoJo speaking, and Cooper
wasn't sure he believed anything the old junkie said. But
even so, every time Cooper had to pee nowadays, he
made sure that any nearby statues were facing the other
way.

Sighing, Cooper leaned back against the trunk of a
Japanese cherry tree and blew into his cold, cupped
hands. Across a quiet stretch of the Tidal Basin, the Jefferson Memorial floated: a big white jellyfish, the pillars
hanging down like tentacles. He could just make out the

statue of the president inside, about to be swallowed.
Thomas Jefferson. The smartest president, people said.
Cooper was smart once, too. At least that's the way he
remembered it.

He reached for his grimy duffel bag and pulled it
closer to his body. Could they be watching him now, he
wondered, even here? With Thomas Jefferson's eyes?
Cooper didn't know who they were or why they were
watching, but he was sure that they had picked him out,
just as they'd picked out the others. He'd already seen
them three times—once at the shelter, once behind the
ginkgo trees in Salazar Park, and then again outside the
Catholic soup kitchen over on Florida Avenue. The second time they were even taking pictures, the telephoto
lens like a finger pointing at him, saying, "You, you are
the next one we choose."

He thought of the old joke—Is it paranoia if they really
are after you?

Cooper closed his eyes. He knew he wouldn't sleep
tonight. He never got a good night's rest in the open air,
especially when he wasn't in his usual territory. But tonight he didn't have much choice. He had a feeling—a
strong feeling—that his time had come finally, that they
were getting close to taking him. At lunchtime the drunk
who called himself Sunshine had seen them hanging
around Cooper's usual soup kitchen, their eyes patrolling
the room. Cooper wasn't there—Thursday was meat loaf
day over at the community center—but Sunshine had told
him all about it later that afternoon on the street. Spooked
by this news, Cooper had decided to walk all the way
across town to escape. It had taken him most of the afternoon, counting bathroom stops at Union Station and
the Smithsonian, where he'd been hassled by a bald-
headed black guard with a gold tooth and a bad attitude.
Eventually, he'd set up here, under the cherry trees across

from the monument. It wasn't a good place for him—there was no food nearby, and the only people around were joggers and tourists, who swerved out of his path before he could even get around to asking them for money. But at least Cooper felt safe here. He was in the other city now, the one you saw on TV, the one the tourists came for. Cooper was a tourist himself here, far from the place of garbage, buckled sidewalks, and broken windows he came from. He couldn't stay here forever—he was sure to be bothered by a cop sooner or later—but at least he could lie low for a night or two. Just until they stopped looking for him and moved on to the next person on their list.

They needed bodies. That's what HoJo and the others were saying—they needed warm bodies. Nobody knew how they chose, but Cooper assumed they had their reasons. He had heard of four people gone already. Two were from his own shelter. One they said was crazy, from that place where they kept the half-wits over in Kingman Park. One was a needle freak. All four had just disappeared, right off the street. And now Cooper was next, for reasons he couldn't even guess at. All he knew was that when they wanted you they came in a big blue car to pick you up. There was nothing you could do to get away. It was your time.

He'd thought about telling someone about it—someone like Fanshawe, the shelter director, or the doctor over at the clinic, Dr. Pfeffer, with the wire-rims and the work shirts he wore to be one of the people. But Cooper was too afraid to tell. He worried that, at the very least, he'd be sent somewhere for a psychiatric evaluation. Besides, he probably couldn't explain it to them even if he tried. Fanshawe and Dr. Pfeffer came from the other side, the other city. The things that happened on Cooper's side these days were impossible even to imagine on the other.

It could never be real for them—this city of secret eyes and men scrabbling like rats under the rubble. Cooper knew this very well. He'd lived on that other side himself once, and knew what things looked like from there.

Cooper yawned and pulled his overcoat tighter around his shoulders. Winter was finally over—the cherry trees all around him would be breaking out in pink any day now—but the air was still cold at night. He remembered what spring was like in South Carolina when he was growing up. It came early and it came pretty and it didn't leave for months, as his mother used to say. Cooper wondered what his mother was doing now, if she and his brothers and sisters still thought about him. It had been eight years since he'd gone on the street. In the beginning, they'd all tried to keep tabs on him, to give him money and find him a place to stay. But nowadays even his mother didn't want to know where he was.

The car, when it came, was dark blue—just as HoJo said it would be. Cooper saw it moving slowly along West Basin Drive, raking the trees with its headlights. When it pulled to a stop near where he sat, he groaned and got to his feet, grabbing the duffel bag that contained everything he owned in the world. The balding man— the one he'd seen with the camera in Salazar Park—got out of the car and held open the back door, smiling. For a second, Cooper considered running away, making a break for the bridge or even jumping into the Tidal Basin and swimming out toward that traitor-president Jefferson. But then two other men got out of the car and Cooper knew that running wouldn't do him any good. They'd find him anyway. It was his time.

Nodding his head, Cooper slung the duffel over his shoulder and started walking toward the car.

ONE

DENNIS SAID HE knew where to get some cocaine.

"Yeah, right," Jason answered. "I'll bet you do."

"I mean it, Jase. I'm a worldly kinda guy."

The laugh took Jason by surprise. Red wine shot up his nose, the sting drawing tears to his eyes. "God," he said, "don't tell me things like that when I'm mid-gulp." He wiped his eyes on his sleeve and then, settling back against the sticky leather seat of the car, held out the bottle for his friend.

"You don't believe me," Dennis said, waving the bottle away.

"It's not that I don't believe you, man. It's just that I know you."

"You don't know shit." Dennis shot him a mock scowl. "You ignorant. You just a ignorant white boy."

"Oh, right, right. The minute we get downtown, Mr. Harvard-bound starts talking like Snoop Doggy Dogg."

"You better watch yourself," Dennis went on. "I be one badass mandingo, don't you know that?"

"Oh yes, Dennis, I'm aware of that," Jason said. "You

so badass you sometimes hand in your homework two days late."

"And you *know* what that can do to a homeboy's GPA."

"I do," Jason said, pounding the cork back into the bottle with his fist. "Badass mandingo. *Please.*"

It was just after ten o'clock on a chilly Sunday night. Jason Rourke and Dennis Monroe, juniors at Robert F. Kennedy High School in northwest Washington, D.C., were sitting in the Monroes' black Audi, stopped at a red light near Union Station. The moonlit city stretched out in front of them—like an offering, it seemed to Jason, an opportunity too good to pass up. An hour earlier, they'd escaped from one of the more excruciating parties in recent memory—the sedate, alcohol-free birthday celebration of their classmate Melinda Parks, a tall, gorgeous, depressingly wholesome girl whose father was minister at a local Baptist church. It was a grisly scene from the very start, with the Reverend himself asking everyone to join hands for an opening prayer of thanksgiving. By the time ten o'clock rolled around and Melinda's mother began shepherding people toward the grand piano to sing "Happy Birthday," the two had reached their limit. "Let's disappear," Jason whispered to his friend, "before they start launching into Rodgers and Hammerstein." Dennis agreed, and the two of them sneaked out without a word to anyone. Jason produced the bottle of red wine, slipped secretly from his father's basement wine rack earlier that night, and opened it with the corkscrew on his Swiss Army knife. Then they got into the car, took a few long, sour chugs of wine, and just started driving, not knowing where they wanted to go but knowing that home was definitely not it.

"Anyway," Jason said now, as they waited for the light

to turn green. "You ever really do cocaine? I mean honestly."

"Honestly?" Dennis looked straight at him for a few seconds, clearly considering a lie or a joke. He had dark, deep-set eyes, sharp cheekbones, and a sloping, wide-nostriled nose that gave him a weirdly exotic look—more Egyptian than black. Jason, with his messy wad of wiry brown hair and sallow cheeks, always felt a little too ordinary next to him. "Nope," Dennis said finally, shaking his head. "Never tried it."

"Me neither." Jason looked down at the wine in his hands. The streetlights outside touched the curves of the bottle with vague Os of light. "I heard that Cory Donahue snorted something before the PSATs. In the boys' room right before the exam started."

Dennis looked interested. "How'd he end up doing?"

"Ninety-fifth percentile, dude. Better than you."

"Shit. Ninety-fifth percentile?"

"Math *and* Verbal. If he had your skin color, they'd be paying *him* to go to Harvard."

Dennis raised his eyebrows. "You're a racist, you know that, Jase?"

"Yeah, I know," he said. "And my cousin Julie in Canada tells me I'm an 'unreconstructed sexist.' What else is new?"

They drove past the pale, hulking facades of the House Office Buildings. The sidewalks were empty at this time on a Sunday night in March, but there were still a few lights on in the office buildings—congressmen, Jason figured, pretending to work late. At the next corner, Dennis stopped and turned east, and the streets changed almost immediately. The big government buildings were suddenly gone, giving way to long lines of tidy row houses on dark, narrower, tree-lined streets. After a few blocks, Dennis turned north again, and Jason glimpsed the stark

white peak of the Capitol dome moving across an intersection, as vivid and incongruous as a UFO.

"Seriously speaking," Dennis said after a while, "now
that we're heading this way, we probably *could* turn up
a few joints. If we wanted."

Jason kept his eyes on the hovering white dome. The
statue on top could have been a border guard, watching
them from its tower.

"I know a promising street corner," Dennis added.

Jason didn't answer for a few seconds. He glanced
over at his friend. Dennis was wearing his "preppy disguise," as he called it—blue button-down shirt, chinos,
some bland oatmeal-colored jacket. Next to Jason, in his
black leather jacket and ratty sneakers, Dennis didn't
look like the one who would hear about the promising
street corners. But Jason, for all his teasing, knew better.

Jason ran his fingers over the raised gold seal on the
label of the wine bottle. He understood that this wouldn't
be the same as buying from the bald Grenadian who hung
around the high school grounds on weekends. They were
heading into Northeast. "It would be one way of saving
this night," he said uncertainly. "And I've got a spare
twenty in my wallet."

"A twenty would do it. If we were so inclined."

The two friends locked eyes for a few seconds.

Dennis smiled. "Or would you rather go back to Melinda's party?"

That did it. "Like shit," Jason said finally. "Consider
me so inclined."

"Really?"

"Really."

Dennis took a slow breath. "Excellent," he said. "Then
let's incline on over there."

They continued north past Stanton Park. Preparing
himself, Jason corked the wine bottle more tightly and

shoved it under the seat. He took the wallet out of his back pocket, removed the twenty, and then pocketed the wallet again. The bill was wrinkled, so he tried to press it smooth against his thigh.

"Don't get it all sweaty," Dennis said. "Dealers in these parts hate wet money." It wasn't even a joke, but Jason laughed anyway—a high-pitched, unnatural giggle that embarrassed him. Don't be a *dick*, he told himself firmly, pressing the bill harder against his thigh.

They continued north for a while longer, the streets turning shabbier and grimmer as they drove. They passed a weed-choked lot, the loading dock of a sheet-metal works, and then an abandoned gas station, the blackened, burned-out shells of its gas pumps lined up like head-stones in a cemetery. This is the city you live in, Jason told himself.

Dennis turned the Audi onto a dismal side street lined with peeling row houses. Almost all of the windows and doorways were boarded up with splintered, graffiti-slashed plywood. Three black men sat on a broken stoop, hunched against the unseasonable cold, each one facing in a different direction. Dennis slowed down. "It should be right around here," he said.

They turned another corner. This block was quieter, the buildings lower and windowless, more industrial. Ja-son felt a sizzle of anxiety in his stomach. He was like an astronaut, he thought suddenly—unmoored and weightless in space. "Shit, Dennis, I don't know about this. Who told you about this place?"

Dennis grinned, looking pleased by Jason's nervous-ness. "Relax," he said. "This is what it's all about, Jason. Grace under pressure. It'll be good discipline for you, trust me." He steered the Audi around a fallen trash can spilling bottles and grease-stained pizza boxes into the street. A few drops of rain spattered the windshield. They

caught the light like tiny beads before Dennis turned on
the wipers and smeared them into blurry arcs.

Then, just before they reached the end of the block,
near a stop sign with its top half bent back in a perfect
right angle, a figure came out of an alleyway and moved
straight toward the curb. "Here we go," Dennis said.

It was a short Latino man with a heavy jaw, a thin
mustache, and a gold hoop earring in the lobe of his left
ear. He stepped toward the car, his hands deep in the
pockets of a brown vinyl jacket. Jason closed his eyes
for a second, bracing himself. He rolled down the window just as Dennis pulled up at the curb.

"This the deaf guy?" the man asked. He stooped to the
open window on Jason's side. "Shit, look what we got
here. This him?"

"Hey, man," Dennis said. "What's up?"

The man peered at Dennis, then at Jason, then back
again. He seemed nervous and uncertain. "I asked you a
question."

"You selling loose joints?" Jason blurted, wanting to
get this over with.

There were little dots of sweat cobbling the man's
broad face. "He don't talk like he's deaf. You guys
fuckin' with me? Where's the deaf guy?"

"Sorry, there's no deaf guy, man." Dennis leaned
across the gearshift. "We're just trying to conduct a little
business with you."

The dealer slammed both hands against the car door.
"I can't believe this shit. You're supposed to bring me
the deaf guy. Did Arlene tell you to fuck with me?"

Dennis straightened up and started putting the Audi in
gear. "Look, I guess we made a mistake."

"Hold on, hold on." The man cleared his throat and
spat a gob of saliva onto the sidewalk. Then he reached
behind his back and smoothly pulled a small pistol from

the waistband of his jeans. "I got a point to make with you little ones," he said, chambering a round.

"Oh Jesus fuck," Jason whispered.

"Okay, take it easy, man," Dennis said slowly. "We didn't want anything like this. We just came to do a little business."

"I don't do no little business, you tell Arlene."

"We don't know any Arlene," Dennis said. "It's a mistake."

"A *mistake*?" The man started shaking the pistol at them. He seemed to be strung out on something, barely in control. "You think I got time to fuck with this? I should shoot the fuckin' *cojones* off both a you." The man reached into the car with his other hand and snatched the twenty from Jason's fingers. "This all the business *we* got together," he said. "Let's have the wallets now."

"Oh Christ," Dennis said. He shot a quick glance at Jason and started fumbling for his billfold.

"Get out the car first!" The man pushed the pistol toward Dennis. "Get out and come on over this side!"

Dennis started to go along, but Jason put his hand out to stop him. The man was mumbling to himself now, shivering and waving the pistol around. It was practically in front of Jason's face. He could see little pink scars on the knuckles, the fingernails milky and thick.

It was like a movie jumping a few frames in his head. Jason found himself reaching up and grabbing the dealer's wrist with both hands, then pulling down as hard as he could. The forearm smashed against the bottom of the window frame. He heard a distinct crack—like a dry stick snapped in two—but the gun didn't drop from the hand. "Go, Dennis!" Jason screamed. "Jesus, *go*!"

The arm was flailing around ridiculously now, like a big, struggling fish. Jason held on with all of his strength,

trying to keep the pistol barrel aimed down and away
from them. Suddenly, a yellow flame jumped from the
barrel and a sharp explosion pummeled his ears. Jason
felt stunned, numb. Dennis was speeding away now, but
somehow Jason was still holding on to the dealer's arm.
The car was dragging him along the curb. Then, with a
sickening thud, the man's body collided with the back of
a parked car. The arm tore itself out of Jason's grasp and
clattered out the window. As Dennis accelerated away,
Jason twisted around in his seat to look back. He saw the
man slumped in the street beside the parked car, the pistol
lying a few feet away from his misshapen outstretched
arm. Jason stared—hoping to see the body move—until
the Audi turned the corner and the scene was eclipsed by
the edge of a brick warehouse.

They were moving fast down the empty street, lights
whizzing by the windows. As they turned the next corner
they almost hit a forest-green Explorer heading slowly
across the intersection in the opposite direction, but Dennis swerved away from it in time. Jason could see a pale
shocked face through the side window as they passed. He
realized only then that Dennis was shouting at him: "You
fucking imbecile! What the fuck was *that*? What do you
call *that*?"

Jason couldn't answer. Dennis's voice sounded fuzzy
and distant. Jason wondered if maybe he *was* deaf now,
if the dealer was somehow right about that after all.

"Jason, say something," Dennis went on then, in a
calmer voice. "Are you okay?"

Jason managed a nod. "I'm, yes. Okay."

Dennis pounded his fists against the steering wheel.
"Don't you know that you're supposed to *cooperate* in a
situation like that, Jason? Didn't they ever *teach* you
that?"

"I was not getting out of this car." He looked over at

Dennis. "The guy would've killed us. I had, like, a premonition."

"You had a *premonition*?"

Was that right? Was it a premonition that made him panic like that? "I thought he was going to kill us," Jason said. "I'm sorry."

"Talk about grace under pressure." Dennis dragged a hand across his forehead. "A premonition! You really are twisted, Jason."

They didn't say anything more for a few minutes. Dennis just kept driving west and south, easing through red lights and stop signs now, heading toward familiar downtown streets.

"We'll have to find where that slug went," Dennis said finally, when they'd put enough distance between themselves and the man lying in the street.

Jason nodded. He could still feel the dull thump of the body hitting the parked car, like a physical memory burned into his arm muscles. "You think the guy is seriously hurt?" he asked.

Dennis shrugged. "Could be dead, for all we know."

"Fuck you! No way he could be dead."

"If that was his skull that hit the car, Jase, he could be dead."

"No way," Jason repeated, turning and looking out the window. They were passing under the elaborately decorated gate on H Street in Chinatown. An old Chinese man in a quilted jacket was standing in the middle of the busy street, looking lost and confused. "Where are you going, anyway?"

"I don't know. I wasn't thinking about it."

"Well, maybe you *should* think about it. Before we wind up somewhere else we don't want to be."

Fifteen minutes later they were driving along M Street in Georgetown. There were people all over here, window-shopping, leaving restaurants, getting into their parked cars. At the light on 31st Street, a Metro Police cruiser pulled up beside the Audi. Jason forced himself not to glance over at the pretty female cop behind the wheel, who seemed to be talking to herself. When the light turned green, the cruiser pulled ahead of them. "Can we get off this main strip?" Jason asked.

"I'll park somewhere," Dennis said. "Then we can see what the damage is."

Dennis turned onto a dark side street and drove until they came to an empty parking space at the curb. "My mother usually has a flashlight in the glove compartment."

Jason found the flashlight and then the two of them searched the interior of the car, running their fingers over the carpeting like sculptors shaping something in clay. After a few seconds, Dennis cleared his throat and held up a little piece of metal. "The shell," he said, turning it in his fingers. Jason nodded uncertainly. "Semiautomatics eject them, revolvers don't," Dennis explained scornfully. "Keep looking for the slug."

"Whatever you say," Jason answered. It didn't take him long to find it. "Here," Jason said. High on the forward part of the footwell on the passenger's side—about an inch beyond the edge of the floor mat—was a surprisingly neat hole in the carpeting, surrounded by what looked like two or three shreds of metal.

"What's this?" Jason asked.

"The casing, I think. Jacketing. Whatever."

"You think the bullet's still in here?" Jason asked. He traced the rough edge of the hole with his index finger.

"I don't know, it might have gone through. But we've got to get it out if it's there."

"Why?"

"Because slugs can be traced, asshole. If that guy back

there is dead, they're going to be looking for the slug
fired from his weapon."

"He's not dead, Dennis." Jason took a deep breath.
"Besides, they don't investigate things like this, right?
This is D.C. The guy was a drug dealer."

Dennis shook his head disgustedly. "Listen, Jason, this
is my mom's car. If the slug is here, we find it and get
rid of it. Then we fix the hole so nobody will see any
damage."

"Okay, fine," Jason said. "Here, hold this." He handed
Dennis the flashlight and then stuck his finger into the
hole in the carpeting. He could feel a tiny, sandpapery
groove in the metal floor of the car. At the end of the
groove, his fingertip nudged the slug, embedded in the
metal. "It's here," he said. "But it's stuck."

"Dig it out with something. Your knife."

Jason took out his Swiss Army knife, unfolded the
hole-punch, and used it to pry the slug from the metal
floor under the carpeting. "Here." He held it up—a misshapen dollop of lead, surprisingly small.

Dennis took the slug from him. "Shit, this could have
been in my brain right now, you dildo."

"So what do we do with it?"

"We make it disappear."

"How?"

Dennis pocketed the various pieces they'd collected
and opened the door. "Follow me."

They got out of the car and walked quickly down the
dark sidewalk, Jason breaking stride to keep up with his
much taller friend. At the corner was K Street, traffic
passing noisily overhead on the elevated highway. Jason
followed as Dennis crossed the street to the Washington
Harbor development. They climbed a flight of cement
steps, past an empty fountain and some closed-up luxury
stores, and then walked out onto the boardwalk over-

looking the Potomac River. A few couples were strolling in the chilly night, serene and oblivious. Below, the river curved away—like a huge silver highway, Jason thought, like a road heading someplace far away. "Here," Dennis said. He handed the shell to Jason and brushed his fingers over the side of the boardwalk. Then he reared back and threw the slug far out toward the river. It disappeared without a sound into empty space. "It's gone now. Forever."

Jason stared down at the river for a few seconds, the cold wind making his collar flap like wings. Then, feeling an odd surge of hilarity, he turned and sidearmed the shell like a flat stone out into the darkness. It didn't carry very far, but the effort felt good, shaking that thump out of his arm muscles. "Disappeared!" he shouted toward the lights of Virginia. He turned back and shoved Dennis hard against the railing. "Call me a dildo, dildo."

Dennis, grinning, shoved back just as hard. "You *are* a dildo."

"Yeah, right," Jason said. Then, as Dennis watched, he started running down the boardwalk, sprinting as fast as he could until he finally had to stop and sit down.

After a few minutes, they left the boardwalk and went back to the car. Before getting in, they checked the outside of the passenger side for blood or scratches, but couldn't find any. "So what about the bullet hole, O great criminal genius?" Jason asked as they settled back into their seats. "Won't your mom see it and start asking questions?"

"See if you can pull the floor mat over it."

After a few tries, Jason found a way to position the mat so that it covered the hole without looking too far out of place.

"That should do us until we can fix it," Dennis said.

"You know that shit they sell on QVC for cigarette burns in your carpet?"

"What? Do criminal geniuses watch QVC?"

Dennis shoved him again. "I think you just cut up some carpet fibers from under the seat and glue them with this binder glue into the hole."

"What about the groove in the metal?"

"Nobody will ever see the groove, Jase."

"You hope."

"No," he said. "*We* hope."

"Right." Jason reached under the seat to find the corked bottle of red wine. Then, in a perfect imitation of the Reverend Parks standing over his daughter's birthday cake, he added: "We hope and pray. Amen."

It was just past midnight when Dennis turned the Audi onto Jason's block, a quiet stretch of Dunhaven Street near Rock Creek Park. The bottle of wine was empty now—they'd poured the rest of it out while stopped at a red light—and Jason was feeling clearheaded and sober.

"God," Dennis said, driving slowly down the street. "I literally thought I'd piss myself when that shot went off."

Jason nodded. "You should have felt the kick in the guy's wrist. Like a jolt. Electroshock or something. Wild." He sniffed his hands. "I can still smell it," he said. The smell reminded him of the anemic Roman candles his father used to set off in the backyard when he was a kid.

"Wash your hands before you go to bed," Dennis said.

"Okay, Dad. And you spray the car with deodorizer when you get home. Maybe you can call QVC and order one of those pine trees that fat salesmen hang from their mirrors."

Dennis pulled up at the curb in front of Jason's house. He idled there for a few seconds as they both looked across the street at a gray cat skulking along a wall. "Seriously, Jase," he said. "This whole thing goes to the grave with us. I mean it."

"Actually, I thought I'd bring it up with my dad at breakfast tomorrow."

Dennis turned his head sharply.

"Joke, joke," Jason droned. "Dildo." He got out of the car. There were tiny spring leaves on the branches of the trees overhead, like lace silhouetted against the yellowy streetlight. He came around to the driver's-side window. "I guess we never got our twenty dollars' worth of weed," he said quietly.

Dennis smiled. "Next time," he said. "Take it easy, asshole."

Jason gave the back bumper a little kick as the Audi moved away from the curb. He waited until the red brake lights flashed at the stop sign and the car finally disappeared around the corner.

He looked down at his hands. The guy was a drug dealer, he told himself for the fifth or sixth time in the last hour. The guy pulled a gun on them. He deserved to get the shit kicked out of him.

Jason looked up at his father's bedroom window. It was dark; the blinds were pulled. That was good. No explanations would be necessary, at least not until tomorrow morning. By then he could make up something convincing, if he had to. If he wanted to.

Feeling composed now, almost relaxed, Jason took a last breath of night air. It's over, he told himself. Then he started walking toward the yellow glow of his waiting front porch.

TWO

GRAHAM ROURKE WAS watching cartoons. He sat in a Barca-Lounger in the television room, leaning forward and scratching his coarse morning stubble with the edge of the remote. "Look at this, look at *this*!" he shouted to the empty room. On the screen, an army of short, red-furred creatures stormed a crenellated castle, firing weapons that looked suspiciously like assault rifles. "This is like Smurfs with Uzis!" Graham shouted. "Here it is"— he looked at his watch—"not even eight A.M. and we've already got a body count."

He watched for a while longer, his indignation rising by the second. The furry creatures were inside the castle now, laying down a line of fire furious enough to let their leader climb the spiral stairway to the prison tower. Halfway up, the little creature encountered two hulking, obtuse-looking, purple-haired guards, whom he quickly pummeled with his rifle butt and pushed over the side of the stairway. "Can you believe this?" Graham asked aloud. "I cannot believe this!"

Finally, just as the red leader reached the cell containing a group of kidnapped, saucer-eyed children, the station cut to a commercial. Graham checked his watch again. 7:50. His son should be out of the shower and dressed by now. Jason's regular school bus had broken down three weeks ago and, of course—the D.C. school system being what it was—hadn't been repaired yet. If he missed the public Metrobus, he'd be late for school. "Keep it friendly," Graham muttered, heaving his 245 pounds up from the lounger. He himself had to be at work for a staff meeting at 8:30. Graham Rourke was executive director of the Foundation for Responsible Children's Programming—or FRCP, as it was better known in the acronym-happy District of Columbia. The cartoon he'd been watching was on the agenda for discussion at the meeting. It was one of the new shows on a renegade cartoon network that had just been picked up by forty cable systems nationwide. The FRCP was considering an official protest.

Graham turned off the television and stepped across the hallway to the closed door of his son's bedroom. "Jason?" he called, knocking. "Jase, you'll miss your first class if you don't get a move on!" His son had come in late the night before—after the understood curfew—but Graham had decided not to make a big deal about it. Battles with Jason had to be chosen carefully. The boy seemed to enjoy reminding Graham that in a year and a half he'd be in college, well beyond the reach of his father's alleged overprotectiveness. These days, Graham tended to concede all but the most crucial conflicts.

Graham knocked again, louder this time. When he didn't get an answer, he felt justified in opening the door. He found Jason sitting on the edge of his unmade bed, talking on the telephone. An unfolded newspaper lay on the bedspread beside him. The boy stopped talking immediately and turned. "I'll be off in a second."

"Who is it?"

Jason shook his head, gave him a look of perfect annoyance, and turned away.

"Ah, the withering glance," Graham muttered to himself. He closed the door and went into his own bathroom to finish getting ready for work. "Be philosophical," he told himself in the mirror. Why, he wondered, was there always such an imbalance of affection in father-son relationships? When Jason was small, it seemed he couldn't get enough of his father. Every night when Graham came home from work, Jason would attach himself greedily to his father, refusing to let go until he'd received his daily share of stories, jokes, and general senseless roughhousing. Graham and Laura, on her better days, had even joked about it—the Barnacle, they'd called him. But now the balance had shifted the other way, and it was Graham who loved Jason too greedily, too sloppily, too much. It was Jason who turned away now, impatient, itching to move on to some better use of his time. Logically, Graham thought, there must have been an interval—maybe a year, a month, even a day—when there had been some equality of affection between them, some unnoticed golden age of emotional parity. But if there had been, Graham had no recollection of it now.

He picked up the can of shaving cream and shot a wet gob of it into his hand. As he spread the foam along his blunt, square jaw, he took a close look at himself in the mirror. He was showing his age these days—his thick dark hair silvering, his grape-green eyes going dull with too many disappointments and sleepless nights. People used to refer to his "rough good looks" in years past, but now those looks were getting rougher, craggier, more ursine than leonine these days. He frowned ironically at himself. In two months, he thought, he would be fifty. In two years, he would be fifty-two—and alone in that house.

Shaking the thought from his head, he tried to concentrate on shaving the deep cleft in the center of his chin. Jason, he hoped, would eventually get through this current stage. He was a good kid—though not particularly popular in school, from what Graham could glean from the boy's almost nonexistent conversation. Remembering the look of thudding annoyance on his son's face a few minutes ago, he wondered if it could possibly be a girl that Jason was talking to on the phone. Three months ago, the boy had broken up with his longtime flame— Sarah Thomas, a statuesque, preppy, and really very appealing blond sophomore—and there hadn't been anyone since, as far as Graham knew. Not that Jason would enlighten his father about any new love interest, even if questioned directly on the subject. Graham regarded his relationship with his son as reasonably close, all things considered, but somehow a pair of males living alone, without a female mediator, didn't seem to share too many secrets with each other. Their meals together tended to be silent and quick—not morose, but just blandly efficient, the conversation rarely extending much beyond "Don't forget I've got orchestra practice after school today," or "You going to eat the rest of that lamb chop?" or "Are there really supposed to be furry green spots in this tomato sauce?" It was always Laura who'd kept the conversation going at mealtimes.

Graham thought again about the murderous cartoon creatures on TV. Maybe he and Jason could talk about *that* at dinner tonight. "I was speechless, Jase," he'd say. "Imagine a cross between Barney and Jean-Claude Van Damme. In psychedelic colors, yet. So much for intelligent life on earth." That last sentence was one of Laura's pet sayings. He wondered if Jason would remember.

Graham finished shaving. He wiped his chin with a dirty maroon towel (Louella would be coming to do laundry on Tuesday) and then stepped into his bedroom to get his sport jacket. He had hung it, as always, on the plush beak of Big Bird in the corner. The seven-foot-tall stuffed beast, which was probably worth a couple hundred dollars, had been presented to him by friends at the public television station in New York after he gave some rousing testimony at a congressional hearing. He'd kept the thing in the attic for a while, but finally, in a fit of perverseness, decided to bring it down to the bedroom. Jason, of course, was mortified by the thought of his father's owning such a thing, and he made a point of shutting the master-bedroom door whenever he had friends in the house. But Graham, a man of large proportions himself, had developed a genuine liking for the huge, benevolent-looking creature. Pitiful as it sounded, the bird kept him company on nights when Jason was out. He'd even started talking to it once in a while, though only in a spirit of high irony. Like now: "So much for intelligent life on earth, Bird, don't you think?" He plucked his jacket from the silent beak and quickly put it on.

It was now almost eight. Past time to leave. Graham straightened his tie in the mirror and then stepped out into the hall. "Jason?" He knocked on his son's door again and opened it. Jason was sitting in the very same spot on the bed, the phone still in his hand, as if he hadn't moved an inch. "Will you be home for dinner?" Graham asked.

Jason looked like someone coming up from a deep and frightening scuba dive. "What?"

"Dinner. The taking of sustenance at the end of the day. Will you be around?"

Jason shrugged. "I guess."

"Veddy good, sah," Graham said in a clownish Indian accent. "I'll pick up some takeout at Delhi Palace. But I've got to go now."

"So go."

Graham paused in the doorway. "Anything wrong, Jase?"

"No."

"Who's on the phone?"

"Just Dennis."

"Well, excuse me, but won't you be seeing him at school in half an hour? Can't you talk then?"

"Yeah."

"Okay. So I'll imagine you hanging up the moment I leave. See you tonight."

"Yeah."

Graham closed the door, knowing enough not to try to kiss his son good-bye. He grabbed his briefcase and headed downstairs. Again, he checked his watch. Assuming decent traffic, he'd still have a few minutes to prepare before the meeting. He wanted to be pithy and convincing on the topic of the cartoon boycott. It was an important gesture, although it was bound to be unpopular with some of FRCP's major funders.

"Smurfs with Uzis," he said aloud as he opened the front door. It was a good line, he thought. Well, maybe not *that* good, but good enough to use at an in-house meeting. He felt for the car keys in his pocket, then pulled the door closed and headed toward his own first battle of the day.

Jason's ears were buzzing, as if that gun from last night had gone off again in front of his face. He shifted the phone to his other ear. "There's no way this can be the same guy, Dennis," he said.

"It *is* the same guy, believe me. It's the same street and the same time of night. It has to be."

Jason picked up the *Post* and reread the headline on page one of the Metro section: UNDERCOVER COP SLAIN IN BRUTAL NORTHEAST ATTACK. "First of all, there's no way our guy could've been a cop. Shit, he was robbing us!"

"We don't know that for sure. He could have been arresting us."

"He grabbed the twenty right out of my hand!"

"Maybe it was evidence. Proof that we were trying to buy from him or something."

The bedroom door creaked open. Jason, who had been trying to ignore his father's calls and knocks, turned to find Graham sticking his head into the room, his thick eyebrows high on his forehead. Jason got rid of him as quickly as he could.

"I'm sorry, Dennis," he went on, "but this is just too much, you know? It says this guy was shot. Fuck, we got the slug, remember? It went into the floor of your mom's car, not into the guy's chest."

"Read the whole article, Jason. It says the guy had two bullet wounds, but the pistol they found had been fired three times."

"So what does that mean?"

"Think about it. The slug in the floor of the car? That's the missing shot. And they say the guy was probably beaten up beforehand—does that sound familiar? As in dragged by a car and smashed against somebody's fender?"

Jason didn't answer. None of this was making any sense to him. What had happened last night was supposed to be over. They'd gotten away from a drug dealer who was trying to rob them. But now it wasn't over, after all. Now it turned out that the guy was a cop. Detective Ramon Harcourt. And he was dead. With two gunshot wounds in him.

"Christ, man, figure it out," Dennis went on. "We left the guy lying on the street with a pistol next to him."

"So you think somebody shot him after we left?"

"It has to be, Jason. This Harcourt's an undercover cop. He's got enemies in the neighborhood. They find him helpless—ping!—they do him for good, and with his own gun. Then they set the guy on fire for good measure."

Jason got up and began pacing back and forth, the phone cord stretching like a tether. "At least that means we didn't kill him," he said.

"How so?"

"I mean, if he was dead when we left him, they wouldn't have shot him."

"Jesus, Jase, you're so fucking naive. Who knows? Maybe some lunatic crack addict found him and put two bullets in him just for laughs."

Jason sat down again on the edge of the spongy bed. "I can't believe this is happening," he said. He started winding the phone cord around his arm, putting deep red impressions in the flesh.

"Jason?" His father again, this time with no warning knocks. Jason turned again and had some kind of conversation about dinner, though he didn't take in much of it.

"So what do we do?" he asked Dennis after Graham had closed the door again.

"I don't like that question, what do we do? Why do we have to do anything?"

"Well, we don't. I guess."

"Exactly. The cop is dead. We didn't do it."

"You just said—"

"Forget what I just said, Jason. It was . . . whatever—hypothetical."

"But if it's a cop."

"So what? We don't know anything useful, right? Who would it help if we told what happened?"

Jason's stomach took a sickening turn. "Shit, you think I could have left some fingerprints? On the guy's wrist? Or on the cuff of his shirt? Can they pick up prints on stuff like that?"

"You're worrying too much, Jason. Besides, if they threw lighter fluid on the guy and lit him up, that would probably erase any fingerprints on him. Don't you think?"

"Yeah. I guess." Jason stared up at the ceiling of his bedroom. I killed a cop, he said to himself, trying to grasp the idea. Something else occurred to him then. "Oh shit," he said.

"What."

"You do that set of calculus problems for Cardinelli's class? I totally forgot."

Jason heard Dennis laughing on the other end of the line.

"Something's funny?" he asked.

"Calculus homework! He's asking me about calculus homework! You scare me sometimes, Rourke."

Jason considered this. "Shit," he said. He started laughing, too. He lay back on the bed and tried to make the laugh penetrate the layer of numbness that seemed to surround his body like a quilt.

"Look," Dennis said after a few seconds, "let's talk about this at school. I'll be late if I don't get off the phone now."

"Yeah. Me too."

"I'll see you in Daniels's fourth period. Then we can talk at lunch."

"Right."

"So Jase, until then, be cool. Okay?"

Jason sighed. "I'll be cool, Dennis. I'll be cool." He said good-bye and put down the phone. Then he sat on the bed for a few more minutes, just looking around his room—at the rack of CDs next to his boom box, at the travel poster of the main square in Brussels, at the carved African mask on the wall that he'd once bought Dennis for Christmas but then felt too self-conscious to give him. This was his room, he reminded himself—the same room it was yesterday morning, the same it would be tomorrow. He got up and walked to his bassoon case leaning against the wall. He had orchestra tomorrow and he hadn't even begun to practice the Mozart piece. You are a bassoon player, he told himself, as if he'd forgotten. Jason had picked up the instrument two years ago, when he first decided to join orchestra. He figured that everybody played violin, flute, or clarinet. But the bassoon would be something unusual, something that would stand out on a college application.

Jason picked up the case and opened it on the bed. Inside, the instrument was broken down into three parts, each one like a segment of burnished, caramel-colored bamboo, nested in a groove cut to its exact shape. The reeds were in a little plastic film can taped to the velvet lining of the case. He imagined some admissions officer reading his application: Jason Rourke. 3.5 GPA. Bassoon Player. Swimmer. Math Team Co-Captain. Plus, he'll fill our quota for undergraduate cop killers.

He shut the case again, snapping the latches closed. The sound reminded him of that other sound—the snap of the man's forearm last night.

Jason closed his eyes. He could hear the lazy buzz of flies outside his window, the mocking caw of a crow in the distance. It was spring; school would be over before too long. He thought of his mother—of the way she used to look forward, almost desperately, to the D.C. spring— and silently told her that there was no reason whatsoever to worry.

Dennis noticed three different Metro Police cars on his way to school that morning. They seemed to be all over—one lurking ten yards back from a busy intersection, one sprawled across the white lines in a church parking lot, another creeping slowly down a residential street. As he steered his bike down McKinley, Dennis told himself that he was just being hyperaware of them, out of sheer paranoia. The District, after all, was always full of cops, not just the D.C. Metro Police, but also the U.S. Park Police, U.S. Marshals, the FBI, the Secret Service, and a security force for every federal agency in town. And just a few blocks north were the Maryland contingents—Montgomery County Police, Maryland State Police, Montgomery County Sheriff's Department. Washington might be falling apart these days, but it wasn't from any shortage of cops. They were everywhere—federal, state, local. And all of them, he knew, gunning for a young black male like himself, waiting for him to make the slightest mistake. . . .

"Oh please," Dennis said aloud, his halfhearted stab at resentment falling flat. He knew plenty of black males— his mother's relatives, in particular—who'd been given a hard time by the police, but he himself had never had any problem. In fact, the only real racism he'd experienced in his life had come from his own race—the kids at school who thought he wasn't black enough for their taste. But Dennis tried not to care much about their opinion of him. He thought of himself as a pragmatist, and he understood that copping ghetto attitude was a loser's game—something that would get him absolutely nowhere in this world. He had plans for his life, and he knew he could go far as Dennis Monroe, the smart, well-dressed, well-spoken African American kid from Chevy Chase, D.C. A credit to his people, as some asshole had once called him at a Scout function.

A Boy Scout. Shit, he had actually been a Boy Scout once.

Dennis turned off McKinley and headed south on 41st. A black Audi pulled into the intersection in front of him. He thought of his mother's car, of the bullet hole in the carpeting. Earlier, she'd called him from work to remind him about an overdue library book, so apparently she hadn't noticed anything on the drive in. As long as she didn't move the floor mat on the way home, he'd be okay. He'd buy something at the hardware store to fix the hole, bring it home after school, and then nonchalantly slip down to the garage after dinner. By morning, the glue would be dry. And that would be that. He'd have saved Jason Rourke's ass once again.

Saving Jason's ass—it seemed he'd been doing a lot of that lately. Just last week Dennis had steered Jason out of a potential free-for-all with some older guys who wanted to take over the basketball court they were using at Rock Creek Park. Jason, the idiot, had got into a shouting match with one of the guys, a huge, square-headed Jamaican who would have crushed him into the asphalt like a cigarette butt if Dennis hadn't intervened. But that was vintage Jason. He had his head so far up his ass sometimes that he didn't calculate, or evaluate, or even *think*. That number he'd pulled with the cop last night was all too typical—grabbing the guy's wrist without considering what could happen. As if the pistol would just fall, the way it does in all the Bond films, when somebody delivers a fake karate chop to the arm of a gun-slinging bad guy.

It could have been all right, Dennis told himself. Going over to Northeast was a mistake—he'd gotten a little too confident, maybe—but it could have been okay if Jason hadn't lost his head. Dennis was sure he could have kept the situation in control, cop or no cop.

Dennis started pedaling faster. He thought about his parents—what they would say if they ever found out what had happened the night before. It would be ugly, no doubt about it. Dennis's mother was a lawyer for the National Labor Relations Board; his father was a politics professor at UDC. They were churchgoers. Members of committees. Dennis could just imagine how they would react to the news that their only son was cruising the drug corners of Northeast on a Sunday night. They would probably think he was rebelling, going through some kind of standard-issue adolescent revolt. His mother would be especially bad. She'd take it as a personal insult, a direct assault on her competence as a parent. She'd look at him with that hurt, disappointed expression on her face, and make him feel like shit.

Squeezing the hand brakes, Dennis slowed and turned down Gulliver toward RFK High School. Something was bothering him. For the past minute or so, he had sensed a car trailing behind him, matching his pace annoyingly. He'd tried to ignore it, but now, as he checked behind him to cross to the other side of the street, he finally saw it—a forest-green Ford Explorer. He thought instantly of the Explorer they'd almost hit last night, just seconds after their run-in with the undercover cop. Rattled, Dennis told himself that it couldn't be the same one. He was being paranoid again, like Jason. He looked forward again, just in time to see a huge pothole in the road in front of him. It swallowed the front wheel of his Raleigh, twisting the bicycle out from under him. As the pavement raced toward his face, he let go of the handlebars and

tried to put his hands out to break his fall. He hit the
pavement, then slid over a patch of wet grass and rolled
onto the sidewalk, his ribs hitting a cracked cement
planter.

"Hey, you okay?"

Dennis rolled over, feeling disoriented. A goggle-eyed,
gray-haired man in a shiny blue sweat suit was staring
down at him.

"Um, what?" Dennis said. He looked up and down the
street. The green Explorer was gone now, lost in traffic.

"You hurt?"

It was a good question. Dennis drew his knees up to
his chest. His left pants leg was ripped and streaked with
grease, but his legs seemed to be all right. He looked at
his hands. The fall had nearly shredded the padding on
the heel of his left riding glove, but his hand wasn't
scraped. Only his shoulder and ribs ached. He reached
up and started kneading his left shoulder.

"You want me to call somebody?"

"No, sir," Dennis said. "I'm okay. Really."

"Good thing you were wearing a helmet," the man said
piously, his sweat suit shimmering.

Dennis looked over at his bicycle. It lay in a heap
against a peeling mailbox, like a dead insect.

A few other people were hurrying over to him now.
"He all right?" asked a young blond woman. "He get
hit?"

"No," Dennis said loudly, feeling embarrassed now. "It
was my fault. I hit a hole."

Dennis got slowly to his feet, with help from the gray-
haired man. "I'm okay, sir, thanks. I'm fine." He brushed
some sand and dirt from his pants—they were ruined
now—and walked over to his bicycle. Close up, he could
see that it wasn't too badly damaged after all. The front

wheel was out of alignment and the chain had come off, but the bike still looked ridable.

Dennis crouched to rethread the greased chain onto the sprockets. "Chalk up another D.C. pothole story, right?" the woman said. Dennis smiled, and the people who had gathered started walking away, shrugging their shoulders and shaking their heads, talking to each other now as if Dennis weren't even there. After a few seconds, he was able to slip the chain onto the sprockets again. He stood and carefully mounted the bicycle. Don't be a jerk, he told himself. Settle down and get a handle on this thing.

"It was a white man, honey."

Dennis turned. A round-shouldered black woman stood at the curb and stared at him, her gray hair peeking out around the edges of a linty black wig. She wore sagging blue knee socks and a dark brown overcoat far too heavy for the weather.

"A white man in a green car, on his way to work, prob'ly."

"Thanks," Dennis said. "But it was my fault. The car didn't hit me." He stuck his right foot into the stirrup and tested the hand brakes.

The old woman was shaking her head. "God forbid anybody get themself in the way of a white man goin' to work," she said, as he started to ride away.

THREE

"WELL, WE HAVE any number of approaches, don't we?"

Renee Daniels leaned back against her desk at the front of the classroom. She crossed her long-boned, black-stockinged legs in front of her and waited for an answer. On the blackboard behind her, the words "Objective/Subjective" were spelled out in her sloppy but legible cursive.

"Don't we?" she repeated. She began shaking the chalk in her hand like dice. It was her signature impatient gesture, the one her students invariably imitated when they played her in the Senior Variety Show every spring. Renee should have been self-conscious about it by now—after eight years of teaching Introductory Journalism at RFK High School—but she had worked long and hard to eliminate self-consciousness from her emotional repertoire. Renee was five feet ten, still fairly presentable (if men in bars were to be believed, which was doubtful), and old enough or arrogant enough not to care what anyone in that school thought of her. Besides, according to the underground student guidebook, she was the third most popular teacher in school (despite her "occasional shrillness and tendency to harangue"). She figured she could afford a few harmless eccentricities.

Renee looked around the classroom, clawing her mane of jet-black hair (another quote from the underground guide: "Looks a little like Sophia Loren—on a bad-hair day"). "Please, anybody?" she said. But no one—not even Jason Rourke, who could usually be relied on to say *something*, no matter how misguided—raised a hand.

Renee moaned aloud. "Okay, my little drones, let's start over with an easier situation." She pushed herself off the desk and walked with admirable steadiness to the blackboard. It had been one of those mornings, the kind when getting her mascara on in a straight line seemed like a small miracle worthy of candles and offerings of fruit. "Let's say we have an accident. Crash! A rush-hour collision between, say, a Volvo and a Mack truck, with two witnesses—somebody driving behind the truck, whose view was almost entirely blocked, and a busybody pedestrian on the street, who saw everything." Feeling a little burst of irrational enthusiasm, Renee began to write short, cryptic notes on the blackboard. "You arrive on the scene and get four different stories—one from each of the two witnesses, one from the truck driver, and one from the driver of the Volvo, which has crumpled up to absorb the shock, just the way they do in those TV commercials. Each person has a different story about what happened and who is at fault. What do you, as the bright young journalist you are, do in this situation? What story—or whose version—do you report?"

After a few agonizing moments of silence, Stuart Franz raised a tentative hand. "The pedestrian's?" he offered.

She pounced like a hawk on a helpless field mouse. "Why?"

Stuart blanched. "Well, because he was, like, the objective witness?"

"Are you asking me or telling me?"

"Telling," he said quickly. "He's the one who saw it all, and he doesn't have any bias. The way, um, the Volvo driver would, since he was involved in the accident."

"Okay, that's one possibility." Renee turned to the board and wrote: "1. Choose a single version and report it."

"Wait!"

Renee turned back to the class hopefully. Leslie Dormund was waving an arm in the air like a windshield wiper. "Yes, Leslie."

"Okay, but we don't know for sure that this one witness is really objective. Maybe he's got his own bias. Say he hates truck drivers or something. Or"—here she smiled at her own attempt at Renee-like outrageousness— "maybe his wife is having an affair with the guy in the Volvo."

Renee raised a plucked eyebrow at her. "Fascinating, by the way, how we're assuming that all of the players involved here are male. But that's another tirade." Renee started shaking the chalk again. "Leslie's made a good point. It's not always clear who, if anyone, is an objective witness. So how would *you* report the story, Leslie?"

"Okay, I'd talk to all of the witnesses and write all four stories into my article. You know—this one says this, that one says that."

"So Leslie votes for the Russian-novel approach," she said. "Let's hope she has a city editor willing to give her as many inches as she wants." Ignoring the snickers that the word "inches" inevitably produced in a mixed-gender high school class, Renee began scribbling on the board again: "2. Present all versions." She turned and looked over the faces of her thirty students. "Anyone else? Dennis?"

Dennis Monroe, who seemed to be affecting an uncharacteristic grunge look today, glanced up from his notebook. "Sorry?" he said.

Renee pinned him with her famous acid glare. Here was another usually reliable participant, lost in Dreamland. "Okay, is *anyone* paying enough attention to help us here?" More silence. Finally, Renee wheeled around and began writing: "3. Unite all versions."

"How about this?" she asked with a flourish. "You do more than just report what other people say. You dig a little into the background. You find some dirt—let's say the pedestrian's wife *is* having an affair with the Volvo driver, as Leslie so pruriently suggested, and that's why the pedestrian's version of the story puts the blame on the Volvo driver. The truck driver, meanwhile, just found out that she's got . . . oh, I don't know, inoperable brain tumors. Is she therefore distracted? Depressed? Experiencing double vision? You could check that out. Meanwhile, the Volvo driver has three DWI arrests on his record. He's driving without a license. How reliable is *his* story? You see where I'm taking this?"

"It's an explanation," Leslie says. "One that unites all versions of the story."

"You read my handwriting beautifully," Renee said. She launched herself back toward the blackboard. "Okay, this approach to the story, number three"—she poked at the number with her chalk, breaking it in two but choosing to ignore that fact—"is what we call investigative journalism. It is, in my not so humble opinion, the highest form of journalism there is. And, unfortunately, it's the kind that most reporters never get to do much of in their careers." She quickly wrote the words "investigative journalism" on the board, aware that she was running out of time before the end of the period. Then she spun around, leaned back against the metal chalk gutter, and crossed her arms and legs. "Make sense? Investigative journalism is what we do when we dig beneath the surface explanation to find the real one underneath. Another phrase for it might be 'good, hardworking journalism.' It's what I want to focus on in the last few weeks of this course. Okay?"

Leslie was nodding, but the rest of the class looked befuddled, unimpressed, or just bored. Renee let her shoulders sag theatrically. This was when the bell was supposed to start shrieking throughout the building. Renee was legendary in the teachers' lounge for timing her lessons to end on a high note, just as the period was over. Out of habit, she looked at the clock, though of course it hadn't worked in months. Nothing did these days— even here, at the best public high school in the District of Columbia, a school that even middle-class families sent their kids to. There were times when Renee had to buy her own chalk for class.

Finally, the hallways resounded with the shrill scream of the bell. "Don't forget," Renee announced as the thirty teenagers in front of her got to their feet and started packing up their books. "I need your profiles by the end of this week. No extensions."

She began erasing her notes on the board. Then she pounced again. "Dennis and Jason," she said icily, not looking at them. "Can you stay behind a minute?"

She turned just in time to see the two boys exchange a meaningful look. "There, right there," she said, pointing a long, red-nailed finger at them. "That's exactly what I want to talk to you about."

The boys looked almost comically sheepish. Tweedle-Dum and Tweedle-Dee. Or, better, Mutt and Jeff, considering the difference in their heights.

Renee waited while the rest of the class wandered out. Then she came around the desk and said, "Something's going on, and I want to know what it is."

"What do you mean?" Jason asked, clearly uncomfortable.

Renee stared at him for a few seconds. "Dennis?" she asked, keeping her eyes on Jason.

"Um, yes?"

"Are you going to be more helpful than your pal here?"

"Don't know what you're talking about, Ms. Daniels. Sorry."

Renee turned her glare on Dennis. At least he could meet her eye without fidgeting like a child, but even so, he couldn't conceal his nervousness. Renee had long ago decided that seventeen-year-old males had more in common with five-year-old boys than they did with seventeen-year-old girls. "You look a little disheveled today, Dennis. Is this a new fashion statement?"

Dennis shrugged. "Fell off my bike."

More silence. Renee lost patience. "Come on, guys. This is me—Renee. Aren't you going to tell me *any*thing? I thought we three were friends."

She could see that Jason was weakening, eyeing Dennis hopefully. But Dennis wouldn't budge. He gave Jason a tiny but unmistakable shake of the head. What a cute couple, Renee said to herself snidely. They could practically be married. She had to admit, though, that these boys were the best of the lot at RFK—smart enough to want to make something of themselves but dignified enough not to brownnose shamelessly, as so many of their AP classmates did. They were the kind of teenagers *she* would have raised, she thought. If anyone had ever dared to marry her.

"It's nothing," Dennis said, without looking at her. "We just like being mysterious."

Renee decided to give up. It probably *was* nothing, she told herself. Maybe the two of them had lost their virginity over the weekend. Or tried Quaaludes. She'd always been curious about Quaaludes, and promised herself, before she died . . .

"Fine," she said then. "I'll just sit here in the dark, don't mind me." She brushed a little dust from Dennis's shoulder. "But by Wednesday's class, you two had better start participating again. Otherwise I'll have to let Leslie Dormund rule the class. God help us all."

She pushed them both toward the door. "Go. And try not to look so relieved."

The boys left, making a show of shuffling as nonchalantly as they could. Renee watched the door slam behind them, then started rounding up her own things. She glanced over her notes for her next class, which started after her lunch period. Expository Writing 1, the class for callow, illiterate freshmen. With her eight years of seniority, she could have let someone else teach the class, but she never allowed herself that luxury. EW1 was her penance. Inmates in prison broke rocks with sledgehammers; Renee taught fourteen-year-olds how to construct intelligible paragraphs.

EW1. God help us all, she screamed silently toward the heavens. Then she gathered up her books and stuffed them resentfully into her purple totebag.

Jason and Dennis met at the Hechinger's on Wisconsin Avenue after school. They found a stock clerk in the carpeting aisle and told him what they were looking for.

"Carpet repair kit?" the clerk asked. He reminded Jason a little of his father—an older man, with hair like steel wool and eyebrows he probably had to comb. "Like what? Patches?"

"No," Dennis said. "You cut up some carpet fibers and mix it with this glue powder and you stuff it into the hole. Then you iron it or something."

The eyebrows moved like furry inchworms. "Never heard of it."

"I saw it on QVC."

"If you saw it on QVC, why don't you buy it on QVC?"

Dennis sighed. "Well, what *do* you have to repair carpets?"

The clerk crossed his arms in front of his barrel chest. "What kind of carpet is it?"

"Basement," Jason put in, at the exact moment Dennis said, "Car."

The eyebrows sank and joined. "You guys wouldn't be jerking my chain, would you?"

"No, it's a car carpet," Dennis said quickly. "We burned a hole in it with a cigarette and it's my mom's car."

The clerk grinned, as if finally grasping the situation. "And now you want to fix it so she doesn't find out you been smoking in her car."

"Exactly," Dennis said.

The clerk looked down and fingered the lapel of his red vest in thought. After a few seconds, he said, "I got something that should work. As long as there's still some left." Dennis and Jason followed him into the next aisle. "Here," he said, handing Dennis a box. "Mom will never be the wiser."

They paid for the kit and left the store. Dennis put the plastic bag in his backpack and stooped to unlock his bicycle, which was chained to a rack on the sidewalk.

"You'll probably need a new front wheel," Jason said, looking at the curving rim.

"I know." Dennis wound the chain and lock around the base of the seat. "You really don't have to help me with this if you don't want to."

"Hey, I'm responsible. I'll help." The two boys started walking up Wisconsin Avenue, Dennis pushing the bicycle. The whole thing shimmied as it rolled, in a way that struck Jason as vaguely obscene. "How will you make sure your mother doesn't catch us?"

"She usually comes home at four and then works in her attic office for a few hours," Dennis said. "The car will be down in the garage."

"What do we do if she walks in on us?"

Dennis shrugged. "We could use the cigarette-burn excuse. She'd throw a fit, but probably just a minor fit."

" 'I'm shocked,' " Jason deadpanned, " 'shocked to discover that there is gambling going on in this establishment!' "

"What?"

"Nothing. Just something my father says when he's trying to get a laugh."

The boys walked on in silence for a minute, the only sound the squeak of the bicycle's front wheel.

"So," Jason began cautiously after a few blocks. "We're sure this guy in the Explorer this morning was a coincidence, right? No way it could be the same one we saw last night?"

"What makes you think it could be the same one?"

"You tell me. *You're* the one who freaked when you saw it."

"Yeah, from talking to you too much. You're poisoning my mind, Rourke. And ruining my car and my bike in the process."

"Right, right. Blame everything on Jason."

A fire engine zoomed down Wisconsin Avenue, moving fast but not making a sound.

"Talk about freaking," Jason added then. "I couldn't believe it when Lois said that about staying after class." "Lois"—as in Lois Lane—was one of their private names for Renee Daniels. "She's got, like, this seventh sense."

"Sixth," Dennis said.

"Sixth. Right. Stupid." Jason knocked himself on the head with his fist. "You know," he went on in a different tone, "that could have been our whole lives last night. If that cop arrested us? Forget college, dude—we'd have been stuck selling CDs at Tower for the rest of our lives."

"He wouldn't have arrested us, Jason. He just wanted to scare us. Teach us a lesson."

"Hey, he looked whacked out enough to do anything. You see the way his hands were shaking?"

"He had no evidence, Jase. It would've been his word against ours."

"Right, and what excuse would we give for being in that neighborhood? We were looking for homeless people to take home with us?"

"We would've come up with something."

"I don't know," Jason said. He looked up at the telephone wires strung loosely over the street. A dozen gray birds were perched in a line on the highest wire, like commuters waiting for a late bus. "It's so fucking easy to screw up," he said. "One little mistake can change everything."

"Or it can change nothing."

Jason shook his head. "You just never know. You ask a guy on the street for the time and you can get yourself shot in the head. It happened just the other night to somebody, over in Southwest. Nobody knows what the fuck is going on. It's like you're in the hands of Fate, you know?"

Dennis stopped walking. "Come on, Jase. Don't get all mystical on me."

"I'm just making a point here," Jason said, his cheeks warming a little. "I mean, life is just weird."

"Yeah, I know it is. But you don't have to make it any weirder, okay?"

They started walking again. Jason looked around, noticing all the flowers coming up in people's yards. After almost a full day of walking around in a haze, he felt he was finally becoming aware of his surroundings again. The weather in D.C. was changing. The wet dirt everywhere was starting to warm up, giving off smells of spring. Enjoy this, he told himself silently. This is your life.

Ten minutes later, they reached Dennis's corner on Quiller. "So," Dennis said, turning his bicycle, "to recap here, try not to screw it up with my mom, okay? If she catches us fixing the hole, just let me do the talking. Don't say a word."

Jason smiled. "Understood, man," he said. "I know I'm not as good a liar as you are. I admit that." He looked over at Dennis, ready to be teased back, but Dennis wasn't paying attention. He was staring at something off in the distance.

"Shit," Dennis said.

Jason turned and followed his gaze. Standing in front of the Monroes' brick colonial was a police car—a white Metro Police cruiser—parked across the entrance to the side alley.

"Shit," Jason agreed.

FOUR

THEY STARED AT the patrol car, its chrome mirrors gleaming in the bright sun. "It could be a coincidence," Jason said, fishing for reassurance. "It could be totally something else."

Dennis steered the wobbly bicycle to the curb in front of his house. Jason followed. The patrol car was empty, parked sloppily across the alley from either hurry or complete apathy. Jason noticed a narrow dent running along the driver's side, distorting the Metro Police emblem on the door.

Dennis threw the bicycle down on the lawn. "Let me handle this. You don't say a word, Jason, okay?"

"Stop saying that."

Dennis didn't even look at him. He headed calmly up the front walk. "Come on."

The door was unlocked, so the boys walked right in and shed their backpacks in the foyer. The Monroe house—a standard D.C. colonial like hundreds of others in the neighborhood—was full of sunlight and solid oak furniture, the walls decorated with tribal baskets and Hai-

tian primitive paintings. At the foot of the stairs facing
the door was a polished table covered with what Dennis
always called African tchotchkes.

"Dennis, honey, is that you?" It was Mrs. Monroe's
voice, coming from the dining room.

"Yeah. What's going on?"

"Come in here a second?"

They exchanged a quick glance and then walked
through the house to the dining room. Standing at the
end of the oak table was a tall, mustached white cop with
a shaved head. He was holding an open pad and pencil.
Dennis's mother, a plump, round-faced woman with intense toast-colored eyes, stood at an awkward distance
from him. Her arms were folded across the lapels of her
ivory-colored blazer. "Perfect timing," she said, with a
cheerfulness that seemed almost sarcastic.

"This the son who had the car?"

"It's the only son of mine I know of. Dennis, this is
Officer Collins and he's—"

"We're just doing a routine canvass," the cop interrupted. He nodded an apology to Mrs. Monroe. "I understand you were driving your mother's car last night at
around eleven o'clock?"

"Yes, sir, I was. Why?"

"Can you tell me where you went?"

Dennis looked at his mother, then at Jason. There was
an expression of perfect bewilderment on his face. "We
went to a party. Jason was with me. Why? What's
wrong?"

"Can you tell me where the party was?"

"At a friend of ours." He gave the address. "Her name
is Melinda Parks. Her father's a minister."

"And when did you leave this party?"

Dennis shot a glance at Jason. "Nine-thirty, ten, I
guess. Somewhere around there, right?"

Jason shrugged, trying to match Dennis's easy attitude.

"And did you come straight home?"

"No. We drove down to Georgetown, down by the river. It was still early."

"God forbid a teenager comes home early," Officer Collins said. "And what did you do there?"

"I don't know, we hung out at Washington Harbor for a while. Along the boardwalk there?"

"You talk to anybody? Is there anybody to confirm this?"

"Just Jason here." He looked at his mother. "What's this all about?"

The cop turned to Jason. "You are Jason . . ."

"Rourke," Jason said levelly.

"Address?"

Jason gave it to him.

"And you were with Dennis the whole time?"

"Yeah. Except when he went in to rob that bank on Wisconsin."

"Jason," Mrs. Monroe said with wide-eyed annoyance.

"You robbed a bank, Dennis?" the cop asked, looking bored.

"Jason's idea of a little joke," Dennis said. He was frowning, but Jason could see that he was impressed with the tactic.

Officer Collins wrote a few more notes on his pad. "So when did you leave Washington Harbor?"

"I guess it was midnight or so."

"You come straight home?"

"Yes, sir. After dropping Jason off."

"And you always stay out past midnight on a Sunday?"

This question seemed to irk Mrs. Monroe. "When your son is a straight-A student, you let him have a little leeway, Officer Collins. You figure they've earned a little trust."

Officer Collins stopped writing. "Didn't mean any offense," he said. He clicked his ballpoint and flipped his notepad closed.

"Can somebody tell me what this is about?" Dennis asked.

Officer Collins slipped the pad and pen into his back pocket. "A police officer was killed last night. We've got a report of a black Audi with D.C. tags speeding in the neighborhood around the time of the shooting."

"So you're checking every black Audi in D.C.?"

"A certain number of them, yeah."

"How many are there?"

"Too many," the cop said. "That's all for now. Unless you want to tell me more about the bank robbery?"

Jason produced a sheepish smile. "I didn't know it was anything serious. Sorry."

"They don't get any more serious than this." The cop nodded then at Dennis's mother. "Thanks for your time."

"I'll show you out." Mrs. Monroe started to lead Officer Collins toward the front of the house while the cop muttered something about the change in the weather. But then, just as he was about to leave the dining room, he stopped. "Actually," he said in a fake offhand tone, "do you mind if I take a quick look at the Audi?"

No one answered for a few seconds. "As I understand it," Mrs. Monroe said, fingering the leather belt of her skirt, "we're under no legal obligation to say yes."

Officer Collins gave her a sour smile. "God, I love dealing with lawyers," he said. "No, you're under no legal obligation to consent, but seeing as Dennis here can't prove his whereabouts last night, it could make people wonder if you didn't."

"Dennis, do we agree to let Officer Collins look at the

car?" Mrs. Monroe asked, as if reciting a line in a play.

Jason understood what this was about. Last summer, Mrs. Monroe had found half a joint in Dennis's shirt pocket while doing the laundry. After what Dennis had called an inquisition, she'd agreed not to tell Mr. Monroe about it. Even so, Dennis had been virtually grounded for a month.

After a pause, Dennis shrugged. "I don't see why not," he said lightly.

"It's in the garage," Mrs. Monroe said.

The four of them went out the front door and around by the alley to the garage, which was under the Monroes' back porch. Mrs. Monroe hit a button on the automatic opener and the red-painted garage door began to open with a groan. The black Audi sat inside at the center of its own grease stain, surrounded by garbage cans, rakes, snow shovels, and three different lawn mowers. "You want me to pull it out into the alley?" Dennis asked.

"It might make things easier."

Dennis pulled his set of keys from his pocket and got into the car. Jason stood back with the two adults near a feeble lilac bush. He noticed that Officer Collins was staring hard at Dennis through the back window, watching every move he made. Finally, after revving the engine a few times, Dennis put the car in reverse and pulled out into the narrow alley. He got out of the car and then gestured like a magician presenting the results of his best trick.

Officer Collins took a slow walk around the outside of the Audi, examining the lights, fenders, and bumpers. As he did this, Dennis walked over to join the two near the lilac bush. Jason felt the faint pressure of Dennis's sneaker on top of his own, but he refused to look at him. High in the maples overhead, birds chirped like the sound track of a movie about spring romance.

After making a complete circle around the car, Officer Collins pulled open the front door on the driver's side. He stuck his shaved head inside and looked around. He pulled open the ashtray and checked the seams of the seats. "Excuse me," Mrs. Monroe said, "but I can't see how this kind of search is helping you determine if this car was the one near your crime scene."

The patrolman pulled his head out of the car and smiled. "Just trying to be thorough, Mrs. Monroe." He stepped back and pushed the door shut.

"I'm sure you always like to be thorough," Mrs. Monroe said in a hostile tone. "Especially with black folk like us."

Officer Collins frowned. He seemed genuinely offended. "It's not about that, Mrs. Monroe."

"It's *always* about that, Officer Collins."

Dennis stepped forward quickly. "Can I put it back in the garage now, officer?"

"A cop was shot, ma'am," the patrolman went on.

"And meanwhile you're looking for marijuana seeds in every Audi in the District, whether the owners are black or white, right?"

"Mom," Dennis said.

Officer Collins gave Mrs. Monroe a long, tight-lipped stare. "Yeah, you can put the car away now, Dennis," he said.

Dennis got in and started the engine. "Thank you for your cooperation," Officer Collins said to Mrs. Monroe. Jason walked with them back to the front of the house. They watched as Collins climbed into the patrol car. He sat for a moment in the front seat, shuffling through some papers. Jason heard the garage door rumbling shut, then saw Dennis striding around the corner of the house.

The three of them stood there while Officer Collins started the patrol car. He rolled down the window and stuck his head out. "Your mother has my card," he yelled toward Dennis. "If you think of anything—like anybody else who can confirm that you were in Georgetown—call me. Otherwise we may have to be in touch again." Then he pulled away from the alley and drove slowly down the street.

After a few seconds, Mrs. Monroe uncrossed her arms and turned around. She looked over Dennis's clothing. "What happened to you?"

"Fell off my bike. No big deal."

She watched him closely for a few seconds. "I meant that, Dennis," she said, the lines visible around her heavily lipsticked mouth.

"Meant what?"

"What I said about trust." She reached out and fingered a loose button on his shirt. Then the tightness seemed to lift from her face and she smiled a warm, totally confusing smile. "You boys are something," she said. "Robbing a bank. But you'd better be careful. Someday, someone just might believe you."

Dennis and Jason sat slouched on the ratty cotton sofa in the Monroes' basement rec room, watching the news. They'd spent the previous half hour in the garage, fixing the carpet of the Audi. Jason had stood guard at the door while Dennis sprawled across the front seats, carefully gluing a circle of carpet into the bullet hole. According to the directions, the glue would dry within six hours. Assuming nobody used the Audi before the smell faded, they'd be all right.

The television was tuned to the local all-news cable station. There'd been a few teasers about the murder but no full report yet, since they'd tuned in late in the half-hour cycle. They'd had to endure a story about decaying bridges, one about allegations of fraud against one of the

District's deputy mayors, a disgustingly cheerful weather report, and a feature about a tiny candy store in Anacostia that was closing after fifty-seven years in business. When the anchors turned to a story about an abandoned car on the front lawn of the Smithsonian Institution, Jason threw a balled-up sock at the screen.

"Relax," Dennis told him. "And keep your hands off my laundry."

They watched as the news cut to a commercial for a local Mexican restaurant. Two Waspy lawyer types were cutting loose after a hard day on Capitol Hill. The guy wore a straw hat and was waving a margarita around as he loosened his necktie.

"We were good with that cop," Jason said then, as if speaking to the pillow he hugged to his chest. "Don't you think?"

"Yeah, excellent. 'I was with him the whole time, officer, except when he was robbing that bank on Wisconsin.' Give me a break."

"Hey, it's called genius. When he heard that, the cop naturally thought we were just a couple of wiseass kids."

"Well, he got it half right."

"What about you, man? 'You want me to pull the car out so you can see better, sir? You want me to suck your dick, too, while I'm at it, sir?' "

Dennis laughed. "You're right, we *were* good."

"I almost lost it, though, when your mom started picking a fight with the guy."

"Good old Mom. Tireless defender of all African Americans against society's injustice."

Jason didn't say anything to this. He thought suddenly of his father, making a big deal about violence on children's television. Everybody had a cause in this town—Greenpeace, Feed the Homeless, Gays for the Ethical Treatment of Animals. Meanwhile, all of it was falling apart anyway, no matter what kind of rescue plans they came up with. Sometimes the whole city made Jason sick to his stomach. "Hey, we shall overcome," he muttered, for no real reason.

The television switched to a station ID—a still of the white-marble Jefferson statue standing in its little gazebo—and then to a shot of a familiar-looking street corner. Jason recognized the bent-back stop sign, and the alley between two boarded-up row houses. A male voice-over was saying, "Still no arrest in last night's shooting of an undercover narcotics officer in Northeast. . . ."

Dennis sat up quickly. "Here we go," he said, grabbing for the remote to turn up the volume.

As they watched, the camera panned across a dark street speckled with ambulance lights. There was a shot of some uniformed police standing around, then a weirdly artistic shot of long ribbons of yellow crime-scene tape twisting in the wind, and then a quick, half-blocked view of a covered body on the sidewalk. The voice-over described the discovery of the body at 3:00 A.M. by a cab-driver who was lost and trying to find a street sign. "And in the most recent development in the case, News Channel 8 has received an unconfirmed report of an internal police investigation into why Detective Harcourt, who was actively engaged in a sting operation involving local drug operators, was apparently working alone without backup at the time of the shooting. Police also refused to comment on another unconfirmed report that the officer may have been carrying a substantial quantity of money at the time of the shooting—money intended for use in the sting operation." The camera cut back to the anchor-man, who announced solemnly, "The shooting of Ramon Harcourt was the ninety-seventh homicide in the District so far this year."

The show cut back to the female anchor, who started

talking about a diet-pill scam in Arlington.

"There's your motive right there—the money," Dennis said. "He was probably waiting to pass off the money to somebody. They knew he had the cash, so they offed him and ran away rich." He got up from the sofa and turned off the television manually, even though he had the remote in his hand. Then he walked over to the ratty pool table near the stairs. He picked up a ball, turned it in his long fingers, and then rolled it against the far cushion. "Let's get out of here," he said. "I need a walk."

They went upstairs and got their jackets. "We're just going out for a while," Dennis shouted upstairs to his mother.

"Your father's bringing home Chinese at seven," she answered from far above. "Don't be late."

"I will obey." Dennis checked for his keys in his pocket and then led Jason outside. Yesterday's cold front was already ancient history, and the evening was turning humid and warm. Daffodils were starting to bloom everywhere, and pink cherry blossoms were already open on some of the trees.

"So you think somebody robbed the guy after we left?" Jason asked finally, as they neared the playground at the neighborhood elementary school. "Robbed him while he was unconscious on the street, and then just shot the guy?"

"Could be."

Jason kicked a half-full soda can out of his path. "Probably wouldn't be the first time something like that happened over there." They walked past some kids crowded around the swing set. Two of the four swings were broken, their chains twisted up into knots or hanging loose. The kids were taking turns on the two good swings. "You don't think he saw us, do you?" Jason asked.

"Who?"

"The guy who killed him." Jason was thinking of the Explorer that had spooked Dennis that morning, and he could tell that Dennis was thinking of it, too.

"We didn't see *him*. That's the important thing. He's safe as long as we can't identify him."

"I did see him."

Dennis stopped walking. "What?"

"I saw *somebody*," Jason said. "On the passenger side of the Explorer. As we were turning in front of it in the intersection."

"Could he tell you saw him?"

Jason considered this for a second. "God, I don't know. Could be, I guess." He looked down at his sneakers, then up at Dennis again. "You think that could have been the deaf guy? The one I saw? The cop kept going on about a deaf guy."

"Who knows what he was talking about? He was coked up or something. Half these narcotics cops are junkies themselves."

"But, I mean, maybe that's important information. It could be something the police could use to find the killer. A clue."

Dennis shook his head. "No, Jason," he said. "Don't even think this way. I'm not ruining my life to give the cops some little piece-of-shit information that probably doesn't even mean anything. We don't know that this green Explorer had anything to do with what happened." He pressed a finger into Jason's shoulder. "You said it yourself, Jason. This could be our entire lives here."

"You're right," Jason said. "Forget I even mentioned it."

"And you forget you even thought it, okay?"

"It was stupid. I agree."

They started walking again. Long stringy clouds

floated over the treetops, the undersides glowing pink in
the late sun. A siren blared in the distance. Two squirrels
raced across the street and scrambled into a rhododen-
dron bush. You could almost forget where you were, Jason said to himself as he looked around. At certain times
of day, on certain streets, you could easily be in a small
midwestern suburb.

"This fucking town," he muttered to himself.

FIVE

RENEE DANIELS PARKED her Civic at the curb on Nevada Street, pulled the red Club from under the seat, and locked it onto the steering wheel. She grabbed her book-filled tote from the backseat and climbed out of the car. It was turning into one of those benign Washington twilights—the kind of calm, humid, blossom-scented March evening that the city could produce every once in a while as evidence of its old southern heritage. She walked back along Nevada to Kitchener, where late rush-hour traffic buzzed past in both directions. At the corner, Renee stopped to pull a cigarette from the pack in her tote, but when she couldn't find her lighter after almost a full minute of rummaging, she threw the cigarette back into the bag and started walking again, down Kitchener this time. Just as she reached the overgrown walkway of her house, some redneck in a pickup with Virginia plates beeped her and shouted something obscene out the window. Renee gave him a halfhearted finger and then started searching for her keys.

Her parrot, Fenton, squawked at her as she pushed the

door open. He was perched in his cage just inside the living room, screeching and digging energetically at his iridescent-green chest feathers. He did this whenever anyone came into the house. Her watchbird, she called him. Fenton was a gift—an inheritance, really—from Karen Wilkes, an old college roommate who had died of breast cancer several years earlier, at the age of thirty-four. Renee saw the bird as an obscure punishment for not visiting Karen during her last few months, when Karen lay dying in a hospital bed in Annapolis. Renee hadn't really liked Karen, whom she had regarded as sneaky and fiercely overambitious, and so, from guilt, she indulged Fenton with every kind of cuttlebone and bird toy imaginable.

She kicked aside the day's mail on the foyer floor, threw her tote onto the pile of newspapers near the door, and shucked off her black cotton jacket. With a quick glance at her answering machine—no messages—she went to the kitchen and poured herself a glass of red wine. From the other room, Fenton let out a shrill little cackle. During her illness, Karen had apparently taught the bird an entire repertoire of laughter—girlish titters, amused chuckles, even something that sounded like a guffaw. And although these various mirthful utterances were probably intended to cheer Karen up, Renee had always found them annoying—and, at times, even vaguely spiteful.

Renee took a cigarette from the extra pack on the counter, lit it, and inhaled deeply. Then, unlocking the well-armored back door, she carried her wineglass and the cigarette onto the patio. The sky was darker now, as if night had fallen in the brief moment she was inside. She lowered herself into a wrought-iron lawn chair and took a sip of wine. Then she sat back, took another drag on the cigarette, and closed her eyes, listening to the distant murmur of traffic and pretending it was a waterfall.

After a few moments, a siren raked across the evening's stillness. She opened her eyes, then smiled grimly to herself. She was still sensitive to the call of a siren, even after all this time. Twelve years ago, after suffering through her requisite two years at a small daily in North Carolina, Renee had come to Washington as a police reporter for the *Washington Sun*. The crime beat had been a mostly male fraternity even in the mid-1980s, and Renee had been obliged to endure the usual rounds of teasing, practical jokes, and blatant but good-natured harassment from her colleagues. Her editor, Lyle Santerelli, used to assign her every rape case deemed worthy of the paper's notice (in other words, every one in which the victim was a middle-class white female living in Northwest), until finally she threatened to quit if he didn't start assigning a few to the other reporters on the beat. "But you understand the victims—our readers appreciate that," Lyle told her, throwing up his hands in exaggerated innocence. To which she responded, "Well, why don't you assign Hill or Anderson or Delmar and let our readers understand the perpetrator for once." The very next rape case—of a congressman's daughter who turned out to be moonlighting as a prostitute—was assigned to Victor Anderson, who rode the story through weeks of front-page features all the way to a six-figure book contract with Simon & Schuster and an equally lucrative movie option.

Renee kicked off her shoes and put her feet up on the glass-topped table. She noticed a hole in the foot of her black stockings. The knuckle of her right middle toe peeked out like a pearl. Renee told herself she should go shopping to buy panty hose and underwear, maybe a new skirt or two. The state of her wardrobe was becoming embarrassing. Too many old clothes, she thought. In fact, she still wore two pairs of black jeans she'd bought in New York back in her journalism-school days—and she didn't know whether to feel mortified by this or proud of it. Cigarettes and nerves, she knew, were the main factors in keeping her weight down. That, and an occasional tendency to let a bottle of cabernet suffice for dinner. The Daniels Diet, she called it. You might die young, but you won't die fat.

"Woo-hoo!" said Fenton weakly, from inside the house.

Renee finished her glass of wine, collected her shoes, and went back inside. She turned on the portable television in the kitchen and started ransacking the refrigerator for something to eat. The news was on—another story about last night's cop killing in Northeast. Renee stopped with a half-rotten bunch of celery in her hand and watched. She had covered her share of cop shootings in her time at the *Sun* and had always regarded them as the most banal stories of all. Each was virtually identical with the last, so that you could practically call up the previous series from the paper's morgue and just replace the names with new ones. First, there was always the breaking news story—the invariably tawdry who-what-where-why-when, which would be repeated endlessly in one form or another in the stories to come. Then the tense vigil-at-the-hospital story, the heartless and manipulative interview-with-the-grieving-widow story, the ritual-appearance-of-the-chief-and-the-mayor piece (complete with tough talk on the need to clamp down on crime, increase cooperation in crime-fighting efforts, involve the community, etc., etc.). Then came the hero-cop profiles—the charities he helped, the kids on the street who loved him, the dogs he saved from half-frozen ponds in winter—along with updates on the investigation. The wake next. Then the funeral piece (a thousand blue uniforms

at the cemetery, the tears, the eulogies, the endless ha-
giography). And, finally, the long drought before the trial
pieces, which few people seemed to care about unless
there were celebrities involved.

Renee kept an eye on the screen as she put the celery
back and grabbed a blueberry yogurt and some three-day-
old salad. This latest shooting, she decided, was more of
the same, although Renee's eye had detected a few subtle
differences. For one thing, there was no grieving widow
here. This cop had been divorced for five years; his ex-
wife, who lived somewhere in Virginia, was apparently
unwilling to weep poignantly for the cameras. And there
also seemed to be a certain restraint in the testimonials
of the victim's fellow officers. Of course, they claimed
that he'd been a good cop and a good human being, but
Renee noticed a definite lack of conviction in the television interviews. This Ramon Harcourt was probably an
unpopular guy, she guessed. A maverick, or maybe just
a prick. There were plenty of those in the Metro Police
force, as she well knew, but it was amazing how rarely
they were the ones who got shot.

Now, now, she scolded herself. He was probably an
honest, hardworking cop. Who just happened to be in that
neighborhood without his partner. With a bag of money
that didn't belong to him.

Then, in the imagined voice of one of her students, her
mind added, *As if.*

Renee turned off the set and carried the yogurt and
salad to the kitchen table. She missed journalism, of
course—real journalism, as opposed to the fluffy feature
stuff she still occasionally produced for the *City Paper*.
On her more hopeful days, she even thought of trying to
get back into the business. Not that it would be easy after
so many years of exile. When she left the *Sun* (when you
were *fired*, she told herself tartly), Santerelli had advised

her to go into another line of work, something more suitable for her "low stress threshold." She had interpreted this to mean that he would be perfectly honest with any prospective employer who might call to check her references. A man of unimpeachable integrity, that Santerelli.

But he wasn't wrong about her stress threshold. At the time Renee was fired, she had already run through several years' worth of accumulated sick days. "Stress" was Santerelli's little euphemism; it was something else she was suffering from—the Big B for Burnout, Anxiety Overload, or, as she liked to call it, her Date with Diazepam. There were mornings, in fact, when she couldn't even leave her Dupont Circle apartment, let alone go out to cover crime scenes.

She had lost her nerve—that was Renee's own best euphemism for what had happened to her. She'd been going along fine for a few years, walking the walk, but then she'd been forced to look down. She saw the thin tightrope she was standing on, the fragile thread of her self-confidence twisting beneath her, and she panicked. She fell.

It was a serial rape case that did it—the Foxhall Phantom Case, as one of the less respectable neighborhood papers dubbed it. Renee had covered it from the beginning, and probably knew the case as well as the investigating detectives did: White male, late thirties, navy-blue ski mask. He would enter a house—usually one of the big, expensive ones off Foxhall Road—through an open or unlocked back window in late afternoon. Wait for victim to return from outing. Pop out of closet, threaten victim with knife, tie her ankles and wrists to the bed legs with panty hose. And then the part that Santerelli and every other editor in town loved: The perpetrator would talk to his victim the whole time—

sweet talk, encouraging and reassuring. He would woo her, flatter her, romance her. Then he would finish and get out before the man of the house was back from work.

It was a big story, and Renee had written a whole series on the case, each article getting better play, first in the local section, then in the front. Eventually, one of her stories jumped above the fold on page one—when the Metro Police finally overcame their usual reluctance and declared it a serial case. Renee was even on the local news once or twice, describing the perpetrator's modus operandi and laying out proper precautions for anyone living in the area ("News you can use," they called it). But she was spooked even then by the guy. She'd interviewed some of his victims, heard them speak about what had happened to them. And no amount of preemptive cynical joking in the newsroom could let her hide from the fact that this guy seemed to have her number.

Literally, as it turned out: The call came at 2:00 A.M. on a Wednesday night. "I like the way you write about me," he began. "I like what you say, how you describe me. I want to hear more."

It was enough. The man never called again, and the police were never convinced that it was him to begin with—probably a hoax, they said, very common in serial cases. But one call was all it took. Twang! Renee fell from the high wire. From that night on, she couldn't concentrate on anything except that smooth, teasing voice on the phone, praising her work, asking to see more. And finally, one evening as she stood outside the house of the Phantom's sixth victim, she decided she just couldn't do it anymore. She was finished. No big drama—no nervous breakdown or panic attacks or hysteria, no retreat to a leafy suburban facility to throw ceramic pots with depressed political wives. Just a flattening out of her will, a loss of spirit shot through with a kind of generalized anxiety. That world—the world of the D.C. streets—was ugly and dangerous, and she decided she didn't want to have anything to do with it anymore. The cost was just too high. Lie down with dogs and you get what you pay for, as her mother used to say.

Renee ate the last spoonful of yogurt and got up to throw the container away. She refused to go over this corrosive territory one more time in her mind. It was old news, for one thing. Nobody even remembered the Foxhall Phantom anymore—not his crimes or even how appropriately he got his due in the end, shot in that sweet-talking mouth by a divorced labor lawyer with a 9-mm pistol in her night table. And Renee, of course, had recovered nicely. She'd gone on to become a teacher, a high school instructor. And a good one, too—a better teacher of journalism than she had been a journalist. There were even times when she believed she was making a real difference in her students' lives. Already, two of her former pupils had gone on to become reporters, one as a sportswriter with a Gannett paper in suburban Virginia, the other—God love him—as a police reporter for the *New York Times*.

Renee walked out into the foyer and pulled a handful of papers from her tote—the thirty-six assignments she'd collected that day from her Expository Writing 1 class. All thirty-six had to be read and graded by the end of the week. She carried them into the kitchen and dropped them onto the table next to the wilted salad. After refilling her wineglass, she sat down, ate a forkful of salad, and pulled the papers closer to her. She'd asked the students to write a three-page profile of "someone they knew and admired." Renee picked up the first one, written by Kathi Pinella, a mousy, thin-lipped girl who always wore Fair Isle sweaters and sat in the front row. The title was "Ms. Renee Daniels: Educator Extraordinaire."

Renee sighed deeply and reached for her wineglass.

SIX

"YOU LIKE THE eggplant?"

"What?"

"The eggplant. Is it good?"

Jason looked down at his plate. "Oh," he said. "I guess so."

"And the lamb curry?" Graham asked. "Not too spicy for you, is it?"

"Which is the lamb?"

"The dish that's not eggplant," Graham said. "Ipso facto, right?"

Jason, who was apparently too preoccupied to take offense, just shook his head. "No, it's good. Not too spicy." As if to prove the point, Jason ate a huge forkful of the lamb and began chewing distractedly.

Graham took a sip of beer, watching his son eat. It was almost eight o'clock—late for dinner, but Graham hadn't been able to get away from the office any sooner. The meeting about the cartoon boycott had been a fiasco. Nobody else seemed to share his indignation at the whole idea of shoot-'em-up cartoons aimed at the three-to five-

year-old set. Reggie Gray, the assistant director, had ful-
minated at length about squandering the organization's
"moral capital," and so Graham had been forced to table
the issue until a later date. In the meantime the little furry
creatures would continue to splatter blood at will.

"So how was school?" he asked then, though he remembered how galling this question had seemed coming
from his own father decades ago.

Jason, as expected, gave him a galled look and said,
"Stimulating."

Graham put his fork down. "Stimulating," he echoed,
pushing his plate aside. There were times when he just
wanted to pick up the skinny kid—who was still five
inches shorter and a hundred pounds lighter than Graham—and hug the breath out of him. "Hey, Jase, this is
Dad," he'd say. "We're family, remember?" But, of
course, he never did that. Graham had been seventeen
once, too.

He looked over at his son's wiry brown hair, hazel
eyes, and those almost too thick, sharply cut lips he'd
inherited from his mother. The boy was a total enigma
to Graham sometimes. He saw how engaging Jason could
be with other people. He could be warm, witty, even
charming—with everyone, it seemed, except his father.
And this fact made Graham feel absurdly jealous, like a
suitor too marginal to be bothered with. Somehow Graham just didn't seem to interest his son anymore. And
despite their shared grief in losing Laura, their shared
loneliness now, Jason remained as familiarly mysterious
to him as the squirrels in the backyard.

Graham pulled his plate closer and started eating again.
Maybe they should take a vacation together. When Laura
was alive, they would sometimes go down to a ranch in
the Great Smoky Mountains to ride horses for a week.
Laura loved riding, and therefore (in the early days of

Jason's adoration of her) so did Jason. The two of them would go off on all-day rides together, while Graham remained—meanwhile, back at the ranch—trying to get some work done. Laura and Jason would show up at the room in the late afternoon, faces flushed, eyes bright, expressions of excited collusion on their faces. It was this feeling of being left out that had persuaded Graham to join them occasionally on their rides, despite his work-load and the fact that Graham and horses generally distrusted each other. Once, during their first stay at the ranch, a bad-tempered stallion had thrown him on what was supposed to be a sedate "family ride," fracturing his wrist. Even so, he would have been willing to give the ranch another try, if he had any sense at all that Jason would enjoy it.

Jason got up suddenly from the table and began walking out of the kitchen without a word, as if his father weren't even there.

"Sit down, Jason," Graham said, angry now.

"I'm finished."

"Sit down."

Jason stared at his father for a few seconds, his expression unreadable. Then he returned to the table, pulled out his chair, and sat.

Graham swallowed another mouthful of beer and began the discussion he'd resolved not to have. "You were out late last night. Way after curfew."

"I know. I got delayed."

"Delayed by what?"

Clearly uncomfortable now, Jason shrugged. "We lost track of time, I guess."

"You guess?" Graham tried a deep breath, but it only seemed to intensify his anger, to lodge it deeper in his chest. "Listen, Jason, we have an agreed-upon curfew. Losing track of time isn't an acceptable excuse."

"An honest mistake isn't acceptable?"

"You've got a watch, don't you? It's even got a little alarm—'Peep peep.' Ten o'clock. Time to get home to Dad."

Jason gave him a withering stare.

"Where were you last night?" Graham asked calmly.

"None of your business."

Graham paused for a second before saying, "Okay, if you can't keep your promise to me about the curfew, then I can't be expected to keep my promise to you about respecting your privacy. Am I going to have to start checking your sock drawers for joints now, too?"

"If you find any," Jason said, looking bitterly amused now, "they're probably yours. I'm not the one who got kicked out of college for smoking dope."

Graham closed his eyes. How many times had he regretted Laura's full-disclosure philosophy of child-rearing? "That's why you should listen to me, Jason," he said slowly. "I know what kind of trouble you can get into."

Jason seemed to find this funny. "You don't have any clue, Dad. Not one fucking clue." And then he stood up and left without another word.

"Jason!" Graham shouted. "Get back here, now!"

He heard the front door slam. He quickly got up and stepped over to the window. Jason was heading down the walk to the street. Graham felt an impulse to go after him, but he knew he shouldn't. There would be a scene on the street if he did, something ridiculous and embarrassing to both of them. So he just watched as his son pushed his hands into his pockets and started walking stiffly down the dark street, disappearing finally beyond the circle of light thrown by the streetlamp.

Graham turned from the window. "You blew it," he

said aloud. "Again." He walked back to the table, sat, and picked up his glass of beer.

He thought of a day, four years ago, when he and Jason had tried to make dinner together. This was about two weeks after Laura's suicide, when it was still an open question whether life could conceivably go on without her. He and thirteen-year-old Jason were downstairs in the basement, standing in the pool of bone-colored light from the open deep freezer. They were looking through the tightly wrapped packages that Laura had labeled and hidden away, searching for something they could cook on the outdoor grill. But they were having trouble deciphering her labels. "Here's one that says 'L of P,' " Jason said, holding up a package while cold mist from the freezer tumbled down onto their shoes.

Graham took the package from him. "Loin of pork, I'd guess," he said. "Too elaborate. Is there anything with an 'F' in it? Fish would be good."

"Mom never froze fish," Jason said. "She said it spoiled the texture. Too mushy."

They paused, contemplating Jason's use of the past tense.

"This one says 'C L times 2,' " Jason said after a while.

"Two chicken legs." Graham took the package from Jason's hands. "That'll be perfect."

They closed the freezer and went upstairs. "You unwrap that and I'll go out back and get everything ready," Graham said.

He stepped out onto the deck and fired up the hibachi, using too much charcoal lighter as usual. But when he came back, Jason was laughing. The sound frightened Graham. "Hey, what's up?" he asked.

Jason turned with the unwrapped meat in his hands— two wet slabs of purple-black meat fringed with rime.

" 'C L times 2,' " he said. "Two packages of chicken livers."

Graham frowned, trying not to think too much of the fact that he'd misread his wife's code yet again. "Two packages of chicken livers," he repeated. He and his son both hated chicken livers. "Want to do the honors?" he asked then, pointing his chin toward the back door.

Nodding in comprehension, Jason gave him one of the slabs of frozen livers and then they pushed through the screen door onto the deck. The hibachi flamed in the corner like a miniature city on fire. They began breaking up the slabs into segments, each individual liver flat and dumpling-sized. And then, in unison, they wound up like baseball pitchers and started flinging the livers one by one over the maples into the yards beyond. After the first few, they took turns, trying to send them farther and higher each time, watching them rise and then sink in the slanting light, into the well-kept yards of their smug, tragedy-free neighbors.

"Raccoon's Night Out," Graham said, after they'd thrown the last liver. "They'll have a feast." He put his arm around Jason's narrow shoulders, and then—feeling something like acceptance, even hope—he and his son walked slowly back inside.

At the time, it had seemed like a turning point—the night of the chicken livers. But now, four years later, he had to admit that it hadn't turned out that way. Graham had somehow made a mess of it with Jason over the years, despite all his good intentions. Without Laura, they weren't a family—just two people sharing the same roof, two members of the same species thrown together by the cosmic zookeepers, sharing nothing except the similarity of their genes.

Graham got up from the table again. "You blew it," he repeated, softer this time. He cleared the table, ran water over the dishes in the sink, and then went upstairs into his bedroom. He reached behind the books on the top shelf of the bookcase behind the stuffed Big Bird. This was where he kept the box, a hammered-tin box he'd picked up on a trip to Mexico. Inside were three joints, sitting side by side like birch logs in a fireplace. He took out one joint and returned the box to its hiding place.

"So, I'm a hypocrite," he said to Big Bird, patting his pockets for a match.

Dennis was in the downstairs rec room, watching television, when he heard a rap at the window. He got up from the sofa carefully. From across the room, he couldn't make out the figure peering through the glass. He moved slowly around the pool table toward the window. "It's me," a muffled voice said. "Jason."

Dennis felt his whole body sag in relief. "Come around to the garage," he shouted. "I'll let you in."

He went into the dusty garage, slipped around the front of the Audi, and opened the side door. Jason appeared after a few seconds. He was wearing no jacket—just a green corduroy shirt and baggy jeans—even though the night was chilly. "What's up?" Dennis asked.

Jason shrugged. "My father was being his usual asshole self, so I left. What's going on?"

"Nothing. Come on in."

He followed Jason into the rec room. Once inside, Jason walked to the television and started watching what was on the screen—a surfing show on ESPN. "So, did your mom say anything to your dad about the cop being here?"

"She mentioned it. At dinner. Then she and my father started talking about the shooting. My mother thinks the guy was probably involved in some kind of shit—not her choice of words, exactly—and that's why he got offed."

"And don't tell me: your father disagreed with her."

Dennis smiled. "He said, and I quote: 'Come on, Annie, he's dead now. Think of the poor man's family.'" Dennis shook his head. "It was so weird, Jason, sitting there and listening to that? I kept getting this urge to say, 'Yeah, well I saw the guy in the flesh and he didn't look like any hero cop to me.'"

"I'm glad you restrained yourself." Jason hesitated a few seconds before saying, "But I know what you mean. It's like we're living on a different plane now or something."

"A different plane?"

"Different from everybody else. My father. Your parents. Everybody."

Dennis just stared at him. First he has a premonition; now he's living on a different plane. The word "twisted" came to mind again.

Shrugging awkwardly, Jason turned away and walked over to the pool table. He started racking up the balls. "You want to play?"

"You can never get enough humiliation, can you," Dennis said, feeling a little relieved. He walked to the rack of cues and took down the two best. "Loser's choice," he said, holding them out to Jason.

They played a game of straight pool. Dennis won by four balls. He was racking them up for a game of eight-ball when Jason asked, "You still think we shouldn't let anybody in on this?"

Dennis stopped with a ball in each hand. "Like who?"

"Come on, you know who."

Dennis dropped the last two balls into the rack and lined them up. He'd been going over this question himself for the past few hours. If the guy in the Explorer really was involved in this thing, and if he knew that

Jason had seen him, they could be in real trouble. "What good do you think telling Renee would do?" he asked.

"She knows about shit like this. From when she was a reporter. Maybe there's something we should be doing. Like what if that cop comes back to take another look at the car? A closer look this time."

Dennis lifted the rack, put it on the windowsill, and grabbed his cue. "It won't happen, Jason."

"You don't know that. And she wouldn't tell anybody. You know Renee."

"Yeah, I do know Renee—enough to know that you can't predict what the hell she's going to do." He lined up his shot and then slammed the cue ball. With a sharp crack, the fifteen balls scattered around the table. The three-ball dropped into a corner pocket. "Look, I'll think about it, okay? Right now, we're the only ones who know about this, and I don't see any reason to change that."

"What about the guy in the Explorer?" Jason asked. "He knows too."

"Forget the Explorer, Jason. It was a coincidence, okay?" He took another shot and missed. "My concentration sucks," he said. "What time is it?"

"Almost ten o'clock."

"You want to turn on the news?"

"Shit, no. Do you?"

Dennis hesitated for a few seconds, then shook his head. "I guess not."

"In fact, I don't want to see another news report in my life." Jason walked around to the other side of the pool table and took a shot. "As your mother once said to me, 'Some things out there you just don't want to know about.'"

Dennis winced. "Oh God, he's quoting my mother now," he said, and smacked the two-ball hard into the far corner pocket.

• • •

Later that night, a little before midnight, Dennis was in his room, typing on the computer in his dark bedroom. He'd connected to a Web search engine and was conducting searches for phrases like "police shootings," "unintentional manslaughter," and "juvenile offender." He wasn't turning up anything useful—or at least not anything that seemed relevant to his and Jason's situation—and was about to sign off when he decided to check his E-mail one last time before going to bed. He opened the program and hit the retrieve icon. Four messages came up and copied to his in-box. One was from Jason—his main correspondent—asking some incredibly minor question about their calculus homework. Two others were junk mail from people peddling sleaze on-line (titled "Are You a Hot Man?" and "Oooh, I'm Waiting for You"). The fourth was from David Goldbaum, a friend from chemistry class. The title was "Check this out," and there was a file attached to it.

Dennis opened the message. "den," it read, "i always knew you'd go bad one day. your parents should have bought american. one question, do black audis make good getaway cars?"

Flustered, Dennis clicked on the attachment. His Web browser came back up on the screen, displaying what looked like a story from an on-line news site. "Police Intensify Search for Cop Killer," read the headline. He scanned through the article until he got to the third paragraph, which David had managed to highlight in bright yellow: "One focus of the investigation is a report of a black Audi sedan seen speeding in the area around the time of the shooting. . . ."

Dennis pushed away from the desk. Was it possible, he wondered, that Jason was right, that the cops would be back to look at the car again? If his friends were making jokes about this, how long would it be before somebody really made the connection?

He went back and reread the article more carefully, but there was nothing else about the black Audi sedan.

Dennis sat three feet away from his desk and stared at the words on the screen, debating with himself—until finally he reached forward and shut down the computer, throwing the room into total darkness.

Okay, he told himself. We should go to Renee.

SEVEN

"**I THOUGHT YOU** guys had some sense," Renee said, rubbing the tight skin around her temples. "Buying drugs over there. That was stupid."

"Okay, we're aware of our stupidity," Dennis said. "That's not the question we're asking."

"Come on, Renee," Jason said impatiently. "No lectures."

She stared at the two boys with a feeling of plunging disappointment. Why did it have to be Dennis and Jason? she asked herself. Why couldn't it be two of those other kids—the jerks who skip class and hang around the video store on Wisconsin Avenue? They were going to end up in jail anyway. "Really stupid," she said again.

The three of them were sitting on boxes of old textbooks in a storage room at RFK High School. The room was lined with metal industrial shelving that reached to the water-stained ceiling, every inch of shelf space crammed with textbooks, examination booklets, ancient copies of *Smithsonian* and *National Geographic* magazines, and rubber-banded sheaves of brittle, long-outdated notebook paper. The storage room, known to students and faculty alike as The Hole, was a depressing place to be at any time—dusty and dimly lit and somehow, to Renee, reeking of the futility of public education in the District of Columbia—but it was the most secluded room in the school.

"We want your honest opinion," Dennis prodded.

Renee pressed her knuckles against her teeth in thought. "Well, look," she said finally. "It's a wild story. I mean, cops don't pull guns like that unless they're in immediate danger—they're trained not to. In fact, it's a big deal if they do."

"But it's pretty obvious that he wasn't a regular cop, right?" Dennis said. "And he sure wasn't out there on official business."

"And he was high," Jason added.

She looked at Dennis. "You think so too?"

Dennis nodded. "Yeah, he was on something. PCP or something. I'm sure of it."

"D.C.'s finest," Renee muttered. She remembered the undercover narcotics cops she'd met during her time as a reporter. Some of them seemed as crazy and unsavory as the people they were supposed to be catching. Santerelli used to say it was like sending German shepherds out with a pack of wolves. If you didn't watch them every minute, it would eventually be impossible to tell the dogs from the wolves.

"Okay," Renee said, leaning forward on the cardboard box. "Let's say we've got a bad cop. If that can be proved, it would give you guys some credibility. He was out there doing some extracurricular stuff when you guys just happened to drive up. There was some kind of misunderstanding, he pulled a gun, and you panicked. You thought you were acting in self-defense. You didn't mean to drag him into a parked car. It was an accident."

"Will people believe that?" Jason asked.

"Y-Yes," Renee answered, instantly regretting her slight hesitation in getting the word out. But she had to admit that she wasn't sure. The fact remained—there was a body in the morgue with two bullets in it. And if Dennis and Jason didn't put them there, people would want to know who did. This Arlene he mentioned? Some unnamed deaf man? A passerby? Renee shot a quick glance at Dennis, then at Jason. Both of them were staring at her, waiting for some kind of answer, as if she could make everything go away with a single sentence. She suddenly felt the full weight of the responsibility they were dumping on her. "Look," she said, "this is obviously complicated. I'm your teacher—and your friend, I hope—and I can advise you as much as I can, but this is something we really have to go into with your parents."

"No," Dennis said immediately. "I can just imagine how my parents would react to this."

"Look, Dennis, there's no room for debate here. You've got to tell your parents. And the sooner the better. I can't be responsible for you."

"See?" Dennis said, looking over at Jason. "I told you she would do this. I never should have said yes to this."

"We're not going to tell our parents," Jason said weakly.

"You *guys*, a cop is dead. That won't go away."

"But we didn't kill him!"

"Well *somebody* put those bullets in the man," Renee said. "And that's part two of what I've got to tell you. There's a lot going on here behind the scenes that we don't understand. That's why you should go to the police, too."

"Oh, Jesus," Dennis said, getting to his feet in disgust.

"For one thing, withholding information like this is probably a crime in itself. And it'll be better for both of you if you turn yourselves in before the police find you. They were at your house yesterday, right?"

"That guy knew squat. If they'd known anything, they would have done something by now."

"Dennis—" she began.

"Wait," Jason interrupted. "It's *our* lives we're talking about here. *We* have to decide."

"I'm not arguing that. I'm just telling you what you *should* decide. What you've *got* to decide."

Dennis turned his back on them. "I'm not changing my mind," he said.

Renee got up from the box and walked over to Dennis. God, she needed a cigarette. A finger or two of scotch would have done nicely, too. "Look," she said, "I've got a friend I can talk to about this—no names, no specifics. He knows the law better than I do, and he'll be able to tell me what will happen to you guys if this comes out. Maybe there's some kind of deal you can make with the police or the prosecutors. I mean, it's possibly not as serious as you think."

"It's serious, Renee," Dennis said. Then he turned and asked, "Who is this guy?"

Renee hesitated. She worried that if she told them the truth—that he was an FBI agent she knew—they'd panic. "He's somebody in law enforcement," she said. "I think it's best to leave it at that."

Dennis stared at her, then looked over at Jason. "Okay," he said. "You talk to your guy and see what he says. Then we'll discuss it again."

Renee closed her eyes in relief. "I'll see him tomorrow—tonight, if I can get him. But then, no matter what he says, we tell at least your parents. Promise me."

"We'll talk again tomorrow," Dennis said. "But I don't promise anything. It's our decision, Renee. Jason's and

mine. You promise us you won't tell this guy who we
are."

Renee frowned. They probably had no idea how much
they were asking of her. "I'll probably lose my teaching
credentials over this," she said at last. "But fine. I promise."

After dinner that night, Dennis borrowed his mother's car
and drove over to the gym for a workout. He changed
quickly in the steamy locker room, pulling on a pair of
red running shorts and a sleeveless white T-shirt. As he
laced up his sneakers he glanced at himself in the full-
length mirror at the end of the line of lockers. The usual
evening contingent of older gay guys was hanging out,
watching him surreptitiously via the complex series of
mirrors arranged around the locker room. By now, these
guys had every angle doped out, and could keep an eye
on naked bodies throughout the entire locker room. Usually, Dennis just ignored them, but tonight he was wary,
wondering if one of these guys might be watching him
for other reasons.

When he reached the crowded Nautilus room, the air
acrid with sweat, Dennis climbed onto an exercise bicycle and started pedaling to warm up for his workout.
He always did his best thinking at the gym, the repeti-
tious movements occupying the top layers of his conscious mind while the deeper part could roam at will.
Tonight, of course, there was only one thing on his mind,
and he hoped that by going over it again and again, sift-
ing through every detail, he would see something he
hadn't seen before. The answer would jump out at him
like the face hidden in the picture puzzles in those children's magazines he read when he was a kid.

Dennis suspected that the right thing would be to take
Renee's advice—to tell everything to their parents, the

police, the whole fucking town. It was probably the most sensible, mature thing to do. But what Renee didn't understand was how much that decision would cost him. Even Jason couldn't understand. Jason was allowed to make a mistake; he would recover, even if it took years. But this would be the end for Dennis. Something like this happens to a black kid, and that's it. Suddenly you're the poster boy for black dysfunction, no matter how many honor rolls you've made or club presidencies you've won. It was unfair—monumentally unfair, *cosmically* unfair—but this wasn't news to anybody, especially not to Dennis. The two of them *had* been stupid, but Dennis had been stupider than Jason, because Dennis had had all of this pounded into his head from early childhood. You've got to be better, his mother had always told him. You've got to be perfect even to hope for success.

Dennis got off the bicycle and went over to the mats to stretch out. He sank into a hurdler's straddle and bent forward, grabbing his sneaker and trying to bring his nose as close as he could to his kneecap. He felt the familiar burn in the tendons behind his knees. After thirty seconds he switched legs. Off to his left, doing reps on the chest machine, was Daryl Fox, a senior who played halfback for the RFK varsity football team. Daryl nodded at him warily, and Dennis nodded back. That was about the extent of the communication Dennis had with most of his African American classmates at RFK—this tiny sign of mutual recognition. Dennis knew that he wasn't popular with people like Daryl, the ones who sat at the all-black tables in the cafeteria. To them, Dennis was an Afro-Saxon, a brother hanging with the white kids, playing at being white. What would these people say, he wondered, when they found out? *If* they found out. According to rumor, Daryl had had a few scrapes with the law over

the years—a couple of disorderly conducts and a DWI—
and now he was having trouble getting into any college
at all, even UDC. Would he and his friends gloat over
Dennis's crash and burn? Or would they suddenly respect
him?

Dennis finished his warm-up and got to his feet. The
leg machines—where he usually started his cycle—were
occupied, so he want over to the biceps machine, reset
the pin in the weights, climbed into the seat, and started
pulling. As he finished his third repetition, a sudden wave
of anxiety washed through him as he remembered the
green Explorer on the street near school. Could he actually be in physical danger? he wondered. Fuck his future, could he actually be putting his *life* in jeopardy by
reporting what happened?

Feeling shaky and unsteady now, he finished a single
set and climbed out of the biceps machine, allowing
someone else to have a turn. The man who was waiting
smelled of sweat and tobacco in a combination that
seemed oddly familiar, but Dennis, preoccupied with his
thoughts, just wiped down the seat with his towel and
moved aside.

"Head in the clouds again, eh, Monroe?" the man said.
Dennis finally looked at him and recognized Harvey
Deutsch, his teacher for American History 3.

"Sorry," Dennis said. "You know me: focus and concentration."

"Yeah, well let's hope you devote some of that concentration to your New Deal paper." Deutsch paused to
wipe his forehead with the damp towel that hung around
his neck. "I'd hate to have to give you a B for the last
marking period of your junior year. Colleges pay close
attention to spring grades, you know."

"Oh, I know that, Mr. D," Dennis said, thinking, Sanc-
timonious asshole. He produced something like a smile

and moved off toward the double-chest machine. He wiped the seat and then settled himself into it. Breathing deeply, he put his wrists up against the vinyl pads and started pumping. The resistance felt good, and he imagined the endorphins flooding his pectoral muscles. At the eighth repetition, just as it was becoming hard to complete the full movement of his arms, he thought of something Jason had said that afternoon. If the cop really did die from being smashed into a car fender, he and Jason would be guilty of something serious—unintentional manslaughter, whatever. They should see a criminal lawyer before going to the police. Maybe Renee would know of one.

Dennis stopped after the tenth repetition and slowly lowered the weights. It occurred to him that he should probably see a lawyer on his own, *without* Jason, since their interests might not coincide here. Would Jason interpret that as a betrayal, he wondered. Would it *be* a betrayal?

Dennis quickly finished the rest of his Nautilus cycle, doing just a single set on each machine.

He got home shortly before ten. He put the Audi in the garage and then climbed the steps to the main floor of the house. His parents were in the family room, watching television. "That you, Dennis?" his mother called out.

"Yeah."

"Jason called earlier. He wants you to call back."

"Okay, thanks."

Dennis went upstairs to his room. He turned on the computer and threw his gym bag into the closet. As the computer booted up, he undressed and got into the sweatpants he slept in. Then he sat down at his desk and went on-line to get his E-mail. There was nothing—a relief. He signed off, and then, remembering what Deutsch had said at the gym, got up to find his history textbook. But when he saw the portable television on his bureau, he decided to have a quick look at the news. Jason may want to hide from this, he said to himself, but somebody has to know what's going on.

What he saw on the screen stopped him midstep. "More reaction to Sunday night's shooting of a D.C. narcotics detective in Northeast," the voice-over began.

Dennis squinted at the picture being shown on the screen. "Oh Jesus," he said, when the significance of this picture sank in.

Feeling overwhelmed, and starting to panic for the first time, Dennis went out into the hallway. He ran into his parents' room, picked up the phone, and started punching numbers. After three rings, Jason's father answered.

"Can I speak to Jason, please."

"Dennis? He's in bed already. And asleep too, I think."

"Can you get him up? It's important."

"What's so important?"

Dennis paused. He knew he shouldn't make Jason's father suspicious. "It's not so important, I guess. I'll just tell him tomorrow."

Dennis hung up and ran across the hall to his room again. He closed the door behind him and looked around for a few seconds, uncertain what to do. His eye fell on the computer. He sat down in front of it and opened his E-mail program. He addressed a message to Jason and then started typing: "this is crazy jason. it's not what we thought. we have to report this now."

EIGHT

FRANK LAROUX ARRIVED ten minutes late for lunch. Renee, who was sitting at a corner table near the kitchen, lifted her arm when he walked into the Indonesian restaurant, but he seemed to know exactly where she was even before he came through the door. He raised his eyebrows in mock surprise and started across the crowded dining room toward her, loping in that familiar, loose-jointed way that even now made something in Renee's chest clamp tight. Despite the standard well-cut dark suit, she could see that Frank had put on a little weight since the last time they'd seen each other—years ago, when Renee was still reporting for the *Sun*—but a few extra pounds didn't make much difference on a six-foot-five black man with shoulders you could build a bridge on.

Renee stubbed out her cigarette and stood as he got to the table.

"Still killing yourself with those things?" Frank said as they embraced. Renee recognized the herby smell of his cologne.

"And what's this?" she asked, slipping her hands under

his suit jacket and squeezing the flesh around his waist.
"You're developing a gut in your old age."

"Beautiful women keep inviting me to lunch. What can
I do?"

"Always the come-on line. You haven't changed a
bit."

"No," he said simply. "I haven't."

They sat down. Frank unfolded his napkin and quickly
surveyed the dining room. Renee saw him nod at someone at another table. The restaurant—on Vesey Street,
not far from the FBI Washington field office—was something of a local Bureau hangout. Renee wished she had
chosen somewhere else to meet.

"You're lucky you got me," Frank went on. "I'm heading to Idaho tonight on some Bureau business." He put
his enormous hands flat on the closed menu in front of
him, as if he were about to press the table down through
the floor. Renee couldn't help noticing the groove in the
skin of his left ring finger. "So, how have you been?"
Frank asked.

"Surviving," she said. She grabbed another cigarette
from the pack on the table. "Mind?"

Frank shrugged. "I always did, and still do, but that
doesn't make any difference to you, does it?"

"No," she said, lighting the cigarette. She took a deep
pull and then, nodding toward his left hand, added,
"You've been married."

Frank let out a bark of laughter. "You amaze me,
Holmes," he said in a bad British accent. He shook his
head and then lifted his hand in front of her. "Married
and divorced in the space of three years."

"I'm sorry," Renee said.

"Not any sorrier than me. Joellen. She's a fine woman,
but she didn't like my line of work. The hours mostly.
I'm on the job *tutti i giorni*."

"Uh, what?"

"It's Italian. *Tutti i giorni*—I'm on the job every day."

"You're learning Italian now?"

"Hey, I've grown since you knew me. I'm into self-improvement now."

"Well, as I recall, there was plenty of room for self-improvement." She tapped a lozenge of ash into the ashtray. "Any kids?"

"A girl. Tricia. She's two now, and the apple of my eye, though I never really know what the hell that's supposed to mean. They live out in Fairfax, so I get to see them whenever I want." He took a sip of ice water. "What about you? No ring, I see."

The waiter arrived to take their order. "Number three lunch special?" he asked Frank. "You got it," Frank said, then looked over at Renee. She'd been too nervous even to open the menu during her wait.

"I'll take the same," she said.

The waiter nodded and disappeared into the kitchen.

"So?" Frank asked again, after an awkward moment of silence. He wiggled his own ringless ring finger at her.

Renee took another drag of her cigarette before saying, "No, no ring. I'm married to my work."

"And how's the sex in that marriage?"

Renee decided to ignore the comment. Eons ago, back when she was a police reporter and Frank was one of her sources on federal drug cases, the two of them had had a brief and—to Renee, at least—very satisfying affair. It had lasted until one of Frank's superiors found out about it and told him that sleeping with a newspaper reporter would not endear him to the FBI brass. So he'd ended it. And Renee had never really forgiven him for it—or at least for the apparent ease with which he'd made the decision. Now Frank was higher up in the FBI chain of command, presumably having refrained from affairs with any other newspaper reporters in the intervening years. Renee wasn't sure exactly what he did these days, and on the phone last evening he hadn't offered to tell her.

"I see your byline in the *City Paper* every once in a while," he said. "That was a nice piece you did on that woman in Prince Georges, the one who grows her own medicinal herbs?"

"Yeah, that's the kind of hard-hitting journalism I do these days: 'The Shaman of Shepherd Avenue.'" She sent a punitive stream of cigarette smoke in Frank's direction. "I consider myself a teacher now. The reporting is a hobby. Just to keep my hand in."

"I see," Frank said. He stared at her for a few seconds, then leaned back and crossed his arms. "Look," he said, "I'd like to think that you were getting in touch again— after, what is it, eight, ten years?—just because you missed my big black ass, but I know you better than that, Renee. You're playing hooky from school for this. So what's up?"

Frank's abruptness had been one of his least appealing features. "I've got a couple of questions," Renee said. Then added, "Hypothetical questions."

Frank's eyebrows rose. He had a broad, square-chinned, smooth-cheeked face—more pleasant than conventionally handsome. "Are there any other kind?" he asked.

Renee glanced at the people sitting at the next table before asking, "You still keep up with your Metro Narcotics contacts?" In the old days, Frank had collaborated frequently with the D.C. force on drug cases. Renee had always heard that Frank was one of the few FBI special agents the local cops could stand, mainly because of his sensitivity to jurisdictional niceties. Back then, the FBI had a habit of taking over an investigation once they were called in, pushing out the local authorities who had developed the case and then taking credit for any and all positive results. But Frank had a reputation as somebody who at least *seemed* to defer to the owners of the original case, all the while convincing them that his own bright ideas about the investigation were actually their own.

"I don't work with them directly anymore," Frank said after a second or two. "But I have people under me who do. Why?"

"Everybody clean over there these days?"

"In Metro Narcotics?"

"Yes."

Frank let out a deep belly laugh—so loud that several people in the dining room turned and looked at them. "You always did make my day a little brighter," he said. He shook his head and then added, "Sweetcake, you've been living out in upper Northwest for too long. You're losing your grip."

"I take it that means no."

"You can take it any way you like. Just don't take it to the newspapers."

She put out her cigarette and reached for another. "Okay, let me ask you this. Let's say you were a cop of less than impeccable integrity—this shouldn't be too much of a stretch for you, Frank—and you decided, say, that you needed a little extra money. For whatever reason. Maybe you don't want to pay alimony anymore or something." Frank winced, and Renee instantly regretted the clumsy attempt at a joke.

She decided to plow onward. "You're a narcotics cop, let's say. So you start doing a little moonlighting out on the street. A little drugs here, a little contraband there. Maybe you even start using the department's sting money for your own purposes—"

"Where did you get this?" Frank asked quickly, interrupting her. His flirtatious grin had lost altitude steadily during her last few sentences. Renee could see that he knew exactly whom she was talking about. "How sure of this are you?"

"Hold on, Frank. This is a story I'm telling you. Let me finish, okay?" She took a quick pull on her cigarette. "So you're on the street freelancing. Probably sticking most of your profits up your nose, too. And you get involved in a deal that goes bad. Two kids from a nice neighborhood, trying to buy some pot. There's a misunderstanding, your gun comes out, there's a skirmish, and you end up dead. But it's an accident. There's no intent on the kids' part to hurt anybody. They just panicked."

"Bull*shit*," Frank hissed, leaning forward toward her. "That guy had gunshot wounds to the face and chest. Not to mention second- and third-degree burns. That doesn't sound like any accident to me. Somebody's been telling *you* stories."

"*Listen* to me, Frank," Renee said. She ground out her cigarette and then explained the story to him, just as Dennis and Jason had explained it to her.

"Wait a minute," Frank said when she had finished. He picked up his napkin and wiped his broad forehead with it. "They claim that only one shot was fired? And that one into the floor of the car?"

"Right. When they left, he was unconscious from the collision with the parked car, with his pistol next to him in the street."

"And then somebody came along and finished up for them, is that it?"

"Well," Renee said, not sure she liked his tone. "Yes."

Frank shook his head. "I don't believe it. Do *you* believe it?"

"Yes, I do, Frank. I know these kids. Certainly well enough to know if they're making up a far-fetched lie."

Renee lowered her voice again. "Look, they're good kids, and they don't need their lives ruined by making a mistake like this. Let's just assume that what they say is true. If they go to the police with this, what can they expect?"

"*If* they go to the police?"

"All right. *When* they go."

"And these are juveniles?"

"They're both seventeen years old."

Frank pulled his chair closer to the table. "Well, people tend to like simple stories, Renee. Judges and police as much as anybody else. A drug deal goes bad, and these kids get a little out of hand—they shoot the guy during a struggle and they panic. They torch the guy to try to cover themselves. That's a lot easier to accept than this other story, with unknown bad guys coming along afterwards."

"But it's not the truth, Frank. The truth is what they told me."

Frank looked up at the ceiling for a long time before going on. "Assuming their story can be proved, they'd still be in a lot of trouble. For one thing, they don't know for a fact that they didn't kill the guy themselves."

"Wouldn't the ME be able to make that determination?"

Frank rolled his eyes theatrically. "You don't read the papers, do you. Haven't you heard about our Medical Examiners Office lately? True story: They had a headless torso and it wasn't declared a homicide for months because the ME couldn't determine a cause of death. They lose so much evidence that people are afraid to send them corpses nowadays—it's like throwing something into a black hole. Never mind that half the staff don't have their licenses. So I wouldn't rely on the ME making a fine distinction in determining cause of death here."

"But I assume the ME can at least find traces of co-

caine or PCP in somebody's blood, and if Harcourt was
on something that night, it would support their claim. He
pulled a gun on them, Frank. They were acting in self-
defense."

"The car might be exculpatory," Frank said then. "Assuming it does have evidence of a slug in the floor, it
could lend weight to their version of the story. Then, if
the rumors about Harcourt turn out to be true . . ."

The waiter arrived with their food. Renee was relieved
to have a few moments to collect herself. She'd already
been more specific with Frank than she had intended. She
remembered the promise she'd made to Dennis.

When the waiter was gone, Frank leaned forward again
and said, "But look, all of this is pissing in the wind right
now. Homicide is focusing on this one. It's a cop killing.
And if your two kids—boys, is it? In one of your classes?"

"Nice try, Frank," Renee answered, frowning. "Let's
just call them 'my two kids' for now."

Frank shrugged. "Not that I couldn't find out who they
were if I had to," he said. "And anyway, if they're connected to this thing, the police will catch up to them
eventually. Metro Homicide isn't much better than the
ME office, but they can still investigate a case compe-
tently, at least if the victim is somebody important to
them. So it's a matter of your kids' turning themselves
in or waiting until they're found out."

"But what kind of charge would they be facing?"

"That may be determined by how they act now. If they
turn themselves in, the prosecutor is bound to treat them
more leniently."

"I understand," Renee said. "It's what I told them myself. But you've got to understand their hesitation here.
They've got a lot to lose."

"They might've thought of that before they cruised

over to Northeast that night." Frank looked down and began spearing some broccoli with his fork.

"There's another thing, Frank," Renee went on after a slight pause. "I'm not sure how much it means, but it's possible that whoever did this is aware that my two friends are potential witnesses." She told him about the green Explorer Dennis had seen near school the day before.

"Shee-it," Frank said softly when she had finished.

"I suppose it could be coincidence. There are lots of green Explorers in this town."

"Especially up in your neighborhood, honey," he said. He put his fork down. "Coincidence or no coincidence, this is something you don't fool around with. You've got to bring the police into this. Or maybe I can talk to your two kids myself, if you think it would do any good. Unofficially."

Renee considered this. "They won't like the sound of that," she said finally. "But let me try to convince them. I'll see them today, after school. I promised them I wouldn't take any new steps without consulting them."

"If you say so," Frank said. "But I want to know exactly what happens here, Renee. You can't stuff this cat back in the bag now that it's half out." He handed her a card. "That's my pager number, cell phone, everything. I'll be back from Idaho tomorrow afternoon. Incommunicado until then, but we'll talk when I get back. And what I want to hear from you is that you convinced these kids to at least talk to the police. I mean it."

"Okay, okay."

They both started eating again. The number three special had turned out to be a spicy vegetable dish, full of broccoli, asparagus, and snow peas. Not what you'd expect a big man like Frank to eat. "So what's with all the vegetables, anyway?" she asked. "Have you turned vegetarian on me?"

"So what if I have," Frank said.

"Really?"

"It's how I keep myself young. God knows how you do it, though. I've gotta say, you're still looking pretty good these days. For an older white woman."

Renee decided to ignore the barb and accept the compliment. "Feeling some regrets, are we?"

He laughed, shaking his head. "Maybe. I've got plenty to regret these days." They ate in silence for a few seconds, but Renee could tell that he was looking at her. "You might even say that Regret is my middle name. Fortunately, though, some mistakes can be rectified."

"Don't even try it, Frank," Renee answered, feeling flustered as she knocked a stray piece of asparagus off her plate.

NINE

JASON GOT UP early on Wednesday morning, feeling restless and sleep-deprived. He wrote a short note to his father and then left the house a little before seven. Deciding to skip his first few classes of the day, he spent the morning in Rock Creek Park. He took the unpaved path north into Maryland, following the creek as it wound between gray, muddy banks, their dullness relieved every once in a while by yellow splashes of wild forsythia. Eventually he reached a playground, where he sat on a bench and watched a couple of Latino guys playing an intense game of one-on-one. The air smelled of warm mud and wood chips, and for some reason the smell reminded Jason of his mother. He had long ago stopped missing her every minute of every day, but there were still times when he felt an unexpected pang of something halfway between sorrow and terror. And he'd realize that it was some reminder of his mother that had triggered it—a smell, a turn of phrase overheard in school, even the sight of dirt-encrusted gardening tools hanging from a Peg-Board. Once, he'd seen a woman on Connecticut

Avenue adjusting the strap of her bag with exactly his
mother's casual, distracted motion, and Jason had found
himself following the woman for blocks past his turnoff,
watching her with a blank, idiotic yearning.

He got to school at the end of third period. Raucous
bunches of students were streaming out of the metal
doors as Jason climbed the cement steps. Two guys from
his history class—Rob Wright and Jordan Kotik—gave
him funny looks as they passed but didn't say anything
to him. It occurred to Jason that he'd have to provide
some excuse for missing his morning classes. A dentist's
appointment was always a good choice. Though they
might ask for a note from his father confirming it. He'd
have to figure something out.

Jason waited for a lull in the outgoing stream of bodies
and then slipped through the door into the school lobby.
The wide, fluorescent-lit hallways were filled with the
echoing noise of interperiod traffic. Students stood at
their open lockers, retrieving jackets or stuffing books
onto the upper shelves or shouting to friends down the
hall. Old Mrs. Dawson, meanwhile, was droning an-
nouncements on the PA system. No one even pretended
to listen.

Resettling his backpack on his other shoulder, Jason
turned and headed down D corridor toward his own
locker. Another classmate, Eden Dressler of the Large
Breasts, walked past, staring, without saying hello.

Puzzled, Jason walked on and turned another corner.
A little way down the corridor, Ty Vance stood in front
of his open locker, staring inside with his usual resentful
expression. He glanced over and saw Jason. "Hey,
Rourke," he said, looking surprised. "The fuck you doing
here?"

Jason stopped in front of his locker. "I live here,
Vance."

"I thought you and Monroe would be miles away by now."

Jason turned. "Why?"

"Shit, man. Don't you know? There was a big scene here second period. Toricelli called a random locker search. And then he called in the cops. Story is they found something in some lockers, including yours. Monroe's too."

"*My* locker?" Jason said.

"Coke or crack is what I hear, my man."

"What?"

"You been busted, Rourke."

"Did they get Dennis?"

"He wasn't here either. I thought you'd be together." Ty slammed his locker shut. "Maybe they arrested him, I don't know. We had cops around all morning."

Jason grabbed his backpack off the floor and began walking toward the front of the school again.

"This won't do much for Monroe's chances at Harvard," Ty said behind him with a laugh.

Jason walked faster down the emptying corridors. The bell rang for the start of fourth period; late stragglers were finding their classrooms. Jason fought the impulse to run. He turned the corner to the front corridor and instantly saw two uniformed policemen hurrying down the hall straight toward him. Without thinking, Jason veered toward the nearest classroom and caught the door just as it was closing. Inside, students were taking their seats. Some algebra teacher he didn't know looked up at him. "Lost, are we?"

"Wait," Jason said. "I thought Journalism was moved to this room for today."

The teacher shook his head sadly. "You've been misinformed. We're doing quadratic equations in here today.

You're welcome to join us, though, if you need a re-fresher."

"No thanks," Jason answered. He turned and went back out the door. The cops were just rounding the corner into the next corridor, the keys and handcuffs jingling on their belts. Jason waited another second, then stepped out into the now deserted hallway. He walked calmly to the front entrance and pushed through the blue metal doors into bright sunshine. There was an empty Metro Police cruiser parked at the curb in front of the school.

Jason took the stairs two at a time, and when he reached the bottom, he started running. He raced across the school's front lawn, past the marquee sign announc-ing the upcoming chorus production of *Big River*. Just as he reached the sidewalk, a second police cruiser turned onto Gulliver Street and pulled up in front of the school. Jason attached himself to a group of underclassmen head-ing off toward lunch.

"Can I help you?" said a blond girl with the smallest, shiniest nose Jason had ever seen.

"Going for lunch somewhere?" Jason asked nervously.

"Well, *duh*."

Jason looked back over his shoulder. The cops from the second cruiser were already mounting the steps to the school's entrance. One of them—a dumpy white guy—was far behind the other, waddling up the steps in slow motion.

"Have a fabulous time," Jason said. Then he peeled off from the group and darted across the street. He walked calmly for a few minutes until he reached Wis-consin Avenue. The sidewalks here were busy with pe-destrians. After stopping for a few seconds to catch his breath, Jason walked north until he found a pay phone. He shucked off his backpack, then rooted around in his pockets for thirty-five cents. When he found enough change, he pushed the coins into the slot and punched in Dennis's home number. He leaned against the glass hood and felt a drop of perspiration ooze from his hairline and trickle down his left temple.

The phone rang three times before Mr. Monroe answered: "Yes?"

Jason didn't say anything for a few seconds.

"Anybody there?"

"Is Dennis home?" he asked, trying to disguise his voice.

"Who's calling?"

Jason turned, holding the receiver tighter to his ear. He looked up and down the street. "A friend."

"What friend?" Mr. Monroe asked. "Where are you calling from?"

Jason hung up the phone and grabbed his backpack. He waited for a break in traffic and then crossed Wisconsin. After turning off the avenue, he tried to lose himself in the quiet residential streets behind the WUSA radio tower. The early-afternoon sun was surprisingly strong, and a sudden gust of wind ripped at the branches of some sweet gum trees along the road. He heard a dull pattering sound, and when he looked up he saw something bizarre—a swirling explosion of seedpods in the air. One of the spiky balls fell at his feet and nearly made him start running again.

It was already past one by the time Jason reached his block of Dunhaven Street. He turned the corner and was halfway up the hill when it occurred to him that he should probably be careful. If the police, or whoever, knew that Jason was involved in this thing, they might be watching his house, waiting for him to show up. He stopped walking for a second and considered turning around, but realized that it was already too late for that. If anyone was watching, they'd recognize a quick retreat as a sure sign that Jason was Jason. So he started walking again, right past the front of his house. Just as he reached the dead rosebush at the end of his front walk, he heard a car door open and saw a man in a gray raincoat getting out of a BMW parked across the street. He was tall—about six four—with sandy brown hair cut short and a chin as smooth and round as a softball. "Are you Jason Rourke?" he asked as he crossed the street.

Jason didn't even pause. He dropped his backpack on the buckled sidewalk and ran.

He crossed his own yellow lawn and pushed through the overgrown yew in the alley between his house and the Davidsons' next door. Picking up speed, he reached the backyard and ducked quickly under the wooden deck. He came out on the other side and crossed the lawn to the fence at the back of the house. He had no idea if the man was following him, but he didn't want to slow himself down by looking back. So he just vaulted over the low chain-link fence and kept going.

The ground fell sharply into the yard of the house behind them. Jason half skied down the slope, flattening daffodils as he went. He jumped off a stone wall and shot a glance back up the slope. The man in the gray raincoat was just coming over the chain-link fence, so Jason kept running. He rounded the side of the house and came out onto Oregon Avenue. Across the street was Rock Creek Park, but there was no path into the woods at this place. Without stopping to think, Jason crossed the road and launched straight into the tangled underbrush. Branches tore at his ears and hands and the fabric of his jacket, but he managed to thrash his way to the sparser growth beyond. Here, the land fell away from the road for about thirty yards and then climbed to the top of a ridge. Jason almost stopped when he saw the obstacle course of shrubs and fallen trees ahead of him. But then he heard the man swatting through the roadside brush behind him, and so he pushed on, jumping over decayed logs and muddy clots of dead vegetation. A few of the bushes were sprouting pale green leaves, but the park's winter nakedness had barely begun to fill out, and there was little cover for him. He'd simply have to outrun this man. There was no way he could just hide.

He reached the bottom of the rise and started climbing, barely keeping his balance as he picked his way over the leaf-slick ground. Sweat stung his eyes, and every breath he took seemed to release something raw and corrosive in his chest. All around him, extravagant loops of kudzu hung down from the trees like trapper's nooses, and he had to concentrate to avoid them, sometimes spinning one way or the other like a running back to avoid being snared.

He was already slowing down when he reached the top of the ridge. By now, his legs seemed heavy and uncooperative. But the man in the gray raincoat had fallen behind. He was older—in his forties at least—and probably not in good shape. Jason stopped long enough to take three long sucks of air and then continued running.

On the other side of the ridge, the woods gave way to an open stretch of mud and trampled grass. Just beyond it was a fenced corral, with two horses standing dead center near a metal tub. Jason knew that there were stables nearby. His father had brought him here once, a long time ago, to take a trail ride through the park. He ran up to the corral and slipped through the decrepit board fence. For a few hopeful seconds he wondered if he could mount one of the horses and ride away bareback, laughing back at his enemy like some half-assed television hero. With this in mind, he sprinted toward the two horses. But as he got near, they took off, each one trotting to a different corner of the corral. Jason could only continue to the other side of the enclosure, slip through the fence, and keep running.

He came to a graveled parking lot, where there was an empty Park Police cruiser, an old abandoned taxi, and a couple of pickups, but no sign of human beings. At one end was a huge pile of logs and some dilapidated vegetable plots surrounded by chicken wire. A paved path led to another stretch of woods. Jason saw the trail sign he was looking for—a mounted rider against a mud-brown background. It was the path to the stables.

He reached the shabby, white-painted buildings in another minute or two. He thought he had made it then, that he'd reached some kind of safety, but there seemed to be no one here either. Where the fuck *was* everyone? he asked himself. There was one vehicle parked beside the building—a black, rusted-out pickup with a U-Haul trailer filled with hay bales—but its driver was nowhere in sight. Most of the horse stalls were closed up, but a couple had the top half of their doors ajar. As Jason approached, two huge heads poked out over the doors of two adjacent stalls. The horses stared at him curiously.

Jason ran to the pickup, but there were no keys in the ignition. He turned then and strained to hear any sounds from behind him. It was hard to distinguish anything over the hum of the wind in the trees, but he thought he could hear running footsteps. Panicking, he ran to one of the open stalls. The horse backed away as he unlatched the door and swung it open. "Easy," he whispered, stepping into the stall. The smell of grain and horse manure was dense, nearly overpowering. He pulled the door shut behind him and latched it. The horse—a huge yellow mare dappled with brown spots—moved uneasily to one end of the small space.

Jason stepped into a corner of the stall—the part that

would be hidden from anyone who just took a quick look in. His sneaker sank into something warm and soft. Flies rose from the floor and buzzed noisily around his head. He felt himself gag. The horse was jittery now, muttering in a low-toned, ominous way and half shying, her front hooves rising and falling nervously.

Jason sank to a crouch in the shadowy corner. Then he sat, pulling his knees to his chest. He tried to catch his breath and listen as the horse settled down. She was eyeing him now—an enormous, hot, breathing presence above him, her smooth, glossy flanks twitching constantly.

After a few more seconds, Jason heard footsteps outside and the sound of heavy breathing. The footsteps came toward the stalls, but then stopped or moved away. Straining to hear, Jason felt a drop of sweat fall from his hairline and patter onto the hay beneath him. The flies were everywhere now, trying to land on his moist face and ears.

Jason heard some banging off to the other side of the stables. He glanced up toward the opening in the top of the stall door. Dust motes were spiraling in the creamy sunlight. It was almost hypnotizing to watch.

Another bang—this one so close that Jason nearly sprang up from his crouch to run. The horse in the stall next door was suddenly stomping and whinnying, the sound muffled by the board wall between the two stalls. That set the yellow mare off again. Jason watched her nervously, unsure if he should be more scared of the horse or the man outside. He looked up at the opening, just in time to see a shadow cross the yellow column of sun. A hand came over the top of the stall door and reached blindly for the inside latch. Jason watched the hand move, hoping that somehow it wouldn't find the metal latch and give up. But, eventually, the blunt fingers

found it and slowly unhooked it. As the stall door opened
the mare reared back silently.

The man in the gray raincoat stepped into the stall and
looked straight at him.

Jason launched himself at the man, hitting him hard in
the ribs with his left shoulder. The body was solid but it
gave, like a stuffed sandbag, and both of them fell to the
floor of the stall, the mare rearing again and whinnying
loudly. Jason rolled away and scrambled to his feet. He
looked over at the man just in time to see one of the
mare's hooves come down heavily on the man's exposed
Adam's apple. The windpipe crumpled like a thin alu-
minum can. The mare, whites showing furious around her
eyes, was stamping and stumbling, trying to get away,
her hooves pounding the man's head and body with awful thuds. Then she bolted through the unlatched door
and galloped away.

Jason looked down in disbelief at the man on the floor
of the stall. He was staring straight up at the rafters with
glassy, shocked-looking eyes. As Jason watched, a blue-
bottle landed on the man's lips and wandered into his
open mouth. Jason turned away. He was confused by
how he felt now—horrified, yes, but also powerful, almost elated. He had killed two men. No one could stop
him.

He turned back to the man in the gray raincoat. What
should he do now? Call an ambulance? The police? But
he was running from the police.

Finally, he knelt and rolled the body onto its side. He
wanted to know who this man was—why he was chasing
him—and he suspected that the man must have some ID
and other useful information in his wallet. "Fuck it," Jason said aloud. He was in this thing way over his head
already. What difference could it make if he took the

wallet? He'd just leave all the cash behind so nobody would think he was trying to rob the guy.

Jason reached into the man's back pocket for the wallet. He took out two hundreds and a bunch of smaller bills and laid them carefully beside the body.

Feeling dizzy now, he got up and pushed through the stall door. Bright sun was all around him. The trees reeled overhead. He pushed the thick wallet into his pocket and then started to run toward the woods.

TEN

RENEE WAS POURING her second scotch when she saw the stark white face at the window in her back door. After nearly dropping her glass, she recognized the face as Jason's—or an exaggerated caricature of Jason's, with larger eyes and thicker, redder lips. His dark, sweaty hair was pushed up on one side, as if he'd slept on it all night, and his leather jacket was streaked with yellow mud. He had the palms of both hands flat against the glass like someone being held up by a mugger.

She walked over and unlocked the back door. Jason strode in past her, nearly pushing her into the wall. "Jason? Did something happen? What's wrong?"

Without saying a word, he stalked into the living room, deeper into the house. She followed, letting him lead her first into the living room, then down the hall to her bedroom. He sat down on the edge of her bed, leaned over, and put his face in his hands. She could see his chest heaving, as if he'd run a long way.

"Hey, you're scaring me, Jason. Is something wrong?"

He nodded, hands still over his face.

Renee came over and crouched in front of him. "What is it?" She pulled his fingers away from his face. They were as stiff and hard as coin rolls.

"They must know about us," he said, looking down at his sneakers. "They know everything. There was somebody waiting outside my house. He chased me. And now Dennis is gone. The police were after both of us."

"Slow down, Jason." She grabbed his chin roughly and forced him to look at her. "Who was waiting outside your house? What are you talking about?"

Jason wiped his nose with his sleeve and pulled something out of his jacket pocket. He handed her a wallet. "He was."

Confused, Renee opened the wallet. There were no bills inside, but there were all kinds of business cards, credit cards, and other identification. Renee found a D.C. driver's license, with a picture of a light-haired man, about forty, with rheumy blue eyes and a prominent chin. The license was issued to a Vincent Osborne, with an address in Foggy Bottom, near George Washington University. "How did you find this?"

Jason got up from the edge of the bed. "He ran after me. We went into the park and then a horse trampled him. I made it happen. He was unconscious or dead or something."

"A horse *trampled* him?" For a moment, Renee wondered if the boy was sick, hallucinating with fever. "An actual horse?"

"I was hiding in the stables in Rock Creek," he said impatiently, as if explaining something to a dense small child. "He came in after me."

Renee nodded, still unsure how seriously to take this information. "But what's this about police? And where's Dennis?"

It took her a good fifteen minutes to get the full story

out of Jason. As he spoke she looked through the rest of the wallet's contents. No pictures, no handwritten lists of telephone numbers, but a security pass for the D.C. Department of Social Services Building down on E Street.

"Stay there," she said to Jason. She left the bedroom and went to the telephone in the living room. Fenton, sensing tension in the house, was moving nervously along his perch, making faint throaty noises. Renee picked up the phone and was about to call Frank Laroux when she remembered what he had said at lunch earlier that day—that he was going out of town and wouldn't be reachable until tomorrow afternoon. "Perfect," she muttered, hanging up the phone.

There were two messages on her own machine that she hadn't listened to. She pressed the play button and waited for the tape to rewind. Fenton was eyeing her suspiciously. "Haw-haw-haw," he ventured.

The first message was from her dry cleaner: "Ms. Daniels, we have two blouses and a skirt here that have been ready for two weeks—" She fast-forwarded to the next message. It was from Julie Kovac, a math teacher at RFK she was friendly with. "Renee, this is Julie. Where were you today? Something happened at school that you should know about. Call me."

I know about it now, Renee said to herself. She pressed the erase button and went back to the bedroom. Jason was standing now, staring into the full-length mirror next to her bed. He had her newspaper in his hand. "Jason, listen to me," she began.

He turned and held the newspaper out to her. "It isn't him," he said.

Unclear pronoun, her mind droned automatically. "Who isn't who?"

Jason shook the newspaper. On the front was a picture of Ramon Harcourt. It had taken the police department until that morning to release the picture, but now it was all over the media. "This isn't the guy."

"What do you mean, Jason?" she said impatiently. "That's the guy—says it right there: Ramon Harcourt."

"This isn't the guy we saw on Sunday night."

Jason seemed to be turning more bizarre every minute. Renee wondered if he could be having some kind of breakdown. "Jason, listen to me—"

"This *looks* like the guy we saw, but it's not him." He shook his head in confusion, but then, after a few seconds, he seemed to come to some kind of realization. "Oh shit. I *knew* our guy wasn't a cop. I said that right from the beginning."

"Wait, you're saying it's a coincidence? Two guys who look like each other just happen to meet with violent attacks on the same street corner on the same night?"

"No, Renee. God, can't you see? The cop never died. It was the drug dealer, the guy we saw, who died. In his place."

It took a few seconds for the meaning of this to register in Renee's mind. "No," she said. "They do autopsies, Jason. They don't get things like that wrong." But even as she said this, a shadow of plausibility passed over her mind. Would it be so difficult to arrange an identity switch? The body was badly burned—second- and third-degree burns over the arms, chest, and head. If a cop—a bad cop—wanted to disappear, and had connections in the ME's office? Or in the police records division? But who, then, was this Vincent Osborne who had chased Jason through the park?

"They must know about us now," Jason said. "They must know we know."

Renee sat down on the edge of the bed. If it really was some drug dealer in the morgue, then Harcourt was still out there somewhere, with the money that was supposed to be used in the sting operation. "The man you saw in the green Explorer that night," she said to Jason. "Could you identify him? If you saw him again?"

Jason shrugged. "Probably."

"And it wasn't this Vincent Osborne?"

Jason shook his head. "No, somebody older. And Osborne had, like, this Jay Leno chin."

It was clear to her now that Jason and Dennis were both in real danger. She silently cursed Frank for being away. Should she take Jason to the police? But it was cops he was running from—cops who presumably were behind whatever was going on here. No, she had to take him out of town somewhere, out of danger, to someone she could trust. And there was only one person she could even dream of asking. "Jason," she said, getting up from the bed. "I think we should get you away from here for a few days. Or at least until tomorrow. I know a place where nobody would ever think of looking for you."

"I can't go back home for anything. They'll be waiting for me."

"You don't have to go home. We'll figure something out. We'll call your father."

"No," Jason said. "You don't know my father. He'll want to take over everything. He'll probably get me killed."

"You can call and just tell him you're all right. But you have to call, Jason."

"Now?"

Renee thought about this before saying, "We'll call from the road. I'm probably being too cautious, but I don't want there to be any call from my number to yours. It's important that nobody know I'm involved in this. The last thing I want is someone tracing you through me." Renee took the newspaper and looked again at Harcourt's picture. Her reporter instincts about this cop had been right after all. "We should go now," she said. "We've got a drive ahead of us."

"Where are we going?"

Renee grabbed her coat from a chair. "To Mom's house," she said.

They drove for a couple of hours—east out of D.C., past Annapolis, and over a couple of bridges to the Eastern Shore of the Chesapeake Bay. Jason was quiet most of the way, trying to empty his mind of what he had been through that afternoon in Rock Creek Park. Renee, apparently sensing his effort, didn't try to make him talk. After upsetting him even more than he already was by telling him about her meeting with the FBI agent, she just pushed a cassette of some classical music into the player and drove.

Somewhere north of Easton, they stopped at a gas station and Jason made his call. Wanting to avoid speaking to his father directly, he conveniently forgot about his father's cell phone and instead called home. As he'd hoped, the machine picked up after three rings. He wondered if his father was out looking for him, driving around in his car, peering at teenagers on every street corner in Northwest D.C. At the beep, he left a short message: "Dad, it's Jason. Don't worry about me. I'm safe. Dennis and I are involved in something—as you know by now, I guess—but it's not what they'll tell you. I'll explain it all. Just don't worry. And don't come looking for me. You'll just screw things up if you do."

It was well after dark when they arrived at their destination—a clapboard town house in some brand-new condo complex. Renee turned off the engine. "We're here," she said.

"You're sure she won't mind?"

"My mother? She'll love your company. The question is, will you mind *hers*?"

They both got out of the car. Jason stopped and looked around. There was something fake and too perfect about the whole complex, with its ridiculously neat flower beds and newly tarred driveways. It was like a small-town neighborhood in Disneyland. Each of the town houses was a different pastel color, but they all had the same immaculate shutters and dormers and clean, undented mailboxes. Renee's mother's house was the pale green one in the group.

"It will only be for a day or so," Renee said. "Until my FBI friend comes back."

Jason followed her up the walk to the porch, her heels tapping on the clean, white-painted steps. She knocked on the screen door. "Mother?" she called into the darkness. As they waited for an answer, Jason looked back toward the street. There were daffodils lining the brick walk, looking washed-out and tangled in the dim yellow porch light. Two ceramic pots of hyacinths stood on the bottom step, their sweet stink thickening the night air. From far off, he heard the slap of a line against a mast and a faint lapping of waves. Water was nearby, but he couldn't tell in which direction.

"Mother?" Renee said again, pulling open the unlocked screen door. Jason climbed the stairs and followed her into the house. It was totally dark and smelled of paint and smoke and lemons.

"In here," someone called from deeper inside the house.

Renee flicked a wall switch and filled the entrance hallway with light. "We're here."

"I was waiting."

Jason followed Renee along the empty hall. They walked into a larger uncarpeted room at the end of it, where Renee turned on another light. The first thing Jason saw was a line of windows on the opposite side of the room, reflecting the light back at them like the mirrored walls of a dance studio. It was a long, high-ceilinged space, a wooden dining table and chairs to the left and a living room with a rattan sofa and chairs to the right. There were tables with empty vases on them, standing lamps with green glass shades, potted ficus trees and yuccas, and piles of books, magazines, and cassette tapes all over. In one corner was a baby grand piano, and behind it a Japanese folding screen with a big rip down the central panel, splitting a stylized peacock in two.

"I was expecting you later. You drove too fast."

It was only then that Jason saw the gaunt old woman sitting in the corner. She was wearing a worn nightgown under a puffy down vest, her long, gray-streaked hair down loose around her shoulders. She had a sharp, angular face, deeply lined, and pale blue eyes that seemed to belong to a much younger woman.

"I drove the way I usually drive, Mother," Renee said as she crossed the room. She leaned over and kissed her mother's cheek.

"Too fast," the woman repeated.

"The only way I know how." Renee beckoned Jason closer. "Mother, this is the boy I was telling you about. Jason Rourke."

Jason walked across the room toward the two women. His footsteps echoed weirdly on the glossy floorboards, as if he were walking through an empty house that was for sale. "Hi," he said awkwardly. He wondered if he should shake the old woman's hand.

"This is my mother, Mrs. Daniels."

"Oh, don't confuse the boy, Renee. My name is Maxie to everyone and I won't hear of being addressed any other way." Renee was fixing the collar of her mother's nightgown but Maxie pushed her hands away impatiently. "Enough," she said. Then, turning toward Jason, she added, "Jason Rourke. That's an Irish name, isn't it? Are you Irish?"

"Well, yes," Jason said.

"Good. I like Irish boys. I even married one once." She got up shakily from the chair. "I'll bet you're sentimental and talkative and charming as can be on top of it. So was he, my first husband, Roddy Dexter—doesn't sound too Irish, does it, but he was, every hair and bone of him. Drank like a typical Irishman too. Always well into his cups by lunchtime."

"Mother, Jason just got here," Renee said, grabbing the old woman's elbow to help her across the living room. "You'll have plenty of time to offend him later."

"Offend? Who's trying to offend? Do I offend you, Jason?"

Renee gave him a little apologetic shrug.

"No, ma'am," he said. "You don't offend me."

"Well, there, Renee, see? Don't be so sensitive." She reached out in Jason's direction. "Come here, Jason, and let old Maxie have a look at you."

Jason obeyed. He stood there awkwardly while the old woman examined him the way she might have examined a piece of furniture in dubious taste.

"We'll get along just fine, I think." She grabbed his forearms and squeezed them so hard that Jason could feel the impressions of her rings in his flesh. She looked up toward the ceiling. "Renee, find an old woman her cigarettes, will you? I left them somewhere, and Hortense always forgets accidentally-on-purpose to put them where I can find them before she goes down for the night."

Maxie held on to Jason as Renee went to get her mother's cigarettes. The old woman pulled Jason closer and muttered to him, "You'll be safe here, Jason. I'll look after you."

She let him go and started moving slowly across the room. Jason wondered if he should follow her, assist her somehow. But she didn't seem to need any help as she cruised through the furniture. "I've got some cookies and tea set out. Come. Renee, is Jason old enough to have vodka in his tea?"

"No," Renee said ominously from across the room.

"Oh, loosen up. It's a tense time for everyone." She reached the dining room table, which was set with three little plates. "Sit there," she commanded, and Jason complied instantly. "As if the boy—what are you, seventeen?—as if a seventeen-year-old Irish boy hasn't had a drink in his life. . . ." Muttering, she shuffled into the dark kitchen, which opened off the dining area of the big windowed room.

Renee came back with the cigarettes and tossed them onto the table. "Are you smoking those little cigars again, Mother?" she asked.

"There's something wrong with little cigars?" she shouted from the kitchen. "I don't inhale them. And besides, they're half the price of regular cigarettes." She emerged with a loaded tray. "Those annoying Democrats don't tax cigars as they do cigarettes."

"Here we go," Renee said.

"Well, it's true. You're not a Democrat, are you, Jason? Oh, you probably are. Roddy was too." The tray landed hard on the tabletop, sending a couple of spoons clattering off their saucers. "You'll love Maryland then. It's a hotbed of old-style liberalism. They won't even let you into Annapolis these days unless you're wearing a Mao suit." She started handing out teacups. Jason took one, and grabbed one of the spoons that had fallen. "You know," Maxie went on, "we have two gay men living in

the Lyle place down the block, and I'm happy to say
they're as Republican as the day is long. Like two little
swishy Alf Landons—"

"Can we talk about something else, please?"

"Fine." Maxie sat down and took a satisfied sip of tea.
"Help yourself to the cookies," she said after a moment.
"Hortense baked them just a few hours ago."

Jason took two cookies from the platter on the tray.
He ate one, then sipped his tea. It was laced with vodka.

"So, did you tell Hortense what I said to tell her?"
Renee asked, after taking a sip of her own tea.

"About Jason? Of course. Jason, my boy, you're the
grandson of my old friend Hallie from California and
you're visiting the East Coast to discover what civiliza-
tion is like—"

"To check out East Coast colleges," Renee corrected
her.

"It amounts to the same thing." Maxie reached for a
cookie. "Not that it makes any difference to Hortense.
We could tell her you're a Romanian fugitive on the run
from Interpol and it wouldn't make the slightest difference to her."

"Still," Renee said. "I don't want her telling tales in
the supermarket."

"Oh, nobody listens to Hortense anyway." Maxie
groped for her little cigars, removed one from the pack,
and lit it with a black lighter in a hungry, desperate way
that reminded Jason of Renee. "So, will you be spending
the night?" she asked her daughter.

"I shouldn't." Renee turned to Jason. "Is that all right
with you? I should get back and do whatever I can to
find Dennis. If he hasn't been arrested, he could be waiting at my back door just the way you were."

"I'll be fine," Jason said, swirling the tea in his cup.
"Maxie will look after me."

"Ha!" Maxie shouted. "I like this boy already, Renee. Thank you for bringing him to me. He knows just what to say."

Renee stayed for about an hour. They talked about logistics—Jason would have to buy some clothing and supplies tomorrow at the nearby mall—then made up a bed on the couch in the television room next to Maxie's bedroom. With two cups of vodka tea in her, Maxie faded quickly, and she shuffled off to bed without a word to anyone. "She does that," Renee apologized. "She'll just disappear into her bedroom for the night whenever she gets tired. Don't take it personally. She just likes to be considered eccentric."

Renee invited him out onto the deck overlooking a quiet bay. The moon had risen by now, and Jason could see a small marina off to the right, sailboats and cabin cruisers rocking gently in the swell. He could just make out some lights on the dark strip of land across the bay— a darker continuation of the star-pocked night sky. Below the deck, across a short stretch of grass broken up by anemic bushes and thin, newly planted trees, was a concrete breakwater that seemed to glow in the moonlight.

Renee took a pull of her cigarette in the darkness. Jason could hear the tobacco crackling.

"Are you scared?" Renee asked.

Jason didn't answer. He looked at the bay, the sand, the boats. A few doors down was a house still in construction, surrounded by tractors and piles of sand. There was dirt where the green lawn should have been.

"It's okay if you are. I know I am."

After a moment, Jason said, "Maybe. A little."

"We'll clear it up, though. Once I get my FBI friend involved. In the meantime, just lie low here. Try to get some homework done."

"I don't have my books with me," he said.

Renee frowned. "So read the newspapers. My mother gets the *New York Times* and the *Washington Post*. She makes poor Hortense read them both to her every day."

Jason breathed in the night air, which was tinged with the smoke of Renee's cigarettes. "You'll bring him here? The FBI guy?"

"Maybe," she answered. "They probably have someplace safe to take you. But I'll talk to him when he gets back tomorrow." She looked over at him. "Jason, this is all going to come out now. You realize that, right? There's no way we can try to keep this secret anymore."

Jason turned from the bay and leaned back against the deck rail. "Yeah. So much for my future, I guess."

"Oh, bullshit," Renee blurted. "Your future won't be spoiled because you decided to buy a joint on the wrong night."

"Two people are dead because of me," Jason said. "There's no way my life's anything but a disaster from now on. Not that I care anymore."

"You're not morally responsible for either one of those deaths, Jason. And trust me, your life is not over." She took a last pull on her cigarette. "Your life is never over until you die, Jason. Unless you give up. Everybody gets a second chance. It's in the rule book." She stubbed out the cigarette on the railing and then tossed the butt into the darkness below the deck.

"You think Dennis is all right?" he asked then.

He heard Renee sigh and could feel her eyes on him. "I don't know," she said. "I hope to God he is." She put an arm around his shoulder, her fingers draping down casually, grazing his chest. Jason felt two distinct pulsebeats in his groin and was completely mortified. "I've got to go," Renee said.

Jason followed her back into the house. He watched her gather up her bag and keys, wanting her to stay. "Tell

Maxie I'll call here tomorrow early," Renee said. She came over and gave Jason a kiss on the forehead. "Try not to worry," she said. "It'll be hard, I know, just waiting here, but you've got to do it. Don't call anybody but me, okay?" She reached into her bag and pulled out a handful of twenties. "Buy what you need tomorrow."

"I've got a credit card," he said. "My father gave me an extra of his."

She shook her head. "Don't use it. It could be traced."

"By who?"

"By whom. By anyone, really. I don't want to take any chances."

He took the money and they walked through the dark hallway to the front door. "I'll let you know as soon as I find out anything," she said, pushing the screen door open and stepping out onto the porch. She turned. "And don't let Maxie get to you. She likes to bait people. It was one of the things that made my childhood a living hell."

"I can handle Maxie," Jason said, sounding more certain than he was.

"Good."

Jason watched her walk down that perfect path toward the perfect street.

After she had pulled away, he closed the screen door and the wooden door behind it, locking the knob and twisting the dead bolt closed. Then, feeling like an intruder in the strange house, he went back to the main room. There were a few dishes left on the dining table, so he carried those back to the sink. Then he slowly walked to his bedroom, turning off lights as he went. He stopped at Maxie's open bedroom door and looked in. She was asleep—with her mouth open and her cheek crushed against the pillow. It occurred to Jason that this

was one of the few times he'd slept in the same house
with a woman since his mother's funeral.

He went into his own room and closed the door. The
walls of the condo seemed thin and fragile around him.
He used the remote to turn on the television and watched
it as he undressed. The news was on, but he quickly
switched to another channel—one playing an old black-
and-white movie in Japanese. Someone was throwing a
suitcase out the window of a fast-moving train. Other
people were looking for him, running up and down the
aisles. Jason watched for a few minutes before turning
off the television and the lamp beside it.

He lay back on the sofabed, which smelled vaguely of
baby powder and tobacco. The vodka in the tea was giving a nice fuzziness to his thoughts. He tried to hold on
to that feeling, but whenever he thought about it, it kept
eluding him, disappearing like evaporating water.

He imagined his mother's face on the dark screen of
the TV. She had her hair cut short and straight, the way
she did when she first went back to her job at the museum, when he was in second grade. He remembered the
time she brought him into the office—it was a school
holiday—and he sat beside her desk all day, feeling her
warmth, watching her go over changes in the museum's
monthly newsletter. "Look at this," she would say, and
hand him a picture of a Buddha statue or a wild-eyed
Chinese lion. "Isn't it amazing? I've never seen one quite
like that." And afterward—after the day's work was
done—she took him upstairs to the galleries. The museum was open late that night, and there were just a few
people scattered around the echoing marble hallways,
making the whole place seem hushed and secretive. She
led him through the cool, glossy-floored galleries, showing him her favorite paintings, statues, and scrolls of cal-
ligraphy. In one room, they stopped in front of a painting

of a sad-looking woman in an ornate red-and-gold gown. "She's a concubine, sort of like a mistress," she explained to Jason. "She's probably out of favor with the emperor, so she's alone all day. But isn't she beautiful? And look at her feet, so tiny. Women's feet were broken when they were very young—see?—and then wrapped up in bandages so their feet never grew properly. It was supposed to be attractive, emphasizing the woman's femininity." He remembered looking up at her, appalled, and asking, "How could they do that?" She kept her eyes on the concubine. To Jason, the feet in the painting looked like small ax blades. "I don't know, actually," his mother answered. "But I'd say that the real question is how the women could let them do it."

Jason rolled over on the sofabed. He didn't want to think about his mother. He didn't want to think about anything.

He fell asleep finally, after another hour or so, trying to erase from his mind the image of a fly crawling into the black hole of Maxie's toothless mouth.

ELEVEN

DENNIS WATCHED THE blue-black wasp struggle across the windowpane. It had been weakening for hours—beating itself against the glass, falling suddenly to the sill, recovering, crawling up the pane, and then taking off to beat itself against the glass again. It was an exercise in slapstick, a joke. Dennis had even laughed aloud once or twice. Ludicrous.

He wasn't afraid. Objectively, he knew that he should be afraid, but somehow he felt only a dull, foggy calm. He knew he wouldn't die; it was impossible. Other people died, that wasp would die, but Dennis wouldn't. He was being tested. Somebody or something out there felt the need to test him.

It was getting late. The brightness was fading from the window's narrow rectangle—as if all the light in the basement room were leaking out through that single opening. Would they come down and turn on a light for him? Or just let him sit in the dark all night, handcuffed to the bracket cemented into the cinder-block wall?

The wasp started up the windowpane again. Its veined

wings dissolved suddenly and it was airborne. It tapped the window twice, fell like a dropped marble to the cement floor, and then looped back up again to hit the window once, twice, three more times. Like Morse code, Dennis thought. Sending an SOS to whoever was out there to see it.

Sighing, Dennis got up from the wooden chair. The handcuff on his right wrist gave him a very limited range of motion, but he could either sit in the chair or stand next to the wall with relative comfort. He couldn't lie flat on the ground—the bracket was too high on the wall for that—and he wondered what would happen when it was time to sleep. He worried that he would have to doze sitting up in the chair, his right hand dangling ridiculously at his side, the ring of metal digging into the flesh of his wrist.

He had lost track of the wasp. He listened for it in the deepening shadows, leaning forward as far as the handcuff would allow, but he couldn't hear it. Dennis felt a sudden deep certainty that nothing really bad would happen to him as long as that wasp was alive. If the wasp made it out of there, Dennis would too. Their fates were locked together.

"Stupid," he said aloud, and sat again in the hard chair. Being stupid, he told himself, was worse than being afraid. Being stupid would hurt him. He knew he would have to think straight to get through this. Dennis put his right foot up on the chair so that he could rest the manacled hand on his knee. The pressure on his wrist eased. He took a few deep breaths and closed his eyes.

They'd grabbed him just around the corner from his house, near the playground. Since his bike was out of commission, he'd been walking to school, thinking about what he had seen on television the night before—the face of Detective Harcourt, but the wrong face, not the face

of the man they'd seen on the street on Sunday night.
Dennis was still trying to figure out what it all meant
when a man—a black man in his thirties, with a shaved
head and a brown bomber jacket—passed him on the
street. A few seconds later, an arm came around his neck
and he felt something hard in the small of his back.
"Don't make a sound," a voice whispered close to his
ear. A car—a green Explorer, *the* fucking forest-green
Explorer—pulled around the corner and stopped at the
curb. The back door opened and Dennis was pushed inside. Another man, white, was waiting in the backseat.
He pushed some kind of cloth hood over Dennis's head
and tied it roughly at the neck. A door slammed and then
hands on both sides of him pushed him to the floor of
the car. "Say one word and we'll shoot you in the throat,"
a voice said, almost gently. Dennis felt the vehicle pull
away from the curb and turn a corner.

Even at that moment—at the very beginning—he had
felt more confused than afraid. He lay in total darkness,
his knee crammed up under his chest, a heavy foot
planted like a dead weight between his shoulder blades.
No one spoke in the car. Dennis could hear his own
breathing, and traffic noises from outside, but nothing
else. He tried to move his knee, to slide it out from under
himself, but the foot on his back pressed down harder
every time he moved. "I just want to get my knee out,"
he said, his voice loud in his own ears. The foot eased
off. "Do it." Dennis shifted on the carpeted floor, moving
his knee, slipping his arms more comfortably under his
chest. And then the foot was there again, digging into his
spine.

They traveled in silence for what must have been thirty
or forty minutes. Finally, after a few quick turns, the
Explorer pulled to a stop. Doors opened, and Dennis was
grabbed by the arms and dragged out. With someone on

either side of him, he was led up some metal steps and into a building. He was pushed through a bare-floored room to a doorway. Here, the man on his right went ahead of him, leading him down some narrow metal steps that echoed under their feet. "Give me your right arm," the voice said, still almost kindly in tone. Dennis heard a ratchety sound and felt the bite of cold metal on his wrist. "Upstairs." Dennis heard footsteps going back up the metal steps. When they were gone, he felt someone tugging at the loose rope around his neck, and then the hood lifted from his head. The sudden light was a surprise. He was in a cement-floored basement, the only light coming from a small, barred window high in the wall across the room. There was nothing in the basement but a wooden chair, a furnace and water heater in one corner, and some metal shelving lined with paint cans and rags. The whole basement reeked of fresh paint and oil from the furnace.

"Sit." Dennis turned. It was a white guy who'd stayed behind with him—dark curly hair, a wrinkled forehead, and brown eyes—but he wore a blue bandanna over the lower half of his face. The man looked like an outlaw in an old western movie.

"Sit," the man said again, pushing Dennis down onto the wooden chair. The man came around behind him and put his masked face close to Dennis's ear. "No one will hear you if you shout. Just sit here quietly and wait." Then he straightened up and started walking toward the foot of the stairs.

"What if I have to pee?" Dennis asked, his voice hoarse from long silence.

The man stopped and turned. "You have to pee?"

Dennis didn't know what to say. "No," he answered finally. "Not now, I mean. But what if I do later?"

The eyes above the bandanna blinked twice. "Then

you'll pee." He turned then and climbed the metal stairs.

Dennis was left alone for several hours. He was just beginning to get hungry when he heard a door opening at the top of the stairs. The same man, face still masked, came downstairs again, carrying a sandwich on a paper plate and a bottle of water. He put the sandwich and water down on the floor, just out of Dennis's reach, and then walked away, toward the light of the window. "Have to pee yet?" he asked.

Watching him carefully, Dennis said, "Not yet."

The man turned back toward him and crossed his arms in front of his chest. "I think some people are very disappointed in you today, Dennis. In case you haven't heard, your principal called a random locker search this morning, and you know what they found in yours?"

Dennis didn't answer.

The man shook his head. "Very disappointing." He took a few steps closer. "A nice college-bound young black man like you with a sock full of coke in his locker."

"It's not mine," Dennis said weakly.

"Well, *I* know that, and *you* know that, but will anyone else believe it? Right now, the Metro Police are out looking for you. For your friend Jason, too. Seems he had a little something in *his* locker too."

"Look, we won't say anything about what we saw. To anybody."

"Kind of late for that, Dennis, don't you think?" He reached into his back pocket and took out a piece of paper. He unfolded it slowly and then read: " 'this is crazy jason. it's not what we thought. We have to report this now.' "

Dennis cringed at the sound of his own words. They'd even been watching his E-mail.

"This kind of thing can make a man like me nervous." He folded the piece of paper and put it into his back pocket again. "Then again, maybe it's not too late after all. Charges in a case like this can be dropped. In fact, I hear it's hard to tell cocaine from baby powder until you do the lab tests. Cops make mistakes. Your records could still be kept clean. Assuming you cooperate."

"It's no problem," Dennis said. "We'll cooperate. I'm not dying to tell anybody about this, believe me."

"Well there *is* a problem. Your friend Jason. He didn't go to school today and nobody can locate him."

Dennis wondered if he should believe this. He'd called the Rourkes' that morning, but Jason was already gone—earlier than usual, according to his father. But if Jason had heard something, why hadn't he warned Dennis?

"If you can tell us where he is, we could do business. We could make a deal and everybody could walk away from this thing. If not, and you two end up in the Anacostia River, there's any number of possible explanations. Two kids trying to sell cocaine in a D.C. school—nasty things can happen."

"How do I know you won't just fuck the deal and get rid of us anyway?"

"You don't," he said. "You don't, Dennis. That's a very good point. I guess you'll have to trust me." He came around the back of the chair, out of Dennis's sight. "So where could he be, Dennis?"

"I don't know."

"Think."

Dennis suspected he knew—Jason would probably have gone to Renee's—but he wasn't about to tell them that. At least not yet.

"Think hard."

"The gym," Dennis said finally. "The gym at the Y. We go there together sometimes." This was a lie. Jason wasn't even a member.

"What Y?"

Dennis told him.

"Anything else?"

Dennis shook his head.

The man walked around the chair, back into Dennis's line of sight. "Think some more about it, Dennis. You're a smart kid. I think you know that some things aren't worth risking your life for." He walked across the basement to the stairs.

"Wait," Dennis said.

The man turned around.

"I have to pee now."

Dennis could see the eyes crinkling above the bandanna. "There's a drain in the floor behind you. Aim carefully. It won't smell so bad if you don't splash."

Dennis held his eye for several seconds. "What about that sandwich?" he asked.

The man came back and picked up the sandwich. With his foot, he shoved the bottle of water within Dennis's reach. "People think better on an empty stomach," he said, walking away again. "If you come up with anything, just holler."

That had been four or five hours ago. Dennis had been alone ever since, with only the wasp for company. He still hadn't eaten anything. The first wave of raw hunger was already past, and now all he felt was a dull tightness in his stomach. He could make it through the night, he knew. He still had half a bottle of water. But he had no idea when or even if they would feed him.

Dennis shifted his position in the chair again, trying to relieve the pressure of the cuff on his wrist. His parents, he thought then, were probably out looking for him at that very moment. He wondered what they were thinking—what his mother was thinking. She'd probably been called at the office. They probably had told her right away about the drugs in the locker, about Dennis being missing. Would she believe that the cocaine was really his? That he was just hiding out now, running from the police? She always talked about having faith in him. Maybe *she* was the one being tested here.

He remembered one morning last summer, the morning after she'd found the joint in his shirt pocket. It was July—school was out, and Dennis was working nights at the Houlihan's off Wisconsin Avenue. His mother came into his room at about nine o'clock and sat on the edge of the bed. Outside, the faint but constant thrumming of lawn mowers had already begun.

"You're late for work," he told her.

"I called in sick," she said. "Don't I look sick to you? Bloodshot eyes?" She gave him a wan smile and said, "I want to talk to you."

"So talk."

She shook her head. "Get dressed. I want to take you somewhere."

Forty-five minutes later, when she pulled the black Audi up in front of the D.C. court buildings on Judiciary Square, Dennis groaned aloud.

"Don't give me any shit, now, Dennis," she said bitterly. This got Dennis's attention. His mother never cursed. "I want you to sit here for a while and just look around."

"I don't have to look around. I *know* what you're trying to tell me. You've said it to me a thousand times."

She reached out and grabbed his chin. "Listen to me," she said, turning his face toward her own. "I'm going to tell you now for the thousand-and-first time, because it's obvious I'm not getting through to you." She turned his head back toward the windshield. "Look around you, Dennis. There are three kinds of black men on this square—the ones in suits, the ones in uniform, and the ones in handcuffs."

"I know, I know," he said.

"I'm not sure you *do* know. It's your choice, Dennis. Some of these people don't have much choice, but you do."

They sat in the car for ten minutes, watching the police cars stop at the curb in front of the court building, the young black men being pulled out of the backseat in handcuffs. He felt his mother's eyes on him the whole time. Dennis didn't need anybody to convince him about being one of the suits—even as a high school freshman he'd been thinking beyond college to law school, or maybe an MBA—but he could never believe that something could go wrong for *him*, that he, Dennis Monroe, could make a mistake and end up as one of the guys in handcuffs.

"You decide what you're worth," his mother said finally. "This city is full of people who aren't worth much of anything to anybody." Then she started the car again. "Okay, I'm through. Nobody likes being preached to, I know. You think I like pontificating like this? I don't. But I'm scared here, so I'm willing to make myself a little ridiculous in your eyes. I don't know what else to do."

That had been almost a year ago. He'd understood his mother's warning—and he'd thought, yes, she was making herself a little ridiculous, driving him to Judiciary Square for extra drama. But here he was now, sitting in a dark basement, handcuffed and hungry, with no one to blame but himself.

Dennis looked down at the handcuff on his wrist. In the fading light, he could see something on his shirt—the wasp, crawling weakly along the bright, almost luminescent white sleeve. Feeling sick to his stomach suddenly, Dennis swept the insect off his shirt and onto the floor. He crushed it under the rubber sole of his scuffed brown boot.

TWELVE

A DOVE WOKE Graham at a quarter to six in the morning. It was cooing insistently just outside his bedroom window, bringing him up from the shallow sleep into which he'd fallen shortly before dawn. Graham opened his eyes and saw the enormous Big Bird staring blankly across the room. Remembering suddenly, he sprang up from bed and hurried across the hall to Jason's room. But Jason hadn't come back. Graham stood in his son's doorway for a full minute before leaning exhaustedly against the frame and sinking to a sitting position on the carpet.

He looked toward the doorway of his own room. He thought of the tin box hidden behind the books on his oak bookshelf. Better remember to get rid of that, he told himself—under the circumstances.

The day before—Tuesday—he had been called out of a late staff meeting at 4:45. Gail the receptionist had looked uneasy handing him the phone in the deserted outer office. The caller—a rough-voiced southerner who spoke in a studiously emotionless tone—identified himself as Lieutenant George Toomy of the D.C. Metro Police. Jason Rourke, the lieutenant said, was in trouble, and now the boy was missing. Graham was expected at Sixth District Police Headquarters immediately.

When he got to the redbrick station house, he was led into a fluorescent-lit room at the back of the building. Leon and Ann Monroe, whom Graham recognized from various high school events, were already there, sitting on folding chairs against the wall, grimly drinking coffee from foam cups. Also in the room were two white police detectives in bad suits—Lieutenant Toomy of Narcotics, looking smaller and thinner than Graham had pictured him, and Lieutenant Douglas Harvey of the Homicide squad. "Homicide?" Graham asked incredulously when Harvey introduced himself. "It's complicated," the detective answered.

Graham sat beside Ann Monroe and listened, dazed and appalled, as Toomy and Harvey told them what had happened. There had been an unannounced locker search at the boys' school that morning. School officials had discovered substantial quantities of cocaine and drug paraphernalia in both students' lockers—a quantity sufficient to establish an intent to distribute. The principal had called in police, but both boys, probably tipped off in advance, were now missing, although Jason had been seen by several witnesses at the school later in the morning.

These details emerged slowly, since the Monroes, who had apparently heard all of this once already before Graham arrived, kept peppering the detectives with questions about illegal search procedures, probable cause, and other technicalities. At several points, Graham was tempted to tell them to shut up so that Toomy could finish. The story he was hearing had no emotional reality yet for Graham—it was a mistake, it had no conceivable connection to his son—but the rational part of his mind knew that he had to listen carefully. He remembered Jason's face the other morning when Graham had walked into his son's room. Jason was on the phone with Dennis, and Graham had seen fear in his son's face. He wondered how he could have ignored that fear.

After a few minutes, the other detective, Harvey, began talking, and Graham's sense of disconnect became even more acute. One of the Monroes' cars, he told Graham, had been impounded. A hastily repaired bullet hole had been discovered in the passenger-side floorboard. The car was still being examined, but given the fact that it matched the description of a car seen at the Ramon Harcourt murder site on Sunday night—and the fact that the boys had admitted being together on that night in the car, with no witnesses to their whereabouts—there was sufficient evidence for arrest warrants in that case as well.

"Wait a second," Graham said, the significance of this turn in the story just penetrating his numbed consciousness. "Are you saying that our sons were involved in the murder of a police detective?"

Harvey looked away from his stare. "We believe so, yes."

Leon Monroe stood up suddenly. "This is ridiculous," he said, and walked across the room to stare out the window into the hallway.

Ann, sitting bleakly silent now beside Graham, put a napkin to her mouth and slowly wiped the gloss from her lips, leaving dark red stains on the edges.

They were there for over three hours. Toomy asked again and again for any information they might have about the boys' whereabouts. Graham was tempted to help them in any way he could—the sooner the boys were found, he felt, the sooner this mistake would be cleared up—but Leon and especially Ann flatly refused to say a word to them. And when the detectives broached the topic of searching the boys' rooms at home, she finally stood up from the chair. "There's no way you're getting into my house without a search warrant, Lieutenant," she said.

"That can be arranged," Lieutenant Toomy told her. "Easily."

"Ann," Leon said from across the room.

Ann turned on him with an expression of icy defiance that seemed to cow him.

"Mr. Rourke?" Toomy asked then. "I hope you plan to be more cooperative."

Graham hesitated. He couldn't understand Ann Monroe's reaction. She was acting as if she believed her son was guilty.

But Graham wasn't naive. "No," he said finally. "I'm getting a lawyer. Let me get a lawyer first and then we'll see."

Outside in the parking lot, Graham tried to speak with the Monroes—to talk this over with them and work out what could possibly be behind it. Leon seemed willing enough, but Ann would barely say a word to him. Finally, when they got into their car, Graham leaned over to her window and said, "Ann, I don't get it. I'm not your enemy in this."

She looked up at him. "I'm sorry, but there's no way we can know that for sure yet."

Then they drove away, leaving Graham alone in the floodlit parking lot.

When he got home, the message from Jason was on the answering machine: "Dad, it's Jason. Don't worry about me. I'm safe. Dennis and I are involved in something—as you know by now, I guess—but it's not what they'll tell you. I'll explain it all. Just don't worry. And don't come looking for me. You'll just screw things up if you do."

And now, early on Wednesday morning, Graham found himself going over the message in his mind again and again. The words on the recording didn't give him much comfort, but the pinched, uncertain voice reminded him of the old Jason, the Jason that had existed just a year earlier, before he cut himself off and headed out into the Neverland of brooding teenage strangeness. It was impossible that this was the voice of a delinquent like the one those detectives had talked about last night. Or was Graham kidding himself here? Was it all wishful thinking—his mind's way of excusing himself for letting Jason go like that, for allowing their connection to wither under the pressure of just getting through their days?

Graham thought—for probably the hundredth time in the past twelve hours—of Laura. He was an agnostic, with absolutely no faith in anything like an afterlife, and yet he did half believe in a conscious, watching Laura, a kind of psychological construct looking down in judgment from a corny, angel-infested heaven. What was this Laura saying now? he wondered. And what would she want him to do next?

The phone rang. Graham, still sitting in the doorway to Jason's bedroom, struggled to his feet and ran to the phone in his own bedroom. "Hello?" he said anxiously into the receiver. He heard only dead air for a few seconds. "Jason? Is that you?" He heard nothing for a few more seconds, then the muffled sound of someone putting down the phone on the other end of the line.

Graham hung up and sat on the edge of his bed. "It's not what they'll tell you," his son had said in his message. But what, then, *was* it? Jason was not a particularly secretive kid, at least not with anyone but his father. When he was small, it was a family joke how bad he was at keeping secrets. No surprise party, no hidden gift was safe while Jason knew about it. It was as if his little

body was incapable of containing secrets; they were forever bubbling out of him, spilling out in a flood of enthusiasm and high spirits.

Graham looked down at the phone. If he could talk to
Laura, he thought—now, on this phone . . .

He looked down at his hand resting on his knee. The
index finger was twitching slightly, the tendon in his
hand jumping like a plucked guitar string. His head was
aching, too, from lack of sleep.

Cursing his own weakness, he got up from the bed and
headed toward the bookcase.

Fenton was terrified of Frank Laroux. The parrot cowered
in the corner of its cage, as far away as it could get from
the enormous black man sticking his finger between the
bars. "You sure this thing can talk?" Frank asked.

"If you stop terrorizing him he might," Renee said. She
was sitting on the couch with the morning's *Post* spread
out in front of her on the coffee table. At the top left
corner of the open page was an article with the headline:
UNIDENTIFIED MAN TRAMPLED TO DEATH BY HORSE IN
ROCK CREEK PARK.

"So?" Frank said, still looking into the cage.

"So, yes. It's obviously the same one." She closed the
newspaper and sat back in the couch, watching him. "It's
exactly what Jason told me—the crushed windpipe,
everything."

Frank sighed deeply. He turned away from the cage
and walked over to the armchair across from Renee. "So
let me get my mind around this a second. We have a
cop—or not a cop—hassling your friends on some godforsaken street corner in Northeast. He's dead. And now
we have a man from District Social Services chasing your
friend Jason through a park, and he's dead too. Remind
me again, who are the victims here?"

"Sit down, Frank," Renee said. "The last thing Jason and Dennis need is for the FBI to start doubting them."

Frank sank heavily into the armchair. "You're absolutely sure these guys are clean?"

"Of course I'm sure." She grabbed a cigarette from the pack on the coffee table. "So, can the FBI get involved?"

"If it's a police conspiracy, you're damn right we can. Public corruption. This is exactly what they pay me for."

"And *is* it a conspiracy? Could Harcourt pull something like this off?"

Frank leaned back and crossed his massive legs. Peeking out between his oxblood wing tips and the cuff of his suitpants were thick brown socks with illustrations of little teddy bears on them. "In most places, probably no."

"But we don't live in most places, God knows," Renee said, "and if a body came in battered and burned . . ."

"Forensic technology has come a long way since you left, Renee. You can't just fake physical evidence."

"But you wouldn't have to fake physical evidence. You'd just have to make sure that Harcourt's real fingerprints and dental records and DNA information or whatever went into the autopsy report. You were the one talking about the incompetence of the ME's office. Rampant incompetence just makes cheating that much easier."

"It wouldn't be all that easy. You'd have to have a full file on the corpse well before it became a corpse."

"Which wouldn't be hard if the corpse had frequent contacts with the criminal justice system."

Just then, Fenton chortled from his perch, but Frank, nervously tapping his fingers on the arm of the chair, didn't even seem to notice. "All right, let's think aloud here for a second." He unfolded his thick legs and leaned forward. "If you're Harcourt, you'd have to have this guy picked out in advance. He'd have to be somebody who looks a little like you, even if the face is going to end up burned beyond recognition—they can reconstruct burned faces from the bone structure if they need to. And he'd have to have roughly the same height and weight and general build. It helps if he's somebody whose disappearance won't be noticed. And then, of course, you'd have to make sure that the guy dies at a convenient time."

"The convenient time being Sunday night," she said. "But one thing is bothering me. If Jason and Dennis stumbled into this thing just before it was supposed to happen, why would Harcourt and his friends go ahead with the plan? Knowing that these two kids had seen the guy who was really going to die. Why wouldn't they just put the whole plan on hold to be safe?"

"You can't delay a murder, honey, if the victim is already dead," Frank said.

"What do you mean?"

"If this drug dealer died from the collision with the parked car—his neck was broken, according to the *Post*—there'd be no way to delay the plan. You'd either have to cancel entirely or just go ahead and hope that the two witnesses don't figure it out. Or, if they do figure it out—as Jason did—hope that you can scare them into keeping quiet."

Renee felt her stomach lurch. "Which means that Dennis and Jason really killed that man after all."

"If so, it would be another big incentive for them to keep quiet."

"Not good," Renee said. This was one aspect of the situation she wouldn't be explaining to Jason for a while. "But can something like this be done, Frank?" Renee asked again.

Frank threw up his hands. "I don't have to tell you what this city is like these days, Renee," he said. "It's not just the ME's office that's broken down. The police can't even locate seven percent of their own goddamn patrol cars. The fire department can't handle more than one fire at a time because a third of their trucks are out of service. You know what I read the other day? A new-born baby has more chance of turning one year old in Sri Lanka than in the District of Columbia. And *you* can say better than I can what the schools are like. You can hide a lot of dirt under cover of that kind of chaos."

Renee nodded. "If God is dead, all things are possible to man."

"Say what?"

"It's a line from Nietzsche. Some show-off history teacher at school quotes it in the faculty room every time we hear of the latest atrocity at a D.C. school."

Those eyebrows went up again. "I'm impressed, Professor. Quoting Nietzsche to me now." He cleared his throat. "Anyway, God sure is dead in the District of Columbia at the moment. And I don't think the control board is going to revive him anytime soon."

"So how many people would it take to do this?" Renee asked.

"Not many. Somebody in the ME's office, certainly. Somebody in records. Maybe somebody on the crime-scene unit to fudge any little irregularities that might come up. Depending on how Harcourt is working it, the ME himself could be entirely clean, though he'd probably be able to detect something fishy during the autopsy. Whoever was involved would probably have changed the guy's clothes after they killed him—put him in the cop's clothing—and something like that should be detectable, if the ME is paying attention. Which he might not be if everybody's working on the assumption that it's the cop. Or if he's being paid not to follow proper procedure. And if the guy's wife or other relative provides a visual ID and the records match, and they felt fairly certain of the ID . . ." He paused for a second, then said, "You know, this makes me wonder about all kinds of things. You remember that other cop shooting a while back? They had five detectives interrogating the suspect for hours. And later, when it came to trial, it turns out that not a single one of them took notes on the interrogation. Not a single one! Basic police procedure, but it doesn't get done. And in a cop killing too."

"One conspiracy at a time, Frank," Renee said blandly. "So what do we do now?"

"Well," he said, putting his hands down flat on her coffee table, "our first priority should be to find this Dennis of yours and to keep Jason out of harm's way. Then we start looking into this Harcourt thing. It was only fifty thousand dollars he was carrying at the time of his death—"

"Disappearance," Renee reminded him.

"Right. Disappearance. Doesn't seem like a hell of a lot of money to go to so much trouble for."

"Maybe Harcourt had other reasons for wanting to disappear. Maybe he's been taking kickbacks or something."

Frank grinned. "You're good, Renee, you know that? You still have good instincts."

"Tell me."

"*Cara mia,* I love it when you get all flushed like that," he said. He reached into the pocket of his suit jacket for his notebook. "I had one of my trusted associates do a little checking after our talk yesterday," he said, flipping through the pages. "Turns out there's an Internal Affairs investigation under way into some unexplained disappearances from the evidence room in Harcourt's district. TVs, VCRs, a little heroin here, a little cocaine there."

"Don't tell me: Harcourt's the prime suspect."

"I don't know that for sure yet. But it would be damned convenient if you could blame it all on a dead man, wouldn't it? As a matter of fact, they could probably pile any number of the Ninth District's sins onto Harcourt's shoulders, now that he doesn't have to answer to anybody."

"Are there so many sins in the Ninth District station house?"

"Honey, you haven't been paying attention. The Ninth District is the least of it. The Deputy Mayor for Finance is about to be indicted for fraud. And I hear our trusted Mayor is making unscheduled stops at friends' houses again. Nothing changes in this town, Renee. With or without a Financial Control Board."

"Where do you plan to start, then?"

Frank leaned forward in the chair and rubbed his hands together. "We've got to bring Metro's IAD into this. We can't act alone, especially since they've already got an investigation going in Harcourt's district. Number two, we've got to find out who really died on that street corner. And three, we've got to get somebody looking into the ME's office."

Renee poked the open wallet on the table with her stockinged foot. "And four, what about Osborne, this Social Services guy? Where does he fit in? You should get a search warrant for the guy's office."

"Slow down, Renee. That's something else entirely. We've got no cause yet to start nosing around every local government office in the District of Columbia."

"What do you mean, no cause? This guy was after Jason. He has to be involved."

"According to what you told me, we don't know why this Osborne was running after Jason. Did he threaten him? Did he have a weapon? Maybe he just wanted to talk to him."

"Oh, come on. He chases Jason a mile through the park just to *talk*?"

"Look, Renee, we've got to move carefully here. This

could be messy, and we've got to minimize procedural mistakes. I can't do much with just the wallet of a man trampled by a horse."

"But we're talking about the lives of two teenagers here, not just some fucking police corruption case!"

"Look, Jason's fine, right? How about this: until I can arrange a safe house for him through the Bureau, I'll post somebody at your mother's place to keep an eye on him."

Renee thought about this for a few seconds. "Okay, sure. I think that would make me feel better."

"I also want to talk to him myself, and maybe get a sketch artist out there to do a likeness of the guy Jason saw in the Explorer that night." He wrote something in his notebook. "And as for Dennis, we don't know where the hell he is. He could be hiding out, too."

"Or else he could be dead or kidnapped or who knows what."

"Exactly. And we won't help him by rushing into something half-cocked. If we marched into this guy Osborne's office and started bagging evidence without solid probable cause, our case is screwed."

"Your case is not the first priority, remember? It's keeping Dennis and Jason safe."

"And I'm going to do that, Renee," he said. "I don't need to be reminded." He stared at her for a few moments in silence. Then he heaved himself up from the armchair.

"Wait, Frank," Renee said, getting up. "What about telling the parents? You want me to do it?"

He looked sick for a moment. "No, I've got to do it." He wrote another note into his book. "In my spare time."

"Well, what should I do, then? I've got to do something."

"It's in our court now, Renee. You've done all you can by bringing it to me." He pocketed his notebook and then rubbed his hands together. "I should go," he said.

"Get the wheels turning, call in every police-connected snitch I've got. I want to have something solid to take to the U.S. Attorney."

He took a step toward her. Fenton, still clinging to the far corner of his cage, fluttered ominously but said nothing. "I still don't believe that thing can talk," Frank said.

"He can talk, all right." Renee reached up to straighten the knot in Frank's tie. "And when the time is right, he'll have plenty to say. I just hope he doesn't reveal all of my dark secrets."

Frank's eyebrows went up. He put his hand over hers and pressed it against the dense muscles of his chest. "Oh, do you have any secrets left?"

"One or two," she said uncertainly. Then, looking down, she pushed him away and turned toward the front door of her house.

THIRTEEN

MAXIE WAS EATING bacon and eggs at the sun-drenched dining table when Jason came out of his room at nine in the morning. She was already showered and dressed, her coarse gray hair pulled back in a long ponytail that reached halfway down to her waist. "Hey, Hortense!" Maxie shouted. "He's finally roused himself. Come on out here."

A tall black woman in her fifties stepped out of the kitchen, wiping her hands on an apron. She smiled warmly at Jason. Her face was amazingly beautiful, her skin flawless and glossy, her eyes almost Asian in shape. "Good morning, Jason," she said in a rich Caribbean accent.

"This is Hortense," Maxie said, gesturing with her long, wrinkled hands. "Don't let the friendly demeanor fool you."

"Oh, Maxie, don' be wicked," Hortense said merrily. "Would you like some breakfast, Jason?"

"I'm okay, thanks," Jason said. "I'll just get myself some cereal."

"Oh, let the woman make you some breakfast, Jason. It's what I pay her for."

"I do have bacon and eggs ready for you, if you like," Hortense said.

Jason shrugged. "Sure. Thanks."

"It will be just a moment," she said, and then went back into the kitchen.

Jason sat in the chair across from Maxie, facing the windows. Some of the panes still had the manufacturer's stickers pasted in the corners. Through the windows, he could see the bay stretching out in the distance, its surface glistening in the morning sun.

"How did you sleep?"

"Not too bad," Jason lied. He'd woken up in a sweat three times during the night—scared, and ashamed of himself for being scared. Each time it had taken him the better part of an hour to doze off again.

"I'm an insomniac," Maxie announced proudly. "But I slept like a stone last night. When I wake at night I listen to books-on-tape on my little Walkman. I'm halfway through one of those seafaring novels by that old Irishman, you know him? You're probably related. Patrick O'Something. When he starts dissertating about flying jibs and the politics of the Napoleonic wars I nod right off."

Hortense came in again with a steaming plate of bacon and eggs and a glass of orange juice. "Patrick O'Brian," she said. "Maxie's favorite."

"He is *not* my favorite," Maxie said. "I admire Jewish writers. Saul Bellow. Ed Doctorow—I met him once."

"We read *Ragtime* in English class," Jason volunteered.

"We had him up to read once at Johns Hopkins when I was working there," she went on, not even listening to him. "A very handsome, courtly man, as I recall."

"You taught at Johns Hopkins?"

"Ha! I wasn't smart enough for that. I worked in the medical library. For twenty-two awful years of blood and suffering."

Jason was interested. "I was thinking of applying there next year."

"Well, don't look to me for any help. Everybody I worked with there is dead now. Either that or they despise me." She chuckled to herself and then asked, "What do you want to study?"

"I thought pre-med. Biochemistry, maybe."

"Oh God, a doctor! You should talk to Hortense here. She's studying to be some sort of supernurse at the University of Maryland."

"Only part-time," Hortense said. She was standing in the doorway to the kitchen, hands on hips, listening. "Though Maxie gives me no rest to study."

"Your mother must be ecstatic—a doctor in the family."

"She's dead," Jason said. He didn't mean it to sound so abrupt, but that's how it came out.

Maxie seemed fazed by this. "Renee didn't tell me that part."

"It's okay. It happened a while ago."

There was an awkward silence. "I'm sorry," Hortense said.

"She worked in museums," Jason went on. "My mother. A lot of different museums down on the Mall."

No one seemed to have any response to this. "Eat your eggs," Maxie said after a few seconds. "Before they get cold."

After breakfast, the three of them carried coffee out to the table and chairs on the deck overlooking the bay. It was a sunny morning, the sky an azure blue entirely empty of clouds. A chilly breeze made the fringe of the yellow shade umbrella flutter. Maxie wore big dark sunglasses, a straw hat, and a light cotton sweater over her narrow, bony shoulders. Sitting there, Jason felt like someone visiting his grandmother in Florida.

"So," Maxie said, taking a sip of coffee, "tell us about your little predicament with the law."

Jason looked nervously at Hortense, then back at Maxie.

"Oh, she knows everything," Maxie said. "Renee likes her little secrets, but Hortense doesn't care, do you, Hortense?"

"I care about keeping Jason away from harm," she said.

"See? You're among friends here, Jason. So spill. Tell us all about it—all the details that Renee left out."

Jason hesitated. He didn't know these women. He felt that he probably shouldn't tell them anything at all about what had happened. And yet he found himself—to his surprise—wanting to tell them everything. He liked the feeling of these two women fussing over him, taking an interest in him, worrying about him. So he told them the story. As they sat on that sunny deck, looking out over the Chesapeake Bay, Jason held forth, encouraged by Maxie's intent stare and Hortense's little sighs and cooings of concern. And when he'd finished—explaining about the call to his father's answering machine from the gas station in Annapolis—he felt a huge surge of relief. He had been as honest as he could be with them. Whatever these two women thought of him now—whether they were horrified by what he had done or not—he would accept their judgment of him. If they rejected him, it would only be what he deserved.

Hortense was staring out toward the water. Maxie was looking up as if inspecting the eaves of the house. For a few seconds, neither one said anything. Jason felt a little

seed of dread sprouting inside him. Maybe they *were*
horrified by him, he thought. And maybe the rest of the
world would feel the same way.

Hortense got up and began collecting their coffee cups.

"Come here, Jason," Maxie said finally. She stood up
shakily from her chair, the breeze fluttering her shirt collar and the brim of her straw hat.

Jason got up and went over to her.

"You've made a mess of things," she said to him. "But
I suppose recklessness isn't the rarest of adolescent traits.
And you've got guts and good manners on top of it."

Then she reached up and, with her bony, ring-cluttered
fingers, pinched Jason's cheek—hard. "You'll do all
right," she said, while Hortense, giving Jason a dazzling
smile, gently tucked the old woman's shirt collar under
the neck of her sweater.

Sometime in the afternoon—Dennis guessed it was
around two o'clock—they brought in another hooded
prisoner.

Dennis had been alone for most of the day. The curly-
haired white man had come down only twice since sunrise, once with some plain rice and another plastic bottle
of water for breakfast, then again with some leftover meat
loaf, creamed spinach, and zucchini in Boston Market
containers. Each time, Dennis had expected the man to
interrogate him about Jason's whereabouts, but he'd said
nothing at all. He'd just put the food down within Dennis's reach, collected the used plates, and walked back
upstairs. Dennis wondered if something had happened
overnight. Maybe Jason had turned himself in to the police already. Or maybe these guys had found him and
were keeping him somewhere else.

The prisoner was yelling as he was brought in, his
voice muffled by the thick black cloth of the hood. Den-

nis watched as two men—both wearing identical maroon bandannas over their faces—dragged him kicking and cursing down the metal basement steps. The hooded man's clothes were filthy. He wore green fatigue pants, grimy and torn, and a once-white sleeveless T-shirt spotted with bloodstains and something that looked like dried vomit. He smelled powerfully of beer, sweat, and shit.

The two men hauled the prisoner over to the wall opposite Dennis, where there was another bracket cemented into the cinder blocks. One of the men was tall and black, and wore thick, dark-rimmed eyeglasses. The other was stocky and white, with a hoop earring in his left ear visible under the taut cloth of the bandanna. While the one with the earring held the prisoner's arms pinned to his sides, the other let go and fished in his pocket for something. "Hurry up before I lose it here," Earring said. Finally, Glasses brought out a key and unlocked the handcuff on the prisoner's left wrist. Jerking the man's arm up, he hooked the cuff over the bracket and squeezed it closed. "Okay," he said.

Earring let go of the prisoner, who—quiet now— slumped to the ground and practically hung there by his manacled arm. Glasses loosened the rope around the black hood and lifted it off. Suddenly, the prisoner started shouting again, spitting out barely intelligible curses. "Some company for you," Earring said to Dennis.

After they'd gone upstairs, the other prisoner sputtered and kicked and slobbered drunkenly for several minutes. He was black—tall, potbellied, and in his fifties, with long, dirt-matted hair that dangled to his shoulders. A homeless drunk, by the looks of it, and probably mentally ill on top of it. After a while, he seemed to become aware of Dennis and started directing abuse in his direction. But the man couldn't keep it up for very long. Eventually, he quieted down, blurting out a few drunken mutterings every once in a while. Now he stood propped against the cinder-block wall, swaying, holding his stomach and staring at Dennis. "I need a drink!" he shouted suddenly at the ceiling. "I need a drink, you fuckin' aliens!" He muttered a few more curses and closed his eyes.

"Hey," Dennis said after a few seconds of silence.

"Don't say nothin' to me, you alien. I don't talk to no nappy-ass Martians. Fuckin' alien trash . . ." He trailed off again.

"I'm not an alien," Dennis said, feeling ridiculous but not knowing what else to say.

The man opened one eye and stared at him intently. Then he smiled a huge, broken-toothed smile. "Thass what they all say, suckah."

"Come on, I'm a prisoner here," Dennis said. "Just like you."

The man closed his eyes again and heaved a deep, ragged sigh. His odor was already filling the room. It was amazing to Dennis that a single person could generate that much stink.

Dennis tried again: "Where you from?" It occurred to him that this man might be another witness, someone else who saw that the man who died in Northeast that night wasn't the cop. "You come from D.C. somewhere?" he asked. "Somewhere up near Florida Avenue?"

"I be a spy," the man said then. He rattled his handcuffs a few times and added, "I be a spy from the planet Poontang." This seemed to amuse him. He started chuckling. "Oh sweet Jesus," he said. "Thass a good one." He held up the palm of his free hand. "How. I come in peace." Then he lost balance and, with a shout, fell to the floor, his body twisting around the tethered arm. "Oh dear," he said pleasantly. Then he closed his eyes and went to sleep.

About a half hour later, Dennis heard the door open at

the top of the steps. The same two men came down again, Earring carrying a bucket of soapy water and two scrubbing brooms, Glasses a garden hose that must have been attached to a faucet upstairs; he unwound it from his hand as he came down. "Well, shit," he said, "It isn't long enough."

"You got to shoot from there." Earring walked over to the slumped body of the drunk and kicked it. "Hey, Twinkle, wake up!"

"Don't sweat me, fuckah . . ."

"Take your clothes off, Twinkle. It's time for your bath. You smell like shit."

The man on the stairs shot the drunk with a few quick bursts from the hose, but he didn't even stir. The two men looked at each other. Earring shrugged, put down the push brooms, and calmly poured the bucket of soapy water over the drunk's body. This set him off. He started cursing and thrashing around, sending the white man skittering out of his reach. Glasses laughed and then turned the hose on him again from the stairs. The drunk started screaming—a high-pitched, almost girlish scream—as the water hit him.

"Hey!" Dennis yelled over the noise. "He's not some fucking animal!"

Earring turned and looked at him, his eyes intense over the maroon bandanna. "That's your opinion," he said. Then he stooped and picked up one of the brooms. "Now take it easy, Twinkle," he said. "We're gonna clean you up nice."

Dennis could only look on as they scrubbed down the man's skin and clothes, sending fingers of dark, sudsy water across the floor to the gurgling drain.

FOURTEEN

"I THOUGHT YOU didn't do this kind of thing anymore," David Harkley said as he showed his ID to the guard. He beckoned Renee through the metal detector into the cavernous Department of Social Services Building.

"I don't," Renee answered. She gave David a quick kiss on the cheek and then stopped at the building sign-in book. Under the headings "Name and Organization" she wrote: "Clara Niemand" and "The Eleanor Roosevelt Home for Lost Boys," respectively.

David read what she had written. "You haven't changed a bit," he said, in the nasal Virginia drawl he always exaggerated for her benefit.

The two of them walked down a long, dank corridor and up an unswept flight of stairs. Renee was nervous. It had been years since she'd done anything like this, and she wasn't sure she had the stomach for it. Don't think about it, she told herself, as she followed David down another corridor. You're the only one who can do this.

After a few minutes, they reached his office, a dusty, document-cluttered room dominated by a big wooden desk and a window overlooking E Street. "Thanks for getting me in," Renee said, hoisting her bag onto a side table.

"Hey, old times' sake." David walked around his desk and sat in the swivel chair behind it. He and Renee had been classmates at the University of Virginia, where David had always seemed a lot more at home than Renee ever was. As the tall, blond scion of an old Richmond family, David was someone whom Renee would normally regard with a certain amount of suspicion, but he had a number of qualities that intrigued her—namely, that he was extremely smart, gay, opinionated, and as contemptuous of the ACLU as he was of the DAR. They had kept in touch over the years, though Renee had seen him only a few times in the last decade, once at a press conference given by Mayor Humphrey about cuts in the DOSS budget and once at a downtown street fair, where he had introduced her to his charming and very ugly lover. David had been working for District Social Services ever since college, and somehow had managed to retain his sanity and even a shred of enthusiasm. "I don't reckon you'll tell me why you wanted me to get you into this building."

"Sorry, David," she said. "Top secret. Do you have a building telephone directory or something?"

David opened a desk drawer, pulled out a bound booklet, and tossed it on the desk in front of her.

"You're a prince." She sat in the chair across his desk and flipped through the directory until she found the name Vincent Osborne. His body, she figured, would probably be identified by the end of the day, so she knew she'd have to move quickly. "Can I use the phone?"

David shoved the phone in her direction. "Why not?"

Renee smiled her thanks and picked up the receiver. She reached Osborne's voice mail and listened to the message: "Hello, this is Vincent Osborne at the Office of Emergency Shelter and Treatment Services. . . ." She hung up. "Where's the Office of Emergency Shelter and Treatment Services?"

"Third floor. Turn right at the top of the stairs and follow the long hallway to the end."

"Thanks." Renee got up and collected her bag. "I'll tell you what this is about someday."

"Whenever you're ready." He got up and saw her out. "And give me a call sometime. When you aren't asking for a favor."

"I will," she said, and slipped out into the hall, too preoccupied to feel shitty about David's last comment.

She found her way upstairs to the OES offices. She stopped just outside the glass door and took a few deep breaths. Frank, she knew, would certainly disapprove of what she was about to do. As would any ethical journalist, probably. If such a thing existed.

She rang the bell and was buzzed in. The receptionist—an enormous, middle-aged black woman—sat behind a metal desk shuffling papers. "Okay, what now?" she said, as if this were the fifth time Renee had interrupted her.

"I have an appointment with Vincent Osborne?"

The woman frowned at her. "I didn't see him yet today. Let me check." She picked up the phone and dialed his extension. "He's not in," she said, putting down the phone. "He's usually out in the field on Wednesdays anyway. What time was your appointment?"

"He had some files for me," Renee said. "I was just supposed to pick them up. Did he leave an envelope with you, maybe? The name's Preston, Elaine Preston."

The woman threw up her hands. "I don't see anything. Do you?"

"Is it possible that he left the envelope on his desk?

He told me it would be here. It's really important that I have those files today."

Frowning again, the receptionist pushed herself away from the desk and got up. "Okay, I got nothing but time. Let's go have a look."

Renee followed her down a narrow corridor of cubicles, nearly all of them unoccupied. At the end, she walked through a doorway and turned right. This hall was lined with tiny, dingy offices, each one overflowing with papers, books, and files. "This is his," the receptionist said after stopping at one of the offices. They both squeezed inside. "Sorry, honey. No envelope."

"Damn," Renee said. "I guess I'll just have to come again later."

"We close at five on the dot. Don't you show up at four-fifty-nine and make my life any more difficult than it is."

"I won't." Then, as they were leaving the office, Renee said, "Is there a ladies' room I could use?"

"You full of requests today," the receptionist said, not unkindly. "Down that hall and to the right."

"Thanks." Renee headed off in that direction. She turned the corner and waited, her hand against the wall, bracing herself. For a second, her resolve flagged, and she felt a familiar anxiety creeping up on her. Do it, she told herself. And before she could think better of it, she doubled back into the corridor. The receptionist was already gone. Renee slipped back into Osborne's office and gently shut the translucent-glass door behind her.

One entire wall of the office was lined with file cabinets. Renee started with these. After putting on a pair of thin leather gloves, she pulled open a few drawers and flipped through the files inside. They seemed innocuous enough: paper-stuffed files labeled with the names of various shelters—for the homeless, runaways, battered

women—as well as halfway houses and drug
rehabilitation centers. Deciding that anything useful to
her would probably be kept under lock, Renee just
glanced at the files in any unlocked drawers. After a few
minutes of cursory searching, pulling drawers just to see
if they would open, she turned to the desk. The top center
drawer was locked, which made it impossible to open all
but one of the desk drawers. Reaching into her bag, Renee pulled out a thin metal burglar's tool that one of her
old police-reporter colleagues had presented to her on his
retirement from the paper. She shoved the tool into the
space between the top of the drawer and the desktop,
positioned it, and pulled. The lock gave with an excruciating metal groan. She froze, straining to hear if the
sound had attracted any attention. She had no idea what
she would say if someone found her in the office. She'd
probably end up arrested and thrown into lockup somewhere, and she wasn't at all sure that Frank Laroux
would bail her out.

After a tense minute of waiting, she began opening the
drawers of the desk. Most of the contents here looked
innocent, too—a box of Earl Grey tea bags, a pile of
yellowing *Dilbert* comics from the newspaper, catalogs
from computer warehouses and office supply wholesal-
ers. In the bottom left drawer were more files, most of
them unmarked. Renee opened a few and paged through
the documents inside. Then, in the third file, her eye
caught the name "Ramon Harcourt." Without stopping to
read any more, Renee gathered all of the files she could,
from that drawer and the rest of the desk drawers. She
opened her bag and stuffed them inside, along with the
burglar's tool and her gloves. Finally, after adjusting her
skirt on her hips, she turned and headed toward the door.

"Digestion problems?" the receptionist said archly
when Renee passed her desk on the way out.

"What? Oh. No." Renee grinned. "I always take my time in the bathroom. Drives my husband crazy."

The woman made a sound that Renee realized was a chuckle. "You have a good day now," the woman said.

"Can you have Vincent call me if he comes in? He knows the number."

"I'm sure he does."

Two minutes later—feeling the biggest rush of exhilaration she'd experienced in years—Renee was out again in the bright, humid Washington air, running down E Street toward her car.

Renee reached home shortly after three. She parked, as usual, around the block on Nevada and then walked to her house on Kitchener. The excitement of raiding Osborne's office was wearing off now, and she was starting to wonder how much trouble she'd be in if she ever got caught. The receptionist would almost certainly be able to identify her, if it came to that. What was the penalty, she wondered, for stealing government documents? Was it a felony?

She was so preoccupied with these thoughts that she didn't see the man sitting on her front stoop until she'd already turned onto her walk. She stopped, pressing her document-filled bag hard against her ribs.

"Renee Daniels?" the man asked, getting to his feet. He was a large white man in a wrinkled gray suit, with a shock of graying brown hair and a handsome, chiseled face. "Are you Renee Daniels?"

Renee took a step backward. She thought of Jason running from the man who waited outside *his* house, and even considered doing the same herself. But of course she couldn't. She was wearing heels, for Godsake. "Who are you?" she asked as neutrally as she could.

The man wiped grit from the seat of his suit pants.

"I'm Graham Rourke," he said. "Jason's father."

Renee looked nervously up and down Kitchener. She wondered how long he had been sitting on her front stoop, visible to every car coming down the busy road. "Pleased to meet you, Mr. Rourke," she said finally. "Come in. Quickly."

FIFTEEN

As HE WALKED into the house a caged bird in the living room let out a squawk, jangling Graham's already frayed nerves.

"Can I offer you a scotch?" Renee asked him.

"Any chance of a cup of coffee?"

"Fine," she said, throwing her bag into a corner and taking off her jacket. "But I hope you don't mind if I have a scotch myself. I've had a slightly stressful day."

He followed her into the little kitchen and watched her pull the gold filter out of the coffeemaker and fill it with grounds. She was younger than he thought she'd be. Somehow, he'd expected his son's teacher to be his own contemporary, though he should have known better. Even when Jason was in grade school—when Graham and Laura still made a point of knowing the faculty as well as they could—the teachers had always seemed painfully young to Graham. Jason had spoken of this one as "Renee Daniels," never as "Ms. Daniels." Even so, Graham had always imagined her as a wiry fifty-year-old with cardigan sweaters and bifocals on a chain around her neck.

"I'm sorry about all of this, Mr. Rourke," she said nervously.

"Call me Graham," he said. "And I think we should cut through the formalities and get right to the point. I know that Jason's been in touch with you about his current . . . predicament."

She turned with the coffee scoop in her hand. "Has the FBI contacted you?"

Graham stared at her in disbelief. "The FBI? No. Why would the FBI be contacting me?"

"So how did you know to come here?"

"I know my son, Ms. Daniels. Or at least I thought I did. You're the only teacher he talks about, and the only adult he seems to trust."

Her hard stare faltered. Graham knew that he had guessed right.

"He's my son," Graham went on. "I deserve to know where he is. And what the FBI has got to do with this."

She turned back to the coffeemaker, pulled out the carafe, and started filling it at the sink. "I wanted to tell you," she said. "The minute I heard about it myself. But Jason was very insistent on that point. I felt I really had to respect his wishes, at least until I found out more about what was going on."

"Ms. Daniels, he's seventeen years old. He's still legally my responsibility. I can go to the police if I have to."

"That's exactly what you should not do," she said icily.

"Tell me why."

She poured the water into the coffeemaker and turned to him again. "Let's talk about this sitting down, okay? This isn't going to be a picnic for either of us."

They went into the living room. She gestured toward

the royal-blue couch and then took a seat in the matching armchair facing it, crossing a pair of long, well-made legs that must have given her seventeen-year-old students something to think about. Graham watched her closely as she grabbed a cigarette from a pack lying on the coffee table—there seemed to be open packs all over the house—and lit it with a ceramic lighter in the shape of a baseball. There was something about this woman that reminded him of Laura—certainly not in personality, but in gesture and bearing. She was like a harder, more confident version of his wife, and Graham found being in her presence slightly disconcerting. He wondered if Jason had ever noticed the resemblance.

"First of all," she said, "you should know that—"

"First of all," Graham interrupted, with more impatience in his voice than he intended. "I want to know where Jason is right now. Do you know?"

She hesitated, the pinkie of her cigarette hand tracing the edge of her jaw. "The FBI should be telling you this," she said finally. "But I can tell you that he's safe."

"How do you know? Have you seen him?"

"Yes."

"Where?"

She sighed, then said, "He's staying with my mother. Out of town."

"With your *mother*?" Graham looked down at the cigarette pack and considered taking one. He hadn't smoked a regular cigarette in ten years, but the idea still tempted him sometimes. "And Dennis Monroe's there, too? With your mother?"

"No," she said. "We don't know *where* Dennis is. That's what scares me most about this whole situation."

Graham leaned forward on the couch. His hands were shaking again, so he pressed them hard against his knees. "Okay, tell me what situation you're talking about."

A cackle erupted from across the room.

"Shut up, Fenton," Renee said. She got up from the chair. "Listen, Mr. Rourke—Graham—there's a lot to take in here, and before I tell you about it, you have to understand something. You have to understand that you can't go to the police with this. Not until we figure out more about what's going on. But you have my word that the FBI has been told and they're investigating."

Graham was still trying to make sense of this part of the story. He couldn't fathom how Jason could be involved with the FBI. "I want to meet with them," he said. "With the FBI. He's my son, and I have to be in on this. The Monroes, too."

Renee didn't answer for a while. She just stood there, watching the smoking tip of her cigarette. "You're right, of course," she said. "I'll introduce you to the agent who's handling it. But we'll have to let *him* tell the Monroes—how and when he sees fit. It's his case, not mine."

Graham nodded. "Fine."

"I'm sorry," she said, looking at him with a sympathetic expression so like Laura's that he felt breathless for a second. "This has all happened so fast. I've got the interests of a lot of people to juggle here, and I feel like I'm making a mess of it no matter what I do or don't do."

"I hear you. So just start at the beginning and tell me everything."

"Let's get our drinks first," she said. "And it's not too late to reconsider that scotch."

"Detective Harcourt came to the Ninth District in July of that year. In August we have the first reported disappearances from the evidence room—a Motorola cellular telephone, two Glock 9-mm semiautomatic pistols, and a Samsung VCR. On September 17, two kilos of high-grade, uncut powder cocaine went missing. The officer in charge of the evidence room was reassigned, but the disappearances continued. October: Three Uzi semiautomatic rifles—that one made the *Post*, you'll remember. The headline was: WHO'S MINDING THE STORE? or some crap like that." Sergeant Philip Hodges resettled himself in the green vinyl chair. He passed one hand lightly over his gleaming, mahogany-colored head and continued: "November 8: A Moroccan box containing seventeen rocks of crack cocaine. Christmas Day: an ermine fur coat—I'd like to check Harcourt's girlfriend's closet for that one—and another Glock 9-mm semiautomatic pistol. You want me to go on?"

Frank Laroux shook his head as he scribbled furiously in his black leatherboard notebook. He was sitting across from Hodges in the office of Deputy Police Chief Wesley Volker, head of the Metro Police Internal Affairs Division. Volker, an obese veteran cop with a wad of coarse white hair and a red, pore-addled face, was sitting behind his enormous metal desk, watching the two other men with a handkerchief over his nose. He had been head of the IAD for under two years. During Roy Humphrey's early years as Mayor, the division had earned a reputation as a graveyard for reports about the Mayor's drug use and various other corruptions, but after administration of the police was taken away from the local government, Volker had been brought in from the Boston PD to turn the place around. Not that he'd made much progress, as far as Frank could tell. Volker was a bureaucratic animal—slow, cautious, and political to the core—but seemingly honest. And, unlike some of his predecessors, he didn't hate the FBI.

Frank looked up from his notebook. "Did you check back on Harcourt's previous assignments?"

Hodges smiled, revealing a row of mismatched teeth,

each of which seemed to be a slightly different shade of gray. "You better believe it," he said. He flipped a few ink-heavy pages on his yellow legal pad. "Harcourt was with the Richmond PD narcotics squad three years. Funny thing, during that time there were seven instances of disappearing evidence from the unit he worked for."

"And after he left?"

"Nada, Agent Laroux, nada."

"And where'd he go then?"

"He was with Narcotics in the Tenth for a year or two. There we've got nothing. But this could have more to do with the quality of the Tenth's record-keeping than with any sudden religious conversion on the part of Detective Harcourt."

"So this is the guy they end up trusting with fifty thousand dollars' payoff money in a narcotics sting?"

Volker and Hodges exchanged a quick look. "Detective Hahcaught was not supposed to have that money, Agent Laroux," Volker said in his broad New England accent, his voice heavy with a chest cold. "It wasn't signed out. And that sting operation wasn't supposed to go down until three days later. That's why his partner"—he said it *paht-nah*—"wasn't with him. His partner was in Shepherdstown, West Virginia, visiting his mother that night."

"It's possible Harcourt was freelancing here," Hodges said. "Trying to make a buy of his own—when things went sour."

Volker grunted. "This is beautiful. The cop who's supposed to be stinging these pups is making real buys of his own on the side." He blew his nose noisily into the white handkerchief. "No wonder we have PR problems." He turned back to Frank. "So there you have it, Agent Laroux. Now I'm dying to know why the FBI is taking an interest in this case, if you'll oblige us."

Frank hesitated. He didn't like having to show his hand to IAD—to any local entity in the District of Columbia—but he knew he couldn't keep this to himself. "What would you say," he began, "if I told you that Detective Harcourt wasn't dead?"

The two other men exchanged an amused look. "Not dead—as in alive?" Sergeant Hodges asked.

"As in alive and enjoying his fifty thousand dollars someplace even as we speak, yes."

Volker stuffed the handkerchief into the pocket of his suit jacket. He leaned forward and clasped his hands together on the desk. "I'd say that the FBI has been smoking something," he said. "But you got my attention, Agent Laroux. Go on."

"We have a witness who can attest that the man who was killed on Sunday night was not Detective Harcourt."

"Don't tell me. The dead man was Elvis, right?"

"He saw another man, possibly a drug dealer, who physically resembled Harcourt," Frank answered.

Volker puffed his cheeks out and shook his head. "And where is this witness? I assume he's credible, not some neighborhood crackhead trying to cut a deal."

"Let *us* worry about the witness for now. But I'd say his credibility is good."

"And does Homicide know about this witness?"

"One thing at a time. I wanted to come to you first."

Volker starting tapping his thumbs together. "So, what you're saying is that our friends at the ME made a mistake identifying the body, unintentionally or otherwise."

"The body was badly burned, remember; even his ex-wife claimed she couldn't visually ID him. It could be that somebody at the morgue replaced the corpse's ID information with Harcourt's. Or else someone put the dead man's fingerprints and dental records in Detective Harcourt's personnel file."

"Oh Christ," Volker said. He grabbed the handkerchief from his pocket again.

"That's why I'm asking for a full investigation of the Metro Police records department. We're handling the ME end. Fortunately, the body hasn't been released yet. I want our own guys to take another set of prints off the corpse and compare them with what's in the autopsy report. I'd also like to run the new prints through NCIC ourselves. If the dead man was a dealer, he'll probably be in the computer. And I'll need that ID to take to the U.S. Attorney."

"Well, they're gonna love this, I'm sure. The Ninth is becoming Jessup's favorite little police district."

"There have been other problems?"

"We got a police brutality investigation going on over there"—*ovuh they-ah*—"at the request of Jessup's office. They've got some reports of cops from the Ninth beating up on people at homeless shelters and halfway houses over in Stanton Park. It's an embarrassment."

"Was Harcourt involved in that one?"

"No," Volker said, then added, "but his partner is."

"His partner?"

"Detective Stephen Bishop. A twelve-year veteran of the force."

Frank flipped back through the pages of his little black notebook. "The same Detective Stephen Bishop who identified the corpse's clothing as belonging to Ramon Harcourt on the night of the death?"

Volker nodded. "The very same."

"Where is he now?"

"On leave. All officers get leave if they want it after something like this. Their partner getting killed, eck-cetera."

"And these incidents at homeless shelters and halfway houses?"

Volker opened a drawer and pulled out a thick manila folder. "We'll get you a copy of what we have so far. Mostly unsubstantiated accusations, with less than ideal witnesses."

"What do they say they've seen?"

Volker wiped his nose as he glanced over the file. "The usual paranoid crap," he said. "Cops singling out guys to beat up on. One guy claims the Ninth is kidnapping people and selling their bodies to aliens." His blue eyes rose to meet Frank's. "This, I'm guessing, is *before* his weekly electroshock therapy, not after."

"And Harcourt's partner is named in some of these complaints?"

"Most of them, yeah."

Frank wrote a few more notes.

"So what's this all about, Agent Laroux," Volker said. "You think there's some connection here?"

Frank closed his notebook. "Yeah," he said. "I think there's some connection. Sergeant Hodges, I think you and I should speak to the investigator in charge."

Hodges nodded sadly. "I just love it when the FBI comes around and makes my job harder," he said.

Renee retrieved her bag from the foyer the moment Graham Rourke left her house. She poured herself a second scotch, got the box of Triscuits out of the cabinet, and sat down at the kitchen table. Feeling a flush of anticipation, she stuffed a couple of Triscuits into her mouth and washed them down with the whisky. Then she opened the oversized bag and pulled out the files from Osborne's office.

She hadn't told Graham Rourke about the files, but she'd been forthright with him about virtually everything else that had happened. He had insisted on calling Jason immediately, and Renee had agreed, retreating to the living room in a gesture of privacy. But she heard every syllable of Graham's half of the tortured, pause-filled conversation that followed. Afterward, they contacted Frank Laroux on his cell phone. Frank talked to them for almost half an hour, and arranged to meet with them early the next day. Looking somewhat mollified, Graham had finally left, after agreeing not to call anyone—neither Jason nor Frank nor Renee nor the Monroes—from his cell phone or home phone, which quite conceivably could be monitored.

Now, sitting in front of the closed files, Renee wondered how Frank would react when he found out about them—and about how and where she had gotten them. She wasn't quite sure if she had tainted them as evidence. As a police reporter she'd learned a good bit about search-and-seizure law, and she suspected that her obtaining the files—*stealing* them, she corrected herself— without a warrant would not technically exclude them as evidence in any trial, since she wasn't a law enforcement officer. Besides, Frank himself had said that their first priority was finding Dennis. If there was something inside the files that could help them do that, Renee didn't much care if it all turned out to be inadmissible in court.

She took another sip of scotch and slowly opened the file in which she'd seen Ramon Harcourt's name. She had no idea what she was looking for, but she hoped she would recognize it when she found it.

SIXTEEN

"HEY," DENNIS CALLED out across the shadowy basement. "You awake?"

The crumpled figure on the floor stirred but didn't answer.

"Wake up! I want to talk to you." Dennis got up from the chair and stretched his cramped leg muscles. His wrist stung where the handcuff chafed his skin. He had tried to stuff a tail of his shirt into it, cushioning the bony part of his wrist from the metal cuff, but it hadn't made much difference. "Come on, wake up."

The man across the room let out a heavy sigh. His smell wasn't so overpowering anymore—after hosing him down, the two guards had stripped him of his dirty clothes and forced him into a pair of clean blue coveralls—but he had vomited twice since then. Every once in a while Dennis would get a whiff of it: a combination of stomach bile and Thunderbird.

"Leggo." The voice seemed to rise from the pile of flesh and hair and blue denim like a voice from the grave. "Leggo my arm, fuggah."

"It's chained to the wall. There's nothing I can do." Dennis pushed the wooden chair with his foot so that it made a scraping sound against the cement floor. "You want this chair? If you sit in the chair with your knee up, you can rest your arm and the cuff won't hurt so much."

The man didn't say anything for a full minute. Dennis wondered if he'd fainted again—or gone to sleep or whatever it was that drunks did when they lost consciousness. "Who the fuck're you?" the man asked then, in a voice so clear and distinct that Dennis nearly jumped.

"My name's Dennis. I could probably shove this chair over to you. If you want it."

"Dennis." The man chuckled softly. "Dennis the Menace. What you want wit' me, Dennis?"

"I don't want anything, man. I'm locked up here too. See?" Dennis lifted his chained wrist, but the man wasn't looking at him.

"You got a cigarette, Dennis?"

"Sorry."

"Din't think so." The man began to stir. He shifted to a sitting position, his manacled arm raised ridiculously, as if he were a student in a classroom eager to give the answer. He shook his head, making his long, matted hair swing. "Shit, man, this be cruel, you know? This be cruel and fuckin' unusual."

"You want the chair?" Dennis asked.

"Shut the fuck up 'fore I bust yo ass!" he shouted.

Dennis stopped himself from shouting back. There was no point in fighting with this man. So he just sighed and sat down. The light was fading from the window again. It looked as if he'd have to get through another long night in the cellar.

"Okay, gimme the fuckin' chair," the man said then.

Dennis got up. With his free arm, he pushed the chair

gently over onto its side and shoved it across the bare concrete floor. The man grabbed it as it slid toward him. He set it upright, struggled to his feet, and sat.

"What I'm s'posed to do now? My knee?"

"Yeah. Put up your knee and rest your hand on it. Like this." Dennis tried to demonstrate, lifting his knee and balancing on one foot.

"You look like a dog peein' on a wall, you do that," the man said, laughing a phlegmy laugh. He turned the chair so that he could rest his hand on the high back—a better solution to the problem. The man sat for a minute, rubbing his bulging stomach and then his crotch with his free hand. "Lawd, I feel like shit," he said. "These ass-holes kill me. I say I won't go that fuckin' shelter one mo' time an' what they do? They put me in a fuckin' basement wit' Howdy Doody." He started muttering again. "They don't let a man be."

"You live in a shelter?" Dennis asked.

"Gimme shelter, Lawd."

"Listen to me. I'm trying to find out what's going on here."

He grunted in reply to this. "Shit," he said. "I feel like shit."

Dennis watched him for a while, trying to summon up something other than disgust for this man. "What's your name?" he asked.

No reply. Dennis shook his head and sat on the floor. Dust motes were dropping through a column of light from the little window like snow.

"Silas," the man said finally.

"What?"

"Silas. It's a fuckin' Bible name, niggah. You got a problem?"

"No, no problem."

"My auntie gimme that name. 'S a good name."

"It *is* a good name," Dennis said, trying to make it up to him. "Silas. Like Silas Marner."

"Don't know'm."

"He was a character in a book. By George Eliot?"

Silas eyed him suspiciously for a few seconds. "What fuckin' planet you from, anyways?"

Dennis shrugged. "The planet Poontang," he said.

After a long pause, Silas started laughing—a hoarse, ragged laugh that ended in a wrenching cough full of phlegm. "I know it," he said. "I know that place well. I spent some time there myself. In younger days."

"So what shelter do you live in?" Dennis asked after a while.

"No way I'm goin' back there. Too fuckin' dangerous."

"Dangerous?"

"Too many cops beatin' up on the people that place. Then they go, you don' hear nothin' about it."

"The cops?"

"The people. Story is the cops usin' the people for 'speriments—secret government science shit, you know?"

"Yeah, I'll bet."

"Thass where we at now, asshole. Mark my word. They go infect us with somethin'—AIDS, somethin' like that. You watch."

Deciding to try again, Dennis asked, "You see anything a couple nights ago? Somebody getting shot or something?"

"I see everythin', this town."

"You see that Spanish cop get shot?"

Silas made a dismissive noise with his lips. "They workin' for the white man. Like that black cop took down Mayor Humphrey years back? Brainwash against he own people." He yawned loudly, then added. "Shit, you prob'ly brainwash too."

"Why are you here, Silas? You have any idea?"

"See? You workin' for the man, too. You prob'ly so brainwash you don't even know you brainwash." He rattled his handcuff. "You jes' wait 'n' see," he said. Then he closed his eyes, put his head down on his manacled arm, and refused to say anything more.

Dennis watched him for a few seconds, wondering if there was any use trying to get information out of this man. He was exhausted himself now. He looked down at the manacle on his wrist. Keep it in control, he told himself, then closed his own eyes and tried to get some sleep.

Jason and Maxie were on the back deck, drinking vodka tea as a pale lemon-colored sun sank over the bay, when Hortense came to the sliding screen door. "We have a visitor," she said. Jason looked back and groaned aloud. His father was standing behind Hortense in the big room, a battered suitcase in one hand and a cellophane-wrapped bouquet of daffodils in the other.

"I told you not to come," Jason said disgustedly. Graham had called from Renee's house that afternoon, but Jason had made him promise that he would stay in Washington, that he wouldn't try to come out and stick his nose into everything. But now here he was. "This is so typical. I *told* you."

"Don't be rude, Jason," Maxie scolded, scuttling up from her chair. "And introduce me."

Graham put down the suitcase and the flowers. He nodded thanks to Hortense and stepped out onto the deck. "I'm Graham Rourke," he said to Maxie. "I hope you don't mind me butting in here. I want to thank you for taking care of my son."

"Oh, I've had worse houseguests," Maxie said. "Go ahead, Jason. Say hello to your father."

Jason didn't move. He stood there with his arms folded across his chest and said, "This is so unbelievably typical."

"Jason," Maxie snapped. "You're in my house now, and I insist on mature and polite behavior. From everybody except myself, of course."

"It's okay," Graham said. He ran his fingers back through his thick hair—a habit that never failed to annoy Jason. "I know I promised Renee I wouldn't come, but I was careful to make sure nobody followed me. I just had to see him, make sure he was washing behind his ears. And I brought him some clothes and toiletries and schoolbooks."

"Schoolbooks," Jason said. "With all this going on, my father wants to make sure I don't fall behind in social studies."

"Well, as an ex-librarian, I approve of the sentiment," Maxie said. "Stop being so melodramatic, Jason. You're the one who got yourself into this mess, not your father."

Jason felt as if he'd been slapped. He looked away, feeling betrayed, his arms still crossed tightly. There was a small boat puttering toward the middle of the bay, and Jason wished he could somehow be on it, away from there.

"Now, Mr. Rourke, we were just about to sit down to dinner. Would you join us?"

"I appreciate the offer, but I was hoping Jason and I could go somewhere in town for dinner. I'd like to talk to him alone."

"Of course," Maxie said, sounding a little miffed herself now. "Jason, you can take your father to that pretentious little Italian restaurant we showed you today. The one on the way to the mall?"

"Italian's good," Graham said. "Jason? Okay with you?"

Jason didn't answer for a few seconds. He was still looking out at the small boat. It was heading straight toward the sun now, cruising up that path of glittering water. "Fine," he said at last.

"Mr. Rourke has brought you some flowers," Hortense said then from the open screen door.

"They're very beautiful. Put them in a vase, Hortense, if you can find one."

"I noticed all the daffodils on my way in," Graham said. "I guess I should have brought something else."

"It doesn't matter." Maxie reached out and touched Graham's arm. "Now I don't have to ransack my own flower beds to get some color in here."

"It's a very nice house," Graham said. He stepped back and nearly tripped over the leg of a deck chair.

Maxie cackled and grabbed Graham's arm. "You're having a bad day, Mr. Rourke," she said. "It happens."

They went inside. Hortense carried the daffodils into the kitchen and started filling a vase with water. "He's been a very considerate guest so far," Maxie said, walking with Graham to the dining table. She stopped. "Did you bring his bassoon?"

"As a matter of fact, I did. It's in the trunk."

"Jason, did you hear that?"

"I heard, Maxie," he said gloomily.

"This means we can play together." She spoke to Graham then. "I play piano. Do you play an instrument, Mr. Rourke?"

"I played the trombone in high school. I was responsible for the oom-pah whenever the sousaphone was out sick."

"Ha," Maxie said. "When I taught music—in another of my former lives—my students used to make jokes about the kind of man who chooses to play trombone."

"I can just imagine."

Hortense swept into the room with the vase of daffodils. "Please, Mr. Rourke," she said. "Don't ask her to be specific."

Twenty long minutes later, Jason and his father got into Graham's car and started off toward the Italian restaurant for dinner. Jason had barely said a word since his father's arrival. He knew that Graham had come for reasons other than just bringing him a fresh pair of jeans and his schoolbooks. "You shouldn't have followed me," he said, as they reached the exit of Maxie's condo development and turned toward the road back to town.

"Jason, you're my son, and you're in trouble," Graham said. "It's my job to make sure you're all right." Jason felt his father's stare, the eyes steady under those thick graying eyebrows. "You've been on one hell of a ride, Jase. I just wish you came to me."

"You mean you would've given us some pot from your own stash? If we asked nicely?"

Graham didn't answer. He readjusted his rearview mirror carefully, as if biding his time. "Look, Jason," he said finally. "I won't deny that I'm in a difficult position on this issue—"

"Difficult is right. At least I never got arrested."

"Getting arrested was a consequence of my action. Your action has consequences, too. And we have no idea yet what those consequences will be. That's my only point." He ran his hand again through the thick hair over his ear. "Jesus, that doesn't even make any sense, does it." Jason felt his father's eyes on him again. "So, you want to tell me what you're feeling? If you're half as stressed out as I am, you could probably use a good scream or two."

"You ever kill anybody?"

The question seemed to startle his father. "What do you mean? Like in the army?"

"Whatever."

"Nope. You didn't find too many enemy soldiers in Georgia in those days. Though there was this one sergeant..." He hesitated for a second before adding, "None of this is your fault, Jason. The two men dying. You shouldn't feel guilty."

"I don't feel guilty."

"Okay. So how *do* you feel?"

Jason wasn't really sure. He remembered the weird sensation he'd had after seeing the man get trampled by the horse—a feeling of power, as if no one could get in his way without suffering the consequences—but he was ashamed of this and wouldn't admit it to anyone, especially not his father. "Nothing," he said finally. "I don't want to talk about it."

Graham let out a frustrated growl. "You let me know when you want to talk about it," he said. He put his hand down flat on the edge of his seat. Jason could see the hair on his knuckles. It was white. His father was getting old. "Jason, I'm your only close family now," he said. "I'm on your side. You understand that, right?"

Jason didn't answer. He just looked out the window at the mailboxes passing on the side of the road, the big white houses with gables and shutters and porch swings. "I wish Mom was still alive," he said.

"Yeah," Graham answered, keeping his eyes on the road. "Me too."

SEVENTEEN

GRAHAM AND JASON'S dinner at the Italian restaurant near Bristol was not a success. The two of them sat over identical eggplant parmigianas, Graham making occasional, fruitless attempts at normal conversation. An impeccably dressed, silver-haired couple was seated one table away from them, and because of their presence, Jason seemed self-conscious, as if afraid of being overheard. "It's okay, Jase," Graham told him. "They've both got hearing aids. They're not even listening to each other." But Jason still refused to talk about what was going on. Once, Graham even tried speaking in code— "Hey, did you see that TV show about the two teenagers on the run?"—but this didn't work either. Jason just looked at him and answered, meaningfully, "No, it wasn't on in my viewing area." By the time dessert arrived, Graham was about ready to give up.

It was dark when they finally left the restaurant. Father and son silently crossed the parking lot toward the car. An almost full moon had just risen over the horizon, turning the fallow fields a cold silver whenever it cleared the fast-moving, coffee-colored clouds.

"You want to drive?" Graham asked, unlocking the driver-side door. Since getting his permit the year before, Jason had never refused an offer to take the wheel.

"Yes," Jason responded immediately, looking surprised.

"Omigod! He smiled! Notify the media!"

"Don't be a jerk, Dad," Jason said, coming around and taking the keys.

They got into the car. As Jason started the engine Graham glanced at his watch and said, "It's getting late. Maybe after we drop you off at Maxie's I should just find a motel room in town."

Jason eyed him suspiciously. "You told me you were going back to Washington tonight."

"God forbid I spend a night in the same town as you." Graham watched as Jason shifted into gear and then pulled out of the restaurant's parking lot. "I'll be coming back out anyway. Tomorrow, with this FBI agent who's working the case. Hard to believe, isn't it? That we somehow got ourselves mixed up with the FBI?"

"That *I* got us mixed up, is what you mean."

"I didn't say that, Jason." Graham pulled the shoulder strap to loosen the lap belt's grip on his waistline.

"So you talked to this guy? Laroux?"

"I did. He seemed pretty much on top of things, though he's got his hands full. He said he'd talked to you already."

"Yeah." After a few seconds, Jason continued. "He say anything to you about Dennis?"

"Nothing. I think he knows as little about Dennis's whereabouts as we do."

"He's my best friend," Jason said. "My only really close friend."

"I know." Graham pointed out the window. "Here's our left turn," he said.

Jason turned onto the causeway toward Maxie's development. Before long, they were driving out across the marshes. Eight-foot-high reeds swayed on both sides of the road while a strong breeze rippled the sections of open water, wobbling the reflections of distant lights across the marsh. Through the rolled-down window, Graham could smell the thick odors of mud and swamp. They reminded him of the summer vacations he used to take out on the Eastern Shore with his own parents in the 1950s. He had nothing but good memories of those summers, despite his parents' constant battling. He and his sister would run up and down the pebbly beach in front of their rental cottage, collecting pearly oyster shells and the caps of soda and beer bottles. "Hey," Graham said now, looking over at his son. "You want to rent a house out here this summer? For a week or two in August, say? I think they could spare me at the office."

"I'm supposed to work at the Bethesda library all summer," Jason said.

"You could take some time off. Let the books shelve themselves. Come on, it'd be a blast."

Jason shrugged, watching the road ahead. "Maybe. If I'm not in jail."

"You're not going to jail," Graham said. "As soon as I get back to Washington, I'll find us a lawyer. A good, unscrupulous one with a pencil mustache and a thousand-dollar suit. Shouldn't be a problem, right? Throw a rock in D.C. and you'll hit three lawyers, isn't that what they say?" Graham looked over at his son. "Hey, what do they call twenty lawyers at the bottom of the ocean."

"Shit," Jason said.

Graham was puzzled by this. "Good answer, I guess, but not the right one."

"No. Look behind us."

Graham turned and saw the flashing light in the side mirror. A cop. "Ayah," he said aloud. He looked over at the speedometer. Jason was doing forty-five—over the speed limit, probably, though not by much. "I think they got you."

Jason glanced up nervously at the rearview mirror. "I shouldn't stop," he said.

"What do you mean, you shouldn't stop? You've got to stop."

"Maybe it's those people again. Maybe they followed you out here from D.C."

Graham shook his head. "Come on, Jason. You got caught speeding, that's all. We've got to stop."

"I don't want to."

"Jason! Stop the car *now*!"

Looking intimidated by his father's tone, Jason slowed and pulled to the side of the causeway road. The unmarked cop car pulled in behind them, the little flasher still spinning on its dashboard. A uniformed officer pulled himself out and slowly approached their car, one hand on the pistol in his holster. "Jase, you do have your license with you, right?" Graham asked.

The cop halted just behind the open driver's-side window. He was a thin, nondescript man, about thirty, with blond hair and an acne problem. "Can I see your license and registration?"

While Jason got his wallet out of his back pocket, Graham took the registration from the glove compartment and handed it across to the cop. "I didn't think he was going that fast, officer."

The cop didn't answer. He waited until Jason had taken the license out of his wallet and handed it to him.

After looking over both documents, he bent forward and asked, "Been drinking, son?"

Graham leaned over toward the window. "I'm his father. We just had dinner together. He had some Coke."

"I assume you mean Coca-Cola."

Graham frowned. "You assume right."

"And you, sir?"

"Me? I had a glass of wine. One glass. But what has that got to do with anything?"

The cop looked off down the road in front of them, as if considering this question. Then he looked back the way they'd come. "Would you both step out of the car a minute, please?"

Jason shot his father an alarmed look. Graham was worried now, too. There was something strange about this cop, something off. "You want *me* to step out of the car too?"

"Yes, sir. Slowly, please."

Graham leaned farther over the gearshift to get a better look at the cop. "Why do I have to get out too? I'm not the driver."

"Don't argue with me, sir."

"Wait a minute," Graham said. "I think we should see *your* ID, officer. This isn't standard procedure." Graham looked at the patch on the man's shoulder. It was from the Metro D.C. police department. "D.C.? You're a little out of your jurisdiction, aren't you, officer?"

"I'll have to ask you to keep quiet, sir, and get out of the vehicle."

"You have no authority outside the District. I'm—"

It was then that Jason shifted into drive and hit the gas. Graham was thrown back against the seat as the car accelerated, its tires squealing on the asphalt. Struggling to regain his balance, he straightened finally and peered back over the headrest. He saw the cop, looking shocked and ridiculous, standing in the glare of his own headlights. "Good Christ!" Graham shouted, turning forward again. Jason was staring into the rearview mirror, a terrified grimace on his face. "Look forward!" Graham yelled. The car was veering off the road, onto the far shoulder. Jason hit the brakes as Graham grabbed the steering wheel, but they were too late. The left front tire slipped off the edge of the narrow shoulder. The car tipped forward and skidded off the embankment. The hood plowed into a thick wall of reeds at the bottom. The air bags deployed with startling abruptness, punching Graham in the chest and face so hard that he was momentarily stunned. It took him a few seconds to catch his breath.

The car was left poised at an absurd angle, its front wheels down in the water and mud, its rear end sticking up toward the top of the embankment.

"Get out, Dad!" Jason shouted. He was pushing the air bag aside and grabbing at his seat belt buckle. White, powdery smoke was filling the car from the deflating bags. "Get out and run!"

"Wait, Jason," Graham said. He released his seat belt and pushed open his door, clawing at the air bag like a man fighting his way out of a melting marshmallow. When he finally got free, he fell out of the car onto the pebbly slope of the embankment and struggled to his feet. He could see the cop about eighty yards back, running toward them with his pistol drawn. He realized then that his son was right. Graham thought he'd been careful driving out there, but here they were. He had led them straight to Jason.

"Dad!"

"Good Christ," he muttered again, feeling a sharp pang of guilt. Then he turned and followed his son into the cover of the swaying reeds.

"Over here!" his son's voice hissed at him, somewhere to the left. Graham lurched through the dense-growing reeds, his arms thrashing. After four gushing steps along the damp floor of the marsh, his left hand struck something—his son's shoulder. He grabbed Jason and pulled him to his chest. "Listen, Jason, don't get separated!"

"I told you," he said, his eyes wild, his face red and swollen from the abrasion of the air bag. "I knew you would blow it!"

Something tore through the reeds to their left, and they heard the sharp report of a pistol shot from behind them on the road. "Go!" Graham barked at his son. He pushed him deeper into the swamp. "I'll be behind you! Be as quiet as you can!"

They started pushing through the reeds and marsh elders. The edges of the leaves were brittle, stinging Graham's hands and wrists as he cleared the way in front of him. Every third or fourth step, the wet mud would envelop his shoe, chilling it, then sucking at it obscenely when he pulled it out. Another shot ripped through the reeds just behind them. "Go right, Jason!" he said, as loudly as he dared. His son obeyed, and the two of them thrashed through some extra-thick growth until they emerged into a stretch of lower-growing marsh grass. They stopped and listened. The wind was rattling the dry reeds behind them—a clatter almost like applause. Graham strained to hear whether the cop had stayed up on the road or was now coming after them through the reeds, but he couldn't tell. Jason was staring at him, waiting for a signal. Graham looked across the marsh toward a little mudflat and a patch of higher, drier land beyond, covered with bushes and trees.

"Let's go that way," Graham whispered. "Slowly." They stepped out into the marsh grass. Their feet sank into the spongy growth, but the underlying water wasn't as deep as Graham had thought—just up to mid-ankle. He could feel the cold water seep into his shoes and saturate the cuffs of his slacks, turning the cloth heavy and clingy.

They'd gone out about twenty yards when Graham felt a sharp sting on the triceps of his left arm. A muffled shot crackled far behind them, from beyond the stretch of higher reeds. "Run, Jason!" he shouted, grabbing his arm. "We're out in the open now!"

They splashed noisily through the marsh grass, avoiding the narrow channels of open water and little salt-pan pools. Graham was not in very good shape—his heart was thudding in his chest and he couldn't get enough air into his lungs—but sheer adrenaline seemed to be powering his limbs. When they passed another isolated patch of reeds, the mudflat began and the going was easier. Putting on a burst of speed, they reached the dry shore and ran up into the woods. Graham had worried that this was just a small island, but it seemed to stretch back far beyond the marsh. "This way!" he whispered to Jason, whose face looked as pallid and bloodless as the moon's. They moved off to the left, passing under some willow oaks and a stand of high, exotic-looking pines. Then Graham's body decided that it couldn't continue. He reached out and grabbed his son's shoulder. "Over there, in that undergrowth behind the tree," he gasped. "We have to stop."

Jason nodded. Moving swiftly over to the tree, he pulled aside a few branches of sharp-leafed holly to let Graham slide in, then followed him and let the branches crackle back into place behind them.

"Now just listen," Graham whispered. "Don't move unless I tell you."

They crouched in the space between the tree and the holly bush and waited, trying to breathe as quietly as possible. Graham looked down at his arm. The sleeve of his sport coat was stained with blood. He was certain that he'd just been grazed, but the blood was seeping out of him and he worried about losing strength.

They waited for a few long minutes, Graham listening so hard that his jaw muscles ached. The tree was some kind of pine, and whenever the wind combed through its upper branches it sent down a shower of dry needles that pattered the holly leaves around them. Graham squeezed his arm harder and looked over at his son. Jason was staring straight at him, the muscles of his bruised face taut with fear. Graham tried to nod reassuringly, but he wondered what his own face looked like—if his son's expression was simply mirroring his own. He had never before been in danger—raw physical danger—and he had no idea whether he would keep his head.

A pinecone snapped sharply. Jason flinched beside him, but Graham put his bloody hand on the boy's arm and gripped it tightly. They both peered out through a break in the holly branches toward the path they had come by. A figure appeared there—the cop, holding his pistol with both hands, moving slowly but steadily in the cold moonlight. His head and arms were swiveling back and forth, scanning the woods around him. There was a good chance, Graham thought, that he wouldn't see them in their hiding place. But what then? How long would this man stick around looking for them? All night?

They watched as the cop slowly edged down the path. He paused every few steps to kick at the surrounding underbrush, but there were lots of hiding places in those woods, and there was no way he could know where or if his quarry had stopped to hide. For all the cop knew, Graham and Jason could still be running far ahead of him, and Graham was counting on that to keep the cop going forward.

After a few more minutes, the cop went past them, coming within fifteen yards of their hiding place before moving on. They waited, completely motionless, until he had crossed the small hollow and climbed over the low ridge beyond.

When he was out of sight, Jason started to move, but Graham squeezed his arm again, wanting to give it a little more time, in case the cop was lying in wait just over the ridge. Count to one hundred, Graham told himself. Then it would be safe to come out and head back the way they'd come. He figured they were closer to the mainland side of the marsh now, where there was a road—a busier one than the causeway road. If they could just make it to that road. . . .

The sudden electronic warble—so out of place in those dark woods—confused him. It took Graham a few long seconds to realize what it was. His cell phone. It was in the pocket of his sport jacket.

His fucking cellular telephone was ringing.

They bolted from their hiding place without waiting to see if the cop had heard the noise. Jason was ahead of Graham now, running flat out over the log-strewn trail. "Turn! Turn!" Graham shouted as they reached a fork in the path. Jason cut right and they headed up toward another low ridge, Graham scrabbling in his pocket to silence the cell phone's ring.

They ran for another full minute. Graham felt himself tiring again. He wondered if he should tell Jason to keep going without him. Was the cop even following them anymore? Graham felt an increasing sense of strangeness dropping over him like a shawl, as if this experience were edging into the realm of a nightmare. His legs and arms seemed to be tingling now. He could feel the blood pounding in his temples. He was running through the

woods after his son. Was his son running from him now?
Was he chasing his son?

Suddenly, they were out in the open. Graham could
see lights bearing down on them. He recognized them as
headlights. There was black asphalt under his shoes now.
Jason was in the road already, his arms up, stopping a
truck that was barreling toward them, its horn blasting.
Be careful, Graham tried to say aloud. He stopped running and leaned over and put his hands on his knees,
trying to catch his breath. His dizziness gradually sub-
sided. What was that about? Graham wondered. Had he
almost fainted?

Jason was at his elbow. "Come on, Dad."

Graham looked up at him. They were standing in the
truck's headlights now, like actors on a stage. Insects
whirled around them. "Tell him we were camping," Graham said, still panting. "Tell the driver I cut myself and
we just need a ride into town."

"Hurry," Jason said, and pulled his father toward the
bright tunnel of light.

Forty minutes later, a midnight-blue Grand Marquis
pulled to a stop beside the closed gas station where Graham and Jason were waiting, hidden behind a green
Dumpster. The doors opened. "Mr. Rourke," Maxie said
from the backseat, "you get in with me. I've got some
bandages for that arm of yours. Jason, get in front with
Hortense."

As Jason got into the front seat, Graham put his jacket
on the floor of the back and climbed in beside Maxie.
"You sure know how to make an old woman's life interesting," she said.

"We passed your car as we come over the causeway,"
Hortense added from the front. "There are three police
cars around it, lights spinnin' like a carnival."

"Maybe we should go back there and report what happened," Graham said, as Maxie fussed with the torn sleeve of his shirt. "It's probably the local force back there. They could help."

"Don't be dense," Maxie said. "There's an arrest warrant out for Jason, don't forget. The first thing we'll do is take you someplace safe. Then we'll call Renee and her FBI friend. I want you both protected by the real professionals, not some inept local force."

Graham felt a throbbing under his thick eyebrows. "You're sure *you* haven't been followed, the way I was?"

"Hortense tells me she's sure. I think she moonlights as a getaway driver."

Graham felt a pull at his sleeve. Maxie was tearing the sodden cloth of his shirt away from the bullet wound, her hands moving nimbly in the darkness. "Fortunately," she said, "Hortense is studying to be a nurse, so we had all kinds of first-aid supplies in the house."

"It's not bad at all," Graham said. "It just grazed me. Just a flesh wound."

"Ha! I've never heard anyone actually say that in real life. But you're right—it doesn't look serious. Oh, here." She handed Graham a pint bottle of vodka. "This little bit of medicine is my own contribution."

Maxie began tearing open packages of gauze. "I feel awful about calling your cell phone earlier. I didn't know it would be an inopportune moment."

"There's no way you could have known."

"I ran out of my Captain Blacks, unfortunately, and I thought you could stop at the deli on your way back from the restaurant."

"No harm done, Maxie."

"I like my Captain Blacks." And then, as Hortense pulled out into the road again, she added, "You know,

Mr. Rourke, I've always had a weakness for men who get themselves in trouble with the law."

"Oh?" He put the bottle between his knees and unscrewed the cap with his free hand.

"Especially Irishmen," she went on.

Graham took a long drink from the vodka bottle.

"You all exude a certain desperado charm."

"I see," he said, gasping in pain as she dabbed at his wound with a medicated swab.

EIGHTEEN

"PATRICK IANELLI—REAL estate developer under indictment for embezzlement, died in an apparent suicide at Great Falls, December 16 of last year; Lester Gallo—inmate at the Huxley Psychiatric Center in Kingman Park, missing December 14 of the same year."

Renee was standing in Frank Laroux's narrow-windowed downtown office. She threw down two files—one blue, one red—onto Frank's desktop and then pulled out two more.

"Theodore Herscher—partner in the law firm of Saarinen, Herscher, and Dorn, under indictment for fraud and buried under an estimated 1.7 million dollars of debt, died in a house fire of suspicious origin, January 28 of this year; John Williamson—recovering crack addict living at the Stubbs Home, a halfway house near the Navy Yard, reported missing on January 20, this year."

She pulled out more colored files. "Another pair—Stanley Bosworth, restaurateur, victim of another suspicious fire earlier this month; Daniel Cooper, a homeless man, missing the same day. And here's the pair you'll

be most interested in. In the blue file: Ramon Harcourt—
undercover narcotics detective, subject of an internal police investigation for larceny, extortion, and conspiracy,
shot and torched on a Northeast street corner two days
ago; in the red file: James Rodriguez, alleged small-time
dealer for the Brookins–Florida Avenue cocaine organization, former resident of the General Baker Transitional
Housing Program. How much do you want to bet, Frank,
that Mr. Rodriguez is missing now, too? And that he's
the man Jason and Dennis had their run-in with, the one
in the morgue."

Renee dropped the rest of the files on the desk. "There
are at least a half-dozen others, but I haven't had time to
go over them as thoroughly yet. My guess, though, is
that it would be the same thing for all of them—blue
files of big men in trouble who allegedly die, red files of
little men on the margins who disappear."

"God damn," Frank said, shaking his head as he
looked down at the files on his desk. "Good God *damn*."

"You'll notice, too, that the Huxley Center, the General Baker, and the Stubbs Home are all connected to the
Office of Emergency Shelter and Treatment Services—
through something called the D.C. Sharing and Caring
Initiative. Under the program, they have to file regular
reports to the OES." She brushed a few bits of paper
scraps from her hands. "Looks like somebody's got a
nice little business going. Need to escape your troubles?
We'll stage your death and find a substitute corpse somewhere in the social services system that nobody cares
about anyway."

"This is sick," Frank said. "Totally outrageous." He
put his elbows down on the desk and rubbed his face
wearily. He was wearing a starched white oxford shirt,
the sleeves rolled up to the elbows, the collar open at his
thick, tendon-rippled neck. It was late, almost midnight,

and the halls of the FBI Washington field office were eerily quiet. The building had just been renovated, and the nondescript beige carpets still reeked of formaldehyde. The walls of Frank's office hadn't been painted yet, and the gray Sheetrock stood bare, striped with lines of masking tape. "But these files will never be usable in court," Frank said, his voice muffled by his thick hands. He lifted his head and met her eye. "You found them in the course of an illegal search. Fruit of the poisoned tree."

"I'm not a law enforcement officer, Frank, I'm a private citizen. As I remember the law, I don't need probable cause."

He shook his head. "It's not that simple, Renee. You and I were working together. Any lawyer could make a case that you were acting as an agent for the FBI."

"Oh, come off it." Renee crossed her arms tightly over her chest. "I did it without your knowledge. Against your instructions, in fact."

"And how exactly do we prove that?"

Renee didn't know what to answer. She refused to regret what she had done. As far as she was concerned, the legal niceties would have to take care of themselves. What good was the law if it prevented people from finding the bad guys? "Look, Frank," she said. "Let's focus on what these files are telling us. Somebody's out there selling the lives of the underclass, and it's starting to look suspiciously like those somebodies are cops and social services bureaucrats—these OES guys—the same people who are supposed to be protecting their interests. This is what we writing teachers call 'irony.' "

Frank sighed and got up from the chair. On the floor next to his desk was an old framed photograph of himself, looking thinner and almost comically young, shaking hands with a bored-looking William Webster. "I have to call Jessup. It's time for the U.S. Attorney's office to be in on this, no matter how spotty the evidence." He started gathering up the strewn files she had dropped on his desk. "I can see it now. He'll hit the roof when I tell him how I got these files."

"But Dennis's life may be at stake here! I don't care what Jessup thinks. We can't waste any more time."

"You think I've been wasting time? Renee, this is the most rushed piece of business I've ever tried to pull off. Usually we take months on conspiracies like this before we move, trying to make sure we've got all our ducks straight so we don't get massacred in court. You have no idea how many corners I've already cut here."

"But if they've kidnapped Dennis—"

"We have absolutely no evidence that they, whoever the hell they are, have kidnapped Dennis. That's *your* theory."

"If he was just hiding out somewhere, Frank, he'd have contacted someone. He'd have contacted *me*, the way Jason did."

"Maybe, maybe not."

"I'm their friend, Frank. I'm the one they go to. Take my word for it."

"I wish I could, Renee," Frank said. "Believe me, I do." He walked over to the electric kettle and poured some more hot water into his cup. Frank didn't drink coffee—no caffeine, no red meat, no cigarettes or booze—but he consumed something called Ginseng Health and Energy Tea by the gallon. Renee didn't remember his having these good habits back in the days they knew each other, and she didn't like them. She regarded healthy habits—not only his, but everyone's—as a personal reproach directed at her.

"About Jason," Frank continued. "I've got two men lined up to go out there tomorrow to keep an eye on him." He came around to Renee's side of the desk, gently kicking aside the framed newspaper stories, trophies, and plaques that lay piled all over the brand-new carpet. He took a sip of the tea and then leaned back against the edge with the steaming cup in his hand. Standing in front of him, Renee felt like one of those little yappy dogs facing a Great Dane. "Not that I'm sure it's the best use of my limited manpower . . ."

"But I appreciate it," she said in a quieter voice. "And my mother will too. So many men in the house at the same time."

"They won't be staying in your mother's house, Renee. The Bureau can spring for a hotel room for whichever one is not on duty." He reached out then and touched her elbow. "I've got something else I have to talk to you about."

His hand didn't drop from her elbow. Renee felt her body tensing, going to full alert. "Go ahead," she said steadily.

He let go of her elbow and pushed off the edge of his desk. He planted himself in front of her and looked down into her face. "It's about your role here, Renee. I can't have you freelancing like that again—sneaking into government offices, following leads without my knowledge."

Renee looked away from him, feeling oddly let down. She could see herself reflected in the office window, superimposed against the lights of downtown Washington like a doubly exposed photograph. "So that's your idea of gratitude," she said. "If it hadn't been for my freelancing, you wouldn't have those files."

"Look, this is *my* investigation now, and I can't have some nosy ex-journalist screwing things up, no matter who she is."

"Let the big, strong FBI man handle it, is that what you're telling me?"

He smiled. "Something like that. Though I'd probably

put it as 'letting the professionals handle it.' This *is* my job, you know."

Renee didn't move. "I'll make you a deal," she said.

"What kind of deal?"

"I won't do any more freelancing if you agree not to lock me out of your investigation. I don't want to just wait around on the sidelines."

He took a sip of tea, eyeing her over the rim of the cup. "You sure you don't have another agenda in mind here? Besides looking after your two students?"

"Such as?"

"Such as breaking a big story like this in the newspapers. Couldn't ask for a better way to get back into journalism. Real journalism." He hesitated. "If that's what you're trying to do."

Renee felt her face reddening. "I'm not trying to get back into journalism," she said. "Necessarily."

"Having second thoughts about quitting?"

"I didn't really have a choice about quitting at the time, Frank," she said. "Although you wouldn't know that. As I remember it, you'd already decided that I would be a detriment to your FBI career."

His expression was unchanged, but Renee could tell that she'd stung him. "We'll have time to hash out my many sins later," he said. "But right now we're talking about you and what you're looking for here. I've got to protect the integrity of my investigation."

"The integrity of your investigation?" she said, not even sure what he meant by the phrase. "Look, my main concern, obviously, is Dennis and Jason. But I won't pretend that I haven't thought about . . . well, writing something eventually." She looked longingly over at her bag with its stash of cigarettes. "Frank," she continued, "I realized something today, something important. Getting those files, putting myself in that situation and then finding out about this—for the first time in years, I remembered why I wanted to go into journalism in the first place. These are bad, cynical people, Frank—really bad and really cynical—and I want to make sure the world knows about them."

"And *you* have to be the one to tell them about it?"

She frowned. "Fine, yes, maybe I'm trying to prove something to myself, too. But I'm not using anybody—you or anybody else—if that's what you're insinuating."

"Okay, okay," he said. "I just want you to be clear in your own mind about all this."

She looked away from him, her arms still crossed tightly. "Don't lecture me, Frank. It doesn't suit you."

"Well, just remember, we're dealing with some pretty nasty people here. I can show you the autopsy pictures to prove it."

"I realize that."

"I don't want to lose you," he said then.

"Lose me? I wasn't aware that you had me to lose."

Frank took her two arms in his hands then, his thumbs pressing gently but firmly into her biceps. "You know," he said, "I thought about you. After you left the paper. Then again after Joellen walked out. I thought about calling you."

She avoided his eye. She didn't know what she wanted to happen here. "But you didn't," she said. "Good intentions, poor execution."

"You might say that."

"Still worried about what your bosses might think, even now?"

He laughed. "I'm a squad supervisor now, sugar. That's about all I can hope for at the moment." He began rubbing her arms. "I figure if they want to give me my boss's job someday, it'll be for political reasons. They won't let some skinny-assed white woman stand in their way."

"You're very courageous," she said acidly.

He took her face into his hands then. They were warm and dry on her cheeks. "What do you say?" he asked. "Want to give it another try?"

It was a question she hadn't answered for herself yet. Her attraction to Frank—and his to her—was obvious, but Renee knew that becoming involved with him again would create complications in her life. There was the question of their races, of course; any interracial romance in Washington was bound to be regarded as a political statement, and she wasn't sure she wanted that burden on herself. But there were other reasons for hesitation too, not the least of which was that she had doubts about his seriousness. Frank had had a reputation as a trifler back in the old days—the kind of guy who would come on strong until just after the conquest—and her own experience ten years ago had done nothing to disprove it. And yet here he was, putting on the charm, reeling her in again. Would it turn out differently this time?

Feeling confused and tired, she reached up and pulled his hands away from her face. "Not now," she said.

He nodded slowly, accepting this disappointment with apparent good nature. "Whatever you say," he said, moving away from her.

She glanced at her reflection in the window again. She looked small and ridiculous, standing there. The smell of formaldehyde was strong now, almost sickening. "So what happens next?" she asked.

He looked surprised. "I guess we go back to our respective houses and sleep alone."

"Not that, Frank. What happens with these files? Where do you go with them?"

He smiled grimly. "To the U.S. Attorney, if he doesn't

kick me out of his office. We're going to need some paperwork, and pretty quick too." He turned and opened up one of the blue files on his desk. "What worries me," he said, "is that some of these files could still be active."

"What do you mean, active?"

"Who says they've already done the switch on all of these people?" He turned again and looked at her. "Maybe some of these people are still walking around out there."

This idea startled her. She walked over and took the blue file from his hands. "Which means that some of these blue-file people are *about* to disappear—"

"Exactly," he said, not letting her finish. "And some of these red-file people are *about* to die—really die—in their place." He took the file gently from her hands. "Unless we find them first."

"Oh, God, Frank," she said. "We should check death records and missing-person reports for these names. And I was hoping to get some sleep tonight."

Frank shook his head. "Get your sleep," he said, holding the files to his chest. "We're the FBI, honey. You've got to let us do *something*."

NINETEEN

JASON SAT BESIDE Hortense in the vast front seat of the Grand Marquis, watching the blank, stubbled fields go by. His left ear ached, and his arms still stung with something like rope burns from the air bag in his father's car. As he traced the red marks on his forearms, he listened to Maxie and his father murmuring to each other in the backseat. He heard the words "witness," "FBI," and "warrant" and then didn't want to hear any more. All he wanted to do was sleep and forget about all of this. He wanted to start over, to go back to Sunday night, to the moment when he and Dennis decided to turn east instead of west, and do everything differently this time. It would have been so easy, he thought—just a turn of the steering wheel one way rather than the other.

They were driving along back roads. There were no streetlights anywhere, and the occasional houses they passed—most of them farmhouses, lying far back from the road across empty expanses of land—were dark. Every once in a while, they'd pass a brightly lit desolate-looking building—a propane store or a ramshackle church or an isolated brick-bunker funeral home with a huge green Dumpster in its parking lot. Then they'd be back in darkness again, cruising through the fields like a ferry crossing the black waters of a bay.

Once, passing through a little town, they'd driven under some flowering cherry trees. Petals swirled around them—little white spots that caught the headlights—and for a few seconds it was like driving through a freak spring blizzard.

After about an hour, Hortense pulled the car off the road into a dirt driveway. There was an empty boat trailer parked at the end of it, standing between a beat-up red Toyota and an old-fashioned school bus painted blue. Off to the left was a house—a low, single-story place with a flat roof and cinder-block stairs. The patchy, weed-filled yard was cluttered with old machine parts and boats in various stages of dilapidation. As they pulled up the driveway the headlights picked out a flash of raccoon or muskrat scurrying under the back tires of the bus.

Hortense stopped beside an overturned canoe and shut off the engine and headlights. She turned and glanced back toward Maxie in the rear seat. "I'll go an' talk to her first," she said. Maxie nodded but said nothing.

Hortense got out of the car. As she walked up to the house, the porch light came on. The door opened and a woman stepped out. She was a tall, angular black woman with a red kerchief over her head. She walked down the three cinder-block steps and met Hortense on the lawn. The women touched each other in a way that put Jason instantly on edge.

"Whose house is this?" he asked.

"Julia's," Maxie said. "Hortense's friend."

"Her *friend*?"

Maxie frowned. "Oh, grow up, Jason."

"She's putting us up," his father said, as if Jason was

the only one who wasn't in on this plan. "Until Renee's FBI man can find us another place to stay."

Jason looked again at the two women in front of the house. They seemed to be deep in discussion about something, pointing at the house and then at the blue bus parked under the trees.

"It doesn't look very big," Graham said.

"It isn't. Julia's a nurse, too. Over at some godforsaken clinic in Ocean City. She inherited the house from her father."

Hortense and Julia came back toward the car. "It's all right," Hortense said. "We have it worked out."

They got out of the car. Jason's father stepped up to Julia and stuck out his good right arm. "I'm Graham Rourke and this is my son, Jason. We truly appreciate what you're doing for us."

The woman nodded and briefly touched Graham's hand. She had a little diamond stud in her left nostril. "It won't be the first time we've had fugitives from the law in this house," she said.

Hortense was helping Maxie across the stony yard. "Don' pay any attention, Mr. Rourke."

"Let me show you the estate," Julia said.

They followed her into the house. After seeing the yard, Jason expected the interior to be run-down and depressing, but it was fairly nice—a few small rooms full of castoff, mismatched furniture, but clean and freshly painted in different shades of light blue, dark red, and white. There were two hamster cages in one corner of the living room and a fish tank in the other, full of pale, slow-moving fish that looked like smaller versions of the fish you would buy in a supermarket. As they all came in, a fat brown dog clicked across the linoleum in the kitchen and barked a short, throaty bark, just to let everyone know he was there.

"The way we have it figured out," Julia said, "is Maxie in the back bedroom, Jason and Mr. Rourke in the other bedroom."

"I'll sleep out here on the couch," Jason said, mortified at the thought of being treated with the same gingerliness as Maxie.

Julia shrugged. "Whatever you want," she said.

"But where will *you* sleep," Graham asked her.

Julia and Hortense exchanged a look. "Oh, we like it out in the bus," Hortense said sheepishly. "There's plenty of room to sleep seven in there."

"We can't kick you out of your own house," Graham said.

"*I'll* sleep in the bus," Jason said.

Julia put her hands up. "Enough! Just sleep where I say or I'll put you all out on the beach in sleeping bags!"

That seemed to silence everyone. Except Maxie, who said, "Well, I have no compunctions about taking the nicest bedroom. I consider it my due."

Julia nodded at her grimly. "Thank you, Maxie." She turned to Hortense. "Did you get through to Renee?"

Hortense shook her head. "No one home."

"She's probably having her own slumber party, over at that FBI agent's house," Maxie said. "Mr. Rourke, if you give Hortense your cell phone, we can try her again. They can't trace cell phone calls, can they?"

"I doubt it," he said, taking the phone out of his pocket. "Just be careful what you say, in case anyone's listening in on Renee's line."

Renee still wasn't home, so the five of them got busy settling in. Maxie and the two other women disappeared into the bedrooms while Jason and his father made up the couch. As they tucked sheets and blankets under the damp cushions, the brown dog looked on suspiciously from the kitchen.

"You okay?" Graham asked when they had finished.
The bandage on his upper left arm looked ridiculous, like
a big white cocoon.

Jason just shrugged.

His father stared at him for a few seconds before saying, "You want to go outside and look around? I hear
there's a beach just on the other side of those trees out
back. We can talk."

Jason didn't answer. He felt he'd done enough talking
with his father for one night.

"Come on," Graham said. "I can't sleep unless I know
where I am."

They went out the back door and crossed the cluttered
yard. There was a narrow path leading through a stand
of thick, high bushes, and Graham led the way through.
The sense of vast open space hit them as soon as they
got to the other side. A rocky beach stretched out directly
in front of them, pale gray in the moonlight, a squiggly
line of seaweed tracing the high-tide mark like a badly
drawn sine wave. They could see the light of a boat far
out on the water to the left. Fifty yards down the beach
in the other direction a huge slab of concrete extended
out into the water. A couple of wildly twisted reinforcing
rods reached out of the broken ends like the petrified
tentacles of a giant squid. Just over the edge of the slab
was a broken metal chair, lying upside down in a foot of
lapping water.

"Must have been a boat ramp there at one time," Graham said. "Before the Chesapeake monster got its claws
on it."

"I guess." Jason looked down at the line of seaweed
clotted with crushed cans and plastic six-pack holders.
Even in the darkness, he could tell that this was the ug-
liest beach he'd ever seen.

"I know this must be frightening as hell for you," his father said then. "For me, too."

When Jason didn't answer, he went on. "Jason, I don't know why you're so angry with me. I don't blame you for this, if that's what you think."

Jason couldn't believe what he was hearing. "*You* don't blame *me*?" he asked. "*You* let them follow you out here, and then *your* cell phone almost gets us killed, and you tell me that you don't blame *me*?"

Graham seemed about to say something, but stopped himself. He turned away and looked out over the water. "I don't know how to respond to that, Jason. I really don't."

"Then don't respond at all." Jason walked a few feet down the beach and sat down. There was sand in his sock, and it reminded him of other times on the beach— the smell of suntan lotion and the weird, irritating but good sensation of damp sand against hot, sunburned skin. "It's *never* your fault, is it," he said.

"What's that supposed to mean, Jason?"

He rubbed the sand into his ankle. "Mom wasn't your fault either."

His father didn't answer at first. He walked slowly toward Jason and stood over him for a few seconds. Then he sat down heavily beside him. "No, Jason," he said. "Mom wasn't my fault. Mom wasn't anyone's fault. She was sick."

"Yeah, that's what you've always told everybody."

"Depression is a medical condition. We went over this, Jason. Four years ago, I thought we had talked this all out. With Dr. Wellington."

Dr. Wellington was a psychiatrist they had both seen for a few months after the suicide. Jason barely remembered their sessions, but he did recall eventually telling the woman whatever she wanted to hear, so that he wouldn't have to go anymore to that dismal, gray-walled office on Connecticut Avenue. "We didn't have to leave her alone that day," Jason said finally. "If somebody's sick, you stay home and take care of them. That's what a family is supposed to be for. You don't just abandon them."

"We didn't abandon her, Jason. We didn't know—" He stopped for a second. "We just didn't know how bad she was." He looked out over the water. "Jesus, I had no idea you were still doing this to yourself, Jason. I thought we had gotten over this."

Jason was furious suddenly. "I don't want to get over this. *You* might, but I don't." He got to his feet. He remembered what his father was doing the day of the suicide. He was giving a press conference—something about getting rid of cigarette advertising aimed at minors. He'd been preparing for weeks—staying late at the office, barely ever seeing Jason and his mother. It was supposed to be his big triumph. Some piece of legislation that he and his organization had worked on for a long time.

His father was staring up at him now. The man didn't even look sorry.

"I never meant to let you down," Graham said. "You *or* Mom. If that's what I did."

Disgusted, Jason turned and walked away.

"Don't go."

Jason stopped and looked back. Graham was trying to get to his feet, struggling in the sand. Jason could almost feel sorry for him. His father—the big suit in front of Congress, making pronouncements on the TV news— and all he could do now was flounder, a big, gray-haired man in his torn shirt, his bandage, and his expensive shoes, helpless as a beached whale.

TWENTY

"SCUSI, SIGNORE. C'È una farmacia qui vicino?"

Frank Laroux, sitting alone in his dark blue Pathfinder at a red light near the National Building Museum, repeated the phrase slowly: *"Scusi, Signore. C'è una . . .* Hell." He leaned forward and hit the rewind button on the tape player to hear the sentence again. *"Farmacia,"* Frank said, enunciating clearly. *"C'è una farmacia qui vicino?"*

Someone behind him leaned on his horn. The light was green.

"Fongool!" Frank growled to himself, resisting the temptation to flip the man a finger. *Fongool*—or *vaffanculo* in its high Italian version—was one word that wasn't on his language tapes. It was a word he remembered from his childhood days in Anacostia. Back when Frank was growing up, Anacostia was an integrated neighborhood, and the Laroux family had lived surrounded by Manginis and Romanos and O'Connells and Jacksons. That was before all of the working-class whites moved out of the District to the Virginia and Maryland

suburbs, along with a good number of middle- and working-class blacks, leaving the city neatly divided between the middle-class whites on the west side of Rock Creek Park and the poor blacks on the east side. Frank was not one of those Washington sentimentalists—he didn't delude himself that Anacostia in the old days embodied any ideal of racial harmony—but the neighborhood certainly wasn't the hostile, territorial place it was today. His best friend in grade school, in fact, was a white boy—Anthony Indelicato, a scrawny, crew-cut, big-eared Sicilian kid who liked to cover his bony forearms with press-on tattoos. Nowadays Anthony wouldn't last three hours in the old neighborhood without having his intestines wound around his neck like a scarf.

It was a sorry thing to see, especially for somebody like Frank who'd lived in the District all of his life. These days the city jailed more black men than it graduated from high school. People liked to blame it all on Mayor Humphrey—or on the arrival of crack cocaine in 1986—but Frank knew that the decline started long before either one. It started even before the "Negro removal" of the early fifties, when the city's benevolent white fathers bulldozed the Southwest slums and tried to move poor black residents into underfunded public housing in Northeast and Southeast. No, the *real* problem, according to Frank's way of thinking, was the whole idea of the District—this city that couldn't tax the real estate of its major tenant or the income of its commuting workforce. Since the hard money to run the city still had to come as a handout from the federal government, paternalism was practically built into District affairs. Even today, Congress was still playing Dad to the District's wayward teen, doling out allowance money and just waiting for the inevitable screwup, so that Dad could step in and save the day. And certainly Humphrey and his administration had played their part perfectly, right down to the arrogant adolescent strut. It was a travesty, as the world was finally beginning to realize. And one thing Frank knew was that it would take something a lot more radical than a Financial Control Board to solve the underlying problems of the District. He wondered what would happen if the federal government stopped its annual appropriation for the District. Would things change if the local government was allowed to tax whatever and whomever it wanted to, including the salaries of all those congressmen living in Potomac and Fairfield County? Forced to operate like a real city, Washington, he thought, might actually become one.

Frank wiped the sweat from his upper lip as the deep, smooth-voiced narrator on his tape player moved on: *"Dov'è il Pozzo di San Patrizio?"*

"Dov'è il Pozzo di . . . ?" Frustrated, Frank hit the off button and then turned up the volume on the FBI radio. He was looking forward to pushing aside the District's problems for a while, leaving the cleanup to somebody else. In three weeks, he would be leaving for Italy, a trip he'd been promising himself for years now. He'd been hoping to have a lot more Italian at his command before flying over, but between his caseload and his own ineptness at languages he hadn't made much progress.

A thought occurred to him then. What if, when this was over, he asked Renee to go to Italy with him? Would she agree? If so, would he really want her to come?

Frank turned another corner. His destination loomed ahead of him. *"Ecco la* shelter *di* homeless," he said aloud, pulling into a parking spot at the curb.

Fowler House, a shelter run by a coalition of nonprofit organizations, was set up in a disused school building, a depressing pile of beige bricks and rotting windows standing on a surprisingly pleasant tree-lined street off

Florida Avenue. Frank had come here to look for Silas
Whitcomb, a homeless alcoholic whose file was in the
group Renee had collected from the Office of Emergency
Shelter and Treatment Services. As it turned out, he was
the only person who didn't already have a death notice
or missing-person report filed in his name, so Frank was
hoping to find him before someone else did.

Like many emergency shelters, Fowler House discouraged people from hanging around during the daytime, but
many of them didn't wander very far beyond the shelter's
doors. A gaggle of secretive-looking men sat on the front
steps, looking idle and bored. As Frank crossed the street
toward them, he could sense a little rustle of nervousness
running through the group. It always amazed him how
some people could sense a law enforcement officer at
fifty yards. It was the shoes, he thought. It had to be the
wing-tip shoes. One of these days, he'd have to start
wearing something else.

Two men scooted resentfully out of his way as he
mounted the steps, murmuring noncommittal responses
to his hello. Frank was just about to go inside when
something occurred to him. "Hey," he said, turning back
to the men on the stairs. "Anybody know where I might
find a man named Silas Whitcomb?"

No response. One man—a drug-skinny guy with
dreadlocks—looked straight at Frank and said, "Sorry,
officer, I lef' my address book in my other briefcase."

Fongool, Frank said to him silently. He turned and
pushed through the metal front door.

"Who's there?" The voice came from an open office
to the left. Frank stuck his head inside. A young kid was
sitting behind a desk looking over some forms. "Morning," Frank said, showing his ID. "Is the director
around?"

"Down the hall to your right," the kid said, taking in

Frank's suit and shoes. "The office at the end."

Frank followed these directions, down a long, dark corridor reeking of ammonia and something sickly sweet designed to cover up more noxious odors. There were closed doors on both sides of the corridor, but the door to the director's office was open. Frank walked in. No one was at the desk facing the door, so Frank walked around it and stepped up to the open frosted-glass door to the interior office. Inside, a fortyish white man in a blue work shirt rolled up at the sleeves sat at a desk. He had heavy black eyebrows and thick, prematurely gray hair combed forward over his forehead. When Frank walked in, the man looked up in annoyance, quickly taking in Frank's dark suit and, of course, his well-polished shoes. "Can I help you?"

Frank took out his black ID wallet again. "My name is Frank Laroux," he said. "Are you Harry Jeffreys?"

"Correct-o-mento," Jeffreys said. He pushed aside some paperwork and nodded toward a chair. "Have a seat," he said, with a look of faint amusement on his face. "What can I do for the FBI today?"

Frank sat down and pulled out his notebook. "I'm looking for a man named Silas Whitcomb. I understand that this is the closest thing to a permanent address he has."

"Silas!" Jeffreys said with a broad smile. "What did old Silas do this time?"

"He's been in trouble before?"

"Only once I know of. He was heard making threats against the president one night last year over in Lafayette Park. We had two Secret Service men here the next day asking about him."

"And what did you tell them?"

"The truth. That Silas is a harmless old drunk who

couldn't hurt the worm in a bottle of mescal. So what did he do now?"

"He didn't do anything. I just want to ask him a few questions."

"Well, I haven't seen him for days, but I can check the logs. He's a regular." Jeffreys got up and opened a drawer of the filing cabinet behind him. He took out a big ledger book with a black vinyl cover. He paged through it for a minute or two before saying, "Last record we have of him here was Tuesday night."

"Is that unusual? For him to be gone for two nights?"

Jeffreys shrugged. "For Silas, yes. As I say, he's usually pretty regular. Usually stays the thirty-day limit and then is back again as soon as he's eligible. But a lot of the single men come and go. These are people it's hard to keep track of."

"Is it possible that Silas has been staying at some other shelter?"

"Possible. More likely, though, he's just been spending the time in a park somewhere. We get a rough crowd here occasionally and some of the gentler souls decide it's safer to camp out."

"Is there any way I could find out if he's been sleeping at another shelter?"

"Well, the OES is supposed to keep records, but they wouldn't have information that recent. We send over copies of our logs every two weeks. This was one of Mayor Humphrey's bright ideas. Centralized tracking for the homeless and destitute, part of his 'D.C. Caring and Sharing' initiative. What a crock, if you don't mind my saying so. All it really amounts to is more work for us. Now that the whole system's in receivership, OES doesn't have much to do with us administratively—they more or less just funnel money our way—so who knows what they do with the logs once they get them? Probably put them in boxes and carry them out to the trash."

"Who at OES gets the logs?"

"Now that Vincent Osborne is gone, I'm not even sure." He picked up a coffee mug on his desk, then put it down when he realized it was empty. "Talk about bizarre stories. You hear about that? Vincent Osborne? The guy gets trampled by a horse in Rock Creek Park, and somebody steals his wallet while he's lying there."

Frank murmured something noncommittal. "Anybody here a particular friend of Silas's?" he asked then. "Anybody who might know where he is?"

"You can ask the shelter volunteers. Some of them might know. But Silas was pretty much a loner, as far as I can tell."

"Was?"

Jeffreys threw up his hands: "Okay, is. Assuming he hasn't fallen into the Anacostia River or something."

"Any reason you think he might have?"

"Yikes, you feds jump on everything." He folded his hands on the desktop in front of him. "No, I don't know of any reason he might fall into the Anacostia, aside from the fact that the man is blind drunk twenty-four hours a day and can barely walk and talk."

"Any other place you can think of that he might be?"

Jeffreys thought for a moment. "I heard he sells his blood somewhere—or at least he always wears this pin in the shape of a drop of blood. Though they'd probably get more alcohol than hemoglobin out of his veins. Maybe he just likes the pin."

"Do you know where he sells his blood?"

"Sorry, no." He shrugged. "Is that all, Agent Laroux?"

"Just about. Can you give me a list of your shelter volunteers?"

"Well, our computers are down, but we should have a hard copy somewhere." Jeffreys got up from the chair and started pulling open file drawers behind him.

"Anything I can help you with?" The head of a scholarly-looking black man in his twenties poked into the inner office.

"Dean!" Jeffreys said with a look of relief. "I'm glad you're here. This is Frank Laroux of the FBI. He's looking for a list of shelter volunteers."

The young man nodded at Frank. "Dean Kennedy," he said. Then, turning back to Jeffreys: "Third cabinet, top drawer. The one labeled 'Volunteers'?"

"Egg-cellent," Jeffreys said, opening the drawer and pulling out a file. "Here you go."

Frank took the sheet of paper. There were about a dozen names on it, some with addresses, others with phone numbers only. "So," he said to Kennedy, "are you the one who sends the logs over to OES?"

"That's me."

"Who will you send them to now that Vincent Osborne is dead?"

"Talk about bizarre stories," Kennedy began.

"I know," Frank said impatiently.

Kennedy made a face. "I can't say, really," he answered. "I guess I'll just keep sending them 'Attention: V. Osborne.' Who actually will get them, I have no idea. Maybe nobody. They don't like the extra paperwork any more than we do."

"So, Dean," Jeffreys said then, "have you seen His Majesty Silas around lately?"

"Silas Whitcomb? Not in days. Somebody told me he was picked up in Salazar Park."

Frank looked up from his notebook. "Picked up? Who by?"

"The cops, I guess. They do that nowadays. It's one way of dealing with the homeless problem—make it a crime to be down on your luck. Don't get me started."

"Who told you Silas was picked up?"

"One of our regulars here, Boris Yeltsin."

"Come on," Frank said. "No jokes."

"Well, that's what we call him. Looks exactly like the man. His real name's Nick, Nicolai Aaronov."

Frank wrote the name into his notebook. "He around now, by any chance?"

"You'll find him at his office until dinnertime. Third bench from the end in Salazar Park, right across the street."

Frank thanked them and left. He went out through the front door (the men on the stoop were gone now) and then walked across the street into the dusty little park on the other side. An empty fountain stood in the center of it, its statuary of puttis and cherubs scratched and noseless. Frank looked around. There—on the third bench, just as advertised—was a huge block of a man with a blunt, pasty face and thick silver hair combed straight back. He sat with a stuffed duffel bag beside him and a bagged bottle of something between his booted feet.

"Nicolai Aaronov?" Frank asked, approaching him.

The gelatinous, bloodshot eyes swiveled up. "I know you?" Aaronov asked.

"You do now," Frank said. He showed his ID and took a seat at the end of the bench. He had expected a bad smell, but Aaronov looked freshly bathed and brushed.

"There is no law broken here," he said in a rich Russian accent, subtly moving the bagged bottle under the bench with his feet. "Sitting on bench is not crime."

"No, it isn't." Frank crossed his legs and clicked his ballpoint. "I'm just trying to find out what happened to a friend of yours. Silas Whitcomb?"

Aaronov let out a laugh. "As FBI, your information stinks. Silas Whitcomb is no friend of mine."

"But you saw him picked up here? By the police?"

"Picked up, yes. By police, no."

"By who, then?"

"By who? By bureaucrats is by who. Petty bureaucrats."

"How did you know they were bureaucrats?"

"I am from former Soviet Union, I know bureaucrats." He spat a gob of something onto the pebbly ground. "The white man I recognize. Old man with big bald spot. Looks like monk. He always comes here, looks around and writes in big clipboard. Never speaks. Obvious bureaucrat."

"And this man took Silas away? When?"

"Two, three days. Silas make big fuss, but two henchmen take him away, put him in car."

"Can you describe the car?"

"Is blue. Or maybe black."

"But can you tell me what kind of car?"

"Regular car, I don't know. I was going in other direction. I don't want to be next on list."

"How about the men? Can you describe the men?"

"I told you, white man looks like monk. Small nose, big eyebrows, glasses. Black men look like black men. Like you." He gestured then in the direction of Fowler House. "You ask in there, they know this monk."

Frank asked him a few more questions and then got up from the bench. He thanked Aaronov and went back to the shelter, retracing his steps to the director's office. Jeffreys and Kennedy were together in the outer office, each one talking into a different phone.

"One more question," Frank said, leaning into the office doorway.

They both put a hand over the mouthpiece on their respective phones. "Yes?" Jeffreys asked.

"You know a small man comes around here? A government official, maybe. Looks like a monk?"

Both men nodded in unison at the word "monk." "Morgan Zack," Jeffreys said. "He's in here every two weeks or so to check up on us."

"Check up on you?"

"He's from OES. His title is City Inspector. He goes to every Social Services facility in the eastern wards. More sharing and caring stuff—supposedly he's looking for violations or something."

"He ever find any?"

"Naa. If he found any, they'd have to be fixed. He just comes around and looks over the place and everybody in it. Sometimes he takes pictures. The man's deaf on top of it all, if you can believe it. Probably the brother-in-law of some deputy mayor, picking up an easy pay-check."

Frank wrote the name into his notebook. "Thanks," he said.

Jeffreys and Kennedy both waved and started talking simultaneously into their phones.

TWENTY-ONE

SPECIAL AGENT MATTHEW Holly followed Renee out to the Eastern Shore after lunch. Renee tried to keep the young man's car in her rearview mirror the whole way out, but the white Caprice disappeared somewhere outside Easton. Renee pulled over to the sandy shoulder, amazed at the apparent inability of an FBI special agent to follow somebody who *wanted* to be followed. But after a thirty-second wait, Holly pulled up behind her with a cheerful little toot of the horn. This, Renee told herself, was the man who was supposed to protect Jason Rourke from unknown dangers. She shifted into first and pulled back into traffic, spraying Holly's car with a gusher of candy wrappers and roadside grit.

Hortense had reached her by telephone shortly after midnight the night before. The news of Jason and Graham's mishap in the swamp had shaken Renee, and she'd spent the rest of the night on the phone with Frank discussing what to do about this new development. That morning, Frank had sent over Special Agent Holly—a handsome, square-chinned blond who looked around twenty-two years old—and now the two of them were driving out to Julia's house. Agent Holly was supposed to be making sure they weren't followed.

Hortense, Julia, and Maxie were sitting on the cinder-block steps when she arrived at the little house shortly before three in the afternoon. The three women stood up when Renee's Honda came to a stop on the driveway. As Renee got out, Agent Holly pulled up behind her. "At last," Maxie said, sounding annoyed, as Hortense led her across the dusty yard toward Renee.

Renee greeted each of them with a nervous hug.

"Where's the boy?" Agent Holly asked from behind them.

"Hello to you, too," Maxie said sharply.

Agent Holly nodded to her, and then to the other two women.

"He's sleeping," Hortense said. "Inside. He didn' sleep well last night."

"That doesn't surprise me," Renee replied. "And his father?"

"He's out on the beach."

"Are you the owner of the house, ma'am?" Agent Holly asked Julia. "I'd like to have a look around the place, if I may. Then I'd like to talk to the boy."

Julia nodded, looking vaguely displeased. "The boy's name is Jason," she said. "Follow me."

"Well, *he's* quite the charmer," Maxie muttered after a few seconds.

"Leave him alone, Mother. He's just trying to be professional. It's hard being an authority figure when you don't even shave yet."

"Any word on the other boy? Dennis?" Maxie asked.

"No. Frank's checking out some leads."

"Frank? He's 'Frank' now?"

"He's always been 'Frank,' Mother. Don't let your imagination run wild."

The three women walked around to the back of the house. It was a gray afternoon, with darker shreds of cloud moving across the sky to the north. It would rain soon, Renee guessed.

"The Rourkes have been playing out some little psychodrama," Maxie said then in a half-whisper. "You'd think they'd stop bickering at a time like this, but they've been at each other ever since we got here. Apparently they had a little talk on the beach last night, and Jason came back looking furious. The father followed about ten minutes later."

"Jason is seventeen years old. Remember *our* relationship when I was seventeen?"

"Please don't remind me," Maxie said, grasping Renee's arm a little tighter. "You should have told me about the mother's being dead. Was it an accident?"

"Suicide."

Maxie shook her head. "Well, no wonder, then," she said.

Rounding the edge of the bushes, they nearly ran straight into Graham Rourke. He was walking back to the house from the beach, looking tired and disheveled and totally out of place in a borrowed, undersized work shirt and muddy suit pants. "You're here," he said, seeing Renee. "Did you bring the FBI with you?"

"One of them," Renee answered. "He's in talking to Jason now. Agent Laroux will be out late tonight with the other one in tow."

"Good. I want to talk to Laroux."

"About what?"

"About getting Jason out of here. The FBI must have someplace available for this kind of situation." He turned to Hortense. "I appreciate what you and your friend are doing for us here, don't get me wrong," he said, "but I can't see putting everyone in danger over this thing."

"Frank will be here tonight," Renee repeated. "We can talk to him. I know it's something that he wants to arrange, too."

This seemed to satisfy Graham. He turned and looked back through the break in the bushes to the bay.

"How's your arm today?" she asked.

"What? Oh, fine. I was lucky. A glorified scratch. Though it's handy for getting sympathy in a house full of women."

Renee tapped on her mother's arm a few times with her finger.

"Come, Hortense," the old woman said, taking the hint. "I want to feel the breeze off the water. If you'll excuse us, Mr. Rourke."

"Graham," he reminded her, as she and Hortense started moving toward the beach.

"Let's talk," Renee said. She steered him over toward a corner of the yard, where two splintery Adirondack chairs stood under a tree with an old leather swing suspended from its thickest branch. After shaking a cigarette out of her pack, Renee sat in one of the chairs and gestured Graham toward the other.

"I hear Jason's being a little difficult right now," she began.

Graham laughed. "Nothing I'm not used to," he said. "Why should being shot at in a swamp change the basic family dynamics?"

"I thought a common enemy was supposed to bring people together."

"Ah, but it's all my fault, you see? I'm the enemy here. I was the one who led them to Jason. And actually, that's true. That part *was* my fault."

"And was it your fault that he and Dennis were on that street corner on Sunday?"

"Well, this is seventeen-year-old logic we're talking about here," he said.

Renee didn't answer for a few seconds. She looked out across the lawn at the cars that had accumulated in the driveway. "I've been teaching seventeen-year-olds for eight years," she said, shaving the ash of her cigarette on the arm of the Adirondack chair. "I think I'm something of an expert by now. The only thing I can advise is to have patience. He'll come back. As long as you don't try too hard to bring him back."

"Sounds like Hinduism. You can't attain Nirvana unless you stop *trying* to attain it." He leaned forward and started untying one of his shoes. He took it off and shook sand onto the lawn. "You know about his mother?" he asked.

Renee nodded.

"I thought I'd get her back, too. Eventually. I told myself to be patient. But there comes a point. . . ."

"It's different with Jason," Renee said, not at all sure she knew what she was talking about. "As I heard it, your wife was clinically depressed. It was physiological."

"So they told me. So I told myself." He emptied the other shoe and slipped it back on. "But that's my fault, too. According to Jason. And maybe he's also right about that."

"Don't do this to yourself," Renee said.

Graham laughed again. "Okay, okay, enough of that." He pointed at her pack of cigarettes. "Mind if I take one?"

"Sure," she said, handing it to him. "Sorry, I didn't know you smoked."

"I don't." He put a cigarette to his lips and accepted a light from her. She watched as he took a shallow pull.

"Was it totally unexpected?" Renee asked then. "Your wife's suicide?"

"To me, yes," he answered quickly. Then he added, "Well, maybe not so unexpected. She wasn't responding to anything—drugs *or* therapy. And Jason wasn't helping. Although I'd never tell him that."

"Not helping how?"

Graham stared at the end of the cigarette. "The more distant she became, the more he demanded of her. He'd act up in obvious ways to get her attention—wearing ratty clothes to school, making huge messes in his room, things like that—but he couldn't even get her angry at him. I tried to give him what he needed—attention, whatever—but it was a busy time with my job. And he wasn't taking what I had to give, anyway. Hell, there were times I felt like the court jester in the house, trying to lighten things up. But they were a tough audience."

Renee looked over at him. Maybe a court jester wasn't what they needed most, she wanted to say.

"How do you know when your child hates your guts?" he asked then.

She was caught off guard for a second, and actually thought he was looking for an answer. Then she realized it was the beginning of a joke. "I'll bite," she said. "How?"

"They turn thirteen."

She shook her head. "That's a pretty bleak joke."

"My specialty." He took a pull on the cigarette. "She was a beautiful woman," Graham went on. "In a kind of gangly, fragile way. Dark, thick hair—like yours—but very light skin. I remember, when we'd go to the beach, she'd always stay under the umbrella. Jason and I would get brown as sausages in the sun, but Laura would stay a kind of off-white color, like skim milk. You felt you

could look right through to the bones if you looked long
and hard enough."

He paused for a few seconds, staring at his shoes, before continuing. "She was a good mother, too, at least
until the last months. Very involved in everything. Once,
Jason had to do some kind of presentation for English
class, on the poet A. E. Housman. Laura had a boxful of
slides she'd shot on a trip to Shropshire, back before we
were married—mostly fuzzy, overexposed shots of green
hills and sheep, lots of sheep. And so she and Jason put
together a slide show, along with a live performance of
the two of them reading Housman's poetry. They rehearsed it for me in the living room the night before
Jason's class. I remember Jason reading the poem about
somebody getting drunk and losing his necktie, and there
was one line he couldn't get right, no matter how many
times he tried—'And down in the lovely muck I lay,' or
something like that. But Jason kept saying 'down in the
love of muck I lay' and pretty soon the two of them got
silly and couldn't get three words out without bursting
into giggles. I remember sitting on the couch watching
them fall all over each other, and thinking, 'This is it,
Rourke. This is the stuff you'll remember when you're
old.' " He looked over at her then, with an embarrassed
expression on his craggy face. "And I guess I was right.
Because here I am remembering it." He paused, then
added, "Sorry."

"For what? For sharing a nice memory of your wife?
Men amaze me sometimes." Renee stubbed out her cigarette on the arm of the chair. She wondered, as she often
did, what kind of parent she would have made. Probably
a bad one—competitive with the girls, jealously posses-
sive of the boys. "Well," she said, "you haven't failed
Jason as a parent, as far as *I* can tell. Jason's a good kid.
Don't give up on him."

"I haven't," Graham answered. "And I won't." He dropped the cigarette onto the lawn and stepped on it. "Well, I thought a cigarette might help my headache, but it's just made it worse. You have any aspirin?"

"In my bag in the kitchen," Renee said. "It's ibuprofen, though. Not aspirin."

"Fine," he said, "fine." He put his blunt fingers up against his forehead. "Funny, I get hit in the arm and where it hurts most is over my eyebrows."

"It's stress," she said.

He smiled. "Stress? What stress?"

She got up from the chair and said, "I'll bring you the whole bottle."

The FBI man woke him up. Jason was sleeping—the first decent sleep he'd had in days—but the man came right into his room, sat on the edge of the bed, and shook him rudely by the shoulder. "Okay, kid, wakey wakey," he said. Dragging himself up from unconsciousness, Jason opened his eyes to see this blond Nordic type in a dark suit and a colorful paisley tie. He was staring down at him with a smirk on his face. "Uncle Matt is here," the man said.

Jason was in his underwear. Mortified, he got up from the bed and quickly slipped into his jeans.

"You've been a bad boy, Jason," the man went on, watching Jason. "But luckily for you, we're after some even badder ones."

When Jason was finished dressing, the man got up from the edge of the bed. "I'm Special Agent Holly of the Federal Bureau of Investigation. We've got some ground rules to go over."

"This couldn't wait until later?" Jason asked. "Like after I woke up?"

Agent Holly winked at him. "The FBI waits for no

man," he said, in a low, resonant voice, pulling aside the jacket of his suit to reveal a pistol in his shoulder holster. "This where you've been sleeping at night?" he went on, looking around the small bedroom. He walked over to one of the windows, pulled aside the red-striped curtains, and looked out.

"No," Jason said. "I slept out on the couch in the living room last night. My father was in here."

"Not anymore."

"Why not?"

"Too many means of ingress and egress in the living room," Agent Holly said. "I want you in here. I or the other agent will be watching from a car in the driveway, and we can keep an eye on these windows from there."

"You expect somebody to shoot me from a window?" Jason asked.

Holly walked over to the other window, which was open. Shaking his head, he pushed it closed and locked it.

"It'll get hot in here with the windows closed."

"I know. Can't be helped." Holly walked back around the bed and stood right in front of Jason. The FBI man was only a couple of inches taller than Jason, but he was bigger-boned and muscular. Jason figured he probably spent all of his time in the FBI gym, if there was such a thing. "Have a seat," Holly said, indicating the desk chair in the corner.

"I'll stand, thanks."

Holly shrugged. "Fine," he said. He turned away and started looking over the room as he spoke. "Number one: We have to know where you are and what you're doing twenty-four hours a day. When you get up in the morning, we have to know about it. When you go to the kitchen to eat breakfast, we have to know about it. When you go to the john to pee or whatever, we have to know about it." He turned to face Jason again. "Number two: You don't go anywhere outside this house without me or my associate going with you. If you want to take a swim or a walk, you've got to clear it with us first."

"I'm not your prisoner," Jason said.

Holly laughed. He rubbed the smooth line of his jaw for a few seconds as he stared at Jason. "Look," he said. "I don't want to be here. The way I see it, if some rich kid from Chevy Chase gets himself in trouble buying drugs in a bad neighborhood, well . . ." He stopped, apparently thinking better of what he was about to say. "But my job here is to keep your ass alive, and I know how to do it. So if that's understood, let's go over a few more details."

Jason was about to walk out the door, but Holly got there ahead of him and pushed the door shut. "You know, I've got a brother just about your age," he said, "and he doesn't like me, either."

"I wonder why," Jason said.

Holly kept his hand on the door. "Look, we can agree not to like each other as long as we cooperate, okay? We both have the same goal here."

"You started it," Jason said, then felt ridiculous and embarrassed.

"My brother always says that, too." Holly put his hand on Jason's shoulder. "Come on, use your head. People are shooting at you. Do what I tell you."

Jason didn't answer. He just stared at Holly's too-blue eyes.

"I'll talk to your father about moving his stuff out to the living room. Think of it this way: you're kicking your old man out of his bedroom. That should appeal to you, no?"

Jason turned away and put his hand on the doorknob.

After a few seconds, Holly moved away from the door, letting Jason leave.

"Do what I say and we'll get along just fine," he said as Jason left the room.

TWENTY-TWO

HIS TWO KEEPERS had taken off their masks. The maroon bandannas they'd been wearing ever since he arrived were gone now, and Dennis could finally see their faces. He knew this was not a good sign.

"Hey, Twinkle," Earring said as he came down the stairs. As far as Dennis could tell, this was late Friday afternoon. He'd been in the cellar for two days.

"Wake up, Twinkle," the white man said again, gently kicking Silas's crumpled body. He looked back up the stairs at Glasses, who was carrying what looked like a pile of clothing with a pair of shined black shoes on top. "Shit, man, I don't wanna have to dress him myself," Earring said.

"He wants the guy dressed when he gets here."

"Why don't *you* do it?"

"I don't like to get that close to my work. Besides, it's your turn to get your hands dirty."

Earring frowned, crinkling a thick, bulbous nose that looked as if it had been broken a half-dozen times. "I was the one scrubbed him before."

Glasses smiled. "I rest my case."

"Shit." Earring squatted in front of Silas. "Come on, Twinkle, help me out here. We got some classy new clothes for you."

Silas opened his eyes—first one, then the other. He sat up suddenly, then groaned and began scratching his armpit. "Don' want no new clothes," he said.

"Here's the deal. You can be good and get into these classy new clothes, or else we can drug you and put 'em on you when you're unconscious."

Silas, still scratching, stared at the man. "What kinda drug?" he asked.

Glasses let out a loud hoot. He came the rest of the way down the stairs, holding out the pile of clothing. "Tell you what, old man, we'll change the deal. You put on these clothes and then maybe we'll drug you up anyway? How's that?"

"Why you want me in them clothes?"

Glasses shot Dennis a quick look and then said, "Just put them on and be quiet." He pulled the chair over toward Silas and put the clothing neatly on it, placing the well-shined shoes on the floor. "Everything: Underwear, socks, everything."

Silas stared at the clothes for a long time before saying, "You unlock this bracelet first."

"Okay, Twinkle," Earring said. "It's a deal. But you behave yourself." He got the key out of his pocket and unlocked Silas's handcuff. "Now hurry. It's almost dinnertime."

Silas struggled to his feet. Looking first at the two men and then at Dennis, he slowly began unbuttoning his blue jumpsuit, mumbling something about cruel and unusual punishment again. The situation seemed ridiculous to Dennis—three young men in a basement, watching an old, fat man change his clothes.

"Shoes and socks, now," Glasses said when Silas had finished.

Obeying quietly, Silas sat in the chair, pulled on the socks, and started lacing up the shoes, breathing heavily with the effort. Finally, he stood up. He was dressed in an expensive-looking, double-breasted gray suit and a well-starched white shirt. "No tie, man?" Silas asked. "I got to have a tie with a getup like this." He pulled down the cuffs of the suit jacket, looking pleased with himself.

"Looks okay to me," Glasses said.

Silas strutted back and forth a few times. "The shoes, man. They pinch. You got somethin' a little bigger?"

"Fuck you, old man. You're not going to the prom." Glasses turned to his partner. "I'll bring them down," he said. "Keep an eye on him." Then he climbed the stairs out of the basement.

"What's this all about?" Dennis asked.

Earring ignored him.

"Hey, Dennis," Silas said, strutting again. "What you think? Lookin' good, don' you think?"

Dennis shook his head. "My guess is they're dressing you for your funeral, Silas."

"Shut up," Earring said.

Silas eyed him. "That true?" When the man didn't answer, a look of sorrow passed over Silas's bloated face. "Well, shit," he said. He sank into the chair. "An' I thought they was sendin' me on a job in'nerview." He started laughing then—that same phlegmy growl, only a lot more bitter now. "I do need a drink."

The door at the top of the stairs opened and Glasses came down again, followed by two other men—the curly-haired white man Dennis had talked to the first day, and another white man, older, with a fringe of gray hair around a shiny bald spot. The older man had thick, graying eyebrows and sunken cheeks. He wore a neat maroon polo shirt and chinos, and his arms were surprisingly muscular for a man his age.

"He says the shoes are too tight, if that matters to anybody," Glasses told them.

They all stood in front of Silas, who was slumped now in the chair, looking depressed. The older white man took a few steps around the chair, inspecting Silas's outfit. Then his hands began moving. He made little incomprehensible sounds as he gestured fitfully—in quick, energetic jerks.

Curly started gesturing in return.

Dennis remembered what the drug dealer had said the first night, something about a deaf guy.

"Y'all playin' charades or somethin'?" Silas asked as he watched them.

The deaf man was gesturing toward his own head. He must have been about sixty, his face lined and ashen-gray.

"The hair needs to be cut," Curly said. "Otherwise he looks okay."

"Well, hell, I don't know any barbers," Earring said. "What're we gonna do about that?"

The deaf man put his hand on Earring's shoulder and said, in a slurred, nasal, too-loud voice, "You do it."

"It doesn't have to look good," Curly said. "It just has to be short. Close to the head."

"I don' want no haircut," Silas said, sitting up straighter in his chair. "I be like Samson, asshole. You don' touch the hair."

The others kept talking as if Silas weren't even there. "We can get some shears or a razor or whatever," Curly went on. "Improvise, Lewis, you're a smart guy. But it has to be done."

The deaf man was staring over at Dennis now, his eyes intense. He stepped toward him and looked him up and down appraisingly. Dennis felt self-conscious, and more scared than at any time since he'd been taken off the street.

The deaf man started gesturing again. Curly nodded, then turned to the other two. "Get the boy started, too. Both arms."

"What do you mean, both arms?" Dennis asked.

Curly looked at him and smiled. "You'll like this, Dennis, don't worry. The next two days will be the most enjoyable two days of your life." He looked at the deaf man, who nodded. "Get Silas back into his own clothes, too. We don't want him messing up the suit beforehand. This one's got to be perfect. No more fuckups."

"What is this all about?" Dennis asked. When no one answered him, he said, "I'll tell you where Jason Rourke is, okay? We'll make that deal you talked about."

"Oh, we *know* where Jason Rourke is now," Curly said. "So that deal is already off. Actually, you didn't think we'd ever really let you go, did you? Did the masks really fool you?" He turned and made a sign toward the deaf man. Then they both moved toward the stairs.

"Does that mean you're going to kill me?" Dennis asked.

Curly stopped and turned around. "We are, Dennis," he said. "I'm afraid we are. Then again, in a few minutes, you won't really care much. Certain drugs are wonderful that way." He turned. "Go ahead, Lewis."

Earring—or Lewis—took a small black-leather pouch from the inside pocket of his jacket. As he stepped over to Dennis, he took a small syringe out of it. "Lemme start with the left arm," he said, pulling a spoon and a yellow rubber tube from the pouch.

"Don' he get some new clothes too?" Silas asked.

• • •

Frank left Metro Police Headquarters feeling like someone in an antacid commercial—the "before" picture. His
meeting had turned out to be nothing less than a free-for-
all. Janyce and Harvey, the two Homicide detectives covering what they thought was the Harcourt killing, weren't
convinced by Frank's revelations about the identity of
their corpse. After the discovery of the poorly disguised
slug groove in the Monroes' Audi, Dennis Monroe had
become the prime suspect in their minds, and they obviously weren't eager to let go of the idea, especially
after talking to the Narcotics cops about the find in Monroe's school locker. Meanwhile, the IAD investigator
handling the police brutality allegations in the Ninth District—Warner Basinger—seemed confused about the
state of his own investigation. Yes, they had Harcourt's
partner, Bishop, under surveillance, theoretically, but no,
they didn't know where he was at this moment, mainly
because two of the three cars available for the investigation were caught in the repair backlog at the department's motor pool. Even Frank's own man, Special
Agent Jackson, covering the Medical Examiner's Office,
had nothing to offer. The ME was revamping their
record-keeping system and had "temporarily lost track"
of some parts of the Harcourt autopsy file. Frank was
leaving with a briefcase full of incomplete, half-baked,
and often contradictory evidence, some of it of dubious
legality, on what, by his last count, were at least a half-
dozen different felonies. This was what he was supposed
to take to the U.S. Attorney. His only consolation was
that Jessup, after six years as the U.S. Attorney for the
District of Columbia, was probably accustomed to this
kind of muddle.

Frank unlocked the door of his Pathfinder, threw the
briefcase onto the passenger seat, and climbed in. On the
floor was a copy of the day's *Post*. As if to taunt him

even more, the front page carried a story on the city's loss of $55 million in federal block-grant money intended to rehabilitate housing for the poor, all because the Department of Housing and Neighborhood Development lacked the capacity to find or develop projects to spend the money on. Just the week before, there was another piece claiming that the city had lost $1 million a month because of its inability to process Medicaid managed-care contracts. Frank closed his eyes and leaned back against the headrest. There were times when he wished he could be transferred to the Boise satellite office. He could spend his mornings fishing and his afternoons keeping tabs on those government-hating militia groups. He'd be bored within a month, probably, and he wouldn't get to see his daughter as often as he did now, but it was a tempting prospect.

Frank looked at his watch. He wasn't ready to see Jessup yet, but he had little choice, with the weekend coming up. As it was, even if he could convince Jessup about a warrant for the OES office, they'd still have to go through the nightmare of getting the paperwork issued on a Friday, and by somebody with balls enough not to worry about the political nastiness of a federal agency raiding a city government office on a weekend. The imminent danger to the lives of Silas Whitcomb and Dennis Monroe was speculative at best—besides, one was a homeless alcoholic and the other a suspect in both a homicide and a narcotics case—and there was no saying for sure that they would find anything at OES that would lead to either one of them. Simply put, the case was a mess. Frank knew he'd have to be eloquent, persuasive, and confident to get what he needed. He might even have to be a little creative in his presentation of the facts.

Frank pulled out of his parking space and started driving toward Judiciary Square. He had hoped to interrogate

Jason Rourke in person before going to the U.S. Attorney—he found interrogations over the phone less reliable than those conducted face-to-face—but that was just one more detail he would have to fudge. If he finished with Jessup and the judge early enough, he would head out to the Eastern Shore and have another talk with the boy and his father. Renee would be there, and he could fill her in on his progress. He had been thinking about her a lot since their talk the night before in his office. In fact, he had been sitting in bed remembering something—the night of their first sexual encounter, years ago—at the very moment she called at 3:00 A.M. to tell him about the business with Jason and his father in the swamp. He'd been embarrassed when he first heard her voice on the phone, as if she'd read his thoughts and was calling to berate him for not keeping his mind on the job.

She would be trouble, of course—this bone-thin, neurotic, chain-smoking, scotch-guzzling white woman. Maybe more trouble than he wanted right now.

But that was exactly what he had told himself ten years ago, and here he was now, in the very same place. He'd made what he thought was a safe marriage and learned that there was no such thing. Comfort—the absence of surprises—was not enough to build a life on after all.

This case she had brought him was somehow typical of Renee—chaotic, maddeningly ambiguous, and likely to cause him no end of difficulty. It would be like that all the time with her, he knew. Trouble in all caps, as his mother used to say. But maybe that was what he'd been lacking these past years, that sense of opposition, of friction. He'd been easing along for too long—doing his job, waiting for rewards that sometimes actually came, consoling himself with the thought of his gorgeous little daughter and his European vacations and his Capitol Hill town house that was actually starting to look like something after years of weekend renovation. Maybe what he needed was a challenge.

And Renee, he knew, would be nothing if not a challenge.

TWENTY-THREE

THE SITUATION WAS becoming intolerable. There were just too many people in that house. Every time Graham tried to go off by himself, he ran into someone—Maxie and Hortense whispering in the kitchen, Renee napping in one bedroom, Jason stewing in the other. He couldn't even take refuge in the blue bus without being under the eye of that FBI agent. And when he tried to hide out on the beach, he found Julia there, grimly performing calisthenics in a purple leotard.

"Push-ups," she told him, "are an excellent way of releasing tension."

Eventually, hoping to get rid of his persistent headache, Graham decided to take a walk. He got his jacket from the house and then exited by the front door. Agent Holly was sitting in his car in the drive, listening to country music on a little boom box. Graham walked across the lawn to him. "I'm just heading down the road for a little while. Get some air."

Agent Holly turned off the music. "I'd really like you to stay in the house and environs, sir," he said.

"Yeah, well, you're here to protect my son, not me. And I want to take a walk *beyond* the house and environs." He tapped twice on the roof of the agent's car and then started off. Matthew Holly, wisely, didn't try to stop him.

The light was just fading when Graham reached the end of the drive. He turned left and headed up the road, toward a bank of vivid, slate-colored clouds that hugged the treetops to the north. The sun had just sunk below the cloud cover over the horizon, and now the empty fields seemed to glow a yellowish green in the twilight. Graham, a lifelong urbanite, wondered idly what had been planted in these fields, and where the farmers were. A rusty red tractor sat in the middle of one of the fields, as if it had dropped there out of the sky.

As he walked, Graham tried to imagine what his son must be going through now, standing at the center of this swirl of adult craziness. It was something he'd done a lot of in the months after Laura's death—trying to put himself inside Jason's head. Their therapist had recommended the exercise as a way of reconnecting with each other after the trauma of the suicide. But Graham had always found it difficult, if not impossible. And he still did. The scene with Jason last night on the beach—that outburst of bad feelings from years ago—had taken Graham by surprise. Although it probably shouldn't have. The boy was going through the second major ordeal of his short life. The various shocks of the last week had obviously tapped into the same deep currents of emotion in him, so it made sense that the old poisons would well up with the new ones. But what would happen now that all of those feelings were coming back? Graham had a visceral—and probably irrational—certainty that Jason would be physically safe, that they both would get through this calamity in one piece, but what would happen then?

A wave of anxiety left Graham suddenly short of breath. He regarded himself as a reasonably self-sufficient, psychologically healthy person, but he had to admit that the thought of growing old alone disturbed him. He wondered if Jason would even be speaking to him in five years. They had a neighbor on their block—an old marine captain whose wife had died childless decades ago. The man was in his seventies now, but he still lived in the same big colonial, still shopped for himself, cooked for himself, took care of himself. But he was alone. Graham would watch him on Saturday mornings tooling around his flower beds in boxer shorts, black socks, and oxblood loafers. Occasionally, he would hear the man talking to himself—not bitterly or angrily, but conversationally, as if talking to a longtime familiar. His wife, most likely. And there were times when Graham could picture himself in the same situation. Would he, too, eventually disappear down his own rabbit hole of eccentricity, with no one to witness his fall, let alone pull him back?

He shook his head and picked up his pace, as if greater speed would get him past this embarrassing bout of self-pity. He was passing other houses now, each in a different state of dilapidation. People were turning lights on, and he could sometimes see them through their windows, reading newspapers or just standing around, waiting for dark. All the people he saw were black, and Graham wondered what they must be thinking as they looked out their windows and watched him pass—a disheveled, overweight white man, walking along a road where he obviously had no business. His life must seem as opaque to them as theirs was to him. The great racial divide was something no D.C. resident could ever forget, living in a center of white power that just happened to have a population that was over 60 percent black. Even people like the Monroes, upper-middle-class professionals just like himself, remained a mystery to Graham—as had been painfully obvious in the police station on Wednesday night. Could people like Graham and the Monroes ever hope to harmonize their interests, or even remotely *understand* each other's interests? It was a big, unanswerable question, relevant in every American city but especially in the District of Columbia. And the signs didn't look too hopeful to Graham these days, when every debate seemed to carry the taint of racial politics, and even other blacks who criticized Mayor Humphrey were accused of racism if their skin was lighter than his. Would it take new dogs—puppies like Jason and Dennis, maybe—to learn this new trick?

Getting winded now, Graham slowed down and started walking toward a low brick building by the side of the road. At first, he thought it might be a power substation or a small storage warehouse, but then he read the crudely lettered sign over the entrance: ST. MARY'S CATHOLIC CHURCH. He almost laughed aloud. What was this doing here? he wondered. Was this supposed to be some kind of sign from God, plunked down in this unlikely location to save him from his burgeoning sense of helplessness? More likely it was here to torment him. Graham had been raised a Catholic, but the clearest sense of a God in his mind was of some kind of cosmic satirist, toying with the world for His own amusement. God might be Love to other people, but to Graham God had recently seemed more like Irony. And so this little Catholic church deep in Baptist territory was perfectly in character—God's little joke on him at his moment of greatest weakness.

Graham stepped around the corner of the building to

one of the small windows on the south side of it. The
pane was smeared with dust. He put his hand up against
the window and peered in. The room was empty—no
pews, no altar, just a bare, unswept room. More irony—a
church as vacant as his faith. "Very funny," he said aloud
this time, and thought instantly of the old marine talking
to himself in his underwear. Graham stepped back from
the window. He should pray here, he told himself. He
should play a joke back on the old jokester himself. Although Laura would probably not approve.

Graham winced at a sudden throbbing in his head.
Massaging his temples, he walked over to a low brick
wall and sat down. An image came to him then—an old
memory of one of Laura's earliest bad patches, not long
after Jason was born. She had walked into his study one
night after Jason was asleep. They were talking—he
couldn't remember about what—but she had her back to
him, standing at the leaded-glass window behind his
desk. She had placed her hands up on the window, one
palm on each of two small leaded panes. "I'm afraid,"
she said, apropos of nothing, and he watched as the muscles in her arms tightened. Suddenly, he heard an odd,
brittle pop like that of a lightbulb exploding, and then, a
moment later, the far-off tinkle of glass hitting the concrete patio one floor below. She turned to him with
frightened eyes and showed him the streams of blood
trickling down her forearms.

It was an accident—or so she always claimed afterward—but Graham never really believed her. And he
could never shake that sound from his memory. Irony
again: he always thought of that cheerful tinkle as the
sound that marked the beginning of the end of their hap-
piness together.

Graham stood suddenly and looked up at the sky. It
was getting dark now. There were no streetlights, and he

thought he might have some difficulty finding his way back.

He looked again at the little bunkerlike church. Would it really help him feel closer to her, he wondered, to walk into this church—into *any* church—and pray? But even if he did, what would he say to her? "Jason's in trouble, Laura. And I don't know what to do about it." To which she would no doubt smile and answer, "So what else is new?"

Graham turned. Stop it, he said to himself. His head was pounding again, the ache immune to all medication. Moving quickly now, he set off back toward Julia's house, trying not to think of anything but the sound of his own heavy breathing.

Frank arrived at the house on the Eastern Shore at ten, feeling worn-out but strangely exhilarated. He had spent the better part of a day bouncing his evidence around the D.C. criminal justice system—like a pinball player shaking and pushing some huge but sensitive table, always on the verge of triggering the Tilt function that would paralyze the bumpers and send the ball dribbling down a dead gutter into oblivion. He had in fact come close to doing that at least twice. But after almost twenty years in the Washington field office, Frank knew the tolerance level of the system; he had shoved and rattled the table just hard enough to get what he wanted. True, he'd been upbraided by the U.S. Attorney for the District of Columbia and ridiculed by two different federal judges and his own SAC, but by focusing on the "imminent threat" to Dennis Monroe, he'd ultimately gotten what he needed. No one, it seemed, wanted to be held responsible for the death of a middle-class black teenager in the District of Columbia.

Frank parked his Pathfinder at the end of the drive.

Battered briefcase in hand, he walked over to Matthew
Holly's car. The young agent had been sitting with the
windows open, watching the house and smoking. But
when he saw Frank, he quickly got out.

"Matthew," Frank said. The bushes behind Holly's car
seemed to vibrate with the hum of thousands of insects.
"How's it going?"

"Everything under control, sir. All quiet on the western
front. Or should I say the Eastern Shore?"

"You're a real wit, Matthew." Frank looked over at the
glowing windows of the small house. "You've got, what,
six people in that little place? It's amazing they haven't
killed each other yet."

"It *is* a small place, sir." Holly cleared his throat. "So,
is Special Agent Bradley coming in a different Bucar?"
he asked, using the slang for "Bureau car" with the self-
conscious nonchalance of all new agents.

Frank shook his head. "Sorry, Matthew. Agent Bradley's seeing to some other urgent business for me. He
won't be available until tomorrow. Think you can take
another night out here?"

Holly was obviously not happy with this news, but he
was too accomplished a sycophant to complain openly.
"Yes, sir," he said, practically saluting.

Frank laughed. Agent Holly clearly knew what it took
to go far in this man's FBI. "Carry on," he said crisply,
and then started toward the house.

It was Renee who came to the front door in answer to
his knock. "Finally," she said as she opened the screen
door for him. He ducked inside the house. It was a low-
ceilinged place, stuffed with furniture and pet supplies,
and it would have made him claustrophobic even if it
hadn't been crowded with people.

The other women were all sitting around the kitchen
table, cradling coffee mugs. They, too, looked relieved

to see him, as if his arrival might ease the tension that was palpable in the room. Renee introduced him around. Maxie Daniels, whom Frank had heard about but never met, took his hand and wouldn't let go. "I like the handshake," she said. "Firm, but not aggressive."

Frank produced his deep, pleasant chuckle. "That's me in a nutshell, ma'am."

"I'll bet," Maxie answered ambiguously, then released his hand.

"Well," Frank went on, "I want to talk to each one of you about what's been going on, but first I should see Jason. He around?"

"In the bedroom," Renee said, pointing down the hall. "First one on the right. He's in there with his father. I think they'd welcome an interruption."

Frank excused himself and went down the hallway to the first bedroom. He knocked. "Come," said a voice from inside.

Father and son were sitting on opposite sides of the room, staring at each other. Frank got the distinct impression that he had walked in on an argument. Graham Rourke, a striking, burly man around Frank's own age, stood up. "Agent Laroux?" he asked. "It's about time we met in person."

"I agree," Frank said, shaking his hand. He nodded at the boy sitting on the bed. "Jason."

"I told you everything on the phone," the boy said, as if Frank had arrived solely to make his life even more miserable.

"Maybe so. But we've still got lots to talk about." Frank put his briefcase on a bureau and snapped open the latches. "But first, there's something I want you to take a look at." He rummaged around in the briefcase for the photograph one of his agents had faxed him just before he left for the Eastern Shore. He found it and handed it over to Jason, along with several other faxed photographs he'd put together at the office. "I want you to look through these pictures, Jason, and tell me if any of them look familiar to you."

Jason took the photos and leafed through them. "This one," he said after a few seconds. He held up the photograph of Morgan Zack. "This is the guy I saw in the Explorer that night."

"You're sure?"

"Pretty sure," he said. He took another look. "No, definitely sure. I remember now. With the hair, he looks like a monk or something."

Frank took back the pictures. "Yes," he said, "he looks like a monk." He tossed the pictures into the briefcase and pulled out his ink-heavy notebook.

It was already midnight when Frank finished his interviews and finally caught up with Renee. He found her sitting on the beach, her legs sandwiched between two blankets. She was smoking a cigarette and listening to something on a Walkman. He sank heavily onto the chilly sand beside her and heaved a deep breath.

"Hey," she said, taking off the headphones and pressing her half-smoked cigarette into the sand. "I thought you were avoiding me."

"You're the only person in this place I really want to talk to," he said.

She nodded, pulling her hair back behind her shoulders. She was wearing a sleeveless yellow T-shirt. Frank couldn't help admiring the gentle line of her breasts under the cotton fabric. A fine-looking woman, he told himself. At least for a skinny white woman of a certain age.

"It's a pretty tense situation out here," she continued. "Nobody's getting along very well."

"I noticed."

"Even Hortense is getting cranky, and that woman is the closest thing to a saint I know." She pushed the top blanket aside and stretched out her legs. "So tell me the news."

"Good news first?"

"Always."

Frank smiled. "The good news is that we should be able to go in for the OES records tomorrow, in spite of your little fishing expedition the other day. Lord, was it fun explaining *that* to Judge Thorndike."

"And what about that guy from the files? Silas whatever. The one unaccounted for."

Frank picked up some sand and let it sift through his fingers. "That's the bad news. He hasn't been showing up at his usual shelter. That could mean he's sleeping it off on a park bench somewhere, but I don't think so. I've got a witness who saw him picked up in a car."

"So it's going to happen to him too," Renee said. "But who's the double for him? There was nobody in the files he could stand in for, as far as I could tell."

"We must not have all of the files. I'm hoping we'll find something tomorrow."

"Or else we'll read his obituary tomorrow. It really is sick. They'll be eating Irish babies next."

"Say what?"

"Oh, just a literary allusion. What can I say, I'm a schoolteacher." She paused and then asked, "Do you think Dennis is still alive?"

Frank looked out over the dark water. "I have no idea."

"But how can Jason and Dennis still be a threat to these people? The boys didn't see anyone kill anybody."

Frank picked up another handful of sand. "The evidence is terrible in this case," he said. "As far as I've been able to determine, every body except the last one has been cremated, and who knows what's happened to the autopsy reports? Jason and Dennis are the only witness who can put that drug dealer Rodriguez on the street where Detective Harcourt was supposed to have died. And Jason can positively identify the man in the Explorer." He dropped the sand. "I wish they hadn't thrown the slug and shell casing into the river," he said. "We might have been able to at least tie the bullet in the Audi to the ones in James Rodriguez. But without any better evidence, those files you found may be useless in court, even if they turn out to be admissible."

"Come on, Frank. It just so happens that OES has a drawerful of files about dead people and missing people who look like each other?"

"You've been away from the criminal justice system too long," Frank said. "Even with Dennis and Jason's testimony we might not have enough to convict anybody, at least not yet. Catching bad guys is easy; convicting them is hard."

"If it's so easy to catch them, how come you haven't caught anybody yet?"

"I've got somebody in mind."

"Who?"

Frank smiled at her eagerness. "The famous deaf guy. The man Jason saw in the Explorer. His name is Morgan Zack. And get this: he was Vincent Osborne's boss at OES."

Renee looked impressed. "So is he the one behind all of this?"

"Could be. We'll find out more tomorrow, I hope." He paused. "So I'll be heading back to the city now. Lots to do tomorrow."

Renee grabbed her pack of cigarettes and pulled one out.

"Do you have to?" Frank asked. "Never mind what

you're doing to your lungs. I just hate the smell of cigarettes on a woman's breath."

She stopped with the lighter halfway to the cigarette. "Why do you care? Are you planning to kiss me?"

"It had crossed my mind."

Renee gave him a sour look. "Not here, you're not."

"Where, then?" he asked, feeling exasperated.

She stared at him for a few seconds, then tossed her head back toward the bushes behind the beach. "How about down there a little way? Farther from the house."

Frank was nonplussed by the unexpected success. "Seriously?"

"Hurry," she said. She was on her feet already, gathering up the blankets and the Walkman.

He followed her down the beach, appreciating from behind the fluid swing of her hips, the sinewy line of her muscular legs. *Grazie a Dio*, he said to himself. It had been a long time.

"Put your tongue back in your mouth, Frank, and help me spread this out."

They set the blanket in a little recess in the vegetation, half hidden from the rest of the dark beach. "I'm still not sure about this," Renee said. "So I don't want you to read too much into it. Let's think of this as an experiment."

"A physics experiment?"

"More like a chemistry experiment. Just to see what it feels like."

"I'll try to make it feel *real* good," he said, in his corniest Isaac Hayes voice.

Ignoring this comment, she leaned back on the sandy blanket and pulled off her T-shirt. "Let's try not to make too much noise."

Her body seemed familiar to him, even after all these years. She still had the same warm, cream-colored skin, hairless except on her long forearms, which were covered with a fine, translucent down. Her breasts—compact, dense, and sloped gently at the top—still smelled vaguely of nectarines, and her shoulders were spattered with the same tiny freckles that seemed to collect in the hollows of her collarbones. He watched his hands—dark and thick—traveling over her pale body. She was so thin; he felt he could snap her in two if he wasn't careful. Though he knew she was a lot tougher than she looked. "You really ready for this?" he asked, leaning over to kiss the line of her jaw.

"I've been ready for a decade, jerk."

She unbuttoned his white shirt and pulled it off his shoulders. Then she slid down beneath him. "Ow," he said, startled by the sensation of her teeth on his right nipple.

There was a rustling behind them, then a little strangled yell. Alert suddenly, Frank sat up and looked around. He saw someone running away down the beach.

"Fuck!" Renee hissed. She was scrabbling out from under him, pulling up her loose shorts. "Fuck, fuck, fuck!"

Frank looked back at her, momentarily confused.

"It was Jason, goddamn it!" she said. Her breasts swung back and forth in the dim light. "Fuck!" she said again.

Frank didn't know why Renee was reacting this way. "So he saw us. What's the big deal?"

"Trust me, it's bad," she said, grabbing her T-shirt from the rumpled blanket. "It's not what he needed to see right now."

Frank put a hand on her arm. "Don't go after him," he said. "It won't help."

She shook his hand off. "I should talk to him," she said, pulling on the T-shirt.

"And say what?"

"I don't know. But I should talk to him." She slipped her feet into her sandals and started running down the beach after him.

Frank watched her go, feeling disappointed again and hopeless. "Fuck," he said then—a weak echo of Renee's outburst. He pulled his shirt back over his shoulders and started buttoning it. "God *damn* this goddamn case."

He was still sitting on the blanket, looking out at the tiny, sparkling lights across the bay, when she came back a few minutes later. Her thin form appeared out of the darkness, trudging through the sand, sandals dangling from the fingers of her right hand. She fell onto the blanket next to him. "You calm him down?" Frank asked.

"He ran into his bedroom and locked the door. He wouldn't answer when I knocked."

Frank shrugged. "He'll get over it," he said.

The two of them sat there, side by side, for a few silent minutes. Renee was breathing heavily; Frank could see her shoulders rising and falling. He reached out and placed his hand on her narrow shoulder. "You wouldn't be interested in continuing," he asked then. "Now that the world knows about our dark, secret passion?"

She shook her head without looking at him. "It's late," she said.

Frank let go of her shoulder. He dug his heels into the sand and started pushing, hollowing out deep little ditches. "Yeah," he said, lying back on the blanket and putting his hands behind his neck. "It's late."

TWENTY-FOUR

THE LAST RIDE took him all the way into the city, to Adams-Morgan. The driver—a beefy English guy who had picked him up outside Annapolis—dropped him off right at the intersection of Columbia and 18th. Jason had never seen this corner so quiet. It was just after sunrise on Saturday morning. Most of the stores and restaurants were still closed, and there were big piles of the morning *Post* stacked in doorways up and down the block. A few early risers were hurrying along the sidewalks, looking half asleep, and a couple of homeless men were just getting up from their cardboard beds. Outside a twenty-four-hour chicken place, a short Hispanic-looking man was hosing down a pile of blue plastic crates.

Jason stopped on the corner, unsure which way to go. He had planned nothing, had no idea what was going to happen next. Besides the credit card, he had thirty-eight dollars in his wallet and a prepaid phone card that his father made him carry wherever he went. In his backpack was his toothbrush, his English 3 textbook, and a single change of clothes.

When a Metro Police cruiser crawled to a stop at the traffic light, Jason pulled his backpack higher on his shoulder, trying to look as if he knew where he was going.

It was a half-assed thing he was doing—Jason *knew* it was half-assed—but there was no way he could have stayed any longer in that house—that insane asylum—with four pushy women, an asshole FBI agent, and his father. He was better off just making *himself* disappear. Washington was a big city, full of good places to hide. Most of the museums were free, and there were crowds of tourists on every street corner. He could even lose himself in the White House for an hour if he wanted to. And no one would find him—not the green Explorer goons, not the D.C. narcs who found drugs in his locker, not even the FBI. Washington, D.C., would hide him well.

Jason felt a surge of anger as he thought of the black FBI agent. Something Laroux, who had talked to him the night before. The man was supposed to be out there to protect him, but the asshole ends up putting the moves on Renee. On Renee! It was a fucking outrage!

But now that Jason was gone—gone from right under the FBI's nose—the man would look incredibly stupid. They would *all* look incredibly stupid—Laroux, his father, and especially that blond-boy Agent Holly. Jason had left them all behind, asleep on the job. It was priceless. He could imagine them all getting up at that very moment, bleary-eyed and foggy-headed. Gradually, they'd notice his empty room. They'd start running around, looking for him everywhere. Finally, they'd realize he had escaped. And they'd freak. His father would start chewing out the asshole in the car. Maxie and Hortense would wring their hands in worry. And Renee would go to the beach and start chain-smoking her Camel

Filters, telling herself it was all her own fault.

Priceless, Jason said to himself. Too bad he couldn't be there to see it.

He turned and headed downtown. After a few minutes of walking, he left the commercial seediness of Adams-Morgan and came to a quieter, tree-lined neighborhood that seemed to be the world's capital of blond women in ponytails walking their dogs. At New Hampshire, he turned toward Dupont Circle. Feeling hungry, he went into a Starbucks and ordered a regular coffee and some expensive pastry he didn't know the name of. Then he sat at the high counter looking out at Connecticut Avenue and wondered what to do next.

There had to be someone, he thought—someone he could stay with for a few days—but he couldn't come up with any possibilities. Ever since calling it quits with his girlfriend, Sarah, he'd cut himself off from that whole group he used to hang out with—Peter Quigley, Anita Fox, Jamie DeVries. They'd all sided with Sarah after the breakup—all except Dennis, who'd never been Sarah's greatest fan anyway.

Jason closed his eyes and tried to picture where Dennis could be right then. Could he really have been picked up way back on Wednesday, the day Jason was chased through the park? If so, Dennis might not even be alive anymore. Jason took a sip of hot, bitter coffee, trying to shake the thought from his mind. No, he told himself, there was no way that Dennis could be dead. Dennis was the together one of the duo, the one who always knew exactly who he was and where he was going. He had it all planned out—Harvard, then law school, then a high-powered job in government or business. Jason teased him about it, naturally (the Model Minority, he called him), but he'd always secretly admired his friend's certainty, his steadiness of purpose. So there was no doubt in his mind that Dennis had gotten away. He was probably lying low somewhere, waiting for the whole thing to cool down. Dennis had some friends in school—white kids who thought that being friendly with Dennis was some kind of badge of virtue—who would probably put him up with no questions asked. If Jason could figure out where he was, they could even hide out together. And between the two of them, they could figure out what to do.

Jason finished his pastry, tossed the rest of the coffee, and headed out to the street again. The sidewalks were getting busier now; all the Yuppie drones in the neighborhood were up and around now, looking for newspapers and cappuccino. Jason crossed Dupont Circle and continued south on Connecticut, then east on M Street. He stopped at the National Geographic building and spent a few minutes looking at the enlarged magazine covers in the windows. There was one picture he really liked, of a skinny kid with his face painted like the night sky, stars and planets and comets splashed across his deep-blue cheeks. Somehow, the kid reminded Jason of himself, back when he was seven or eight, before his mother died, when he wanted to be an astronomer more than anything else in the world. Why couldn't he still want something that way? he wondered. Why couldn't he be sure about anything?

Continuing east, Jason reached 16th Street. He could see the White House to the south, across Lafayette Square. Maybe the President would take him in, he thought idly. Jason imagined himself settling into the Lincoln Bedroom and living there under the protection of the Secret Service. Oddly comforted by the ridiculous thought, Jason started walking toward the White House, into Lafayette Park. The lawn here was crowded with homeless people and assorted crazies, stockaded behind rag-filled shopping carts, grimy duffel bags, and card-board boxes. Some of them had signs on their little for-tresses—saying things like VETERANS ABANDONED and MORE JOBS LESS MISSILES. "Hey!" someone shouted at him. Jason turned. It was a man with a long, gray beard clotted with grease and spit. He held up a sign: MR. PRES-IDENT, YOU ARE THE CONSPIRATOR-IN-CHIEF!!

Would this be himself someday? Jason wondered. Would he end up with the psychos here, holding up some crudely hand-lettered sign saying TRUST NO ONE? It was a scary thought, although at least he would be safe then. Nobody paid any attention to these people—nobody even seemed to look at them—so he wouldn't have to worry about being found. With all of the suits running around in Washington—lawyers, politicians, lobbyists, and bureaucrats—these people were just lost in the shuf-fle, too insignificant to notice.

Jason wandered for the rest of the morning. First, he spent a couple of hours at the Museum of Natural His-tory. Then he roamed the Mall, making wide circles around the Washington Monument. He bought a hot dog from a vendor near the carousel and sat down on a bench, watching the kids laugh idiotically as they went around and around. Those blank-eyed wooden horses reminded him of the real horse in Rock Creek Park. He remem-bered the mare's nostrils flaring, the whites of her eyes showing as she reared up in the close confines of the stable.

A man sat down beside him on the bench. He was wearing a Baltimore Orioles cap, a white polo shirt, and jeans, although he must have been at least fifty. "How you doin'?" he asked.

Jason shrugged. "Okay."

The man leaned back and crossed his hands over his little paunch. "You from Washington?"

Jason wasn't looking at him, but he could feel the man's eyes on him. "Yeah," he said warily.

"You look tense. Got something on your mind?"

Jason straightened up on the bench. He told himself it wasn't possible that this could be one of them. They couldn't have just found him like this.

The guy leaned forward again and patted Jason's thigh. "Relax," he said. "I'm staying at a hotel a couple blocks from here. You ever have a massage—I mean a really *good* massage?"

"Oh Christ," Jason muttered. He shot up from the bench and started walking away, toward one of the red Smithsonian buildings. When he reached the entrance, he stuffed the napkin and the rest of the hot dog into a garbage can. Then he pushed through the big doors into the building.

He found himself in a little courtyard centered on a burbling fountain. Jason walked up to it and put his hands into the cool water.

He would have to find someplace to go. He realized now that he couldn't just wander around the city for days on end. He would have to find someone to stay with, someone he could trust. It depressed him, and then scared him, that he had no idea who that someone might be.

Renee hit the curb hard with her right front wheel as she parked in her usual place on Nevada. She reached back for the red Club but then decided against using it. She'd be at the house for only a few minutes. The rest of the afternoon she would spend driving around, looking for Jason. She had a few ideas about where he might have gone, though she realized that her chances of actually finding him were remote.

She got out of the car and retrieved her briefcase and overnight bag from the trunk. Her notes on the case—

she was keeping notes, even though she still told herself
she wasn't going to write anything about this—were
sticking halfway out of the briefcase. Tucking them back
inside, she wondered how she would ever handle this
latest development in the story. How would she, as a
journalist, explain what had made Jason disappear from
Julia's house last night? Talk about gonzo journalism—
she would have to explain that her own dissoluteness,
her own selfishness, had made the boy run off by himself
with half of Washington, D.C., gunning for him.

Frank, of course, had been furious when Renee called
to tell him about it. He had gone back to the city after
midnight, and Renee's early-morning call—the second in
as many nights—had woken him out of a deep and probably deserved sleep. When he commanded her to put
Matthew Holly on the phone, she just handed the receiver
to the sweating young agent and walked out of the house.

But now, back in Washington, she was nursing a vague
hope that at least this latest disaster could be cleared up
quickly. There was an outside chance, she knew, that she
would find Jason sitting in one of the wrought-iron chairs
on her back patio, waiting for her to come home. If he
was there, she would bundle him up, apologize (though
for what, she wasn't exactly sure), and drive him immediately to the FBI Washington field office. Frank—
judging by his mood on the phone—would probably put
the boy in a locked cell for the duration of the case.

She reached the porch of her house on Kitchener. After
unlocking it with her keys, she pushed the sticky door
open. The first thing she saw—through the cluttered
kitchen—was the back door standing wide open, its glass
pane broken. For a second, she thought it might have
been Jason who'd broken in, but then she took a quick
look around. The house had been ransacked. Cushions,
books, and papers were strewn all over the floor of the

living room; in the kitchen, cabinets had been flung open and the contents pulled down onto the counters. Renee felt queasy suddenly. She stepped into the kitchen, her shoes grinding spilled sugar into the linoleum.

Then her mind became aware of an absence—a sound that should have been there but wasn't. She stepped out of the kitchen and headed toward the living room. The birdcage lay on the floor upside down. Inside, stretched out on the thin metal bars, was Fenton. She knelt and opened the door to the cage. Reaching in, she gently took the bird in her hand and pulled it out. It was like holding a fistful of lint—practically weightless. The bird's neck had been snapped, and its head lolled obscenely back and forth like a small, limp toy in her hand.

When the phone rang, she placed the dead bird on the edge of the coffee table and got up to answer it. As she shakily picked up the receiver she thought of another phone call—the one she had received almost a decade ago: "I like the way you write about me . . ."

She couldn't speak. "Hello?" said a male voice on the other end of the line. A strange male voice. "Is anybody there?"

Feeling panicked, Renee turned and saw her long bread knife sticking out of the side of a bookcase.

"I can hear you breathing," the male voice said. "I know someone's there."

Renee hung up. She scrabbled for her bag and then raced toward the front door. There was traffic going by on Kitchener, and a woman pushing a stroller, but no sign of anyone else. Could that really have been them? Were they watching the house even now? Without waiting another second, she burst out of the house, pulled the door closed behind her, and then ran across her lawn back toward her car on Nevada.

TWENTY-FIVE

THE OFFICE OF Emergency Shelter and Treatment Services looked deserted when Frank Laroux and his team arrived shortly after 1:00 P.M. on Saturday. The glass entrance to the third-floor suite of offices was locked, and there was no one at the receptionist's desk to buzz them in. Frank knocked loudly, pressed the nonfunctioning bell next to the door, then knocked again. Finally, a couple of heads rose above cubicle partitions around the office to see what the racket was. None of the attached bodies, though, seemed willing to come to the door, despite Frank's forceful enunciation of the letters F-B-I. He was about to consider breaking down the door when a small, nervous-looking man finally came to the front and let them in.

Frank stuck his ID and his warrant in front of the man's bewildered face. "FBI," he repeated. "We're here to exercise this warrant." His six men pushed in behind him and immediately fanned out to all corners of the office suite. "Can you direct us to the offices of Vincent Osborne and Morgan Zack?"

"I'm new," the man stuttered. "I just came over from the Taxicab Commission last week." He looked disconcerted by the sight of federal agents buzzing through his office. "Are you really FBI?"

"Is there anybody here who has worked in this office *longer* than a week?" Frank asked.

"I can help you." Frank turned and saw a stunning young woman with flawless coffee-colored skin and tight cornrows. Feeling a little disconcerted himself now, Frank showed her the warrant and ID. She scanned them, obviously not taking in the full contents, and then looked up at him. "Is Morgan in trouble?"

"Everyone here will be in trouble if I don't get cooperation."

The woman raised an eyebrow at him. "Well, Agent Frank Laroux," she said, "you've really put the fear of God into all of us. Follow me."

She led them briskly through a warren of cheaply constructed cubicles. "You're lucky there's anybody here except the janitor," she said. "But our computers were down until yesterday afternoon and we had to catch up." She stopped at a hallway of small offices near the back of the suite. "That one is Zack's and this one was Vincent Osborne's. Nobody's gotten around to cleaning it out yet."

"Good," Frank said. Then, turning to two of his agents, he said, "Brande, Singer, make sure you don't miss anything." The two men stepped into the office. They started opening file cabinets and pulling out folders by the fistful.

"They're very eager. I'm glad *my* name isn't on that little warrant of yours."

Frank sent two more agents into Zack's office. "Afraid of what I might find in a search of your personal effects?" he asked her.

"Don't you wish." She raised her perfect eyebrow at him again. "Anyway, I guess it figures that the biggest ballbusters in the office are the ones involved in whatever this is."

"That sounds like a confession to me," Frank said.

The woman let out an unself-conscious honk. "Touché. I didn't think you FBI types went in for subtle verbal abuse."

"We're full of surprises. May I ask your name?"

Her nostrils flared slightly. "Joyce," she said. "Joyce Conley."

"And you work with Zack and Osborne?"

"Not really. Nobody works with anybody in this office. We call it the Mayor Humphrey management model. It's how the Mayor keeps the Control Board's auditors from gaining the upper hand around here—total confusion."

"I'd like to ask you a few questions anyway. You seem to know a lot about what goes on here."

Joyce Conley looked at him for a few seconds, her mouth pursed in thought. "No," she said finally. "I don't think I'll talk to you, Agent Laroux."

"That's your choice. But I have to say, it doesn't look good to refuse cooperation."

She shrugged. "I'm a lawyer, Agent Laroux. I'm used to not looking good."

"Sir?" It was Agent Cross, one of the men searching Zack's office.

Frank kept his eyes on Joyce Conley. "In a minute," he said to Cross. He folded up his warrant. "You sure you don't want to talk to me?" he asked.

"I'm sure I'm sure." She flashed him a sarcastic little smile and waved. "See you around, Agent Laroux."

Frank watched as she turned and walked away. What was it about women like this? he asked himself. Why was it always the wiseasses with hard mouths and long, hard legs who rang his little bell?

"Sir," Cross insisted again, behind him now.

"What is it?"

"We've got a couple locked drawers in here."

Frank sighed. "Well then, let's get out the old hardware," he said, putting an arm around Cross's shoulders. "I guess we're going to have to make a little mess."

Four hours later, Frank was sitting across from Ann and Leon Monroe in their book-lined living room.

"You mean you've known about this since Thursday," Ann Monroe was saying, "and you're just telling us now?"

"We haven't known anything, Mrs. Monroe. And we still don't. That's the problem. We turned up some files and records this morning that *could* tell us something. But I can't say for sure that they will."

Frank squirmed in the uncomfortable armchair. This was not a visit he'd been looking forward to. As he saw it, he was in a thankless position here—morally obligated to tell the Monroes something about their son, and yet having nothing at all concrete to say. "Our team is looking over the documents now. They'll contact me immediately if they turn up anything."

Ann Monroe was sitting beside her husband on an overstuffed couch subtly embroidered with intertwining roses. It was obviously a prosperous household—solid, tasteful furniture, lots of African art and pseudotribal crafts on the walls, a bolt of kente draped over the back of an armchair. All of it a little self-conscious, it seemed to Frank—as if this upper-middle-class African American couple needed to convince themselves that they hadn't forgotten their heritage.

"It's Saturday, Mr. Laroux," Ann Monroe said then. "You've kept us in the dark for over two days."

"We've been in the dark ourselves."

She stood up. "That's nonsense. You've known a hell

of a lot more than we have." She walked over to the bay window looking out on a well-kept backyard. Frank could see a rock wall out there, covered with ivy. "A hell of a lot more," she repeated.

Leon Monroe leaned forward on the couch. "You've got to understand, Agent Laroux. The police have been telling us since Wednesday that Dennis is guilty of some serious crimes—we've had to live with that, get our minds around the possibility. Meanwhile, you've known all along that it wasn't true. And you don't think this was information worth telling us?"

"It's not that I didn't think it was worth telling you," Frank began, annoyed that he was letting himself be put on the defensive.

"So what are we supposed to feel now, relieved?" Ann Monroe asked. "Wonderful. Our son isn't a homicidal drug dealer. Of course, he may be kidnapped or dead, but at least he's not a criminal."

"We have no evidence that he's either kidnapped or—"

"We had a right to know everything as soon as you knew it."

"I understand—"

"No, you don't understand. You don't understand a thing."

"Ann," Leon Monroe muttered from the couch.

"So what are you doing now?" she continued, ignoring her husband. "What steps are you taking to find Dennis?"

"As I said, our people are going through some documents we picked up today."

"Where did you get these documents?"

Frank put up his hands. "I really can't tell you that, Mrs. Monroe."

"You can't tell us that either."

"I can tell you that we're doing everything we possibly can—"

A look of disgust crossed Ann Monroe's face. She took a step toward Frank. "If anything happens to my son, Mr. Laroux, you won't ever hear the end of this. I promise you that." Then she turned and walked out of the living room.

Frank and Leon Monroe sat in silence for a few seconds. "Agent Laroux—"

"Please explain to your wife that threats won't help any of us," Frank said, feeling genuinely angry now. "I don't know why this has to be adversarial."

Leon Monroe looked down at his hands. "Agent Laroux," he said. "My wife's brother was killed about twenty years ago—shot down on a street corner over in Capitol Heights. He was eighteen at the time, working at a gas station. The police never caught the murderer, never even came up with a suspect. And you know what the police told her and her parents? The exact words? That they were doing everything they could."

"And maybe they were," Frank said.

"Yes, maybe they were. But somehow I doubt it, don't you?"

"I have no way of knowing that, sir."

"You don't? You really don't? This was 1975, the D.C. Metro Police. My wife's brother was a young black male from a working-class neighborhood. I don't think you have to ask if they were really doing everything they could."

"Well, this is 1997, sir. Twenty-two years later."

"Yes, and you're still doing everything you can."

There was nothing Frank could say to this. He got up and grabbed his briefcase from beside the chair. "I'd better go."

"I'll see you to the door," Leon Monroe said.

• • •

Graham Rourke was not a man of small proportions. As he made his way through Eastern Market, he found he could barely squeeze through the closely spaced rows of flower and vegetable stalls. It was like an obstacle course, with huge bunches of pussy willows and forsythia branches in plastic pails, wide flats of impatient on spindly card tables, precariously stacked crates of organic potatoes and figs from God knew where. His big graying head ("like the prow of a Viking ship," as Laura always described it) grazed the potted spider plants hanging from the overhead scaffolding, making them spin like pinwheels on their hooks.

He had no idea why he was here. Once, when Jason was small, Graham and Laura had brought him here for a hot dog at Market Lunch, and the boy had seemed intrigued by the bustle of the place—the noise and clutter and good-natured commerce. It didn't seem likely, of course, that Jason would even remember that sunny afternoon, let alone be moved to come back here a decade later to hide out. But Graham didn't know where else to look. He'd been driving around the city for hours in a rented Ford Taurus, checking out every place that might be construed as shelter in his son's seventeen-year-old brain. He'd been to Georgetown, the National Building Museum (which Jason had once described as "bizarrely cool" in a ninth-grade English paper), Pershing Park, and Jason's favorite pizzeria on Wisconsin. He'd been to the Aquarium, Chinatown, and Gallery Place. He'd even sat outside the Uptown Cinema on Connecticut and watched people leaving the early matinee. But he'd seen no sign of his son. All he had to show for his time was a parking ticket and a dime-sized ding in the door of the rental car from a trash can outside a Tower Records.

Feeling dizzy and exhausted—and still suffering from

the headache he'd had for what seemed like days—Graham reached the door of the redbrick warehouse. Inside, the vast, sunny space was filled with food places—little stalls selling everything from designer hot sauce to olives of seventeen different varieties. A few boys of Jason's age were hanging out near a stall specializing in exotic herbs and teas. They were grungily dressed, smoking, slumped against the side of the stall with an almost aggressive nonchalance. Graham found himself staring at them, thankful that at least his son had not turned out like this.

Graham moved on, deeper into the building. Panic was beginning to set in, gripping his head and chest in thick, tight bands. Why was this happening to him, he asked himself. For the second time in his life, one of the only human beings he really loved was running away from him. Was Graham deficient in some way, unfit for any kind of intimacy or family responsibility? God knows, he worked hard at fatherhood, sweating everything, trying not to take anything for granted. He never thought of himself as one of those workaholic Washington types whose families suffered on the rack of the breadwinner's ambitions. He was a *decent* man, a conscientious father and husband. His wife and his son had needed him, obviously, but he seemed not to know how to give them what they needed.

"Can I help you, sir?" Graham looked up. He was standing in front of a gourmet coffee stand. Open barrels of freshly roasted beans stood at his feet. "We're having a special today on hazelnut Colombian. Would you like a taster?"

Graham stared at her—a pretty Asian woman with ruby lipstick and dangling gold earrings.

"Sir?"

"Coffee," he said. "Regular coffee, with milk and three sugars."

As he took the cup and handed her his money, he noticed that his hands were shaking again. I should go home, he told himself, sipping the lukewarm coffee. He could sleep for a few hours at home and then start searching again.

He stopped and drank the full cup in three long gulps. Then he pushed his way out of the warehouse and back onto the crowded street.

Jason, he decided, would probably not come to a place like this. He'd be too scared to hide in plain sight, and so would find someplace secluded and private. Unless, of course, he had hopped a plane or a train. But Graham couldn't even consider that possibility. That his son could be absolutely *anywhere* was not a useful proposition. Jason had to be here, in Washington. There was no way to go on unless he believed that.

Graham edged through the flower stalls and crossed 7th Street. He walked south for a few blocks and turned onto the street where he had parked. After his rest, he would go back to the movie theater. The thought of Jason sitting in a big dark room seemed right to him. He could imagine his son feeling secure there, watching a film— something that would give him an hour or two of rest.

Two young men were sitting on the hood of his rental car. They looked like brothers, both of them with buzz-cut red hair and pimply foreheads. "Sorry," Graham said, jingling his keys. "You'll have to find someplace else to sit."

The two of them looked at Graham, but didn't move.

"I'm sorry," Graham repeated. "I have to go." He didn't need this. He didn't need a fight now.

"Asswipe," one of them said. They pushed themselves

off the car and started to lope away like twin hyenas reluctantly giving up a kill.

Graham turned back toward the car, feeling angry now. He groped in his pocket for the keys, and was reminded suddenly of the swamp—of the sea of reeds he and Jason had run through the other night. The smell of salt and marsh gas seemed to envelop him then. He felt dizzy. His arm went numb. And then the pain blossomed in his head, making his body go rigid. He tried to speak, to shout to the men who had just left, but he couldn't produce a sound. You're sick, he admitted to himself finally, as he twisted to the pavement beside the car's front wheel.

TWENTY-SIX

IT WAS ALREADY dark when Sarah Thomas and her mother pulled into the driveway of their house on Middagh Street. They had obviously been shopping—Sarah climbed out of the passenger seat with a Hecht's bag in her hand, and her mother took two more from the trunk of the car. Jason watched them from his hiding place in the yew bushes across the street. Sarah looked so good to him—her long blond hair pulled back, her blue jeans tight around her hips, her breasts shaping the fabric of her black cotton top. He wondered how he ever could have broken up with her.

As they climbed the steps to the front door of the house, Sarah and her mother started laughing about something. Jason felt a stab of betrayal. Sarah must have known about the trouble he was in. How could she be laughing at a time like this, even if they *had* broken up? Had he meant so little to her?

He waited for them to get inside. When the front door closed, he got up from behind the yews. Hoping that no one was watching, he calmly crossed the street and walked up the alley between the Thomas house and the one next door. Sarah's room, he knew, was on the second floor, with a window overlooking the backyard. He hoped that she would go there right away, to try on whatever new clothes she had bought at Hecht's. If she didn't—if she stayed downstairs and helped her mother with dinner, or whatever cute little families like the Thomases did together at six o'clock on a spring Saturday—he'd have a long wait ahead of him.

He came around the back of the white-painted brick house and stood under her open window. In a few minutes, he heard what could have been Sarah moving around in there. Trusting to his luck, he picked up a twig from the lawn and flung it at her window. When he didn't get any response, he found another, bigger twig and threw it. It hit the upper pane just as her startled face appeared at the window.

She lifted the sash higher. "Jason!" she hissed at him. "What is going on?"

"Can you meet me at the playground on Oppenheimer? Five minutes?"

She looked uncertain, even a little afraid—not of him, Jason hoped. After a second, she said, "Five minutes," and closed the window.

Jason ran back down the alley to the street and started off toward the park.

There were two kids—about twelve, Jason guessed—sitting on the swings when he walked into the fenced playground, but they got off and walked away the minute he showed up. Jason wondered if he really looked that bad, like somebody worth avoiding. He sat on one of the swings and started idly twisting back and forth, watching the chains overhead braid together and then jolt apart. It was a cloudy night, and chilly, though there wasn't any wind. The houses across the street looked fake, like the houses in the old Lionel train scene his father used to set up in the basement every Christmas—peaceful, safe, totally forgotten.

After a few minutes, he saw Sarah round the corner of her block and come toward him. She had her hands sunk into the pockets of a big brown cardigan. Jason watched her, wondering how she was going to react to him. Would she be friendly? Distant? Suspicious? A thought occurred to him: maybe she'd already called the police and told them to come by the Oppenheimer playground to pick him up.

She walked toward the swings and then stopped about twenty feet away, hands still deep in her pockets.

"Hello," Jason said, feeling embarrassed at the formal tone of his voice.

"Hi." She stared at him for a few seconds, then—to his enormous relief—came right up to him and put her arms around him. He felt every muscle in his body relax. He remembered her good, clean smell—the scented lotion that always reminded him of the beach. Fuck you, Renee, he said to himself.

"What the hell have you been up to, Jason?" Sarah asked.

"It's a long story." He didn't want to let go of her, but after a few more seconds, she gently disentangled herself from his arms. God, she looked beautiful to him, her face scrubbed, her hair clean and shiny—the look of decent, normal life.

"Everybody's been going crazy, talking about it. You and Dennis, the drugs in your lockers."

"I never had any drugs in my locker. Dennis didn't either."

"Is he with you?"

Jason shook his head. "I haven't seen him in days. I think they have him."

"Who's they?"

"I don't know exactly." He struggled to keep a sob out of his voice. "You wouldn't believe what's been happening to me. What I've been going through."

"My parents are being total jerks about it. They're both looking at me all the time and saying, like, Thank God you two broke up, and things like that."

"Is that what you think too?" he asked.

Sarah didn't answer at first. She buried her hands in the pockets of the big sweater again. "We both decided to break it off," she said. "It was you as much as it was me."

"I've missed you," he said, and instantly regretted the comment. It wasn't a lie, but he worried that it might sound like one.

"I've missed you, too."

"I have a favor to ask," he said then, looking away. "You can say no if you want to. I wouldn't blame you if you said no."

"What kind of favor?"

"I need someplace to stay. For a day or two, until some things get worked out. Is that room over your garage still empty?"

"Ye-es," she said, hesitating noticeably. "My mom was thinking of having it painted, but they won't get their act together for weeks, probably."

"You think I can sleep there for a while?"

She took a deep breath and looked toward the jungle gym. "God, Jason," she said. Then, looking back: "I guess so. If you really need it."

"I really need it."

"You'll have to be, you know, really quiet. No lights at night, no TV. If my parents ever found out about it, they'd go ballistic."

"They won't find out. I'll just go in late at night to

sleep. And I'll be out early in the morning. Before anybody's up."

"Actually, you can be in there all day if you want.
Tomorrow, at least. My parents are taking my brother to
the aquarium in Baltimore. Just keep a really low profile
from six to eight-thirty in the morning. And then late
afternoon, too. After they're back."

"Okay," he said.

She smiled at him and pulled something out of her
pocket. It was a sandwich. "You hungry? It's grilled
chicken with Dijon mustard. I only ate half of it at lunch.
I brought it for you."

He took the wrapped sandwich. "Thanks."

She put her hand into her other pocket and pulled out
a key. "The lock sticks sometimes, so you might have to
jiggle it."

Jason laughed. "You knew I'd be asking?"

She nodded.

"You're great," he said. "You are so fucking great."

"So fucking crazy is more like it." She handed him the
key, which was warm from her fingers. "If you need anything, you can call the house from the phone in the room.
It's a separate line and I think it's still connected. If my
mother or father answers, just hang up. But I'll try to
pick up whenever I hear the phone." She flapped the
cardigan open and shut a few times, as if she were about
to take off and fly. "Do you have money?"

"I have enough to get by for a couple days."

They didn't say anything else for a little while. Jason
just sat there on the swing, looking at her, while she
stared down at her shoes and flapped the sweater a few
more times.

"Does your father know that you're okay? I saw him

on the street the day after you went missing, and he looked pretty awful."

"My father," Jason said with an exaggerated roll of his eyes. "I guess he knows I'm okay. I was with him until last night."

Sarah looked at him with a puzzled expression on her face. A little vertical line appeared between her eyebrows. "Part of that long story?" she asked.

"Yeah."

Jason started unwrapping the sandwich.

"Jase," she began then. For a second, she looked unsure how to continue. "There's a rumor that you and Dennis had something to do with that cop who got shot last week. That can't be right, can it?"

He didn't know how to answer. "What do *you* think?"

"I don't know what to think. It doesn't sound possible to me."

"Well, it's not true. At least not in the way you think."

She seemed content with this answer. She fingered the top button of the cardigan. "I should go back now."

"Okay," he said, feeling a keen disappointment.

"Try not to go into the room until later. And if you cut through the yard behind our house there's less chance that my mom or dad will see you. The Waynes live back there and they're away on vacation."

"Okay."

"And be careful, okay?"

"I'll be careful."

She shrugged, and pulled her hair back behind her ears. She was wearing a pair of earrings he had given her—little silver parrots. Jason wondered if she had put them on just before coming to meet him. "Okay, then," she said. "I'll see you later."

"Right."

She turned and started walking away.

"Hey," Jason called out to her. She turned around. "Thanks for this," he said.

She smiled—that smile that always used to kill him. "What's an ex-girlfriend for?" she said quietly, tugging at her earring.

TWENTY-SEVEN

FRANK WAITED UNTIL just before midnight to take the house in Anacostia.

There had been little discernible activity in the place for hours. At about seven, a single man—black, tall, glasses, slender build—had come out the back door, climbed into a white Toyota Camry, and left. The agent who followed the car reported that the man had simply driven to a garden apartment in Prince Georges County— probably his own home—and gone inside, where he'd remained ever since. After that, nothing had happened in the house except for lamps going on and off. Now, at 11:47, there were lights showing in the kitchen and in the basement, nothing on the second floor. Frank guessed that Dennis and Silas were being kept in the basement, which had a single small window too narrow to allow access.

If they were there at all. A few hours after starting surveillance on the house, Frank had sent an agent posing as a meter reader into the alley to try to get a glimpse in the window. But the man had come back frustrated. The

best angle he could get showed only an empty corner of
the basement; he couldn't see more without going right
up to the window and peering in—a chance Frank wasn't
willing to take. He was hoping he'd get lucky, that the
subjects in the house would actually try to move their
prisoners while Frank and his team were watching. If that
happened, he could take them down just as they were
loading the prisoners into the car, and there would be
less chance of anyone getting hurt. Frank knew that rushing the house would be dangerous, not only for his men
but for the prisoners inside as well. He'd even considered
doing the operation as a knock-and-announce, but these
people, with numerous murders behind them, weren't
likely to come out nice and slow with their hands up. It
wasn't an easy call, but Frank felt certain that a knock-
and-announce would put the prisoners in greater danger,
not less. That is, *if* they were inside. *If* they hadn't been
killed already. *If* Frank wasn't totally wrong about this
whole situation.

He had found this house through the files turned up in
the OES raid, but although he'd had enough evidence to
persuade a judge to issue a warrant, there was no way
he could know for sure that this was where Zack would
hold Dennis and Silas. Frank was normally a careful man.
In an ideal situation, with plenty of time to prepare, he'd
have put together a large, well-organized effort here, with
sheaves of advance intelligence reports, a Critical Incident Negotiation Team on hand, maybe even the Hostage
Rescue Team up from Quantico. Instead, all he had was
a hastily briefed SWAT team and a van full of listening
devices and nighttime optical equipment that seemed incapable of telling him anything useful. Frank always had
nightmares about raids gone wrong—he'd heard about
one just a few nights earlier, with a D.C. Metro team
breaking into a suspected crack den that turned out to be

the home of a quiet, law-abiding family—and he certainly didn't want one on his own record. Fortunately, his boss's boss, SAC David Blakely, had given the operation his personal okay. But even so, Frank hated working in an atmosphere of so much uncertainty.

He thought again about what he had told Ann Monroe that afternoon: "We're doing everything we possibly can." The statement was seldom true in law enforcement, but in this case it really was. In Frank's opinion, they were doing *more* than they possibly could—more, in fact, than they probably *should*. Because a teenager's life just *might* be at stake.

The radio in his car crackled, and the voice of Special Agent Bolling reported a vehicle coming down the block from the south. Frank turned around in his seat and watched it go by, a beat-up Chevy with a single African American male driving, looking bored. He didn't stop. That, Frank said to himself, was all they would need—a civilian stumbling onto their little operation before it was set to start. He reached forward and grabbed the radio. "Five, this is One. Will somebody stop the goddamn traffic before it turns onto the street, please? Five?" He put the radio down. "Jesus," he said aloud. He shifted in the seat, his heavy vest irritating the nipple that Renee had bitten the night before. Talk about flying blind. Frank wondered just how foolish he was, taking up this old romance with Renee. It had already burned him once; Jason Rourke's disappearance the night before was going to look bad for him, no matter how he spun it in his report. Agent Holly was *his* man, *his* responsibility.

The radio crackled again. Through the static, Frank heard the words ". . . light going on in the bathroom." It was what he'd been waiting for. At least one occupant of the house would now be out of the way. It was enough to increase their odds of success, however slightly.

Frank looked at his watch. 11:56. "This is One," he announced. "It's time to go in. Repeat: it's time to go in."

Frank upholstered his 9-mm pistol and got out of the car. He watched as two of his SWAT men—Walsh and Zucker, both carrying assault rifles and dressed in jet-black combat fatigues and body armor—hustled toward the brown-brick row house. They stopped at the front door. After counting to five, Frank gave all of them the signal to go.

It was over in seconds. Frank listened to the tumult over his radio—the disembodied shouts and shuffles raking through the static in a chaotic jumble. He hated having to sit there helplessly, watching the windows as his men put themselves under fire inside, but as case agent he had to hold back and let the SWAT team do its job. Finally, after an agonizing wait, the sounds died down and he got the all clear.

No shots fired, he told himself with satisfaction as he headed toward the house.

Agent Walsh had two men on their knees in the living room, and Agent Zucker was bringing another one down from the second floor, but Frank headed straight into the kitchen. It was a mess; dishes and pots were piled in the sink and all over the counters, and there were empty cereal boxes and chip bags all over the floor. The door to the basement stairs stood open beside the grimy stove. Frank could hear shouting from below. He ran down the stairs. Agent Grand had someone spread-eagled against the cinder-block wall. As he reached the bottom step, Frank surveyed the whole basement. He cursed aloud. They weren't there. No Dennis Monroe, no Silas Whitcomb. He had guessed wrong.

Frank walked over to the wall and pounded the cinder blocks with the heel of his hand. More agents were coming down the steps now, making a huge noise. "We got four," Agent Zucker said. "That's all she wrote." Frank nodded. No shots had been fired—thank God at least for that—but he certainly wasn't happy. What a fucking screwup this entire case was, he told himself. A screwup from beginning to end.

Then Frank saw the brackets cemented into the wall and the clothes piled in a heap on the floor across the basement. He walked over and picked up a shirt. There was a pin on the collar—a little red teardrop. Silas. So he hadn't been wrong, after all.

He turned and looked around the dismal basement. They had been here—or at least one of them had. But they'd apparently been moved.

And that, Frank knew, was not a promising development.

It took him a long time to realize that what he was hearing was waves and not wind. The regular pulse of water seemed to match his heartbeat's rhythm. He was standing in a padded box. He remembered warm light streaming around him like a school of silvery, blank-eyed fish. He knew that the fish would not hurt him, so he laughed.

Dennis turned onto his side. It was over now. It had been over for an hour, maybe two, and he didn't want to think about how much he wanted it to start again. He was coming back now—coming down, coming up—and he wondered if they were going to give him more. *When* they were going to give him more. It didn't make sense to him. There was a hiss somewhere. Someone had left the gas on. Or the TV, and now there was static. Like insects drumming. Tiny little bongos.

He wasn't hungry, but he was very, very thirsty.

They had moved him, he remembered that part. He and the other prisoner, the fat crazy one with the name.

Dennis remembered being dragged up the stairs and out into the light—a gray, swimming light, like the glow of a pool at night—and being shoved into a truck. He remembered this, and at the time he knew it was happening to him, but it was like watching everything from a window somewhere, the way you'd watch as your neighbor was moving, shoving furniture into a truck parked at the front curb—mildly interesting, maybe, but just a momentary distraction.

In the truck he must have fallen asleep. Time had passed. It was light now, but he had a sense of a night (two nights?) having gone by, the darkness coming and going like a long, lazy blink. An eclipse.

Dennis opened his eyes. The drumming was louder now. The sky over him was cement. He was inside. The lightbulb sun was on and it all smelled like oil. He could have drunk oil, he was so thirsty. His wrist hurt. His neck muscles ached. His body felt empty now, as if all the juice had been sucked out of it, leaving him hollow and sore.

He touched his cock and was relieved to find it was still there.

"I want a drink," he said aloud, his own voice croaky and ridiculous. The phrase sounded familiar. The other guy had said the same thing. Silas. Silas had wanted a drink, too.

Something hit the floor next to his head and rolled to his ear. He turned his head, his ear scraping the cement floor. It was a plastic water bottle, plump with water. He grabbed it, pulled up the spout with his teeth, and drank until he choked and had to sit up. Bad idea. He lay back down. But the water was too good. He tried drinking again, slower this time, and managed to get some water down his parched throat.

"Don't drink it all or you'll puke it right back up

again," said a voice over his head, behind him, through the drumming. The drumming was rain. Dennis rolled onto his side again and looked back. He saw boots, legs, a chair. The guy—Earring, the white one with the shaved head, the one they called Lewis—was sitting behind him. He was rocking back and forth on the rear legs of the folding chair, cradling a pistol in his hands.

It wasn't over yet.

"I smell oil," Dennis said aloud, irrelevantly.

There was a window above Lewis's bald head, and through its wobbly pane Dennis could see the low-hanging branches of some kind of tree, rain dripping from little buds on the end of its fingers. The rain was hard and loud now. There must have been a tarp out there, and the drops were drumming on the taut plastic.

Dennis pushed against the cold cement floor and sat up again. He was in an empty garage—a big one, wide enough for two cars. He held out the plastic bottle. "More," he said.

Lewis smiled. "Say please."

Feeling a surge of rage, Dennis reared back and threw the bottle at him. It hit the wall with a hollow pop and skittered to the floor, missing its mark by several feet.

"Turnin' into a mean son of a bitch," Lewis said, shifting in the chair. He aimed the pistol at Dennis and pretended to shoot.

"You fuckin' junkies are all mean as shit when you're comin' down."

"Why are you doing this?" Dennis asked. "What's the point?"

Lewis nodded his shiny head and grinned. "We've got our reasons," he said. He got up from the chair and took a few steps to stretch his legs. "How's your balance, Dennis?"

"What?"

"Oh, never mind." He kicked Dennis gently in the knee and started waving the pistol toward a door. "Come on. Get up and let's go."

Dennis let himself be pulled to his feet, the sudden change in altitude dizzying. He closed his eyes, trying to dampen the nausea that was groping its way up his ragged throat.

"Come on," Lewis said, and pushed him toward the door.

They walked into a finished basement room, the walls covered with cheap paneling and the floor with scuffed maroon-and-gray linoleum tiles. There were four or five people here. Dennis recognized the deaf man, and Curly. "He's back," Lewis said. Everyone in the room turned in their direction.

What Dennis saw then momentarily bewildered him. Standing side by side, in identical gray, double-breasted suits, were Silas and a man who could have been his twin. Silas's long, dusty dreadlocks had been shorn, leaving him with a neat, close-cropped haircut similar to that of the man standing next to him. Both were tall, potbellied, fifty-something black men, but Silas looked much more weather-beaten and wrinkled. The other man had a pampered look, as if he'd never known any real hardship in his life. He also had an air of authority about him, very different from Silas's sorry, whipped-dog bearing. Dennis could see by the expression in Silas's eyes that he had finally figured out what was happening—that he was going to die for this other man.

"So he's the fly in my ointment?" asked Silas's double. He had a deep, rich, musical voice, like someone who could play God in a movie.

"One of them," Lewis said.

He shook his head. "I don't like this part. I really don't. It lacks elegance."

The gray-haired deaf man was sitting on the sofa against a far wall. He got to his feet and clapped his hands at the others, then started signing.

"Can somebody help me out here?" Silas's double asked.

"He wants you to stop worrying," Curly said. "It's for the best."

"You're sure you can make it convincing?"

More signing between the deaf man and Curly. "They'll find him in an alley in Baltimore with needle marks up and down his arms. A heroin overdose. Just another good kid gone bad."

"And when do you take him up there?"

"After what happens here," Curly said. "It'll work out, believe me, sir."

"And you'll find some way of taking care of his friend, right? We've got some heavy-duty damage control to do here. I want to be sure Morgan understands that."

"He understands."

Silas's double then turned to Dennis again. "It's a shame, son, that this has to happen. I really am broken up about it. But you brought it on yourself. It was a beautiful thing we had going here, a beautiful thing." He turned away and started walking toward the stairs.

"I know you," Dennis said. "I've seen you on television."

The man turned slowly back toward him. "Then you know why all of this has to happen," he said. He smiled a broad, toothy smile. "Think of yourself as a sacrifice, son. You're kind of a hero, in fact. Sacrificing yourself for the greater good of the city of Washington, D.C."

He turned away then and rubbed his hands together.

"I'll be sorry about this place," he said to Curly. "You see this paneling? I put this up myself. Every weekend for about a month. Pretty good job, wouldn't you say?" He shook his head. "A waste," he said. "A terrible waste."

TWENTY-EIGHT

JASON CROUCHED AT the window of his room over the Thomases' garage. In the driveway below, Sarah's parents and her eight-year-old brother, Bobby, were getting ready to go to the aquarium. It was something to watch. Bobby kept remembering things he absolutely had to take on the trip—a baseball cap, a stuffed dolphin— and each time he did, Mrs. Thomas had to go back into the house, through the drizzling rain, to get them. Meanwhile, Mr. Thomas waited beside their Honda van under a dripping umbrella, stewing. Every once in a while he'd reach in the open window and hit the horn to make his wife move faster. All told, it took them almost half an hour to get out of the driveway. As the car backed away to the street, Jason looked at his watch. 10:25 A.M.

Two minutes later the phone rang.

Jason wasn't going to pick up at first, but then he realized who it must be.

"Hi," Sarah said. "They're gone."

"I know."

He heard her sigh. "It's always like that when they go someplace with Bobby. Totally absurd."

"It *was* kind of excruciating." Jason sat down on the white cotton couch, where he had slept the night before. The room was simple but immaculate—just the couch and a chest of drawers and a desk with swivel chair. This was where Sarah's au pairs had lived when she was little, and the walls were still covered with their castoffs— cheap macramé wall hangings, posters of hometowns like Düsseldorf and St. Thomas, a shelf of paperback romances in three different languages. "So what are you doing today?" he asked.

"I don't know, really. Laurie is supposed to call me this morning, Laurie Fein? I said we might do something together."

Jason started pulling on his socks. "You want to come over and visit for a while?"

Sarah hesitated, but then said, "Sure. I can put on the call forwarding to that phone, in case she calls."

"Good."

"Well, okay. I'll see you in a few minutes, I guess."

"Use the knock, so I know it's you," he said. The knock was a secret three-then-two signal they had always used when they were bored in class or at a party. In the middle of a crowd, Jason would casually tap the signal on his leg or on a desk to show that he was thinking about her.

"Right," Sarah said. "As if it could be somebody else."

After they hung up, Jason slipped into his jeans and shirt. He was feeling better this morning—more relaxed, in control. Last night he'd gotten a decent night's sleep. As he laced up his sneakers, he decided that leaving the house on the Eastern Shore had been the right decision. He was clearly better off on his own. He had space to think now, to plan things out. His life was going to change. Once he got through this, he would decide what he wanted his life to be and then go after it, the way Dennis would. Jason would stop just letting things happen to him. That had always been his problem. Even breaking up with Sarah had been like that. The two of them had started drifting apart—one weekend, she annoyed him by not wanting to go to the beach with Dennis and a bunch of people from school, then he annoyed her by going anyway. And so they broke up. He never even sat down to ask himself if breaking up was really what he wanted. He just let it happen. And that, he told himself now, was going to change.

A few minutes later, he heard the familiar knock.

Sarah, dressed in a powder-blue raincoat, was standing at the top of the wooden steps. She had a grease-stained paper bag in her hand. "Breakfast," she said.

He let her in and helped her take off the dripping raincoat. Under it, she was wearing shorts and a maroon, raw-silk Chinese-style blouse they'd bought together at Eastern Market last summer. "There are bagels and Danish in the bag, and some orange juice," she said, squeezing the rain out of her hair.

"Thanks. I'll have them later." Jason gestured with exaggerated hospitality toward the couch. "Would you like to sit down?"

"Thank you, sir, I would." She went to the couch and sat, crossing her muscular tennis-player legs. Sarah was wearing sneakers with no socks, and he could see her birthmark—a square patch of strawberry skin—above her inside left ankle. "I trust you had a pleasant night."

"Very pleasant," he said. He sat down at the other end of the couch. The distance between them was awkward— too close for polite conversation yet too far away to be natural. "A lot better than sleeping on the street, which was my only other choice."

"You're really in trouble, I guess."

"Yeah, I'm really in trouble."

"But how did this happen? You wouldn't believe the stories that are going around."

"I can imagine," he said. He leaned forward and put his elbows on his knees. "I can't really go into it right now. All I can tell you is that I didn't do anything wrong—not really wrong, anyway." He looked over at her. "Do you believe me?"

She pulled her hair back behind her ears. "Yeah. I guess."

"You guess?"

She frowned. "Okay, I believe you."

Jason sat back against the cushions, feeling satisfied. "So what do you think?"

"About what?"

"I don't know. What are you feeling?"

She uncrossed her legs and self-consciously recrossed them the other way. "Worried," she said. "I don't want anything to happen to you."

"Really?"

"Really," she said. Then she asked, "Remind me again why we broke up?"

He put his arm around her and pulled her head to his lips. He could smell her same old shampoo—something with mangoes. "I can't remember," he said. "It must have been something stupid."

"Maybe we both just got bored. It happens."

"Are you bored now?" he asked.

She shook her head. "Are you?"

As an answer, he kissed her again, on the chin this time. She put her head down on his shoulder, burrowing closer into him, and he pressed his cheek against the sheen of her clean blond hair. The warmth of her head and body against him felt right and good. He put his free hand down on her thigh. It was warm, too, and still damp from the rain.

He undid the shoulder buttons of her Chinese blouse, and the silk peeled away from her skin, unwrapping the glossy knob of her collarbone.

"Wait," she said, pulling the silk fabric from his grasp. "Take your time, buddy. I've got to get used to this again."

"Whatever you say," he whispered, and stopped her from saying anything else with a kiss.

They were lying on the couch an hour later—Sarah's leg jigsawed over Jason's hipbone, her shoulder wedged into his armpit, her warm temple against his cheek—when the telephone rang. Sarah's head lifted from his. "Should I answer? It's probably Laurie."

Jason shrugged, though he really didn't want to move yet. Not for another day or two.

Sarah untangled herself from him and got up. He watched her as she stepped barefoot across the room in her bra and shorts, her skin flushed and perfect.

"Hello?" Sarah turned and grimaced comically. "Oh hi, Laurie. I thought you were supposed to call hours ago." She sat on the swivel chair and crossed her legs, pointing her curved, red-toenailed foot at him.

He noticed the muscles in her leg tensing suddenly. "No," she said. She cast a worried look at Jason. "Are you sure?"

"What?" Jason mouthed from the couch.

She shook her head. "Oh God. No, I have no idea where he is. I don't know if he knows. What hospital is it?" She grabbed a pencil and scribbled something on a piece of scrap paper.

Jason sat up nervously. "What?" he asked, aloud this time.

"Listen," Sarah went on. "I'll call you later. I have to go. Later." She put down the phone.

"What is it?" Jason was getting seriously worried now. "What happened?"

She swiveled in the chair to face him. "God, Jason. It's your father. He's in the hospital. He had a stroke."

The word didn't make sense to Jason at first. He could conceive of his father being shot, after what had happened to them, but a stroke? Jason got to his feet. "Is he okay?"

"Laurie's mom heard it from one of your neighbors. He's at the hospital now. In intensive care."

Jason turned and looked out the window at the Thomases' tidy green lawn. "It's not fair," he said. "This is so fucking unfair."

Frank stepped into his office, slipped around his desk, and fell wearily into his chair. He reached for his cup on the desk and drank a few sips of cold ginseng tea. Then he unknotted his necktie and pulled it out from under his collar like a crabber pulling in his line.

They were getting nowhere with the interrogations. They had four men from the house in Anacostia—each in a separate interview room on the top floor of the Washington field office—and although Frank and his team had tried every interrogation tactic they knew, none of the prisoners was showing any signs of giving in. The man from Jessup's office had offered one of them—a retired security guard who was obviously just a hired hand— total immunity, but even that hadn't worked. The four of them weren't saying a word, with or without their attorneys. Whoever was in charge of this thing had done a good job of training his subordinates.

It was probably too late now, anyway. If Dennis had in fact been held in that basement with Silas—and

Frank's instincts told him that he had—there was only one reason to move him. Whatever they were going to do with Dennis and Silas was going to happen soon.

Frank leaned forward and pushed aside some files until he found the one on Silas Whitcomb. He opened it and took out the picture inside. It had been taken at night—surreptitiously, or so it seemed, with a long lens. Silas wore a navy blue watch cap in the picture, his graying dreadlocks snaking out of it like logs of unbroken cigar ash. He wasn't a particularly distinctive-looking man, but obviously someone thought he'd do for the purpose. He had high, smooth cheekbones that shone in the bad light. And his eyes were cloaked and suspicious.

Frank put the picture down and started riffling through the stack of pink message slips on his desk. Nothing from Renee. He sighed. Another disappearing act. He picked up his phone and punched in her number, but he got nothing, not even her answering machine. He wondered if she had just turned off the phone and crawled into bed with the blinds closed. It was something he was tempted to do himself.

Agent Brande appeared in his doorway then.

"Any luck?" Frank asked.

"Niente." Agent Brande, one of Frank's best men, came from an old Italian family in Baltimore. He was supposed to be helping Frank with his Italian lessons, but so far had only taught him the words for "whore" and "machine gun" in Sicilian dialect.

Frank handed him the picture of Silas Whitcomb. "He remind you of any prominent citizen you know?"

Brande glanced over the photograph and handed it back. "No prominent citizen I *want* to know, at least." He rubbed his eyes and yawned. "So tell me, Frank," he said. "How do we come to have four obvious thugs in our interview rooms, each one of which seems to be

drawing a paycheck from either D.C. Social Services or
the Metro Police?"

"Good question."

"Anything you're not telling us about this operation?"

Frank shook his head. "You know as much as I do,"
he said. "As far as I can tell, it was like a business.
They'd get a client—somebody who wanted to disappear—and then they'd go out and look for a close match.
Morgan Zack and Vincent Osborne and whoever else at
OES would be in a perfect position to do it. Thanks to
this D.C. Sharing and Caring Initiative, they're out every
day inspecting shelters and halfway houses and other
places, supposedly for the city. They see somebody who
could stand in for their client—some drunk or schizo
whose disappearance wouldn't cause much of a stir—and
bingo."

"Talk about entrepreneurial spirit," Brande said.

"It's proactive. Isn't that what Mayor Humphrey says
we need more of in District government?"

Brande laughed. "Figures that the one thing that works
in D.C. government is something like this. Whose idea
was this Sharing and Caring thing, anyway?"

"That's something I'd like to find out." Frank wrote
himself a note. "If I remember right, it was set up pre–
Control Board. But there's no saying that the program
was created with this little permutation in mind. Maybe
somebody like Morgan Zack just saw the potential, once
it was up and running."

"Or up and not running," Brande offered, "which is
more likely in this town." He moved toward the door.
"You want some more hot water for tea?"

Frank shook his head. "No, I want those guys upstairs
to tell us something useful. So get back to work."

"Jeez," Brande muttered as he left the room, "sounds
like somebody needs a vacation in Italy."

After Brande was gone, Frank picked up the photograph again. He put his hand over the lower part of the face, then over the upper half. Nothing. It seemed odd to him that Silas Whitcomb's was the only red file for which they'd found no blue-file equivalent. It was possible, of course, that the blue file was just lost or misfiled. But somehow Frank had a sense that there was more of an explanation. Here was a stand-in for which there was no client. So who was Silas standing in for?

He was about to throw the photograph aside, but something made him hesitate—something about the set of the eyes, the slope of the man's jawline. Suddenly, recognition snapped into place, and a familiar face seemed to jump out at him from the picture.

He picked up his telephone and punched in the number of the field office's librarian. "Connie, this is Frank Laroux. You have copies of the *Post* from the last couple of weeks?"

"We have only the last few days on hand," she said. "The rest are at the bindery already. But everything's accessible electronically."

"Can you get me some information on somebody? I forget his name, but he's that District politician they're investigating."

"Well, that narrows it down to several dozen," Connie said blandly.

"You know, the finance guy. Assistant Mayor for Finance, I think his title is."

"Cashen," she said. "Dwight J. Cashen, Deputy Mayor for Finance. I'm glad to see your civics lessons haven't been wasted, Frank."

"Can you find me a picture of the man ASAP? It's an emergency."

"I'll do my best."

Ten minutes later she was at his door with a file in her

hands. She removed a picture from the file and placed it on the desk. The picture of Silas Whitcomb was already there. "Hmm, separated at birth?" Connie said.

The resemblance was too close to be a coincidence. "I've got to get the man's number. It's Sunday, can you find me his home phone number?"

Connie pulled a note card from the file. "Home, office, cell phone, and E-mail address. Would you like to know his mother's maiden name?"

Frank grabbed the phone and punched in the cell-phone number. No answer. He hit the disconnect button and dialed the home number. A woman picked up after four rings.

"Hello, may I speak to Mr. Cashen, please."

"Who's calling?"

"My name is Joshua Daniels," Frank improvised. "I work for the Oversight Committee and we just had to reach Mr. Cashen to ask him a question."

"Well, he's gone out to the place in Indian Shores."

Frank paused. "Would you be able to give me that number?"

"Well, I don't like to give out that number. Even government officials have to have a personal life, you know."

"It's important, Mrs. Cashen."

"No," she said hesitantly. "I'd really rather not." Frank considered trying to bully the number out of her, but he didn't want to make her suspicious. "All right, then. Please tell him I called. He has the number. Thank you very much."

"You're very welcome."

Frank hung up. "Well, Connie, here's something you *didn't* have in your files," he said. "Cashen has a week-end place in Indian Shores."

"I'm mortified."

"You can redeem yourself by finding the address. That shouldn't be beyond your powers, should it?"

She snatched the note card from his hand. "Give me ten minutes," she said again.

TWENTY-NINE

HIS FATHER WAS still unconscious when Jason arrived at the Warrington Hospital ICU. Graham lay motionless in a tangle of hoses and wires on a high inclined bed, surrounded by machines that clattered, beeped, and sighed. A plastic tube jutted from his pale, chapped lips, and his head, which had been shaved clean, was wrapped in a thick white bandage that was taped to his forehead and chin. His arms and legs had also been shaved. They looked pale and soft and plump, like giant slugs asleep beside him on the bed.

Jason didn't want to go into the room. He stood in the doorway, looking across at this unrecognizable person. Sarah stood beside him, her fingers wrapped around his wrist.

"Are you the son?"

A nurse had appeared behind them. She was dark-skinned—probably Indian or Pakistani—and so thin that she looked like a patient herself. "How is he doing?" Jason asked.

"Let me page the doctor for you," she said. "Your

mother is here. She's downstairs in the cafeteria."

Jason lost his breath for a second. "My mother?"

"Ms. Daniels? She said she was your father's ex-wife. I thought she was your mother. I'm sorry."

Renee. She must have lied to get into the ICU. They were admitting only immediate family, and even getting Sarah up to the room had been a struggle. "It's okay," he said, turning back toward his father. There were two metal-framed black chairs beside the bed. "I have to sit down."

He and Sarah lowered themselves awkwardly into the two chairs. From where he sat, Jason could see his father's face framed by the metal tubes of the guardrail. He reached out and briefly put his fingers on his father's shaved arm. He didn't know where to look then, so he stared at the monitors around the room and tried to decipher the readings. After a few seconds, a little alarm sounded on one of them. He and Sarah exchanged an anxious look, but no one came into the room. Then, after a little while, the alarm stopped.

Sarah squeezed his wrist. "He'll be all right," she said lamely.

Jason didn't answer. He was staring at his father's feet now. They were sticking out of the sheet at the bottom of the bed. His father had thick, horny, discolored toenails, like the shell of a tortoise. They had always disgusted Jason.

It occurred to him suddenly that if his father died he would be an orphan. An official, textbook orphan. He wondered what would happen then. Would he be turned over to his aunt Emily in Vancouver? Or was he old enough now to live on his own? There was plenty of life insurance—his father had told him about it many times—so money wouldn't be a problem. And he'd be going to college soon anyway. Would they let him live alone in the house until he left for school?

He thought of the huge Big Bird in his father's bedroom. Jason's throat closed up. He looked down and rubbed his eyes with his dry fingertips. He didn't want to live alone in the house. He wasn't ready. He swore to himself that he wouldn't let things turn out that way.

When Renee walked in the door, Jason shot to his feet.

"Thank God," she said.

He was still furious with her, and his body went rigid as she put her arms around him. She smelled of alcohol and cigarettes.

"What's going to happen?" he asked her.

"I don't know. I wish I could tell you."

"We came as soon as we heard," Sarah said.

Renee looked at Sarah curiously, as if just noticing her. "Of course," she said. "It makes sense. I should have thought of it." She took a deep breath and then said, "Jason, your father is in critical condition. They operated and took a blood clot from behind one of his ears—"

"Has he been awake?" Jason asked.

"Once or twice, for short periods. The doctors say—"

"Did he mention me? Did he ask about me or anything?"

Renee's mouth tightened. "He can't speak, Jason, and one side of his body seems to be paralyzed."

"Oh, great." Jason sat again. He crossed his arms tightly in front of his stomach. "This is my fault."

Renee crouched in front of his chair and grabbed him roughly by the shoulders. "That's not true," she said.

"He was out looking for me, right? When this happened?"

"This was probably coming on for days now, even weeks. It would have happened anyway."

Jason didn't believe her, but he didn't have the energy to argue. "Is he going to die?" he asked.

She let go of his shoulders. "They don't know. The next twenty-four hours, then they'll know."

"Then they'll know," he repeated quietly.

The same alarm—an anemic little buzz—sounded again for about ten seconds and then stopped.

Renee stood up shakily. "I have to ask you some things, Jason," she said, steadying herself against the bed rail.

"Like what?"

"Relatives. We have to let your father's relatives know. Nobody here knew anyone to call."

Jason cleared his throat and said, "I'll do it. There aren't many, and they all live way out West. But I have the numbers somewhere."

"The other thing," she went on, "is that you've got to accept FBI protection. I'll call and have them send somebody over. But, Jason, you can't disappear like that again. I mean it."

"I know. It's okay. I understand." Then he asked, "Did they find Dennis yet?"

Renee shook her head. "They're getting close, I hope. But nothing definite yet."

Jason looked over at his father asleep on the bed. "It was just last Sunday. One week ago exactly. It's so weird to think about it."

Sarah moved her chair closer to his. It seemed natural to Jason—the feeling of having Sarah there. It was the only natural thing in that whole situation.

Renee was watching them. "I'll call the FBI now," she said, and walked out of the room.

"This is falling apart."

"It's not falling apart, Mr. Cashen."

"Take it from someone who knows about disaster, son. If they've got Osborne's files, it's falling apart."

"We don't know that they have the files. It's possible that Osborne moved them before his . . . whatever. Accident. Morgan couldn't find them on Friday, so it's not likely that the FBI found them yesterday."

"Then how did they know about the house in Anacostia? And now that they've got Bishop and the others in custody, it's just a matter of time. You think Bishop won't strike a deal eventually?"

Dennis was sitting on the floor of the basement room, his arms and legs bound with rough twine. Curly and the man they called Mr. Cashen—Dennis recognized him now as the Deputy Mayor for Finance, the one who was under investigation—were arguing with each other on the other side of the room. Dennis's brain was still fuzzy from the heroin, but he was alert enough to hear if not understand everything they said.

"For all we know, they could be on their way here right now."

"I don't think so, sir. You're insulated. We were careful about that. Your name is nowhere."

"I'm *insulated?*"

"You're insulated."

"I don't share your optimism. We've got to pull the plug. Now. And head straight for the boat."

"We've got the kid to drop off in Baltimore."

"The kid can die here."

"Bad move, sir. We don't want any possible connection made between you and the boy. If he dies here, it's messy. It automatically lends credence to Jason Rourke's story."

"Credence? *Credence?* You don't get it, son. They *know*. It's just a matter of getting our own asses out of here before they find us. Dumping the kid in Baltimore means two extra hours of exposure before we get on that boat. I say we do what we have to here and get going."

Curly was shaking his head. "We shouldn't panic. What they know and what they can prove are two different things. We've got a plan, and I think we should stick with it as closely as possible. Then, if they *don't* know about your connection to the business, your death might still pass as an accident."

"But the boy—"

"Fine, we can leave the boy here. Shit, we'll make it look like he broke in or something. He's a fugitive, on the run from the law, and if there's anything left to autopsy, they'll find heroin in his blood. It'll look like he broke into the empty house to sleep here, in the basement."

Cashen paused for a few moments, considering this. "Okay," he said finally. He looked over at Dennis. "What about the twine around his hands and feet? Won't that look, you know, *suspicious*?"

"It won't exist. Afterwards, I mean. We've done this before and the twine burns completely. We help the explosion along to make sure."

"I'll take your word for it." Cashen pulled his suit jacket from the back of a wooden folding chair. "So he'll be down here and I'm upstairs?"

"Right. You'll be napping, with the dishwasher on. It's the electronic ignition on the hot water heater that sets it off."

Dennis was listening to this conversation carefully, but he couldn't make sense of it. They'd taken Silas upstairs an hour ago, still dressed in his new suit. Silas was going to be Cashen, obviously, but was Dennis supposed to be anybody? He tried to concentrate, to pierce the cocoon of artificial well-being the drug had wrapped him in. This is real, he told himself. This is happening.

Curly looked at his watch. "I should give him one more shot," he said. "To put him out for the duration." He got the leather satchel from the cabinet and carried it over to where Dennis was sitting. Cashen followed, the suit jacket draped over his arm like a waiter's cloth.

"Who am I?" Dennis asked, slurring his words.

"Who *are* you?" Cashen shot a glance at Curly. "What's this? Some kind of amnesia?"

"He's just confused, I think. Don't pay any attention."

Dennis tried to be more precise. "Who am I supposed to be?"

"He *is* confused," Cashen said. He bent over and stared into Dennis's eyes. "Anybody home?" He straightened up and looked at his watch. "Hard to believe. In a few minutes, my life will be over. This life, at least." He pulled his shirt cuffs down over his wrists. "I can't help thinking it's the end of an era."

"That it is, sir," Curly said.

"Not that I haven't seen it coming. With those Control Board prigs looking over our shoulders all the time. I've been saying it to him for a while now. They've taken all the fun out of it."

Curly filled the syringe with brown liquid from the spoon and tapped the needle. Dennis watched him, wondering why he couldn't feel anything like fear.

"Accountability," Cashen went on. "They're all talking about accountability now—openness, order. Responsible, accountable government. But you ask any businessman, he'll tell you about accountability. Why do you think they're all running to Russia and Eastern Europe nowadays? It's the chaos." He pulled on his suit jacket. "Chaos is just another word for opportunity, that's what the man himself said to me once. The weak person's crisis, he said, is the strong person's opportunity."

Curly grabbed Dennis's arm. "Just one more," he

whispered. "And then it will be over." Dennis watched as the skin on his own forearm gave under the point of the needle, going concave for a second before the tip penetrated and Curly pressed the syringe home.

"It's been historic, though," Cashen said, as the cold heat spread up Dennis's arm. Dennis could see the men's faces dissolving into air. "D.C. in the nineties. It'll go down in the history books as a golden age, at least for those of us who knew how to take advantage of it. But now they've gone and ruined it all. Pretty soon D.C.'s going to look like a city in Switzerland."

Curly stood up. "It's time to start, Mr. Cashen. We can stick around just long enough to make sure it goes right, then we can go to the boat."

Cashen stared at Dennis for a few seconds more. "The end of an era," he repeated. Then he added, "He wants me to call him. At home. Before I leave."

"Better not to, sir. He's got to be insulated too. Especially him."

"Oh, he'll insulate himself," Cashen said, chuckling.

Dennis gratefully felt himself slipping away.

"He's always been very good at insulating himself," the deep voice said, as Dennis lay back on the hard linoleum and let the warmth wrap around him again.

Frank hit eighty-five miles per hour on Route 50, weaving in and out of traffic, his blue dash light spinning. The wipers were on high, but he still had trouble seeing through the flooded windshield. He hoped the rain would stop by the time he got to the coast. Indian Shores, he knew, was three hours from Washington under normal circumstances. He was going to try to make it in two.

Number 2 Oceangate Terrace. It was the address that Connie had given him. Frank knew roughly where this was—on an exclusive part of the beach where a lot of bankers, real estate developers, and other D.C. heavy hitters had weekend places. Rows of modern imitation-rustic monstrosities anchored in the sand dunes, far enough away from each other to assure privacy.

Frank looked at his watch. His men and the SWAT team would be about a half hour behind him. Frank would have time to do some reconnaissance on his own and work out a plan. Assuming he wasn't already too late.

He remembered the picture of Dennis Monroe he had seen at the Monroes' house the day before. The boy looked a little like his sister's son, Jamal. Probably about the same age. Jamal would be going to college in two years. The kid wanted to be a stockbroker. "Or a merchant banker," he would say whenever Frank visited. "There's a future in merchant banking." Frank wasn't even sure what a merchant banker *was*.

Leaning closer to the windshield, Frank passed another car and accelerated until the needle hit ninety.

THIRTY

AT NINE O'CLOCK, Jason asked Sarah to go home. Her parents and brother would be back from Baltimore by now. They'd be worried about her. "I can handle everything here," he said. "You've been great. Really."

Sarah shook her head at first. But then she looked over at Renee in a way that said yes, she wanted to go home, but no, she didn't want to admit it.

"I'm okay now," Jason insisted. "I've got Renee and the FBI agent outside to look after me."

Renee got up from the chair where she'd been reading the newspaper. "I'm going down to the cafeteria," she announced tactfully, and left.

Jason put his hands on Sarah's shoulders. "Go home," he said. "I'll let you know if anything happens."

"You'll really be all right?"

He smoothed back her hair. "I'll be fine. Just do me a favor. Tell your parents I'm not evil, okay?"

He kissed her and ushered her into the open area outside, where the nurses were stationed. "Good night," she said. "And call me." He heard her say good night to the nurse and to the FBI man—Agent Cross—as she left.

Jason turned back into his father's room. The overhead light crackled when he hit the off switch, throwing the room into gray half-darkness. Jason crossed to the little table in the corner and turned off the lamp. His father was still in the same position on the bed, the plastic tube in his mouth making him look like a napping sword-swallower.

Jason glanced at his watch. They said the next twenty-four hours would be key. That was eight hours ago. Twenty-four minus eight is sixteen. So if his father survived until lunchtime tomorrow, he would live.

Jason turned from the bed and looked up at the television, which he'd had the nurses turn on for his own sake rather than his father's. He took the remote from the rolling bedside table and started changing channels until he found the all-weather channel. They were reporting on late-spring snowstorms in the Midwest. A reporter was standing on a street corner in Chicago, up to his knees in snow. Jason sat down and watched for a while, with the volume low. The television threw fast-moving blue shadows all over the walls and ceiling of the darkened room. It reminded him of the nights when he and his father would watch *Frasier*—the only show they both liked—sitting on the couch together and trying to make conversation during commercials.

A few minutes later, when he glanced over at the bed, he noticed that his father was awake. "Dad!" he said, getting to his feet. Graham's eyes were wide open, and he had a startled expression on his gray face.

Jason grabbed the bed guard and leaned over his father. "Dad? I know you can't talk. That's okay." He took his father's arm, but it was heavy and cold in his hands, like a piece of meat.

"Dad, everything's under control now," Jason told

him. Then he said something he'd been preparing to say for hours. "Dad, I want you to know that I'm all right. What I said to you on the beach over at Julia's? It was bullshit. You understand?"

Graham was looking around the room. When his eyes met Jason's, there was no recognition in them. He seemed confused. He looked down at his arm as if it didn't belong to him.

Jason stepped back from the bed. "Nurse? Hey, nurse?" he called.

She appeared in the doorway—a plump, middle-aged black woman who had taken over for the day nurse.

"There's something wrong with him," Jason said. "He's in a trance or something. He doesn't recognize me."

Sighing, the nurse went over to the other side of the bed. "Mr. Rourke? Try to squeeze my fingers." She held up two fingers and placed Graham's hand around them. "Squeeze now." The hand dropped back onto the sheet. "Press that button over there," she told Jason.

He obeyed. "What is it? What's happening?"

"Mr. Rourke? Come on, now, try to squeeze. Concentrate."

Graham didn't seem to understand anything she was saying. He just looked at her, the way you'd look at some moderately interesting museum exhibit. After a few seconds, he tucked his chin and put his hand to his chest, as if he were trying to swallow something too big to go down. His head came up again, and he had a strange, puzzled expression on his face.

"Mr. Rourke?"

Graham's mouth opened. A deep gurgle rose from his throat, as if he were being strangled. He threw his head back against the pillows, and his body began trembling, shaking the whole bed. The nurse's thick black arm went across his chest.

"Oh God," Jason said, backing farther away. The monitors around the room seemed to be buzzing in chorus now.

"Move! Please!" Somebody pulled him away from the bed. There were people all over the room now, blocking his view. But he could still hear that gurgle from the bed—a sound totally unlike his father's voice.

"Fuck, what's going on? Give him something! Somebody give him a shot or something!"

"Get the boy out of here!" a nurse shouted, and then a pair of hands grabbed Jason from behind and pulled him out of the room. It was Agent Cross. "Take it easy, Jason," he said.

"What's happening to him?"

Agent Cross led him away from the doorway and pushed him up against the wall of the nurses' station. He held him there, his beefy hand pressed to Jason's chest.

"What's going on?" It was Renee. She was back from the cafeteria.

"The father is having a seizure or something," Cross said. "Can you help me take him somewhere and calm him down?"

Renee grabbed Jason's arm. "Come on," she said. "There's nothing we can do here. Let's go outside."

Jason allowed himself to be led past the nurses' station, through the electric doors, and out of the ICU. There was a waiting room here—empty at this time of night. While Agent Cross waited outside the door, Renee steered Jason to a sofa and sat him down. "It's a seizure, Jason," she explained to him. She sat beside him and took his hands. "Just try to calm down."

"He's dying," Jason said.

"We don't know that." Renee's voice was something

to hold on to. He wanted her to keep talking. "He's having a seizure. It sometimes happens with people in this situation, after brain surgery. It doesn't mean he's dying."

"How do you know?"

"They said this could happen. His doctors." She squeezed his hands. "Listen to me. Drink some water. You want to drink some water?"

He didn't answer. She got up and walked over to the drinking fountain. When she came back she handed him a little paper cup and a pill. "Here," she said. "Take this."

"What is it?"

"Just take it, Jason. It's a Valium. You're lucky I've got any left after today."

He took the pill from her hand and placed it on his tongue. Then he grabbed the paper cup and drank.

Renee sat beside him again and put her arm around his shoulders. "You're scared," she said to him quietly. "It's understandable. I know what that's like. Believe me."

It was about half an hour later that the doctor came into the waiting room to see them. He had glossy crew-cut hair and a big mole on his left cheek. His expression was neutral, careful.

Jason and Renee stood up at the same time, as if they'd rehearsed this move beforehand. "Tell us quickly," Renee said.

The doctor shook his head. "This is the hardest part of my job," he began.

Jason sank back onto the couch and slowly looked up at the ceiling.

THIRTY-ONE

FRANK LEFT HIS Pathfinder at the edge of the beach about four blocks north of the Deputy Mayor's house. After checking his watch, he followed a wooden walkway up over the low dunes toward the water. This stretch of beach was sparsely populated—just a few year-round residents in sweaters and jackets, most of them walking dogs. It was a Sunday night in March, so most of the weekenders had already gone back to the city. The earlier rain had tapered off, leaving the damp sand as rough and pockmarked as a cheese grater.

Feeling hopelessly conspicuous in his gray trench coat and black wing tips, Frank trudged down the beach toward the house with his hands in his pockets. His pistol was in its underarm holster, the clasp undone. As nonchalantly as possible, he scanned the beach and the dunes, looking for sentries. But they were either not there or very good at concealing themselves.

After a while, he saw the house he had driven past a few minutes earlier—2 Oceangate Terrace, a flat-roofed architectural statement in glass and weathered gray wood, with huge windows looking out on the beach. The house was mostly dark, but the big windows glowed just brightly enough to suggest a light burning somewhere inside. Frank walked along casually, his head facing forward but his eyes taking in everything about and around the place. He kept walking past the house and continued a few more blocks before heading inland again on another walkway, as if he were going back to the street.

He had seen no one around the house. It was possible, he reasoned, that they were all inside, since they had no cause to suspect that anyone knew where they were. But it was also possible that the Deputy Mayor was alone in his living room, innocently doing some paperwork or just relaxing from the rigors of city governance with a glass of wine and something peaceful on the stereo. Maybe Dennis and Silas were two hundred miles away. If so, Frank would have a lot of explaining to do. There were ten FBI special agents speeding toward this house right now. Frank wouldn't relish having to tell them to go home and forget he'd ever brought them out here.

Moving through the dunes as quickly as he dared, Frank made his way back to the house. When he was a block away, he sank to a crouch. Fortunately, it was a relatively dark night, with an indistinct smear of moon showing behind a thin layer of clouds. If anyone in the other beachside houses saw him—a black man, no matter how well-dressed—crawling around these dunes, they'd probably have the local cops on him in a second. Police response tended to be quick in wealthy neighborhoods.

Frank reached the last dune before the house and, feeling slightly ridiculous, crawled up the side of it commando style. He looked over the crest and saw nothing unusual—just the quiet house, throwing its faint glow onto the sand.

He would have to approach the house and have a look

inside. There was no way he could have his SWAT team besiege the place unless he knew he was right about Cashen. He slid back down the gentle slope of the dune and emptied the damp sand from his shoes. After lacing them up again, he got to his feet and started.

A bank of scrubby bushes bordered the property, so Frank headed for them first. Using the bushes as cover, he moved toward the back of the house away from the beach. There was a driveway here, with a single car parked in it—a black BMW sedan, the kind of car a deputy mayor would be expected to drive. Frank experienced a moment of gnawing doubt. Maybe he really was wrong about this whole thing.

He checked his pistol one last time. It was FBI policy not to discharge a firearm unless the intent was to kill. In fact, Frank hadn't fired his pistol at a real human being in over eight years—and this was just as well, since he wasn't a very good marksman. Once, in his second year at the Bureau, he'd shot at a perpetrator's chest and ended up shattering the man's kneecap. As his instructors never tired of telling him, he had a tendency to shoot low.

After saying a quick, all-purpose prayer, Frank slipped from behind the bushes and headed toward the quiet house.

He could smell the gas from twenty feet away. Frank stopped walking. The window in the back door of the house, up three steps on a wooden porch, had been smashed, meaning that someone had probably broken in. This confused Frank. His resolve wavering suddenly, he crept up the wooden steps to the door and peered inside.

In the dim light of the house's interior, he could just make out Deputy Mayor Cashen standing in the living room beyond the kitchen. He was dressed in a suit, his arms tied behind him around a thin decorative pillar.

The realization came a few seconds later. It wasn't Cashen, of course. It was Silas Whitcomb.

There was no time to wait for backup. Frank knew he had to move now. He also knew that it would be suicide to fire his pistol in that gas-saturated house. So he holstered his weapon, reached through the broken window to unlock the door, and rushed in.

Silas looked up at him with wide, bloodshot eyes. "Who the fuck're you?" he said. Frank didn't answer. He picked up a heavy wooden chair and flung it with all of his strength at one of the big windows facing the beach. The pane cracked, but didn't break. And there didn't seem to be any other way of opening the windows.

"Shit, you the cavalry, ain't you," Silas said.

"FBI," Frank announced. "The boy, Dennis Monroe. Is he here?"

"Basement. Down through there." Silas pointed with his chin toward a doorway just inside the kitchen.

"Anyone else here?"

He shook his head.

Frank ran back into the kitchen and pulled open the door to the basement. The smell of gas was even stronger here. It was dark, and Frank was about to hit the light switch when he stopped himself. It might have been enough to set off the gas.

He raced down the stairs two at a time. There was enough ambient light from upstairs to make out shapes around the basement. Frank saw the hulking furnace, a washer and dryer, a shelf of paint cans. A dark bulk lay on the linoleum floor near the washer—just the right size for a teenage boy. Frank grabbed the limp body of Dennis Monroe and heaved him over his shoulder. Moving quickly, he carried him up the steps and through the kitchen into the living room. He threw the boy onto the couch, took out his pocketknife, and started sawing away at the twine tying Silas's wrists. His head was already swooning from the gas.

"What the hell you doin', FBI?" Silas shouted at him. "Get that boy out first. I ain't goin' nowhere." Frank didn't stop sawing, but the twine was tough. "You deaf, FBI? I say get him out. Git!"

Frank stopped sawing, put the knife down, and grabbed Dennis again. He carried the boy over his shoulder through the kitchen and out the back door. After vaulting down the three steps, he ran about thirty yards over the first dune and dropped the boy onto the sand. Then he turned back. For a few seconds, he hesitated. He knew that going into that house again would be a big risk—his own life against that of some old homeless alcoholic.

He was inside again within seconds, pressing his handkerchief over his nose and mouth. He went to the living room, picked up the knife, and began sawing at the twine again. His progress was agonizingly slow, but he finally cut through the restraints.

"Ow, fugger," Silas said. "That hurt."

"Go!" Frank pushed Silas ahead of him, but the man was moving too slowly. "Come on, you fat-assed old man!" They got through the kitchen and out the back door. As they jumped from the porch, Frank was aware of the movement in his peripheral vision, but he didn't break his stride. He pushed Silas ahead of him until they were over the first dune. "Down!" Frank said. "Get down!" He fell to the sand and pulled the old man after him. Five seconds passed. Nothing happened. Silas pushed away from him and struggled to his feet. "Well, shit, FBI," he said. "Looka that. We had all the fuckin' time in the world."

Frank started to get to his feet.

He heard an enormous *whoosh*. Then the sky seemed to fill with light. He watched in amazement as Silas was lifted off his feet and flew backward through the damp, reeking air.

THIRTY-TWO

FRANK HEARD SHOUTING through the whiny buzz in his ears. It took him a moment to place himself. He was lying on his back on a bed of salt grass. He had been thrown backward onto a sand dune, and was looking straight up into an inky sky streaked by light.

"Goddamn fuggin' ankle shit *dawgie!*" Frank glanced over toward Silas. The old man, his beautiful suit torn and sandy, was lying beside him in the salt grass, shouting incoherently at no one in particular. Before them, what was left of Cashen's house was in flames.

Frank rolled himself over, spitting wet sand from his mouth. His shoulder ached and he felt a pang in his bad left knee. The handkerchief he'd been holding was now snagged on a small driftwood fence behind him, moving in the breeze like a miniature flag of surrender.

Frank stood up slowly. He noticed that one of his shoes was missing, and he had no idea where it was. He looked over at Silas. The old man seemed to be all right, despite the stream of obscenities coming out of his mouth. He was clutching his ankle with both hands, as if he'd broken it.

Frank thought of Dennis then, and of the movement he'd seen just before the explosion. Still feeling dazed, he ran over to the place where he'd dropped the boy. But Dennis wasn't there. Frank saw only thick-treaded tire marks leading toward the beach.

Turning back, he climbed up to the top of one of the higher dunes. He could see a dune buggy speeding northward up the beach, several hundred yards away already.

Leaving Silas where he lay, Frank ran down off the dunes toward the house. He started cutting through backyards, weaving past backyard grills and outdoor shower stalls. It seemed minutes before he reached his Pathfinder. He climbed in, scrabbled for the keys in his pocket, and started it up. Then, after buckling himself in, he shifted into gear and drove straight toward the spindly fence separating the dunes from the street.

The Pathfinder jounced so violently as he crested the dunes that his head nearly hit the roof several times. Once he got stuck going over one of the steeper mounds of sand, but he backed up and tried again. This time he made it over. He sped down the other slope onto the flatter, hard-packed sand of the beach. Then he turned north and headed toward the taillights of the dune buggy far ahead, dousing his own lights so that they wouldn't see him coming.

He accelerated gradually but continuously, not wanting to lose traction on the damp sand. There were more people on the beach now, and every one of them seemed determined to wander into his path. Frank didn't want to warn them with his headlights or his horn, so he just maneuvered around them. As he picked up speed, a dog broke free from its owner and bounded toward him from

the left side. Frank veered sharply away from the animal,
just missing it. He recovered and sped up again.

Frank got on the radio. He called out on the FBI fre-
quency, hoping that his team was near enough to receive
it. But he heard nothing except static in reply to his hail.
He was about to broadcast again when a voice pierced
the static—Agent Brande, asking for his location.

"I've got suspects heading north on the beach—repeat,
on the beach—now about two miles north of the target
site. I'm in pursuit. Can you intercept?"

There was another long pause, and then Brande's voice
came on again. "We'll try. We're coming from that direction."

"It's a dune buggy kind of thing," Frank shouted. "I
don't know what the hell else to call it. I think they've
got the boy inside."

"Ten-four, we'll give it a try."

Frank put the radio handset back in its cradle. The
taillights ahead were closer now. But when he got to
within fifty yards, the taillights suddenly swerved to the
left. The dune buggy began speeding up. They had seen
him.

Frank leaned forward and turned on his headlights.

The dune buggy swung sharply to the left again and
headed toward the narrow band of dunes behind the
beach. Frank followed until it climbed the first sand hill
and turned north again. The dunes were lower on this
part of the beach, but Frank knew that his Pathfinder
wouldn't be able to keep up in that terrain. So he stayed
down on the flatter beach, following along at a distance,
keeping the dune buggy in sight. Soon he had pulled
almost even with it.

The dune buggy slowed then and started to make a
sharp circle. In response, Frank spun the wheel of the
Pathfinder, spraying a shower of damp sand. They had

turned around completely and were heading south now. Frank regained control and tried to catch up. Just when he had pulled even again, the dune buggy turned once more, straight toward the beach, straight toward Frank. *"Bastardo!"* he shouted aloud, the Italian coming to him from some remote nook of his brain. Both of his side windows shattered as someone shot at him three times. Frank was showered with glass, but he wasn't hit. He pumped the brakes and spun the wheel hard to the left. The dune buggy was trying it on the flat sand now, heading north again. Frank sat low in his seat and followed, pressing the accelerator to the floor with his shoeless foot.

Another shot hit the windshield of the Pathfinder, instantly webbing the glass with a thousand hairline cracks. Frank could barely see now. He was about to try sticking his head out the side window when he saw different lights—high beams—directly ahead. The dune buggy, trying to avoid a collision, veered sharply to the left. Frank saw it go over, bouncing and tumbling on the sand. He jammed his own brakes and felt the Pathfinder float out of his control. He did a half turn before the side of the Pathfinder's rear end smashed into something. Frank was thrown into the door. Pain seared his shoulder, and he found himself almost strangled by the shoulder belt, covered with pebbles of glass.

Slowly, he reached over and opened the door. He heard shouts outside—the reassuring sounds of a SWAT team kicking ass. He crawled out of the wrecked Pathfinder onto the sand. What he'd hit turned out to be the SWAT van. There was a dent in its side panel the size of a small refrigerator.

Frank got to his feet. Two other vehicles were pulled up beside the toppled dune buggy a few yards ahead. Three men with black FBI jumpsuits had their weapons aimed into the upside-down dune buggy.

Frank hobbled over as best as he could, his pistol in his aching hand. Agent Brande was pulling Dennis out of the dune buggy. He was bleeding, but conscious now. "You okay?" Brande asked as Frank came up to him.

The SWAT team seemed to be doing a little dance around the dune buggy. Frank stooped and looked inside. There were three men lying pinned under the vehicle, looking dazed. Frank recognized one of them as Deputy Mayor Cashen. "Good evening, sir," Frank said. "I'm Special Agent Laroux of the Federal Bureau of Investigation. And you, sir, are under arrest."

Frank straightened up then, but he must have come up too quickly. "Oh Lord," he said. The pistol fell from his hand as his knees wobbled and he pitched sideways onto the sand.

THIRTY-THREE

FRANK WAS ASLEEP when Renee walked into his hospital room on Monday morning. He lay in bed half upright, his left arm in a sling, his right wrist bandaged and braced. His head was turned against the pillow and he was drooling—adorably, she thought—on the white hospital linen.

I should let him sleep, she told herself. But she couldn't wait to talk to him, so she shook him awake anyway.

"Wha?" he said, his eyes opening slowly.

"Wake up, Hero Cop, it's one of your admiring fans."

His eyes focused on her and he smiled. He wiped the drool from his mouth with his bandaged wrist. "I'm no cop. I'm a federal agent."

"Tell that to the newspapers," Renee said. "The Moonie rag has the best callout line—KIDNAPPING PLOT THWARTED BY FBI ACE. She tossed a copy of the day's *Post* and *Washington Times* onto the bed at his feet. "It's not the way I'd play the story. My headline would read:

BUNGLING G-MAN ALMOST KILLS KIDNAPPED TEEN WHILE
TRYING TO SAVE HIM."

"How's the kidnapped teen doing?"

"Just fine." Renee sat down on the edge of the groaning hospital bed. "He's dehydrated, and they had to put
ten stitches in his shoulder from the accident, but he's
okay. For someone who's been drugged and gassed and
kept in various basements for five days."

"And how's his head?"

"You mean inside? Amazingly good. He was shaken
up, naturally, but he seems surprisingly chipper. Who
knows, maybe the heroin did him some good. Took the
edge off the trauma."

"Piece of advice, Renee," he said. "Don't share that
theory with anyone but me."

"I won't." She put her hand out and rested it on his
chest. "You heard about Graham Rourke?"

"Brande told me this morning. Tough break for Jason.
How's *his* head?"

"He's not doing as well as Dennis," she answered.
"But still pretty well, considering the circumstances. I'm
learning a thing or two from both of them."

"How so?"

Renee shrugged. "I don't know. I'd be a wreck in their
situation. I'm already a wreck in mine, and it's nothing
by comparison." Renee still hadn't worked up the cour-
age to go back to her own ransacked house. She'd spent
the past two nights at Julie Kovac's apartment in Bethesda. But today, she told herself, she'd go back and
start cleaning up. Though maybe with the phone un-
plugged.

"Jason's aunt flew in this morning from Canada," she
went on then. "I haven't met her yet, but she's with him
now."

"That's good," Frank said. He gently pushed her hand

from his chest and grabbed the newspapers. "So, are they going to let me out of here today?"

"Your doctor says probably so. They've already released Silas Whitcomb. Aside from a few cuts and bruises, he was apparently in better shape than he's been in for years. Especially after he had a couple of drinks."

"They gave an alcoholic alcohol in a hospital?"

"Somebody did."

Frank scowled at her.

"Oh, don't be such a prude, Frank. The day after a near-death experience is not the time to go on the wagon."

"They have a word for people like you," Frank said.

"Pragmatist?"

"I was thinking of 'enabler.' "

"Spare me." She started reaching for a cigarette and then stopped herself. This was a hospital. "He's actually a charming man. And your colleagues were not being very nice to him. I had to remind them that Silas was a victim here."

"They're just doing their job," Frank said distractedly. He tried sitting up in bed. "Ouch."

"What hurts?" Renee asked.

"What doesn't." He pushed his leg against hers. "Move a minute. I want to get up."

"You're sure?"

"Just move."

Renee stood and pulled the loose sheet aside so Frank could get out. As she helped him toward the door, she slipped her hand under his hospital gown and squeezed the hard, warm curve of his ass. "Watch that," he said, looking genuinely scandalized. Then he added, "Are there any slippers or shoes or something?"

She retrieved a pair of hospital slippers from the little closet in the corner. "Don't take this as a precedent,

Frank. I won't be fetching your slippers after you're healthy again." She put them on the floor so that he could slide his feet into them. When he started shuffling toward the door, she asked, "Where are you going anyway?"

"I want to see Dennis," he said, disappearing out the door.

Ann and Leon Monroe were sitting on either side of Dennis's bed when Frank and Renee got to his room on the floor below. "Dennis," Renee said as they entered. "I don't think you two have been formally introduced. This is Special Agent Frank Laroux."

Looking relieved at the interruption, Dennis smiled gratefully. His shoulder was also bandaged, and there was a glucose drip taped into his arm. "Hey there, Agent," he said. "Do I call you Agent?"

"You call me Frank."

"Okay. Frank." He gave a little salute. "Thanks for saving my life."

Both parents had gotten up from their chairs. "You're the man of the moment, Agent Laroux," Leon said. "How are you feeling?"

"I'm fine, fine." He turned back to Dennis. "How about you?"

"Tired."

"About that," Leon said. "Your men have been coming in here all day with books of mug shots, asking Dennis to identify people, but we've been trying to put them off. The boy is exhausted."

"Dad," Dennis said, obviously mortified. "I'm fine. It doesn't take much energy to look at pictures."

"Can't they wait until he's gotten a little more sleep?" Leon asked.

Frank flashed Dennis a quick, commiserative glance and said, "I'll talk to them." This seemed to satisfy the Monroes. "Anyway," Frank went on, "I just wanted to say hello. I've got to go back and get some sleep myself." He patted Dennis's foot under the sheet. "I'll talk to you again before we get out of this place."

Frank and Renee were halfway down the corridor when they heard someone call. It was Mrs. Monroe. She quickly caught up with them. "I just wanted to say," she began, then stopped. This was obviously hard for her. "I wasn't particularly friendly to you the other day, when you came to see us. I don't want you to take it personally."

"Your son was missing, Mrs. Monroe," Frank said expansively. "You don't have to explain yourself."

"I won't say that what I said was untrue," she went on, speaking carefully. "But it *was* unfair." She put her hand to her hair and cleared her throat. "And we *are* grateful to you for everything you've done."

"He seems like a terrific kid, Mrs. Monroe," Frank said. "You should be proud."

She nodded, then turned and walked back down the hallway.

Renee looked up at him and made a face.

" 'It wasn't untrue, but it *was* unfair,' " Frank repeated under his breath. "You're the intellectual. *You* explain what that means."

"It was an apology, Frank, and you should be grateful for it. It's more than I got, and I stole documents from a government office to find her son."

Frank looked amused. "Thanks for reminding me. We're still trying to figure out if what you did was a federal crime. We've all decided that you'd look terrific in a prison jumpsuit."

"Shut up, Frank," Renee replied, and pulled him along back toward the elevators.

• • •

That night, Renee showed up at Jason's house with a pan of lasagna. She'd made it herself—in her own newly reorganized kitchen, after giving Fenton a decent burial in the backyard. Her little acts of bravery for the day.

"Thanks," Jason said when he saw the foil-wrapped pan. His face looked red, as if he'd been sitting in an overheated room. He took the lasagna from her and carried it into the kitchen, where he stuffed it into the freezer next to a dozen other prepared dishes. "Good thing we've got a deep freeze downstairs," he said.

He introduced Renee to his aunt and cousin, and the four of them sat around in the living room for twenty minutes or so, awkwardly discussing funeral arrangements. Jason's aunt Emily, Graham's younger sister, was as husky and handsome as her brother, and her daughter was a virtual carbon copy of herself. Renee wondered how Jason had turned out so different—so slender and fine-boned. She wondered what Jason's mother had been like.

After an acceptable interval, Renee got up and asked Jason if he wanted to take a walk. He shrugged, then said, "Yeah," and got his jacket. "We'll be back soon," Renee told Emily as they left.

They walked along the dark street for a few minutes in silence. The sky was still overcast, obscuring the moon and stars, but the air had turned warm again. It wouldn't be long before the six-month Washington summer set in with a muggy vengeance.

"So," Renee began. "Have you guys been discussing logistics?"

Jason seemed confused for a second. "Oh. You mean after-the-funeral logistics?"

She nodded.

"Aunt Emily says she can stay here with me through June, so I can finish the school year here. Then she wants me to go to Vancouver and live with her. So I'd do my senior year out there."

"And how do you feel about that?"

He didn't answer for a while. He picked up a stick from the curb and began twirling it in his fingers, trying hard to be nonchalant. "Okay, I guess," he said finally. "I think I'd be fine living here on my own, though. It's just one year. Then I'd be going to college anyway."

"You'd rather stay in Washington and finish high school here?"

"Sure. Of course. I mean, my friends are here and everything."

Renee stopped walking. "Jason," she began cautiously. "I don't know how you'd feel about this—or how your aunt would feel—but I'd love to have you stay with me next year." She looked over at him, but the expression on his face was hard to read. She'd thought a lot about this in the hours since Graham Rourke's death. It was probably a reckless offer, but it was one she wanted to make. "Would that interest you at all?"

"I would live with *you*?"

"Yes. There's plenty of room in my house. I mean, it's a small house, but it's a house, and I'm only one person." Renee felt foolish, babbling on like that. She sounded like a nervous freshman asking a boy on a first date. "It would have to be something you and your aunt both agree to, but I'd like it very much. Just for the year. Then, as you say, you'd be heading off to college anyway."

Jason seemed to be going over the possibility in his mind. She found it vaguely insulting that he didn't jump at the chance.

"I don't know," he said. "Let me talk about it with my aunt."

"Only if it's something you really want to do," she

said, a little tartly. "And naturally, you wouldn't be able to take my Journalism 2 course if you did stay. I couldn't have you in my class if you were living in my house."

"I'd survive. Without Journalism 2, I mean." He turned and they started walking again. "I'll think about it. I've got a lot of decisions to make."

They were silent the rest of the way back to Jason's house. Renee stopped when they reached the end of the walk. "You want to come in?" he asked her.

She shook her head. "Just say good night to your aunt and cousin for me."

"Okay."

She turned and started heading toward her car.

"Thanks," he said from behind her.

She turned and looked back at him.

"Thanks for the offer," he went on, standing in the yellow glow of the porch light. "And for the lasagna."

"Don't mention it. Bake it for a full hour at four hundred degrees. Don't defrost it ahead of time."

"Four hundred degrees. One hour. Got it." Then he asked, "Would I have my own room?"

It took her a moment to unravel the non sequitur. "Yes, you'd have your own room," she said. "In the finished basement. So you'd have plenty of privacy."

"And you wouldn't, like, try to be my mother or anything, would you?"

"No, Jason. I wouldn't presume. I'd be your friend. Your older, wiser friend, full of sage advice to keep you out of trouble."

Jason nodded. He seemed maddeningly blasé about the whole thing. Seventeen-year-olds, she told herself—not for the first time—could be the most infuriating creatures on earth.

"I'll think about it," he said again, fingering his house key.

She nodded and turned away to watch a cat slink across the side lawn. But then, looking back again, she saw Jason sitting on the top step of the porch with his face in his hands. She ran back to him, almost tripping on the uneven pavement. She sat down beside him and put her hand on his hunched right shoulder. "Go ahead," she whispered. "There's nobody watching you here. Take your time."

THIRTY-FOUR

JASON GAVE THE eulogy at his father's funeral. He stood beside the gray, burnished casket on a sunny Wednesday afternoon, speaking about his father as honestly as he could. As the hot wind tugged at the lapels of his new sport jacket, he reminisced about a day, shortly after his mother's death, when he and his father had tried to find something to eat in the freezer. They'd opened a package of what they thought was chicken legs, but it had turned out to be something else, something they both hated—chicken livers. He and his father had carried the livers outside and tossed them, one by one, over the back fence for the raccoons.

"My father seemed to think this was some kind of symbolic act—something really major," Jason said, reading from his notes. "He was like that—always looking for hidden meanings in everything. I didn't have the heart to tell him that, for me, I was just relieved that I didn't have to eat the livers. My mother had always forced me to eat them. For the vitamin A."

Jason finished the eulogy and stood for a few seconds,

staring at the mechanical winch that would lower his father's casket into the freshly dug grave. Take care of Mom, he told his father silently. And do a better job of it than you did the first time.

He looked up then. Most of the people he knew in the world were standing there—his aunt and cousin, his father's colleagues from work, teachers and friends from school, Sarah and her mother. Dennis and his parents were also there, standing next to Renee and Agent Laroux, and Maxie and Hortense and Julia. Even that other FBI guy had shown up—Agent Holly the asshole. They were all watching Jason, looking embarrassed at the lameness of his eulogy.

Jason didn't know what he was supposed to do next. So he just stepped away from the casket and stood next to his aunt and cousin on the lawn. The priest waddled up and started saying something generic and grandiose. And then the casket went down into its hole.

Afterward, as everyone was heading slowly across the cemetery to their cars, Jason moved away from his relatives and caught up with Renee and Agent Laroux. "Hey," he said. "I talked to my aunt."

"And?"

"And she wants to talk it over with you, but I think she's willing. She looked kind of relieved, actually, when I told her about it."

"I'll talk to her," Renee said. "As long as you're sure that it's what *you* want."

When they got to Renee's car, Jason said, "Yeah. It's what I want."

"Good," she said, and kissed him on the cheek. "We'll be roommates."

Jason opened the door for Renee and let her get in. "I'll see you back at the house."

Then he turned away and jogged over to Sarah, who

was waiting for him at the edge of the grass, looking gorgeous in a tight black dress.

Later that night, after the guests had gone home and his aunt had cleaned up the mess from the after-funeral gathering, Jason met Dennis and the two of them rode their bicycles over to Rock Creek Park. A couple of white guys in their thirties were playing basketball on the court, but the rest of the playground was entirely deserted. Jason and Dennis went to the far corner of the second court and sat down with their backs against the chain-link fence. For a while, they just watched the pitiful white guys trying to pretend they were teenagers again. One of them had his shirt off, and the flab around his waist wobbled every time he ran down the court.

"Let me ask you something," Dennis said after a while. "My parents are trying to talk me into going to see some shrink they know, just to talk things out for a couple of months. They say he might be able to help me through some things—'some issues raised by my ordeal,' as dear old Mom puts it. You think I should?"

Jason seemed surprised. "You've got issues?"

Dennis shrugged. He looked over toward the bicycles. "I've got a few new ideas."

"Ideas like what?"

"I don't know. I've been rethinking the plan of going right to college after high school. Maybe I should do something else for a year or two before heading off."

Unbelievable, Jason thought. Just when he himself was starting to be sure of things, here was Dennis going in the opposite direction.

"*You* saw a shrink, right?" Dennis asked. "When your mother died?"

"Yeah."

"Did it do anything for you?"

"No."

"Oh."

They sat in awkward silence for a few minutes, watching the basketball game. "I almost forgot," Dennis said then. He put his hand into the front pocket of his shorts and pulled out two thick joints. "You interested?"

Jason was so stunned he couldn't speak for a few seconds. "Shit, man," he said. "You are insane, you know that? After everything that's been happening?"

"What do you mean? We deserve a little recreation after all we've been through. You can't tell me you're going to be a Boy Scout the rest of your life."

Jason just stared at him. "You know, you really do need a shrink."

"Maybe so."

After a few seconds of hesitation, Jason sighed and took one of the joints.

Dennis smiled broadly. "Actually, it's tobacco. I was just testing you."

"Shit," Jason said. He looked at the fake joint more closely. "I guess I just failed."

"You did. Typical."

They lit up the hand-rolled cigarettes and smoked in silence for a while. Then Dennis asked, "Are you really going to move in with Lois Lane?"

"Looks like it. For a year, at least."

"Mind-boggling," Dennis said. "Hey, maybe if you're lucky, you'll get a little nooky on the side from her."

Jason, who had taken a pull on the cigarette, began coughing uncontrollably. "A little *nooky*? Did you say a little *nooky*?"

"It's a perfectly legitimate word, hoser. Look it up."

"You are such an unbelievable dinosaur, Dennis, you know that?"

"You're the one moving in with an older woman."

"I don't know why I hang with you, Dennis, I really don't."

Dennis shook his head. "Asshole," he said.

Jason flicked away the cigarette. "Asshole," he said.

Frank and Renee were sitting on the couch in Renee's living room, watching excerpts from the Mayor's news conference. Humphrey was grandstanding as usual. Congress and the media, he intoned, were using the arrest of the Deputy Mayor for Finance as an excuse for another "racist assault on the idea of democracy and self-rule in the District of Columbia." He reminded everyone that Deputy Mayor Cashen, though appointed by the Mayor, had been approved by the Financial Control Board, and that his administration would in no way accept full blame for the scandal. And he assured the public that neither he nor any of his close aides had any knowledge whatsoever of the Deputy Mayor's misdeeds or of the "horrendous alleged conspiracy" in the police and social services departments that had been reported in the newspapers. The D.C. Sharing and Caring Initiative, he maintained, was a sound idea whose goals had been perverted by the greed and venality of a few individuals. The real conspiracy, he went on, was among those who would use anything they could find to further weaken the D.C. government and the ability of the citizens of the city to govern themselves.

"*Fongool* a-you!" Frank shouted, gesturing in disgust at the screen. "I can't believe he's turning it into the same old bullshit!"

The Mayor turned away from the microphones and introduced Silas Whitcomb.

"Oh, here it comes," Frank moaned. They watched as Silas—looking spiffy and well-groomed in a new dove-gray suit—stepped up to the podium and accepted an award from the Mayor for personal bravery. He waved to the crowd and mugged with the Mayor for a few minutes, showing off. "Let this award be a symbol," Humphrey said into the microphone, "of the city's continuing commitment to the less fortunate members of our community."

On the screen, Silas stepped up to the microphone. He hit it twice with his finger and blew into it in the age-old way of public speakers. Then, smiling his gap-toothed smile, he cleared his throat and said, "I wanna take this time to announce my candidacy for mayor."

Roy Humphrey burst into laughter and embraced Silas as a thousand camera flashes exploded around the room.

"I can't stand this," Frank said finally. He reached for the remote and hit the off button. Renee, sitting next to him, said, "Excuse me, I was watching that."

"You like to see people lie through their teeth?"

"What, you think Humphrey was involved in all of this? You think he knew?"

Frank put down the remote. He leaned back against the cushions and put his feet up on the coffee table. "Hell, I don't know. There's no evidence that he did know. But when you're up to your eyeballs in shit, who can say what shit you see and what shit you don't see."

"My, how eloquent." Renee moved closer to him on the couch. She kissed him on the jaw, but he seemed too upset even to notice. "Did you read that piece in the paper this morning?" she asked. "They're starting to talk about a possible D.C. budget surplus for next year. Can you believe it? They may even find enough money to fix the roof at RFK High."

"Right. This time next year we'll all be living in that shining city on the hill. Can't wait." He drummed his fingers a few times on his knee. "I should go," he said then, in a quieter voice. "I've got all kinds of unfinished business to contend with at the office. The paperwork on this thing is going to be a nightmare."

"It's ten-thirty, Frank. You're not really going in now, are you?"

"I should, Renee. Nobody's been able to locate Harcourt yet, and Jessup is all over me. He wants to get this thing put away as quickly as we can."

Renee got up from the couch and grabbed her pack of cigarettes from the coffee table. "As I recall," she said peevishly, "there was some other unfinished business you had to attend to."

He looked up at her. "Now?"

"What do you mean, 'now'? If it's not too late to go to the office, it's certainly not too late for what I have in mind." She lit the cigarette and took a long drag. "Besides, you heard the Mayor. It's a time for healing."

"Yeah, and the healing won't start until we track down all the bad guys in this mess."

"That's not the kind of healing I was thinking about, Frank," Renee said. "And get those goddamn lawyer shoes off my coffee table."

Frank stared at his shoes for a few seconds. Then, slowly, he got to his feet, groaning. "Okay, you win." He walked over to her, took the cigarette out of her mouth, crushed it in the ashtray, and then grabbed her around the waist. "I could get used to this," he said.

Renee wormed out of his grasp. "Come on," she said. She took his hand. "No interruptions this time. I promise."

"You really think these are lawyer shoes?" he asked, following her toward the hallway.